W

Edited by
Claude Lalumière
and
Marty Halpern

FOUR WALLS EIGHT WINDOWS
NEW YORK

Published by
Four Walls Eight Windows
39 West 14th Street, room 503
New York, N.Y., 10011

Visit our website at http://www.4w8w.com

First printing April 2003.

Library of Congress Cataloging-in-Publication Data:

Witpunk/edited by Claude Lalumière and Marty Halpern
p. cm.
ISBN 1-56858-256-0
1. Science fiction, American. 2. Fantasy fiction, American. 3. Science fiction, Canadian.
4. Fantasy fiction, Canadian. I Halpern, Marty. II. Lalumière, Claude.

PS648.S3 W58 2003
813'.08760817—dc21

2002192768

10 9 8 7 6 5 4 3 2 1

Typeset by Pracharak Technologies (P) Ltd.
Printed in Canada

Table of Contents

Preface

This all started in June 2001, when, on an e-forum called *fictionmags*, someone asked, "When did reading SF/fantasy stop being fun?" *Witpunk* coeditor-to-be Claude Lalumière took exception to this question and especially to the point of view that it represented; namely, that science fiction was no longer as much fun as it used to be. He promptly posted a list of recent genre novels that were fun in a variety of ways, from over-the-top adventure tales and goofball satires to sardonic pastiches and dark comedies.

Using that list as a template, fellow fictionmaggers Marty Halpern and Claude Lalumière began to think about assembling an anthology that gathered together classics of hard-hitting sardonic fiction with new stories exemplifying that contemporary fiction – any kind of fiction, be it genre or so-called "mainstream" – was as much fun as it ever was, if not more so. And we (pardon the abrupt switch from third to first person) settled on *Witpunk* as a suitably facetious name for such an enterprise. But we're getting ahead of ourselves.

Back to the question that started it all. This is an oft-heard complaint: that [fill in the blank] isn't as much fun as it used to be. To which we say: bullshit.

When people complain like this, what they're really saying is: "When I was younger, I discovered science fiction (or rock music, or sitcoms, or whatever), and it fixed in my mind exactly what SF (rock music, sitcoms, etc.) should be. Any deviation from this model is a debasement of the form, and in my self-involved geekhood I will proclaim any such deviation an abomination, an insult to my right that creators everywhere bow to the tastes I developed in my earlier years!"

Contrary to their stated claims of wanting things to be fun, such people have become anti-fun police, ready to destroy anything new and exciting, to denigrate anything that doesn't conform to their one-note idea of entertainment. Of course, you *Witpunk* readers are above such petty sentiments. You all equate fun with being challenged and surprised, while rote reiterations of tired old tropes bore you to death.

And you seek out fiction that satisfies your need to be entertained with new ideas, merciless irony, transgressive wit, and engaging storytelling.

In this book we've gathered twenty-six such stories by twenty-four writers, ranging from established veterans to first-time authors. While some of these authors will slap you sardonically silly upside the head with their in-your-face humor, others weave more subtle tales of dark irony. Although most of the writers in *Witpunk* are active in the SF and fantasy genres, not all of the stories in this book are fantasy or SF. Several, in fact, take place in the here-and-now, but their characters, ideas, and attitude are too daring to be labeled "mundane" or "mainstream."

But, come to think of it, all of the stories in *Witpunk* are SF: Sardonic Fiction, that is.

Claude Lalumière and Marty Halpern, January, 2003

The Teb Hunter

ഌ

Allen M. Steele

"The trick," Jimmy Ray says, "is not to look 'em in the eye."

The truck hits a pothole just then, jouncing on its worn-out shocks and causing stuff to skitter across the dashboard: shotgun shells, empty chewing tobacco cans, wadded-up parking tickets ignored since last May. A little plastic bear swings back and forth beneath the mirror; Jimmy Ray reaches up to steady it, then glances back to make sure nothing has come loose in the back of the truck. Satisfied, he takes a swig from the box of Mountain Dew clasped between his thighs.

"That's why I don't take kids," he continues. "I mean, it's just too much for 'em. My boy's too young for this anyway . . . next season, maybe, after he gets a gun for Christmas . . . but a couple'a years ago, I tried taking my nephew. Now Brock's a good kid, and . . . hang on . . ."

Jimmy Ray twists the wheel hard to the left, swerving to avoid another pothole. A can of Red Man falls off the dashboard into my lap. "Gimme that, willya?" I hand it to him; he pops the lid off with his thumb, gives the contents a quick sniff, then tucks it in his hunting vest. "Like I was saying, Brock's bagged a couple'a deer with no regrets, but I got him out here and he took one look at 'em, and that was all she wrote. Just wouldn't shoot, no matter what. Fifteen years old, and here he is, bawlin' like a baby." He shakes his head in disgust. "So no kids, and I'd just as soon not let anyone else shoot. No offense, but if you can't look 'em in the eye, it ain't worth the hassle, y'know what I mean?"

The woods are thick along either side of the dirt road, red maples shedding their leaves, tall pines dropping cones across the forest floor. We slow down to pass over a small bridge; the creek below is fogged with early morning mist, its clear waters rushing across smooth granite boulders. Jimmy Ray slurps the last of his Mountain Dew, then tosses the empty box out the window. "God, what a beautiful morning," he says, glancing up through the sunroof. "Great day to be alive." Then he winks at me. "Less'n you're a teb, of course."

Another quarter-mile down the road, he pulls over to the side. " 'Kay, here we is." The door rasps on its hinges as Jimmy Ray shoves it open; he grunts softly as he pries his massive belly from behind the wheel and climbs down from the cab. Another few moments to unrack his rifle from the rear window – a Savage .30-.06 bolt-action equipped with a scope – before sauntering over to the back of the truck. The canopy window sports stickers for the NRA and a country-rock band; he throws open the hatch, then pulls out a couple of bright orange hunting vests and a six-pack of Budweiser.

"Here. You can carry this." Jimmy Ray hands me the beer. He reaches into his jacket pocket, produces a laminated hunting license on an aluminum chain; briefly removing his dirty cap to reveal the bald spot in the midst of his thick black hair, he pulls the chain around his neck, letting the license dangle across his chest. He removes the chewing tobacco from his pocket and uncaps it, then pulls out a thick wad and shoves it into the left side of his face between the cheek and his teeth. He tosses the can into the back of the truck, slams the hatch shut. "Hokay," he says, his inflection garbled by the chaw in his mouth, "les' go huntin'."

About fifteen feet into the woods, we come upon a narrow trail, leading east toward a hill a couple miles away. "Got my blind set up that way," he says quietly. "We may come up on one'a them 'fore that, but it won' matter much. This is real easy, once y'know how to do it. All y'need is the right bait."

We continue down the trail. We're a long way from the nearest house, but Jimmy Ray is confident that we'll find tebs out here. "People git sick of havin' 'em 'round, so they drive out here, set 'em loose in the woods." He turns his head, hocks brown juice into the undergrowth. "They figger they'll get by, forage for berries and roots, that sort of thing. Or maybe they think they'll just up and die once winter kicks in. But they 'dapt to jus' 'bout any place you put 'em, and they breed like crazy."

Another spit. "So 'fore you know it, they're eatin' up every-thin' they can find, which don't leave much for anythin' else out here. An' when they're done with that, they come out of the woods, start raidin' farm crops, goin' through people's gar-bage . . . whatever they can find. Hungry lil' peckers."

He shakes his head. "I dunno what people find cute about 'em. You wanna good pet, you go get yourself a dog or a cat. Hell, a fish or a lizard, if that's your thing. But there's something jus' not right 'bout tebs. I mean, if God had meant animals to talk, he would'a . . ." He thinks about this a moment, dredging the depths of his intellect. "I dunno. Given 'em a dictionary or sum'pin."

Jimmy Ray's not particularly careful about avoiding the dry leaves that have fallen across the trail, even though they crunch loudly beneath the soles of his boots. It's almost as if he wants the tebs to know he's coming. "Talked once to an environmentalist from the state wildlife commission," he says after awhile. "Said that tebs are what you call a weed species . . . somethin' that gits transported into a diff'rent environment and jus' takes over. Like, y'know, kudzu or tiger mussels, or those fish . . . y'know, the snakeheads, the ones that can walk across dry land . . . that got loose up in Maryland some years ago. Tebs are jus' the same way. Only diff'rence is that they were bio . . . bio . . . whatchamacallit, that word . . ."

"Bioengineered."

"Thas'it. Bioengineered . . . so now they're smarter than the average bear." He grins at me. "'Member that cartoon show? 'I'm smarter than the average bear.' I sure loved that when . . ."

Suddenly, he halts, falls silent. I don't know what he's seen or heard, but I stop as well. Jimmy Ray scans the forest surrounding us, peering into the sun-dappled shadows. At first, I don't hear anything. Then, just for a moment, something rustles within the lower limbs of a maple a couple dozen yards away, and I hear a thin, high-pitched voice:

"Come out and play . . . come out and play . . ."

"Oh, yeah," Jimmy Ray murmurs. "I gotcher playtime right here." He absently caresses his rifle as if he's stroking a lover, then glances back at me and grins. "C'mon. They know we're here. No sense in keepin' 'em waitin'."

A few hundred yards later, the trail ends in a small clearing, a meadow bordered on all sides by woods. The morning sun touches the dew upon the autumn wildflowers, making the scene look like a picture from a children's storybook. And in the middle of the clearing, just where it should be, is a small wooden table with four tiny chairs placed around it. Kindergarten lawn furniture, the kind you'd find at Toys "R" Us, except that the paint is beginning to peel and there are old bloodstains soaked into the boards.

"Hauled this stuff out here two seasons ago," Jimmy Ray says, pushing aside the high grass as we walk toward it. "Move it around, of course, and clean it off now and then, but it works like a damn." He smiles. "Learned it from *Field and Stream,* but this part is my idea. Wanna gimme that beer?"

I hand him the six-pack; he rips the tops off the cartons and carefully places them on the table. "Book says you should use honey," he explains, his voice a near-whisper, "but that's expensive. Bud works just as well, maybe even better. They can smell the sugar, and the alcohol makes 'em slow. But that's my little secret, so don't tell anyone, y'hear?"

The bait in place, we retreat to a small shack he's put up on the edge of the clearing. No larger than an outhouse, the blind has a narrow slit for a window. The only decoration is a mildewed girlie poster stapled to the inside wall. Jimmy Ray loads his rifle, inserting four rounds in the magazine and chambering a fifth, then lines up five more rounds on a small shelf beneath the window. "Won't take long," he says quietly, propping the rifle stock against the windowsill and focusing the scope upon the table. "First one saw us, so now he's tellin' his friends. They'll be here right soon."

We wait silently for nearly an hour; Jimmy Ray turns his head now and then to spit into a corner of the blind, but otherwise he keeps his eye on the table. The shed is getting warm, and I'm beginning to doze off when Jimmy Ray taps my arm and nods toward the window.

At first, I don't see anything. Then the tall grass on the other side of the clearing moves, as if something is passing through it. There's a soft click as Jimmy Ray disengages the safety, but otherwise he's perfectly still, waiting patiently for his prey to emerge.

A few moments later, a small figure crawls into a chair, then hops on the table. The teb is full-grown, nearly three feet tall, its pelt black and soft as velvet. Its large brown eyes cautiously glance back and forth, then it waddles on its short hind legs across the table until it reaches the nearest beer. Leaning over, the teb picks up the carton, sniffs with its short muzzle. Then its mouth breaks into a smile.

"Honey!" it yelps. "Oh boy, honey!"

Jimmy Ray steals a moment to wink at me. Honey is what tebs call anything they like; either they can't tell the difference, or more likely their primitive vocal chords are incapable of enunciating more than a few simple words which they barely understand, much the way a myna bird can ask for a cracker without knowing exactly what it is.

Now more tebs are coming out of the high grass: a pack of living teddy bears, the result of radical reconfiguration of the DNA of *Ursus americanus*, the American black bear. Never growing larger than cubs and bred for docility, they're as harmless as house cats, as friendly as beagles. The perfect companion for a child, except when people buy them for all the wrong reasons. And now the woods are full of them.

"Honey! Oh, boy, honey!" Now the tebs are clambering onto the chairs, grabbing the beer cartons between the soft paws of their forelegs and draining them into their mouths. A perfect little teddy bear picnic. They're happy as can be, right up until the moment when Jimmy Ray squeezes the trigger.

The first bullet strikes the largest teb in the chest, a clean shot that kills it even before it knows it's dead. The teb sitting in the next chair hasn't had time to react before the back of its head is blown off; the first two gunshots are echoing off the trees when the other tebs begin throwing themselves off the table, squeaking in terror. Jimmy Ray's third and forth shots go wild, but his fifth shot manages to wing a small teb who was a little too slow. It screams as it topples from its chair; by now the rest of the pack are fleeing for the woods, leaving behind the dead and wounded.

"Damn!" Jimmy Ray quickly jams four more rounds into the rifle, then fires into the high grass where the tebs are running. "Quick lil' bastards, ain't they?"

He spits out his chaw, then he reloads again before slamming open the shed door and stalking across the clearing to the table. He ignores the two dead tebs, walks over to the one he wounded. It's trying to crawl away, a thick red smear against the side of its chest. Seeing Jimmy Ray, it falls over on its back, raises its paws as if begging for mercy.

"I . . . I . . . I wuv you so much!" Something it might have once said to a six-year-old girl, before her father decided that keeping it was too much of a hassle and abandoned it out here.

"Yeah, I wuv you too, Pooh." And then Jimmy Ray points the rifle muzzle between its eyes and finishes the job.

We spend another half-hour stalking the surviving members of the pack, but the other tebs have vanished, and before long Jimmy Ray notices vultures beginning to circle the clearing. He returns to the picnic table and checks out his kills. Two males and a female; even though he's disappointed that he couldn't have bagged any more, at least he's still within the season limit.

So he ties their legs to a tree branch, and together we haul the three dead tebs back to his truck. Jimmy Ray absently whistles an old Lynyrd Skynyrd song as he dumps two of the corpses in the back of the truck; for the hell of it, he lashes the body of the biggest one to the front hood, just to give him bragging rights when he drops by the bar for a quick one on the way home.

He's pleased with himself. Three pelts he can sell to a furrier, some fresh meat for his dogs, and another head for the collection in his den. Not bad, all things considered. He climbs into the truck, stuffs some more Red Man into his face, then slaps a CD into the deck.

"But y'know what's even more fun?" he asks as we pull away. "Next month, it's unicorn season. Now there's good eatin'!"

Then he puts the pedal to the metal and away we go, with a dead teddy bear tied to the hood and "Sweet Home Alabama" blasting from the speakers. It's a great day to be alive.

Coyote Goes Hollywood

꧁꧂

Ernest Hogan

Fade in. (My memories always start with a fade-in, because I grew up in front of a TV set.) Night. I'm on a redeye Greyhound from Phoenix to Hollywood (see, I also remember in present tense, like a script or a rerun). The only light comes from the stars, making the bus seem like a spaceship crossing some interstellar gulf.

The seat next to me is empty, so I'm stretched out over it, drifting off into sleep, but the bus stops in some middle-of-nowhere desert town. A big Indian gets on, walks past the family of rednecks who've been on the bus all the way from Kentucky, the black woman with a baby on her lap, several Mexicans – or maybe some type of Central American refugees – all wearing cowboy hats, and the Hindu mother and daughter who both have scorpions tattooed on their right hands to the only empty seat left – the one that my legs, jacket, and sketchbook are in.

I pretend to be sound asleep. He asks, "Can I sit here?" in a deep, dopey voice. I groan, pull my legs, jacket, and sketchbook out of the way so he can sit down.

Close up of the cover of my sketchbook: a cartoon portrait of an anthropomorphic coyote wearing sunglasses with the stub of a cigarette and his tongue hanging out of his mouth, above it there's COYOTE COMIX in big, clunky letters, all in blazing magic marker.

"What's that?" he asks, his voice sounds like it could have been created by Mel Blanc, his finger points at the sketchbook.

"My sketchbook," I say, going into a nodding-off-into-sleep act. I'm not in the mood to hear anybody's life story and/or philosophy even though I'm trapped, helpless here, light-years from Phoenix and Hollywood.

He squinted. "Coyote Comix? What's a white kid like you know about Coyote?"

Something new there. I'm Irish-Mexican with black, kinky hair. I've been called "nigger" often enough, but this is the first time I've been called "white."

"To my girlfriend I'm brown; to you I'm white. Pretty confusing."

"So's Coyote. What do you know about him?"

"He's the Great Native American Trickster Spirit. A distant ancestor of Bugs Bunny, Daffy Duck, Woody Woodpecker, and other smartass talking animals. I've been wandering around the Southwest, getting inspired and fooling around with a cute, little blonde from Phoenix, but now I'm running short on cash and have to go back to civilization to try to make money and art – not necessarily in that order."

"Oh, you're an artist."

"Smile when you say that, pardner. And let me get some sleep."

He points to my sketchbook. "Lemme see it. I'm not sleepy."

"Okay," I hand it over, a bit nervous because I've never shown any of my Wild West stuff to any real, live redskins before. Sleep becomes impossible. I lean into the window, see the Indian flipping through my sketchbook reflected against the desert night blacker than intergalactic space. Maybe he'll get bored. I start to doze. He chuckles; a ridiculous horselaugh.

Lap-dissolve to: The Indian handing the sketchbook back to me. "Kind of interesting. You don't draw like a rich phony and you seem to know something about the spirit of Coyote. And it's kind of funny, too. Ya going to L.A. to work in the cartoon biz?"

"Yeah." I'm starting to give up on the idea of sleeping. "I'm going all the way to Hollywood."

"How'd ya get interested in Coyote?"

"Ran across him in some books. Seemed like great cartoon material."

He laughed again, sounding more cartoonlike.

"I wanted to bring Coyote into the modern times."

More wacky laughter. Then: "What makes you think that Coyote ain't alive and well and living in these here modern times of yours?"

I gasp. Now *I'm* getting cartoony.

"Spirits," he says, "or myths, to use your whiteman word, live, even in the twenty-first century, the twenty-second, the twenty-third . . ."

"Uh, I don't get it." I shudder even though the bus driver has the heater blasting us with tropical air. "Could you give me an example?"

"Heh-heh," he says, leans back, gets comfortable, and tells a tale.

We lap-dissolve (my TV-shaped imagination kicking into action again) to a 1940s-style cartoon bar. Swingy jazz plays squeaky and squawky, droning merrily along in the background. The camera pans across the bar showing lazy cowboys, Indians, horses, rattlesnakes, and scorpions drinking mugs of foamy beer and brushing the flies away; it stops on Coyote, who's surrounded by empty, long-necked beer bottles, slumping in his chair.

He burps.

The Indian narrates in voice-over: "Y'see, after the war things weren't going good for Coyote. I don't know, maybe it had something to do with the atomic bomb, but it seems that people, even his own, were forgetting him. Drinking helped him forget, but little did he know somebody he never expected was thinking of him, and coming for him . . ."

Cut to the desert, humanoid cacti dance to the beat of the music that's in tune with the wiggling rays of the smiling sun. A long, black car slides down the winding road from the horizon like a big, black snake; comes to the bar, coils around it a few times, the door opens, and out hops the Mouse with a busty, pink French poodle on each arm.

The Mouse is jet-black, without the white face makeup that the studio makes him wear in his cartoons. He's wearing a black tuxedo, and his usual white gloves and bulbous, red shoes.

The poodles have tall, elaborate hairdos, heavy makeup, and wear tight halters and stretch-pants.

The three grope and lean on each other like a delirious six-legged creature and enter the bar, causing the doors to swing and flap.

"Hey!" the Mouse yells, his voice deeper than the one he uses in the cartoons. "We got plenty of gas, but we're fresh outta fuel for *us!*" His left eyeball gets real big and scans the bar with a dotted line, seeing cowboy-looking Indians and Indian-looking cowboys. "Say, this looks like the Wild West! What kind of high-powered firewater you got in these parts?" The dotted line brushes across Coyote, past him, and then back on him, then disappears.

The Mouse lets go of his poodles, who embrace each other as soon as he slips out of reach, and they start fondling each other's breasts and kissing, their tongues twining like pink snakes.

"Well, I'll be dipped," the Mouse says. "Aren't you Coyote, *the* Coyote?"

Coyote looks at the poodles, who are passionately rolling in the sawdust on the floor, and says, "Yup. Coyote, that's me. You know me?"

The Mouse thrusts his three-fingered, white-gloved hand into Coyote's face. Coyote looks at him with blood-shot eyes.

"Of course I know you," says the Mouse as he reaches for and grabs Coyote's paw. "The humans in the cartoon biz may not be aware – at least not on the conscious level – but we characters know about our roots. Let the humans think they've invented something new – we know it's all just genetic memories bubbling to the surface."

"Why," Coyote says, "you're that Mouse I've seen at the pictures, but you look different."

The Mouse rubs his black face. "They make me paint my face white for the cartoons. Afraid people'll think I'm a nigger or something.

"Anyway, Coyote, ol' boy, all of us funny animals from Hollywood have had a deep respect for you, this continent being your home turf and all. A lot of us have dreamed about working with you." A light bulb appears over the Mouse's head. "Hey! That's brilliant!" The Mouse leans over to Coyote. "How would you like to come to Hollywood with us? Now that the war is over, there's all kinds of money to be made. And you're sure to be a hit. Who could be more American than you? After all, you did help make this continent!"

"I don't know," says Coyote.

The Mouse walks over through the crowd of cowboy-looking Indians and Indian-looking cowboys that are watching the poodles roll around in the sawdust. The Mouse picks the poodles up, pulls them apart, and tosses one of them at Coyote. With a fallout of sawdust, she lands on Coyote's head, her breasts wrap around his neck, her arms and legs around his torso, and she sucks his ear.

"Think about it, Coyote," says the Mouse. "There's a lot more like her in Hollywood. And a lot of other things, too. And you can have it all."

Dissolve to me and the Indian back on the Greyhound.

"What is this?" I ask. "Did you make this up, or is it a new myth they tell on the reservations?"

"Heh, heh, heh," says the Indian. "It's a story, what you call myth, and a smart guy like you should know how these things are. They just sort of happen. They grow. They live!"

"Uh, yeah," I say. "So what happened when Coyote got to Hollywood?"

"Problems . . ."

Dissolve to an office of one of the biggest cartoon studios in Hollywood. Out of the window, palm trees dance to the music, now a slicker, more polished kind of jazz; the sun wears shades and smokes a cigarette.

Behind his aircraft-carrier-sized desk sits the Producer: a short, fat, bald man who smokes a big cigar and wears a pin-striped suit and a wide tie with gold dollar signs all over it. He smiles, his teeth becoming as big as the chrome grill of a car, his cigar hovering in place. Stepping onto the desk, he walks across it, aiming a big hand at Coyote.

"Ah yes, Mr. Coyote!" he says. "The Mouse told me all about you. I'm glad to meet you."

Coyote doesn't extend his paw, so the Producer grabs it, squeezing it, sending off little stars of pain.

The Producer looks Coyote over, picking him up and turning him around. "Yes, yes, you're perfect for the cartoon business! But let's check a few things before you sign our standard five-year contract." He puts Coyote down, darts over to the desk, presses a button on the intercom, and says, "Bubbles, bring in the suit!"

The door springs open, and Bubbles, the Producer's secretary, slinks in on her long, shapely legs, her ample breasts and bleach-blonde hair bouncing. She smiles so brightly that Coyote and the Producer have to cover their eyes as she holds out a suit that looks like Coyote's body, only without any genitals.

"What is that?" asks Coyote. "It's disgusting!"

"It's the suit we want you to wear in the cartoons," says the Producer. "You know, to cover up your wahzoo."

"My what?"

"You know," the Producer points between Coyote's legs.

"You mean my member and my manhood. You want me to look like I don't have them!"

"Look, don't get upset. All the big cartoon stars wear similar suits: the Rabbit, the Pig, the Woodpecker, all the Ducks . . ."

"Like the way you make the Mouse paint his face white?"

"Yeah. You gotta realize, this is civilization. We got standards to uphold. Appearances to maintain."

"I'll wear anything else – but not that!"

"Okay, okay! So we put clothes on ya. Bubbles, the loincloth."

She reaches deep into her cleavage, pulls out a brightly colored loincloth, and hands it to Coyote with a flirtatious wink.

As Coyote puts the loincloth on, his genitals grow so that they stick out from under it.

"What is that?" screams the Producer.

"It's magnificent," says Bubbles, her eyes bugging out like miniature versions of her breasts.

"Sometimes my member has a mind of its own," says Coyote.

"You and a lot of other guys," says the Producer. "You're supposed to have the power to change things. Make it change back the way it was!"

Coyote closes his eyes and concentrates. Beads of sweat fly off his brow. His genitals only grow larger until they are bigger than his body.

"Cut that shit out, smartass!" says the Producer.

Bubbles starts drooling.

"Uh, sorry," says Coyote, "but this always happens when I try to change things; they change, but then go out of control!"

The Producer's head turns bright red, steam spews out of his ears. He grabs the contract, tears it into confetti that flies all over the office.

"Get out of here!" he screams. "We can't use you! *Kids*, like to watch our cartoons, for God's sake!"

"But this," Coyote says, pointing to his member, "is where children come from."

"Bubbles, get him out of here!" the Producer shouts, his entire body quivering out of shape.

"Come," says Bubbles, putting an arm around Coyote. "This way." And once she's out of the door she leans over and whispers into Coyote's ear, "Let's go to my place. Maybe I can help you with this" – she caresses his member – "problem."

Dissolve back to the bus.

"So Coyote didn't break into the cartoon business," I say.

"Naw," says the Indian, "and what was worse than the humiliation of being dragged out to Hollywood and rejected was that a few years later they created a pale imitation of him that played the fool for a bird that was so stupid it couldn't even talk!"

"Hey! Could that other coyote be Coyote's son, you know, his and Bubbles's kid?"

"Who knows. It's hard to check these things out."

"Too bad Coyote couldn't have gotten even with them."

"Oh, he did."

"Really, how?"

"He disguised himself as a technician, went around to various electronics labs and helped invent television – and you know what that did to the major cartoon studios!"

"Coyote invented television?"

"Yeah. Why not? The technology was around before that. He just put the right things together."

"But the studio cartoons were shown on television; they influenced a whole generation."

"Yeah, as usual, when Coyote tried to change things, the unexpected happened. All the kids saw these new talking animal myths every day during their formative years. It affected their brains. Made them into weird things . . . like hippies."

"Hippies?"

"Yeah. They must have sensed Coyote's connection to the cartoons that made them what they were. They were attracted to him. Sought him out. It bothered him, nearly drove him crazy."

Dissolve to a Cinemascope panorama of a psychedelic version of the Southwestern American desert. The sky strobes back and forth between purple and yellow. Rocks and mountains change into humanoid figures that dance to the acid-rock-with-lots-of-fuzz-tones soundtrack. Rainbows leap from pink-orange clouds that flow and merge and separate like oil-on-water patterns in a lightshow. The Sun's rays are long hair and a beard that flow out in all directions; from his eyes you can tell he's stoned.

All over the desert are hippies, ranging from Day-Glo Pop Art images to figures from all the great underground cartoonists. They mill around, having all kinds of sex, smoking dope, playing electric guitars plugged into glowing rocks.

In the middle of it all is Coyote. His eyes are flashing wavy stripes like an Op Art display. A joint hangs from his mouth.

The hippies crowd around him, saying:

"Coyote, please fuck me!"

"Coyote, y'know where we can get some of that peyote stuff or some magic mushrooms?"

"Could you come live in our commune?"

"Could we come live with you?"

"Why don't you change the universe again?"

Coyote screams long and loud, ending in a supersonic howl.

A well-dressed hippie with a tape recorder hands Coyote a recording contract. "Sign this, Coyote. You'll go platinum, and we'll all be rich."

Coyote tears up the contract and throws it in the air.

"Right on, Coyote!" say hippies dancing under the pieces of the contract. "Don't sell out, man!"

"Can we make a movie about you?"

"Could you, like, stop the war?"

Coyote leaps to a high, thin mesa and says, "I can't stand this anymore! I gotta do something to stop all this!"

"Yeah, stop the war, Coyote!"

"Yeah, you crazy white kids keep saying that all this is about the war in Vietnam. Maybe if I could end that war, you'll all go home and leave me alone; but how can I do that?"

"Go to Washington, Coyote!"

"Talk to the President, man!"

"Coyote for President!"

"Yeah," says Coyote. "I'll go to Washington and talk to the President!" And he changes into a multicolor Day-Glo ICBM and flies off, leaving a psychedelic vapor trail.

"Far out," say the hippies.

Above the White House, Coyote changes back into himself, crawls into a window, and goes looking for the President.

"Will the President talk to a Coyote?" he wonders, so he changes into a cartoon version of the President.

In the Oval Office, he bumps into the real President, who turns and screams.

"First my reflection starts looking like all those caricatures of me," says the President, "my jowl's getting heavier, my five-o'clock shadow showing up fifteen minutes after I shave, my nose looking like a limp dick with an ass at the end of it – now I'm seeing myself!"

Coyote changes back into himself.

"Oh no," says the President, "I'm turning into a werewolf!"

"Don't be stupid," says Coyote. "I just disguised myself as you so I could get in to see you."

"What are you?" The President looks Coyote over.

"I am Coyote. One of the important native spirits of this continent."

"A spirit! A ghost! They've finally done it! Some damned hippies slipped me some LSD!"

"I'm not a hallucination! I am Coyote!" He howls and gets bigger and uglier, his fangs and claws long and sharp.

"No, please! I can't help it; being the President drives you insane! I thought it would make me powerful, but I'm helpless – I'm beginning to want to quit politics, and just write books and give interviews. There's good money in that media stuff – but right now it's as if I'm totally controlled by unseen forces!"

"I am one of those unseen forces!" Coyote snarls. He picks up the President by the throat. "If you don't do what I say, I'll make myself look like you again, and I'll go all over America, making you look like the biggest asshole that ever lived!"

The President shudders. "I'll do anything – just tell me."

"End the war."

The President laughs. Coyote puts him down.

"Is that all you want? Sure, I'll do that. I was planning on bringing our troops home anyway. It's not working. Not even the bombing. I don't even think the Bomb would help. I don't know what went wrong – it seems that the whole world's gone crazy!"

"I sure know that. The hippies keep coming to me, bothering me."

"You too? Is that why you want the war stopped; you want to make a deal or something?"

"I am Coyote. I have the power to change things. If I can get you to stop the war, not only will the hippies stop bothering me, but they will change."

"Change? How?"

"That's easy for me. I have my power, and they have their heads so full of mass-produced spirits and gods that they can't help but change with just a little prodding from me."

"Mass-produced spirits and gods? I don't get it."

"What you call the media – television and all that stuff."

The President runs a hand over his heavy stubble. "Yeah, the media, television has power. I know it."

"So do we have a deal?"

"Yeah," the President sticks out his hand; Coyote slaps it with his paw.

Dissolve back to me looking puzzled on the bus.

"You mean Coyote ended the war in Vietnam?"

"That's what I told you," says the Indian.

"And what happened to the hippies – the yuppies – was also Coyote's doing?"

"Yeah, you know how it is when Coyote changes things; it gets out of control and the unexpected happens."

I shake my head. This is all too weird to believe. "So what's Coyote done lately?"

"Well, haven't you been following the news? There's been a hell of a lot of change going on in the last few years. The world is getting stranger and stranger. Hey, they elected a movie star President, didn't they? Then there was that President who acted like a movie star! Hollywood is taking over the world. And the Internet is really screwing things around. And because things work that way, it all came back to Coyote."

(My mind makes like a TV set jammed between channels, then . . .)

Dissolve to a slick contemporary-style cartoon backdrop of a desert road. A car that looks like all the other foreign and American cars do these days – except it's too big – cruises down the road to the sound of techno music. There is no one driving it. It heads for Coyote's house, which has a brand-new satellite dish next to it.

Cut to inside Coyote's house. Coyote is seated before a state-of-the-art home entertainment system, using his remote control to flick through all broadcast channels and cable networks that his satellite dish can access. He can't find anything he wants to watch, just keeps switching channels.

"Maybe it wasn't such a good idea trading in my antique pick-up truck for all this shit," he says.

The *beep-beep* of an amplified electronic car horn blasts.

Coyote goes outside to see what it is. There's the too-big generic contemporary car, idling with no driver, or passengers.

"A car that drives itself," Coyote says. "It figures."

The car makes some metallic squawks and parts of it unfold and separate until it transforms into five Japanese-style robots each with built-in calculators, document processors, and briefcases.

"Excuse me, sir," says Robot #1 in a pure Hollywood accent. "Are you Coyote?"

"Uh, yeah."

"Very good. My associates and I have been scanning for you a long time."

Cameras, microphones, and radar antenna sprout out of Robots #2 through 5, wiggle around, making beeping noises, and retract.

"Uh, yeah. What do you want with me?"

Robots #2 through 5 circle around Coyote, who turns around, looking suspiciously at them.

"We represent a Large Multinational Corporation," says Robot #1. "And would like to discuss business with you."

All the robots extend their arms with the built-in briefcases and rotate them to horizontal positions. The briefcases open revealing portable computer terminals inside. The screens light up and start flashing diagrams.

"Our Corporation has holdings of many different kinds, all over the planet and, hopefully soon, beyond," says Robot #1. "Among these are real estate, mining, construction, high-tech industries . . . and entertainment."

"Uh-oh," says Coyote.

"Primarily, we would like to negotiate with you on behalf of a holding of ours that produces animated cartoons."

Coyote shakes his head. "No way. Tried to make a deal years ago; it didn't work out. Ask the Mouse."

"We own the Mouse. We have for years. He is the one who told us about you."

"Hope he didn't tell you any lies."

"No. What he said made a lot of sense. About your ability to cause change, about your mythic connection to this most important continent . . ."

"What about why the studio wouldn't have anything to do with me?"

"Ah, Coyote, times have changed. This is the twenty-first century. Communications technologies are more varied. And that is part of our problem."

"Problem?"

"Yes, Coyote. Modern mass media, the Net, and the Web have not only sped up communication but also the process of mythmaking. As we go about our business, creating products, we create new mythologies, new gods, new realities. It can be very disruptive. It cuts into our profit margins."

"And you think I can do something about that?"

"That power to change that the Mouse told us of, you could use it to edit out realities that we find disruptive."

Coyote laughs. All the robots extend sensing devices and rows of question marks fill their computer screens.

"What's so funny?" asks Robot #1.

"It don't work that way," Coyote says, holding his sides to keep from laughing. "Every time I change something, it triggers the unexpected. I can't control it. Nothing can."

"Our R&D departments will get to work on it, Coyote. That glitch can be solved."

Coyote laughs more.

"Please, listen to us. We not only can offer you money but can also make you part of some of the biggest deals in history. Just look at our screens."

Coyote gets dizzy spinning around trying to look at all five screens at once. Image after image flashes on them: storyboards for Coyote cartoon shows, Coyote dolls, Coyote designer underwear, Coyote theme parks, Coyote condominiums, Coyote shopping malls . . .

"Stop! Stop!" says Coyote, staggering around as if he were drunk. "What is all this stuff?"

"Things that could result from your association with us."

"Wait a minute! The amusement parks, condos, and shopping malls – where are you gonna put all that?"

"Why, right here. Through you we are going to obtain the rights to all this undeveloped land. There's so much we could do here and lots of raw materials – some even radioactive – and it disturbs us to see all this land going unused and not generating any profits."

"Get out of here!" says Coyote.

"But we are willing to let you have a share of the profits!"

"I've heard all of this before, and it always ends the same way – with me getting taken for more and more of what I've got!"

"So you refuse to even negotiate with us?"

"You betcha."

Robots #2 through 5 make some beeping noises.

"Yes," Robot #1 says. "We have no choice but to implement plan B."

"Plan B?" asks Coyote.

The robots refold themselves into new shapes, then link up into one giant Megarobot.

"Plan B," says the Megarobot in a booming, amplified voice, "provides for us to take you and your property by force. This is all vital to maintaining our profit margins and saving the world economy. We have no choice."

"Same old story," says Coyote.

The Megarobot raises its arms, retracting its hands and firing missiles into the sky. Lasers shoot out of its eyes and barely miss Coyote. Then it vomits napalm all over the place.

"No!" roars Coyote, as he summons his power of change and conjures up a thunderstorm and tornado that are both several times larger than the Megarobot.

The storm and tornado converge on the Megarobot, knocking it down, shorting out its circuits with water and lightning, sandblasting through its armor, and, with the help of traces of radioactive elements in the flying dust and mud, causing the Megarobot to fuse into a great robot-shaped rock formation.

Dissolve to me and the Indian on the Greyhound.

"So, is that it?" I ask, fascinated, but barely able to stay awake. "The Coyote stories brought up to date. Is Coyote retired now?"

The Indian laughs. "Hell no. Coyote is alive and well and . . ."

I fall asleep.

Dissolve to a dream. I am waiting at a bus stop in the middle of a desert that is drawn in the style of my own Coyote cartoons. Coyote comes up, carrying a big suitcase, sits next to me.

"You Coyote?" I ask.

"Yeah," he says.

"So what happened after you defeated the Megarobot?"

"Well, I got to thinking about what they, it – whatever – said about mass media and the Internet speeding up the making of myths and gods and realities. I realized that this *is* my business. Of course, I couldn't do it on their, or anybody else's terms, but it is what I should do, only *my* way."

"*Your* way?"

"Yeah, with me doing my usual trickster game of changing things around and letting the unexpected happen, with nobody to try and control it."

"How are you planning on doing that?"

"Easy, kid! I'm going to plug into corporations that own the communications and entertainment industries through the World Wide Web! Start my own mythology/god/reality business."

"Wow! That'll *really* change the world! So where you heading?"

"Where else? Hollywood."

Dissolve to me waking up on the bus. The Indian is gone. The only thing left on his seat is some animal fur.

The bus pulls into the Hollywood Greyhound station that, for all its mythic reputation, is small and unimpressive. I stagger out dazed, squinting at the blinding Southern California daylight. I can barely see and don't know where to go or what to do next.

For a while I think I see a coyote crossing the street.

Then there is a flash of light. I'm afraid that I've come all the way to Hollywood, just to be nuked. Was it world war? Terrorism? Foreign? Domestic? It doesn't really matter when you're being vaporized . . .

My eyesight comes back, and dingy, old Hollywood now looks like a Technicolor dancing cartoon backdrop. The street people, hookers, and bus passengers are all now cartoon characters.

I look at myself.

I am a cartoon character.

There's a spooky laugh, like the Indian's. I turn and see . . . Coyote!

He's a cartoon Coyote, in a three-piece suit, wearing sunglasses and smoking a cigar.

"Hey, kid," he says, "how do you like it? And this is only the beginning. There's a lot of work to do. We can use a few good cartoonists. Ya want a job?"

I say yes.

And now, in real present tense, because it isn't the tick-tock whiteman's time anymore, but something like a cross between Indian time and Einstein's space-time, with the past and future happening now. The myth and dreamtime happen before my very eyes, as I draw it. I'm doing my part in Coyote's new, improved mythotech trickster business.

Fade out, but not to black – fade to brightness.

Spicy Detective #3

ꕥ

Jeffrey Ford

On the bleary-eyed, whiskey side of midnight, when even the shadows have shadows and ghosts die of loneliness only to return as pale, flypaper memories of their former selves, when triggers are cocked and cocks are triggered, and all the dames left standing after sleep has swamped the world have a pile of bleached coif like a hair hive abuzz with stingered schemes of revenge and lust and greed, before the lipstick melts into a trickle of blood and the mascara mixes with tears to write lines of graveyard poetry on pancake masks (elegies of regret to be read by the first rays of a sun that might never rise), after the dirty cash has passed hands and the whispered promises are made with fingers crossed and gams uncrossed, leading to the split-tongued French kiss of Mephistopheles, Rent Johnson, of the square jaw, the double-breasted pinstripe and existential malaise, private eye, sniffer out of the why of treachery, the how of betrayal, the who gives a flying fuck of good gone bad and bad gone worse like a shiv in the kidneys, a brass knuckle sandwich for grandma, a pair of concrete galoshes for a sad sack on a losing streak, whose present case was the search for Sammy Anole, the Lizard King, a stout dwarf of a heinous killer with serpent eyes and twin six-foot iguanas in his basement that cleared the flesh from his victim's corpses like two green-scaled Hoover uprights with needle teeth and blood colder than the beer at The Swan Dive, cleaved, with his flesh, snub-nose special, the hair-rimmed portal of soft wetness belonging to Winter Darling, Anole's current squeeze, spelunking her well-traveled cavern path, in and out, like one of those dying ghosts caught between coming and going, the bed springs in the flop house dive overlooking Pork Chop alley, bathed in blue neon from the Pabst sign across the street, squealing out a half-assed version of the "Boogie Woogie Bugle Boy (of Company B)," and caught, in the reflection of Miss Darling's glass eye, Sammy's dragon stare in the doorway, which made him reach, with lightning speed, for his ankle-holstered piece, and shoot over his left shoulder, while shooting down below, directly drilling the thimble heart of the Lizard King, whose first sound heard through ghostly ears was the gasping, passionless sob of Winter.

Auspicious Eggs

ꕥ

James Morrow

Father Cornelius Dennis Monaghan of Charlestown Parish, Connie to his friends, sets down the styrofoam chalice, turns from the corrugated cardboard altar, and approaches the two women standing by the resin baptismal font. The font is six-sided and encrusted with saints, like a gigantic hex nut forged for some obscure yet holy purpose, but its most impressive feature is its portability. Hardly a month passes in which Connie doesn't drive the vessel across town, bear it into some wretched hovel, and confer immortality on a newborn whose parents have grown too feeble to leave home.

"Merribell, right?" asks Connie, pointing to the baby on his left.

Wedged in the crook of her mother's arm, the infant wriggles and howls. "No – Madelaine," Angela mumbles. Connie has known Angela Dunfey all her life, and he still remembers the seraphic glow that beamed from her face when she first received the Sacrament of Holy Communion. Today she boasts no such glow. Her cheeks and brow appear tarnished, like iron corroded by the Greenhouse Deluge, and her spine curls with a torsion more commonly seen in women three times her age. "Merribell's over here." Angela raises her free hand and gestures toward her cousin Lorna, who is balancing Madelaine's twin sister atop her gravid belly. Will Lorna Dunfey, Connie wonders, also give birth to twins? The phenomenon, he has heard, runs in families.

Touching the sleeve of Angela's frayed blue sweater, the priest addresses her in a voice that travels clear across the nave. "Have these children received the Sacrament of Reproductive Potential Assessment?"

The parishioner shifts a nugget of chewing gum from her left cheek to her right. "Y-yes," she says at last.

Henry Shaw, the pale altar boy, his face abloom with acne, hands the priest a parchment sheet stamped with the Seal of the Boston Isle Archdiocese. A pair of signatures adorns the margin, verifying that two ecclesiastical representatives have legitimized the birth. Connie instantly recognizes the illegible hand of Archbishop Xallibos. Below lie the bold loops and assured serifs of a Friar James Wolfe, M.D., doubtless the man who drew the blood.

Madelaine Dunfey, Connie reads. *Left ovary: 315 primordial follicles. Right ovary: 340 primordial follicles.* A spasm of despair passes through the priest. The egg-cell count for each organ should be 180,000 at least. It's a verdict of infertility, no possible appeal, no imaginable reprieve.

With an efficiency bordering on effrontery, Henry Shaw offers Connie a second parchment sheet.

Merribell Dunfey. Left ovary: 290 primordial follicles. Right ovary: 310 primordial follicles. The priest is not surprised. What sense would there be in God's withholding the power of procreation from one twin but not the other? Connie now needs only to receive these barren sisters, apply the sacred rites, and furtively pray that the Fourth Lateran Council was indeed guided by the Holy Spirit when it undertook to bring the baptismal process into the age of testable destinies and ovarian surveillance.

He holds out his hands, withered palms up, a posture he maintains as Angela surrenders Madelaine, reaches under the baby's christening gown, and unhooks both diaper pins. The mossy odor of fresh urine wafts into the Church of the Immediate Conception. Sighing profoundly, Angela hands the sopping diaper to her cousin.

"Bless these waters, O Lord," says Connie, spotting his ancient face in the baptismal fluid, "that they might grant these sinners the gift of life everlasting." Turning from the font, he presents Madelaine to his ragged flock, over three hundred natural-born Catholics – sixth-generation Irish, mostly, plus a smattering of Portuguese, Italians, and Croats – interspersed with two dozen recent converts of Korean and Vietnamese extraction: a congregation bound together, he'll admit, less by religious conviction than by shared destitution. "Dearly beloved, forasmuch as all humans enter the world in a state of depravity, and forasmuch as they cannot know the grace of our Lord except they be born anew of water, I beseech you to call upon God the Father that, through these baptisms, Madelaine and Merribell Dunfey may gain the divine kingdom." Connie faces his trembling parishioner. "Angela Dunfey, do you believe, by God's word, that children who are baptized, dying before they commit any actual evil, will be saved?"

Her "Yes" is begrudging and clipped.

Like a scrivener replenishing his pen at an inkwell, Connie dips his thumb into the font. "Angela Dunfey, name this child of yours."

"M-M-Madelaine Eileen Dunfey."

"We welcome this sinner, Madelaine Eileen Dunfey, into the mystical body of Christ" – with his wet thumb Connie traces a plus sign on the infant's forehead – "and do mark her with the Sign of the Cross."

Unraveling Madelaine from her christening gown, Connie fixes on the waters. They are preternaturally still – as calm and quiet as the Sea of Galilee after the Savior rebuked the winds. For many years the priest wondered why Christ hadn't returned on the eve of the Greenhouse Deluge, dispersing the hydrocarbon vapors with a wave of his hand, ending global warming with a Heavenward wink, but recently Connie has come to feel that divine intervention entails protocols past human ken.

He contemplates his reflected countenance. Nothing about it – not the tiny eyes, thin lips, hawk's beak of a nose – pleases him. Now he begins the immersion, sinking Madelaine Dunfey to her skullcap . . . her ears . . . cheeks . . . mouth . . . eyes.

"No!" screams Angela.

As the baby's nose goes under, mute cries spurt from her lips: bubbles inflated with bewilderment and pain. "Madelaine Dunfey," Connie intones, holding the infant down, "I baptize you in the name of the Father, and of the Son, and of the Holy Ghost." The bubbles break the surface. The fluid pours into the infant's lungs. Her silent screams cease, but she still puts up a fight.

"No! Please! No!"

A full minute passes, marked by the rhythmic shuffling of the congregation and the choked sobs of the mother. A second minute – a third – and finally the body stops moving, a mere husk, no longer home to Madelaine Dunfey's indestructible soul.

"No!"

The Sacrament of Terminal Baptism, Connie knows, is rooted in both logic and history. Even today, he can recite verbatim the preamble to the Fourth Lateran Council's *Pastoral Letter on the Rights of the Unconceived.* ("Throughout her early years, Holy Mother Church tirelessly defended the Rights of the Born. Then, as the iniquitous institution of abortion spread across Western Europe and North America, she undertook to secure the Rights of the Unborn. Now, as a new era dawns for the Church and her servants, she must make even greater efforts to propagate the gift of life everlasting, championing the Rights of the Unconceived through a Doctrine of Affirmative Fertility.") The subsequent sentence has always given Connie pause. It stopped him when he was a seminarian. It stops him today. ("This Council therefore avers that, during a period such as that in which we find ourselves, when God has elected to discipline our species through a Greenhouse Deluge and its concomitant privations, a society can commit no greater crime against the future than to squander provender on individuals congenitally incapable of procreation.") Quite so. Indeed. And yet Connie has never performed a terminal baptism without misgivings.

He scans the faithful. Valerie Gallogher, his nephews' *zaftig* kindergarten teacher, seems on the verge of tears. Keye Sung frowns. Teresa Curtoni shudders. Michael Hines moans softly. Stephen O'Rourke and his wife both wince.

"We give thanks, most merciful Father" – Connie lifts the corpse from the water – "that it pleases you to regenerate this infant and take her unto your bosom." Placing the dripping flesh on the altar, he leans toward Lorna Dunfey and lays his palm on Merribell's brow. "Angela Dunfey, name this child of yours."

"M-M-Merribell S-Siobhan . . ." With a sharp reptilian hiss, Angela wrests Merribell from her cousin and pulls the infant to her breast. "Merribell Siobhan Dunfey!"

The priest steps forward, caressing the wisp of tawny hair sprouting from Merribell's cranium. "We welcome this sinner – "

Angela whirls around and, still sheltering her baby, leaps from the podium to the aisle – the very aisle down which Connie hopes one day to see her parade in prelude to receiving the Sacrament of Qualified Monogamy.

"Stop!" cries Connie.

"Angela!" shouts Lorna.

"No!" yells the altar boy.

For someone who has recently given birth to twins, Angela is amazingly spry, rushing pell-mell past the stupefied congregation and straight through the narthex.

"Please!" screams Connie.

But already she is out the door, bearing her unsaved daughter into the teeming streets of Boston Isle.

At 8:17 P.M., Eastern Standard Time, Stephen O'Rourke's fertility reaches its weekly peak. The dial on his wrist tells him so, buzzing like a tortured hornet as he scrubs his teeth with baking soda. *Skreee,* says the sperm counter, reminding Stephen of his ineluctable duty. *Skreee, skreee:* go find us an egg.

He pauses in the middle of a brush stroke and, without bothering to rinse his mouth, strides into the bedroom.

Kate lies on the sagging mattress, smoking an unfiltered cigarette as she balances her nightly dose of iced Arbutus rum on her stomach. Baby Malcolm cuddles against his mother, gums fastened onto her left nipple. She stares at the far wall, where the cracked and scabrous plaster frames the video monitor, its screen displaying the regular Sunday night broadcast of *Keep*

Those Kiddies Coming. Archbishop Xallibos, seated, dominates a TV studio appointed like a day-care center: stuffed animals, changing table, brightly colored alphabet letters. Preschoolers crawl across the prelate's Falstaffian body, sliding down his thighs and swinging from his arms as if he's a piece of playground equipment.

"Did you know that a single act of onanism kills up to four hundred million babies in a matter of seconds?" asks Xallibos from the monitor. "As Jesus remarks in the Gospel According to Saint Andrew, 'Masturbation is murder.' "

Stephen coughs. "I don't suppose you're . . ."

His wife thrusts her index finger against her pursed lips. Even when engaged in shutting him out, she still looks beautiful to Stephen. Her huge eyes and high cheekbones, her elegant swanlike neck. "Shhh – "

"Please check," says Stephen, swallowing baking soda.

Kate raises her bony wrist and glances at her ovulation gauge. "Not for three days. Maybe four."

"Damn."

He loves her so dearly. He wants her so much – no less now than when they received the Sacrament of Qualified Monogamy. It's fine to have a connubial conversation, but when you utterly adore your wife, when you crave to comprehend her beyond all others, you need to speak in flesh as well.

"Will anyone deny that Hell's hottest quadrant is reserved for those who violate the rights of the unconceived?" asks Xallibos, playing peek-a-boo with a cherubic toddler. "Who will dispute that contraception, casual sex, and nocturnal emissions place their perpetrators on a one-way cruise to Perdition?"

"Honey, I have to ask you something," says Stephen.

"Shhh – "

"That young woman at Mass this morning, the one who ran away . . ."

"She went crazy because it was twins." Kate slurps down her remaining rum. The ice fragments clink against each other. "If it'd been just the one, she probably could've coped."

"Well, yes, of course," says Stephen, gesturing toward Baby Malcolm. "But suppose one of *your* newborns . . ."

"Heaven is forever, Stephen," says Kate, filling her mouth with ice, "and Hell is just as long." She chews, her molars grinding the ice. Dribbles of rum-tinted water spill from her lips.

"You'd better get to church."

"Farewell, friends," says Xallibos as the theme music swells. He dandles a Korean three-year-old on his knee. "And keep those kiddies coming!"

The path to the front door takes Stephen through the cramped and fetid living room – functionally the nursery. All is quiet, all is well. The fourteen children, one for every other year of Kate's post-menarche, sleep soundly. Nine-year-old Roger is quite likely his, product of the time Stephen and Kate got their cycles in synch; the boy boasts Stephen's curly blonde hair and riveting green eyes. Difficult as it is, Stephen refuses to accord Roger any special treatment – no private trips to the frog pond, no second candy cane at Christmas. A good stepfather doesn't indulge in favoritism.

Stephen pulls on his mended galoshes, fingerless gloves, and torn pea jacket. Ambling out of the apartment, he joins the knot of morose pedestrians as they shuffle along Winthrop Street. A fog descends, a steady rain falls: reverberations from the Deluge. Pushed by expectant mothers, dozens of shabby, black-hooded baby buggies squeak mournfully down the asphalt. The sidewalks belong to adolescent girls, gang after gang, gossiping among themselves and stomping on puddles as they show off their pregnancies like Olympic medals.

Besmirched by two decades of wind and drizzle, a limestone Madonna stands outside the Church of the Immediate Conception. Her expression lies somewhere between a smile and a smirk. Stephen climbs the steps, enters the narthex, removes his gloves, and, dipping his fingertips into the nearest font, decorates the air with the Sign of the Cross.

Every city, Stephen teaches his students at Cardinal Dougherty High School, boasts its own personality. Extroverted Rio, pessimistic Prague, paranoid New York. And Boston Isle? What sort of psyche inhabits the Hub and its surrounding reefs? Schizoid,

Stephen tells them. Split. The Boston that battled slavery and stoked the fires beneath the American melting pot was the same Boston that massacred the Pequots and sent witchfinders to Salem. But here, now, which side of the city is emergent? The bright one, Stephen decides, picturing the hundreds of Heaven-bound souls who each day exit Boston's innumerable wombs, flowing forth like the bubbles that so recently streamed from Madelaine Dunfey's lips.

Blessing the Virgin's name, he descends the concrete stairs to the copulatorium. A hundred votive candles pierce the darkness. The briny scent of incipient immortality suffuses the air. In the far corner, a CD player screeches out the Apostolic Succession doing their famous rendition of "Ave Maria."

The Sacrament of Extramarital Intercourse has always reminded Stephen of a junior high prom. Girls strung along one side of the room, boys along the other, gyrating couples in the center. He takes his place in the line of males, removes his jacket, shirt, trousers, and underclothes, and hangs them on the nearest pegs. He stares through the gloom, locking eyes with Roger's old kindergarten teacher, Valerie Gallogher, a robust thirtyish woman whose incandescent red hair spills all the way to her hips. Grimly they saunter toward each other, following the pathway formed by the mattresses, until they meet amid the morass of writhing soulmakers.

"You're Roger Mulcanny's stepfather, aren't you?" asks the ovulating teacher.

"Father, quite possibly. Stephen O'Rourke. And you're Miss Gallogher, right?"

"Call me Valerie."

"Stephen."

He glances around, noting to his infinite relief that he recognizes no one. Sooner or later, he knows, a familiar young face will appear at the copulatorium, a notion that never fails to make him wince. How could he possibly explicate the Boston Massacre to a boy who'd recently beheld him in the procreative act? How could he render the Battle of Lexington lucid to a girl whose egg he'd attempted to quicken the previous night?

For ten minutes he and Valerie make small talk, most of it issuing from Stephen, as was proper. Should the coming sacrament prove fruitful, the resultant child will want to know about the handful of men with whom his mother connected during the relevant ovulation. (Beatrice, Claude, Tommy, Laura, Yolanda, Willy, and the others were forever grilling Kate for facts about their possible progenitors.) Stephen tells Valerie about the time his students gave him a surprise birthday party. He describes his rock collection. He mentions his skill at trapping the singularly elusive species of rat that inhabits Charlestown Parish.

"I have a talent too," says Valerie, inserting a coppery braid into her mouth. Her areolas seem to be staring at him.

"Roger thought you were a terrific teacher."

"No – something else." Valerie tugs absently on her ovulation gauge. "A person twitches his lips a certain way, and I know what he's feeling. He darts his eyes in an odd manner – I sense the drift of his thoughts." She lowers her voice. "I watched you during the baptism this morning. Your reaction would've angered the archbishop – am I right?"

Stephen looks at his bare toes. Odd that a copulatorium partner should be demanding such intimacy of him.

"Am I?" Valerie persists, sliding her index finger along her large, concave bellybutton.

Fear rushes through Stephen. Does this woman work for the Immortality Corps? If his answer smacks of heresy, will she arrest him on the spot?

"Well, Stephen? Would the archbishop have been angry?"

"Perhaps," he confesses. In his mind he sees Madelaine Dunfey's submerged mouth, bubble following bubble like beads strung along a rosary.

"There's no microphone in my navel," Valerie asserts, alluding to a common Immortality Corps ploy. "I'm not a spy."

"Never said you were."

"You were thinking it. I could tell by the cant of your eyebrows." She kisses him on the mouth, deeply, wetly. "Did Roger ever learn to hold his pencil correctly?"

" 'Fraid not."

"Too bad."

At last the mattress to Stephen's left becomes free, and they climb on top and begin reifying the Doctrine of Affirmative Fertility. The candle flames look like spear points. Stephen closes his eyes, but the effect is merely to intensify the fact that he's here. The liquid squeal of flesh against flesh grows louder, the odor of hot paraffin and warm semen more pungent. For a few seconds he manages to convince himself that the woman beneath him is Kate, but the illusion proves as tenuous as the surrounding wax.

When the sacrament is accomplished, Valerie says, "I have something for you. A gift."

"What's the occasion?"

"Saint Patrick's Day is less than a week away."

"Since when is that a time for gifts?"

Instead of answering, she strolls to her side of the room, rummages through her tangled garments, and returns holding a pressed flower sealed in plastic.

"Think of it as a ticket," she whispers, lifting Stephen's shirt from its peg and slipping the blossom inside the pocket.

"To where?"

Valerie holds an erect index finger to her lips. "We'll know when we get there."

Stephen gulps audibly. Sweat collects beneath his sperm counter. Only fools consider fleeing Boston Isle. Only lunatics risk the retributions meted out by the Corps. Displayed every Sunday night on *Keep Those Kiddies Coming,* the classic images – men submitting to sperm siphons, women locked in the rapacious embrace of artificial inseminators – haunt every parishioner's imagination, instilling the same levels of dread as Spinelli's sculpture of the archangel Chamuel strangling David Hume. There were rumors, of course, unconfirmable accounts of parishioners who've outmaneuvered the patrol boats and escaped to Québec Cay, Seattle Reef, or the Texas Archipelago. But to credit such tales was itself a kind of sin, jeopardizing your slot in Paradise as surely as if you'd denied the unconceived their rights.

"Tell me something, Stephen." Valerie straps herself into her bra. "You're a history teacher. Did Saint Patrick really drive the snakes out of Ireland, or is that just a legend?"

"I'm sure it never happened literally," says Stephen. "I suppose it could be true in some mythic sense."

"It's about penises, isn't it?" says Valerie, dissolving into the darkness. "It's about how our saints have always been hostile to cocks."

Although Harbor Authority Tower was designed to house the merchant-shipping aristocracy on whose ambitions the decrepit Boston economy still depended, the building's form, Connie now realizes, perfectly fits its new, supplemental function: sheltering the offices, courts, and archives of the archdiocese. As he lifts his gaze along the soaring facade, Connie thinks of sacred shapes – of steeples and vaulted windows, of Sinai and Zion, of Jacob's Ladder and hands pressed together in prayer. Perhaps it's all as God wants, he muses, flashing his ecclesiastical pass to the guard. Perhaps there's nothing wrong with commerce and grace being transacted within the same walls.

Connie has seen Archbishop Xallibos in person only once before, five years earlier, when the stately prelate appeared as an "honorary Irishman" in Charlestown Parish's annual Saint Patrick's Day Parade. Standing on the sidewalk, Connie observed Xallibos gliding down Lynde Street atop a huge motorized shamrock. The archbishop looked impressive then, and he looks impressive now – six foot four at least, Connie calculates, and not an ounce under three hundred pounds. His eyes are as red as a lab rat's.

"Father Cornelius Dennis Monaghan," the priest begins, following the custom whereby a visitor to an archbishop's chambers initiates the interview by naming himself.

"Come forward, Father Cornelius Dennis Monaghan."

Connie starts into the office, boots clacking on the polished bronze floor. Xallibos steps from behind his desk, a glistery cube of black marble.

"Charlestown Parish holds a special place in my affections," says the archbishop. "What brings you to this part of town?"

Connie fidgets, shifting first left, then right, until his face lies mirrored in the hubcap-size Saint Cyril medallion adorning Xallibos's chest. "My soul is in torment, Your Grace."

" 'Torment.' Weighty word."

"I can find no other. Last Tuesday I laid a two-week-old infant to rest."

"Terminal baptism?"

Connie ponders his reflection. It is wrinkled and deflated, like a helium balloon purchased at a carnival long gone. "My eighth."

"I know how you feel. After I dispatched my first infertile – no left testicle, right one shriveled beyond repair – I got no sleep for a week." Eyes glowing like molten rubies, Xallibos stares directly at Connie. "Where did you attend seminary?"

"Isle of Denver."

"And on the Isle of Denver did they teach you that there are in fact two Churches, one invisible and eternal, the other – "

"Temporal and finite."

"Then they also taught you that the latter Church is empowered to revise its sacraments according to the imperatives of the age." The archbishop's stare grows brighter, hotter, purer. "Do you doubt that present privations compel us to arrange early immortality for those who cannot secure the rights of the unconceived?"

"The problem is that the infant I immortalized has a twin." Connie swallows nervously. "Her mother stole her away before I could perform the second baptism."

"Stole her away?"

"She fled in the middle of the sacrament."

"And the second child is likewise arid?"

"Left ovary, two hundred ninety primordials. Right ovary, three hundred ten."

"Lord . . ." A high whistle issues from the archbishop, like water vapor escaping a tea kettle. "Does she intend to quit the island?"

"I certainly hope not, Your Grace," says the priest, wincing at the thought. "She probably has no immediate plans beyond protecting her baby and trying to – "

Connie cuts himself off, intimidated by the sudden arrival of a roly-poly man in a white hooded robe.

"Friar James Wolfe, M.D.," says the monk.

"Come forward, Friar Doctor James Wolfe," says Xallibos.

"It would be well if you validated this posthaste." James Wolfe draws a parchment sheet from his robe and lays it on the archbishop's desk. Connie steals a glance at the report, hoping to learn the baby's fertility quotient, but the relevant statistics are too faint. "The priest in question, he's celebrating Mass in" – sliding a loose sleeve upward, James Wolfe consults his wristwatch – "less than an hour. He's all the way over in Brookline."

Striding back to his desk, the archbishop yanks a silver fountain pen from its holder and decorates the parchment with his famous spidery signature.

"*Dominus vobiscum,* Friar Doctor Wolfe," he says, handing over the document.

As Wolfe rushes out of the office, Xallibos steps so close to Connie that his nostrils fill with the archbishop's lemon-scented after-shave lotion.

"That man never has any fun," says Xallibos, pointing toward the vanishing friar. "What fun do you have, Father Monaghan?"

"Fun, Your Grace?"

"Do you eat ice cream? Follow the fortunes of the Celtics?" He pronounces "Celtics" with the hard C mandated by the Third Lateran Council.

Connie inhales a hearty quantity of citrus fumes. "I bake."

"Bake? Bake what? Bread?"

"Cookies, Your Grace. Brownies, cheesecake, pies. For the Feast of the Nativity, I make gingerbread magi."

"Wonderful. I like my priests to have fun. Listen, no matter what, the rite must be performed. If Angela Dunfey won't come to you, then you must go to her."

"She'll simply run away again."

"Perhaps so, perhaps not. I have great faith in you, Father Cornelius Dennis Monaghan."

"More than I have in myself," says the priest, biting his inner cheeks so hard that his eyes fill with tears.

"No," says Kate for the third time that night.

"Yes," insists Stephen, savoring the dual satisfactions of Kate's thigh beneath his palm and Arbutus rum washing through his brain.

Pinching her cigarette in one hand, Kate strokes Baby Malcolm's forehead with the other, lulling him to sleep. "It's wicked," she protests as she places Malcolm on the rug beside the bed. "A crime against the future."

Stephen grabs the Arbutus bottle, pours himself another glass, and, adding a measure of Dr. Pepper, takes a greedy gulp. He sets the bottle back on the nightstand, next to Valerie Gallogher's enigmatic flower.

"Screw the unconceived," he says, throwing himself atop his wife.

On Friday he'd shown the blossom to Gail Whittington, Dougherty High School's smartest science teacher, but her verdict proved unenlightening. *Epigaea repens,* "trailing arbutus," a species with at least two claims to fame: it is the state flower of the Massachusetts Archipelago, and it has lent its name to the very brand of alcohol Stephen now consumes.

"No," says Kate once again. She drops her cigarette on the floor, crushes it with her shoe, and wraps her arms around him. "I'm not ovulating," she avers, forcing her stiff and slippery tongue inside his mouth. "Your sperm aren't . . ."

"Last night, the Holy Father received a vision," Xallibos announces from the video monitor. "Pictures straight from Satan's flaming domain. Hell is a fact, friends. It's as real as a stubbed toe."

Stephen whips off Kate's chemise with all the dexterity of Father Monaghan removing a christening gown. The rum, of course, has much to do with their mutual willingness (four glasses each, only mildly diluted with Dr. Pepper), but beyond the Arbutus the two of them have truly earned this moment. Neither has ever skipped Mass. Neither has ever missed a Sacrament of Extramarital Intercourse. And while any act of nonconceptual love technically lies beyond the Church's powers of absolution, surely Christ will forgive them a solitary lapse. And so they go at it, this sterile union, this forbidden fruitlessness, this coupling from which no soul can come.

"Hedonists dissolving in vats of molten sulfur," says Xallibos.

The bedroom door squeals open. One of Kate's middle children, Beatrice, a gaunt six-year-old with flaking skin, enters holding a rude toy boat whittled from a hunk of bark.

"Look what I made in school yesterday!"

"We're busy," says Kate, pulling the tattered muslin sheet over her nakedness.

"Do you like my boat, Stephen?" asks Beatrice.

He slams a pillow atop his groin. "Lovely, dear."

"Go back to bed," Kate commands her daughter.

"Onanists drowning in lakes of boiling semen," says Xallibos.

Beatrice fixes Stephen with her receding eyes. "Can we sail it tomorrow on Parson's Pond?"

"Certainly. Of course. Please go away."

"Just you and me, right, Stephen? Not Claude or Tommy or Yolanda or *anybody.*"

"Flaying machines," says Xallibos, "peeling the damned like ripe bananas."

"Do you want a spanking?" seethes Kate. "That's exactly what you're going to get, young lady, the worst spanking of your whole life!"

The child issues an elaborate shrug and strides off in a huff.

"I love you," Stephen tells his wife, removing the pillow from his privates like a chef lifting the lid from a stew pot.

Again they press together, throwing all they have into it, every limb and gland and orifice, no holds barred, no positions banned.

"Unpardonable," Kate groans.

"Unpardonable," Stephen agrees. He's never been so excited. His entire body is an appendage to his loins.

"We'll be damned," she says.

"Forever," he echoes.

"Kiss me," she commands.

"Farewell, friends," says Xallibos. "And keep those kiddies coming!"

Wrestling the resin baptismal font from the trunk of his car, Connie ponders the vessel's resemblance to a birdbath – a place, he muses, for pious sparrows to accomplish their avian ablutions. As he sets the vessel on his shoulder and starts away, its edges digging into his flesh, a different metaphor suggests itself. But if the font is Connie's Cross, and Constitution Road his Via Dolorosa, where does that leave his upcoming mission to Angela Dunfey? Is he about to perform some mysterious act of vicarious atonement?

"Morning, Father."

He slips the font from his shoulder, standing it upright beside a fire hydrant. His parishioner Valerie Gallogher weaves amid the mob, dressed in a threadbare woolen parka.

"Far to go?" she asks brightly.

"End of the block."

"Want help?"

"I need the exercise."

Valerie extends her arm and they shake hands, mitten clinging to mitten. "Made any special plans for Saint Patrick's Day?"

"I'm going to bake shamrock cookies."

"Green?"

"Can't afford food coloring."

"I think I've got some green – you're welcome to it. Who's at the end of the block?"

"Angela Dunfey."

A shadow flits across Valerie's face. "And her daughter?"

"Yes," moans Connie. His throat constricts. "Her daughter."

Valerie lays a sympathetic hand on his arm. "If I don't have green, we can probably fake it."

"Oh, Valerie, Valerie – I wish I'd never taken Holy Orders."

"We'll mix yellow with orange. I'm sorry, Father."

"I wish this cup would pass."

"I mean yellow with blue."

Connie loops his arms around the font, embracing it as he might a frightened child. "Stay with me."

Together they walk through the serrated March air and, reaching the Warren Avenue intersection, enter the tumble-down pile of bricks labeled No. 47. The foyer is as dim as a crypt. Switching on his penlight, Connie holds it aloft until he discerns the label *A. Dunfey* glued to a dented mailbox. He begins the climb to apartment 8–C, his parishioner right behind. On the third landing, Connie stops to catch his breath. On the sixth, he sets down the font. Valerie wipes his brow with her parka sleeve. She takes up the font, and the two of them resume their ascent.

Angela Dunfey's door is wormy, cracked, and hanging by one hinge. The mere act of knocking swings it open.

They find themselves in the kitchen – a small musty space that would have felt claustrophobic were it not so sparely furnished. A saucepan hangs over the stove; a frying pan sits atop the icebox; the floor is a mottle of splinters, tar paper, and leprous shards of linoleum. Valerie places the font next to the sink. The basin in which Angela Dunfey washes her dishes, Connie notes, is actually smaller than the one in which the Church of the Immediate Conception immortalizes infertiles.

He tiptoes into the bedroom. His parishioner sleeps soundly, her terrycloth bathrobe parted down the middle to accommodate her groggy, nursing infant; milk trickles from her breasts, streaking her belly with white rivulets. He must move now, quickly and deliberately, so there'll be no struggle, no melodramatic replay of 1 Kings 3:27, the desperate whore trying to tear her baby away from Solomon's swordsman.

Inhaling slowly, Connie leans toward the mattress and, with the dexterity of a weasel extracting the innards from an eggshell, slides the barren baby free and carries her into the kitchen.

Beside the icebox Valerie sits glowering on a wobbly three-legged stool.

"Dearly beloved, forasmuch as all humans enter the world in a state of depravity," Connie whispers, casting a wary eye on Valerie, "and forasmuch as they cannot know the grace of our Lord except they be born anew of water" – he lays the infant on the floor near Valerie's feet – "I beseech you to call upon God the Father that, through this baptism, Merribell Dunfey may gain the divine kingdom."

"Don't beseech *me,*" snaps Valerie.

Connie fills the saucepan, dumps the water into the font, and returns to the sink for another load – not exactly holy water, he muses, not remotely chrism, but presumably not typhoidal either, the best the underbudgeted Boston Water Authority has to offer. He deposits the load, then fetches another.

A wide, milky yawn twists Merribell's face, but she does not cry out.

At last the vessel is ready. "Bless these waters, O Lord, that they might grant this sinner the gift of life everlasting."

Dropping to his knees, Connie begins removing the infant's diaper. The first pin comes out easily. As he pops the second, the tip catches the ball of his thumb. Crown of thorns, he decides, feeling the sting, seeing the blood.

He bears the naked infant to the font. Wetting his punctured thumb, he touches Merribell's brow and draws the sacred plus sign with a mixture of blood and water. "We receive this sinner unto the mystical body of Christ, and do mark her with the Sign of the Cross."

He begins the immersion. Skullcap. Ears. Cheeks. Mouth. Eyes. O Lord, what a monstrous trust, this power to underwrite a person's soul. "Merribell Dunfey, I baptize you in the name of the Father . . ."

Now comes the nausea, excavating Stephen's alimentary canal as he kneels before the porcelain toilet bowl. His guilt pours forth in a searing flood – acidic strands of cabbage, caustic lumps of potato, glutinous strings of bile. Yet these pains are nothing, he knows, compared with what he'll experience on passing from this world to the next.

Drained, he stumbles toward the bedroom. Somehow Kate has bundled the older children off to school before collapsing on the floor alongside the baby. She shivers with remorse. Shrieks and giggles pour from the nursery: the preschoolers engaged in a raucous game of Blind Man's Bluff.

"Flaying machines," she mutters. Her tone is beaten, bloodless. She lights a cigarette. "Peeling the damned like . . ."

Will more rum help, Stephen wonders, or merely make them sicker? He extends his arm. Passing over the nightstand, his fingers touch a box of aspirin, brush the preserved *Epigaea repens,* and curl around the neck of the half-full Arbutus bottle. A ruddy cockroach scurries across the doily.

"I kept Willy home today," says Kate, taking a drag. "He says his stomach hurts."

As he raises the bottle, Stephen realizes for the first time that the label contains a block of type headed *The Story of Trailing*

Arbutus. "His stomach *always* hurts." He studies the breezy little paragraph.

"I think he's telling the truth."

Epigaea repens. Trailing arbutus. Mayflower. And suddenly everything is clear.

"What's today's date?" asks Stephen.

"Sixteenth."

"March sixteenth?"

"Yeah."

"Then tomorrow's Saint Patrick's Day."

"So what?"

"Tomorrow's Saint Patrick's Day" – like an auctioneer accepting a final bid, Stephen slams the bottle onto the nightstand – "and Valerie Gallogher will be leaving Boston Isle."

"Roger's old teacher? Leaving?"

"Leaving." Snatching up the preserved flower, he dangles it before his wife. "Leaving . . ."

". . . and of the Son," says Connie, raising the sputtering infant from the water, "and of the Holy Ghost."

Merribell Dunfey screeches and squirms. She's slippery as a bar of soap. Connie manages to wrap her in a dish towel and shove her into Valerie's arms.

"Let me tell you who you are," she says.

"Father Cornelius Dennis Monaghan of Charlestown Parish."

"You're a tired and bewildered pilgrim, Father. You're a weary wayfarer like myself."

Dribbling milk, Angela Dunfey staggers into the kitchen. Seeing her priest, she recoils. Her mouth flies open, and a howl rushes out, a cry such as Connie imagines the damned spew forth while rotating on the spits of Perdition. "Not her too! Not Merribell! No!"

"Your baby's all right," says Valerie.

Connie clasps his hands together, fingers knotted in agony and supplication. He stoops. His knees hit the floor, crashing against the fractured linoleum. "Please," he groans.

Angela plucks Merribell from Valerie and affixes the squalling baby to her nipple. "Oh, Merribell, Merribell . . ."

"Please." Connie's voice is hoarse and jagged, as if he's been shot in the larynx. "Please . . . please," he beseeches. Tears roll from his eyes, tickling his cheeks as they fall.

"It's not *her* job to absolve you," says Valerie.

Connie snuffles the mucus back into his nose. "I know."

"The boat leaves tomorrow."

"Boat?" Connie runs his sleeve across his face, blotting his tears.

"A rescue vessel," his parishioner explains. Sliding her hands beneath his armpits, she raises him inch by inch to his feet. "Rather like Noah's Ark."

"Mommy, I want to go home."

"Tell that to your stepfather."

"It's cold."

"I know, sweetheart."

"And dark."

"Try to be patient."

"Mommy, my stomach hurts."

"I'm sorry."

"My head too."

"You want an aspirin?"

"I want to go home."

Is this a mistake? wonders Stephen. Shouldn't they all be in bed right now instead of tromping around in this nocturnal mist, risking flu and possibly pneumonia? And yet he has faith. Somewhere in the labyrinthine reaches of the Hoosac Docks, amid the tang of salt air and the stink of rotting cod, a ship awaits.

Guiding his wife and stepchildren down Pier 7, he studies the possibilities – the scows and barges, the tugs and trawlers, the reefers and bulk carriers. Gulls and gannets hover above the wharfs, squawking their chronic disapproval of the world. Across the channel, lit by a sodium-vapor searchlight, the USS *Constitution* bobs in her customary berth beside Charlestown Navy Yard.

"What're we doing here, anyway?" asks Beatrice.

"Your stepfather gets these notions in his head." Kate presses the baby tight against her chest, shielding him from the sea breeze.

"What's the *name* of the boat?" asks Roger.

"*Mayflower*," answers Stephen.

Epigaea repens, trailing arbutus, may flower.

"How do you spell it?" Roger demands.

"M-a-y . . ."

". . . f-l-o-w-e-r?"

"Good job, Roger," says Stephen.

"I *read* it," the boy explains indignantly, pointing straight ahead with the collective fingers of his right mitten.

Fifty yards away, moored between an oil tanker and a bait shack, a battered freighter rides the incoming tide. Her stern displays a single word, *Mayflower,* a name that to the inhabitants of Boston Isle means far more than the sum of its letters.

"Now can we go home?" asks Roger.

"No," says Stephen. He has taught the story countless times. The Separatists' departure from England for Virginia . . . their hazardous voyage . . . their unplanned landing on Plymouth Rock . . . the signing of the covenant whereby the non-Separatists on board agreed to obey whatever rules the Separatists imposed. "*Now* we can go on a nice long voyage."

"On *that* thing?" asks Willy.

"You're not serious," says Laura.

"Not me," says Claude.

"Forget it," says Yolanda.

"Sayonara," says Tommy.

"I think I'm going to throw up," says Beatrice.

"It's not your decision," Stephen tells his stepchildren. He stares at the ship's hull, blotched with rust, blistered with decay, another victim of the Deluge. A passenger whom he recognizes as his neighbor Michael Hines leans out a porthole like a prairie dog peering from its burrow. "Until further notice, I make all the rules."

Half by entreaty, half by coercion, he leads his disgruntled family up the gangplank and onto the quarterdeck, where a squat man in an orange raincoat and a maroon watch cap demands to see their ticket.

"Happy Saint Patrick's Day," says Stephen, flourishing the preserved blossom.

"We're putting you people on the fo'c'sle deck," the man yells above the growl of the idling engines. "You can hide behind the pianos. At ten o'clock you get a bran muffin and a cup of coffee."

As Stephen guides his stepchildren in a single file up the forward ladder, the crew of the *Mayflower* reels in the mooring lines and ravels up the anchor chains, setting her adrift. The engines kick in. Smoke pours from the freighter's twin stacks. Sunlight seeps across the bay, tinting the eastern sky hot pink and making the island's many-windowed towers glitter like Christmas trees.

A sleek Immortality Corps cutter glides by, headed for the wharfs, evidently unaware that enemies of the unconceived lie close at hand.

Slowly, cautiously, Stephen negotiates the maze of wooden crates – it seems as if every piano on Boston Isle is being exported today – until he reaches the starboard bulwark. As he curls his palm around the rail, the *Mayflower* cruises past the Mystic Shoals, maneuvering amid the rocks like a skier following a slalom course.

"Hello, Stephen." A large woman lurches into view, abruptly kissing his cheek.

He gulps, blinking like a man emerging into sunlight from the darkness of a copulatorium. Valerie Gallogher's presence on the *Mayflower* doesn't surprise him, but he's taken aback by her companions. Angela Dunfey, suckling little Merribell. Her cousin, Lorna, still spectacularly pregnant. And, most shocking of all, Father Monaghan, leaning his frail frame against his baptismal font.

Stephen says, "Did we . . . ? Are you . . . ?"

"My blood has spoken," Valerie Gallogher replies, her red hair flying like a pennant. "In nine months I give birth to our child."

Whereupon the sky above Stephen's head begins swarming with tiny black birds. No, not birds, he realizes: devices. Ovulation gauges sail through the air, a dozen at first, then scores, then hundreds, immediately pursued by equal numbers of sperm counters. As the little machines splash down and sink, darkening the harbor like the contraband tea from an earlier moment in the history of Boston insurgency, a muffled but impassioned cheer arises among the stowaways.

"Hello, Father Monaghan." Stephen unstraps his sperm counter. "Didn't expect to find you here."

The priest smiles feebly, drumming his fingers on the lip of the font. "Valerie informs me you're about to become a father again. Congratulations."

"My instincts tell me it's a boy," says Stephen, leaning over the rail. "He's going to get a second candy cane at Christmas," asserts the bewildered pilgrim as, with a wan smile and a sudden flick of his wrist, he breaks his bondage to the future.

If I don't act now, thinks Connie as he pivots toward Valerie Gallogher, I'll never find the courage again.

"Do we have a destination?" he asks. Like a bear preparing to ascend a tree, he hugs the font, pulling it against his chest.

"Only a purpose." Valerie sweeps her hand across the horizon. "We won't find any Edens out there, Father. The entire Baltimore Reef has become a wriggling mass of flesh, newborns stretching shore to shore." She removes her ovulation gauge and throws it over the side. "In the Minneapolis Keys, the Corps routinely casts homosexual men and menopausal women into the sea. On the California Archipelago, male parishioners receive periodic potency tests and – "

"The Atlanta Insularity?"

"A nightmare."

"Miami Isle?"

"Forget it."

Connie lays the font atop the bulwark, then clambers onto the rail, straddling it like a child riding a see-saw. A loop of heavy-duty chain encircles the font, the steel links flashing in the rising sun. "Then what's our course?"

"East," says Valerie. "Toward Europe. What are you doing?"

"East," Connie echoes, tipping the font seaward. "Europe."

A muffled, liquid crash reverberates across the harbor. The font disappears, dragging the chain behind it.

"Father!"

Drawing in a deep breath, Connie studies the chain. The spiral of links unwinds quickly and smoothly, like a coiled rattlesnake striking its prey. The slack vanishes. Connie feels the iron shackle seize his ankle. He flips over. He falls.

"Bless these waters, O Lord, that they might grant this sinner the gift of life everlasting . . ."

"Father!"

He plunges into the harbor, penetrating its cold hard surface: an experience, he decides, not unlike throwing oneself through a plate glass window. The waters envelop him, filling his ears and stinging his eyes.

We welcome this sinner into the mystical body of Christ, and do mark him with the Sign of the Cross, Connie recites in his mind, reaching up and drawing the sacred plus sign on his forehead.

He exhales, bubble following bubble.

Cornelius Dennis Monaghan, I baptize you in the name of the Father, and of the Son, and of the Holy Ghost, he concludes, and as the black wind sweeps through his brain, sucking him toward immortality, he knows that he's never been happier.

Timmy and Tommy's Thanksgiving Secret

ꕥ

Bradley Denton

Timmy and Tommy were best friends. They lived on a farm in the Great Midwest with Daddy Mike, Mama Jane, Buster and Scotty the Farm Dogs, several pigs, a few chickens, and Maybelle the Moo Cow. Timmy was five years old and belonged to Daddy Mike and Mama Jane, but Tommy was younger, and an orphan. Even worse, he couldn't talk.

But Timmy didn't feel sorry for Tommy, because Tommy was just like one of the family. Mama Jane called him Timmy's adopted brother. Tommy even went out with Timmy every morning to watch Daddy Mike milk Maybelle the Moo Cow, and Daddy Mike would surprise them both with squirts of milk in their faces.

"Ha ha!" Daddy Mike would laugh. "Look alive, there!"

Then Timmy would laugh too, and Tommy would do the best he could.

And even though Mama Jane had said that Timmy didn't have to share his room with Tommy, Timmy was glad to do it anyway. At night after they went to bed, he and Tommy whispered secrets that they promised never to tell anyone else – secrets about all the adventures they'd had together.

And oh! What adventures!

They fought pirates on the banks of Muddy Pond . . .

They chased buffalo across Grassy Meadow . . .

They explored deserts that looked just like Rocky Pasture . . .

And best of all, they scaled the dizzying heights of Towering Grain Silo.

That is, Timmy did. Tommy always refused to climb the shaky ladder. So Timmy would go up alone, and when he reached the very tip-top, he would look down and shout, "Tommy is a chicken! Tommy is a chicken!"

At this, Tommy would always look very indignant, and sometimes he would even stalk off in a huff. A chicken, indeed! What an insult!

But by bedtime, all would be forgiven, and Timmy would lie awake in bed and whisper secrets across the room to where Tommy slept on a pallet on the floor. And although Tommy couldn't talk the way normal people did, sometimes he would jabber nonsense in response to Timmy's whispers. At least, Daddy Mike said that it was nonsense, but Timmy knew better. After all, Tommy's jabbering sounded just like Mrs. Krunholtz at Sunday Church when she rolled around on the floor and spoke in tongues. And no one ever said that Mrs. Krunholtz was jabbering nonsense.

One November morning while it was still dark, Timmy woke up to the sounds of the kitchen door banging shut and Daddy Mike's boots clomping into the barnyard. Timmy was surprised. Daddy Mike got up early every morning to milk Maybelle, but never this early. Timmy didn't know what to make of it.

"Come on, Tommy!" Timmy cried, throwing off his blankets and grabbing his pint-sized coveralls from the bedpost. "Let's go see what Daddy Mike's doing! Maybe we can help!"

Tommy jabbered in agreement, and together they hurried downstairs, almost tumbling over one another in their excitement.

When they reached the kitchen, they found that Mama Jane was up and about, too. She was putting a big pot of water on the stove.

"Oh good," Mama Jane said when she saw Timmy and Tommy. "I'm glad you two are bright-eyed and bushy-tailed! There's a lot to do today!"

"Why?" Timmy asked. "What's today?"

"Well, my goodness, child!" Mama Jane said. "It's Thanksgiving! Now, run out and help Daddy Mike. The sun's coming up, and my whole family will be here before you can say Jack Robinson – so hop to it!"

Timmy and Tommy hopped outside, and then Timmy saw Daddy Mike, along with Buster and Scotty the Farm Dogs, standing in the barnyard beside the old oak stump that Timmy and Tommy used as the deck of their battleship. So Timmy dashed out to the stump with Tommy hurrying close behind.

"Why, there you are!" Daddy Mike exclaimed when he saw Timmy and Tommy. "I thought you were going to sleep the day away!" And with that, he grabbed Tommy by the feet and slammed him onto the stump.

"Daddy Mike!" Timmy cried. "Is Tommy in trouble?"

"In a manner of speaking," Daddy Mike said. Then he picked up a hatchet that had been hidden on the far side of the stump, and with one quick stroke, he chopped off Tommy's head. Tommy's head flew away and tumbled to the dirt, and Tommy's blood spurted from his neck onto Daddy Mike's hand.

Then Buster and Scotty the Farm Dogs began making quite a ruckus. They were fighting over Tommy's head.

"Timmy, take Tommy's head and put it in the trash barrel down by the barn," said Daddy Mike. "If Buster or Scotty got hold of it, they could start choking, and then I'd have to get the gun."

So Timmy picked up Tommy's head and went down to the barn with Buster and Scotty nipping at his heels.

"Tommy?" Timmy said to Tommy's head. "What did you do to get in trouble?"

But Tommy's head didn't even jabber. It just gazed up at Timmy with one glassy black eye.

"Timmy!" Daddy Mike cried then. "Come look at this!"

Daddy Mike sounded excited, so Timmy dropped Tommy's head into the trash barrel and ran back to the old oak stump as fast as he could. When he got there, he saw Tommy staggering toward the house, leaving a squiggly trail of blood behind him. Before long, though, Tommy flopped over and lay there twitching.

"Did you ever see the like?" Daddy Mike asked.

But Timmy didn't have a chance to answer, because Buster and Scotty the Farm Dogs came running back from the trash barrel, snarling and biting at each other all the way.

"Quick, Timmy!" Daddy Mike said. "Pick up Tommy and take him to Mama Jane while I have a talk with Buster and Scotty!"

So Timmy went to Tommy and tried to pick him up while Daddy Mike had a talk with Buster and Scotty. But Tommy was big and heavy, so Timmy had to grab him by the feet the way Daddy Mike had done, and then drag him to the house.

This was hard work, but Timmy finally got Tommy into the kitchen, where Mama Jane was waiting. Her big pot of water was boiling now.

"My goodness, child!" Mama Jane exclaimed. "You've left a bloody smear all across my kitchen floor!" Then she scooped up Tommy and dropped him into the boiling water. Tommy's feet stuck up out of the water and wiggled.

"Why are you doing that, Mama Jane?" Timmy asked. "And why did Daddy Mike chop off Tommy's head?"

"My goodness, child!" Mama Jane exclaimed again. "How you do go on!" With that, she put on a pair of heavy rubber gloves, pulled Tommy from the water, and plunked him onto the sideboard. Then she started yanking out all of Tommy's feathers.

"Doesn't that hurt?" Timmy asked.

"It would if I wasn't wearing gloves," Mama Jane said.

After all of Tommy's feathers were gone, Mama Jane used a cleaver to cut off Tommy's feet. Then she took a shiny knife, sliced Tommy open, and yanked out his guts. She put most of the guts into a pan and gave the pan to Timmy.

"You can take these to Buster and Scotty if you like," Mama Jane said.

So Timmy did just that. He watched Buster and Scotty play tug-of-war for a while, and then he went down to the barn. He found Daddy Mike milking Maybelle the Moo Cow, and while he sat in the corner to watch, Daddy Mike sprayed him in the face with milk.

"Ha ha!" Daddy Mike laughed. "Look alive, there!"

Later, Grandma Eula, Uncle Augie, Aunt Pearl, and Cousins Fred, Earl, Cookie, and Poot all came over for Thanksgiving dinner. Tommy had been cooked all golden and crispy on the outside, and when Mama Jane placed him in the center of the table, Daddy Mike cut him up into juicy, steaming chunks.

"Give me a drumstick," said Cousin Fred. "That's the best part."

"No, no," said Cousin Cookie. "The neck is the best."

"You're both wrong, children," said Grandma Eula. "There's nothing better than a nice plump thigh."

"It's a slice of breast for me," said Aunt Pearl.

"I'd prefer a wing, myself," said Cousin Poot.

"You're all loopy," said Uncle Augie. "I dibs the gizzard. That's really the best part. Did you remember to fry up the gizzard, Sister Jane?"

"I surely did," said Mama Jane, and she brought Tommy's gizzard to Uncle Augie on a special silver plate.

"Yum!" Uncle Augie exclaimed, and he gobbled up Tommy's gizzard in three quick bites. Then he leaned back and gave Timmy a big grin. "And now," he said, "it's wishbone time!"

"What's that?" Timmy asked.

So Uncle Augie showed him. He held one side of the wishbone while Timmy held the other, and then they both pulled. The wishbone broke in two.

"You got the big half!" Uncle Augie cried. "You get your wish!"

"What did you wish for, Timmy?" Grandma Eula asked.

"I wished for rattlesnakes to bite all of you until you swell up and stink like Maybelle's calf Pansy did," Timmy said.

So Mama Jane said it was all right if Timmy went outside to play, and he did just that. After a while he wandered down to the trash barrel by the barn and pulled out Tommy's head.

Timmy walked across the barnyard with Tommy's head cupped in his hands, thinking that perhaps he would take Tommy to the top of Towering Grain Silo at last.

But then Daddy Mike came down from the house, calling, "Timmy! You can come back now! We have punkin pie!"

Timmy didn't want Daddy Mike to know that he had pulled Tommy's head from the trash barrel, so he did the first thing he could think of, which was to pop Tommy's head into his mouth, chew it up as best he could, and swallow it. By the time Daddy Mike reached him, Tommy's head was all gone.

"It's time for dessert," Daddy Mike said. "And then we're each going to say what we're thankful for. Can you think of what you're thankful for, Timmy?"

"Yes I can, Daddy Mike," said Timmy. "I'm thankful that I'm not adopted."

But as they walked back to the house, Timmy realized that there was something he was even more thankful for. He was thankful because he and Tommy now had one more secret, the biggest one ever, that only the two of them shared.

The secret was this:

No matter what anyone else thought, the *head* was the very best part of all.

Savage Breasts

Nina Kiriki Hoffman

I was only a lonely leftover on the table of Life. No one seemed interested in sampling me.

I was alone that day in the company cafeteria when I made the fateful decision which changed my life. If Gladys, the other secretary in my boss's office and my usual lunch companion, had been there, it might never have happened, but she had a dentist appointment. Alone with the day's entree, Spaghetti-O's, I sought companionship in a magazine I found on the table.

In the first blazing burst of inspiration I ever experienced, I cut out an ad on the back of the *Wonder Woman* comic book. "The Insult that Made a Woman Out of Wilma," it read. It showed a hipless, flat-chested girl being buried in the sand and abandoned by her date, who left her alone with the crabs as he followed a bosomy blonde off the page. Wilma eventually excavated herself, went home, kicked a chair, and sent away for Charlotte Atlas's pamphlet, "From Beanpole to Buxom in 20 days or your money back." Wilma read the pamphlet and developed breasts the size of breadboxes. She retrieved her boyfriend and rendered him acutely jealous by picking up a few hundred other men.

I emulated Wilma's example and sent away for the pamphlet and the equipment that came with it.

When my pamphlet and my powder-pink exerciser arrived, I felt a vague sense of unease. Some of the ink in the pamphlet was blurry. A few pages were repeated. Others were missing. Sensing that my uncharacteristic spurt of enthusiasm would dry up if I took the time to send for a replacement, I plunged into the exercises in the book (those I could decipher) and performed them faithfully for the requisite twenty days. My breasts blossomed. Men on the streets whistled. Guys at the office looked up when I jiggled past.

I felt like a palm tree hand-pollinated for the first time. I began to have clusters of dates. I was pawed, pleasured, and played with. I experienced lots of stuff I had only read about before, and I mostly loved it after the first few times. The desert I'd spent my life in vanished; everything I touched here in the center of the mirage seemed real, intense, throbbing with life. I exercised harder, hoping to make the reality realler.

Then parts of me began to fight back.

I reclined on Maxwell's couch, my hands behind my head, as he unbuttoned my shirt, unhooked my new, enormous, front-hook bra, and opened both wide. He kissed my stomach. He feathered kisses up my body. Suddenly my left breast flexed and punched him in the face. He was surprised. He looked at me suspiciously. I was surprised myself. I studied my left breast. It lay there gently bobbing like a Japanese glass float on a quiet sea. Innocent. Waiting.

Maxwell stared at my face. Then he shook his head. He eyed my breasts. Slowly he leaned closer. His lips drew back in a pucker. I waited, tingling, for them to flutter on my abdomen again. No such luck. Both breasts surged up and gave him a double whammy.

It took me an hour to wake him up. Once I got him conscious, he told me to get out! Out! And take my unnatural equipment with me. I collected my purse and coat, and, with a last look at him as he lay there on the floor by the couch, I left.

In the elevator my breasts punched a man who was smoking a cigar. He coughed, choked, and called me unladylike. A woman told me I had done the right thing.

When I got home I took off my clothes and looked at myself in the mirror. What beautiful breasts. Pendulous. Centerfold quality.

Heavy as water balloons. Firm as paperweights. I would be sorry to say goodbye to them. I sighed, and they bobbled. "Well, guys, no more exercise for you," I said. I would have to let them go. I couldn't let my breasts become a Menace to Mankind. I would rather be noble and suffer a bunch.

I took a shower and went to bed.

That night I had wild dreams. Something was chasing me, and I was chasing something else. I thought maybe I was chasing myself, and that scared me silly. I kept trying to wake up, but to no avail. When I finally woke, exhausted and sweaty, in the morning, I discovered my sheets twisted around my legs. My powder-pink exerciser lay beside me in the bed. My upper arms ached the way they did after a good workout.

At work, my breasts interfered with my typing. The minute I looked away from my typewriter keyboard to glance at my steno pad, my breasts pushed between my hands, monopolizing the keys and driving my Selectric to distraction. After an hour of trying to cope with this I told my boss I had a sick headache. He didn't want me to go home. "Mae June, you're such an ornament to the office these days," he said. "Can't you just sit out there and look pretty and suffering? More and more of my clients have remarked on how you spruce up the decor. If that clackety-clacking bothers your pretty little head, why, I'll get Gladys to take your work and hers and type in the closet."

"Thank you, sir," I said. I went back out in the front room and sat far away from everything my breasts could knock over. Gladys sent me vicious looks as she flat-chestedly crouched over her early-model IBM and worked twice as hard as usual.

For a while I was happy enough just to rest. After all that nocturnal exertion, I was tired. My chair wasn't comfortable, but my body didn't care. Then I started feeling rotten. I watched Gladys. She had scruffy hair that kept falling out of its bobby pins and into her face. She kept her fingernails short and unpolished, and she didn't seem to care how carelessly she chose her clothes. She reminded me of the way I had looked two months earlier, before men started getting interested in me and giving me advice on what to wear and what to do with my hair. Gladys and I no longer went to lunch together. These days I usually took the boss's clients to lunch.

"Why don't you tell the boss you have a sick headache too?" I asked. "There's nothing here that can't wait until tomorrow."

"He'd fire me, you fool. I can't waggle my femininity in his face like you can. Mae June, you're a cheater."

"I didn't mean to cheat," I said. "I can't help it." I looked at her face to see if she remembered how we used to talk at lunch. "Watch this, Gladys." I turned back to my typewriter and pulled off the cover. The instant I inserted paper, my breasts reached up and parked on the typewriter keys. I leaned back, straightening up, then tried to type the date in the upper right-hand corner of the page. *Plomp plomp.* No dice. I looked at Gladys. She had that kind of look that says *eyoo, ick, that's creepy, show it to me again.*

I opened my mouth to explain about Wilma's insult and Charlotte Atlas when my breasts firmed up. I found myself leaning back to display me at an advantage. One of the boss's clients had walked in.

"Mae June, my nymphlet," said this guy, Burl Weaver. I had been to lunch with him before. I kind of liked him.

Gladys touched the intercom. "Sir, Mr. Weaver is here."

"Aw, Gladys," said Burl, one of the few men who had learned her name as well as mine, "why'd you haveta spoil it? I didn't come here for business."

"Burl?" the boss asked over the intercom. "What does he want?"

Burl strode over to my desk and pushed my transmit button. "I'd like to borrow your secretary for the afternoon, Otis. Any objections?"

"Why no, Burl, none at all." Burl is one of our biggest accounts. We produce the plastic for the records his company produces. "Mae June, you be good to Burl now."

Burl pressed my transmit button for me. I leaned as near to my speaker as I could get. "Yes, sir," I said. With tons of trepidation, I rose to my feet. My previous acquaintance with Burl had gone farther than my acquaintance with Maxwell yesterday. Now that my breasts were seceding from my body, how could I be sure I'd be nice to Burl? What if I lost the company our biggest account?

With my breasts thrust out before me like dogs hot on a scent, I followed Burl out of the office, giving Gladys a misery-laden glance as I closed the door behind me. She gave me a suffering nod in return. At least there was somebody on my side, I thought, as Burl and I got on the elevator. I tried to cross my arms over my breasts, but they pushed my arms away. A familiar feeling of helplessness, one I knew well from before I sent away for that pamphlet, washed over me. Except this time I didn't feel my fate lay on the knees of the gods. No. My life was in the hands of my breasts, and they seemed determined to throw it away.

Burl waited until the elevator got midway between floors, then hit the stop button. "Just think, Mae June, here we are, suspended in midair," he said. "Think we can hump hard enough to make this thing drop? Wanna try? Think we'll even notice when she hits bottom?" With each sentence he got closer to me, until at last he was pulling the zip down the back of my dress.

I smiled at Burl and wondered what would happen next. I felt like an interested spectator at a sports event. Burl pulled my dress down around my waist.

"You sure look nice today, Mae June," he said, staring at my front, then at my lips. My breasts bobbled obligingly, and he looked down at them again. "Like you got little joy machines inside," he said, gently unhooking my bra.

Joy buzzers, I thought. Jolt city.

"You like me, don't you, Mae June? I can be real nice." He stroked me.

"Sure I like you, Burl."

"Would you like to work for me? I sure like you, Mae June. I'd like to put you in a nice little apartment on the top story of a real tall building with an elevator in it." As he talked, he kneaded at me like a kitten. "An express elevator. It would only stop at your floor and the basement. We could lock it from the inside. We could ride it. Up. Down. Up Down. Hell, we could put a double bed in it. You'd like that, wouldn't you, Mae June?"

"Yes, Burl." When would my mammaries make their move?

He bent his head forward to pull down his own zipper, and they conked him. "Wha?" he said as he recoiled and collapsed gracefully to the floor. "How the heck did you do that, Mae June?"

I decided Burl had a harder head than Maxwell.

"Your hands are all snarled up in your dress. You been taking aikido or something?"

"No, Burl."

"Jeepers, if you didn't like me, you shoulda said something. I woulda left you alone."

"But I do like you, Burl. It's my breasts. They make their own decisions."

He lay on the floor and looked up at me. "That's the dumbest-assed thing I ever heard," he said. He rolled over and got to his feet. Then he came over, leaned toward me, and glared at my breasts. The left one flexed. He jumped back just in time. "Mae June, are you possessed?"

"Yes!" That must be it. The devil was in my breasts. I wondered what I had done to deserve such a fate. I wasn't even religious.

Burl made the sign of the cross over my breasts. Nothing happened. "That's not it," he said. "Maybe it's your subconscious. You hate men. Something like that. So how come this didn't happen last time, huh?" He began pacing.

"They were waiting to get strong enough. Oh, Burl, what am I going to do?"

"Get dressed. I think you better see a doctor, Mae June. Maybe we can get 'em tranquilized or something. I don't like the way they're sitting there, watching me."

I managed to hook my bra without too much trouble. Burl zipped me up and turned the elevator operational again. "Do you hate me?" I asked him on the way down.

"Course I don't hate you," he said, shifting a step further away from me. "You're real pretty, Mae June. Just as soon as you get yourself under control, you're gonna make somebody a real nice little something. I just don't want to take too many chances. Suppose what you've got is contagious? Suppose some of my body parts decide they don't like women? Let's be rational about this, huh?"

"I mean – you won't drop the contract with IPP, will you?"

"Shoot no. You worried about job security? I like that in a woman. You got sense. I won't complain. But I hope you got Blue Cross. You may have to get those knockers psychoanalyzed or something."

He offered to drive me to a doctor or the hospital. I told him I'd take the bus. He tried to get me to change my mind. He failed. I watched him drive away. Then I went home.

I picked up the powder-pink exerciser and took it to the window. My apartment was on the tenth floor. I was just going to drop the exerciser out the window when I looked down and saw Gladys's red coat wrapped around Gladys. My doorbell rang. I buzzed her into the building.

By the time she arrived at my front door I had collapsed on the couch, still holding the exerciser. "It's open," I called when she knocked. My arms were pumping the exerciser as I lay there. I thought about trying to stop exercising, but decided it was too much effort. "How'd you know I'd be home?" I asked Gladys as she came in and took off her coat.

"Burl stopped by the office."

"Did he say what happened?"

"No. He said he was worried about you. What did happen?"

"They punched him." I pumped the exerciser harder. "What am I going to do? I can't type, and now I can't even do lunch." I glared at my breasts. "You want us to starve?"

They were doing push-ups and didn't answer.

Gladys sat on a chair across from me and leaned forward, her gaze fixed on my new features. Her mouth was open.

My arms stopped pumping without me having anything to say about it. My left arm handed the exerciser to her. Her gaze still locked on my breasts, Gladys gripped the powder-pink exerciser and went to work.

"Don't," I said, sitting up. Startled, she fell against the chair-back. "Do you want this to happen to you?"

"I – I – " She gulped and dropped the exerciser.

"I don't know what they want!" I stared at them with loathing. "It won't be long before the boss realizes I'm not an asset. Then what am I going to do?"

"You . . . you have a lot of career choices," said Gladys. "Like – have you ever considered mud wrestling?"

"What?"

"Exotic dancing?" She blinked. She licked her upper lip. "You could join the FBI, I bet. 'My breasts punched out spies for God and country.' You could sell your story to the *Enquirer.* 'Double-breasted Death.' Sounds like a slick detective movie from the thirties. You could – "

"Stop," I said, "I don't want to hear any more."

"I'm sorry," she said after a minute. She got up and made tea.

We were sitting there sipping it when she had another brainstorm. "What do they want? You've been asking that yourself. What are breasts for, anyway?"

"Sex and babies," I said.

We looked at each other. We looked away. All those lunches, and we had never talked about it. I bet she only knew what she read in books too.

She stared at the braided rug on the floor. "Were you . . . protected?"

I stared at the floor too. "I don't think so."

"They have tests you can do at home now."

I thought it was Burl's, so my breasts and I went to visit him. "You talk to them," I said. "If they think you're the father, maybe they won't beat you up anymore. Maybe they're just fending off all other comers."

Between the three of them they reached an arrangement. I moved into that penthouse apartment.

I shudder to think what they'll do when the baby comes.

I Love Paree

ᘓᘐ

Cory Doctorow and Michael Skeet

Day 1: The Night the Lights Went Out in Dialtone

Gay Paree was in full swing when the Libertines conscripted the trustafarians. Me, I should have seen it coming. After all, that's what I do.

I was an OPH – Old Paree Hand – there before the Communards raised their barricades; there before the Boul' Disney became a trustafarian chill zone; a creaking antique expat who liked his café and croissant and the *International Times* crossword in the morning. I loved Paree, loved the way I could stay plugged into everything while soaking in the warm bath of centuries. I loved the feeling of being part of a special club; we OPHs always managed to look out for one another, always managed to find the time to play at baseball in the Bois de Boulogne when the weather was good. Not even civil war had been able to change that, and that I loved about Paree most of all.

Normalement, I would've been in bed when the Club Dialtone was raided. But that night, I was entertaining Sissy, a cousin come from Toronto for a wild weekend, and Sissy wanted to see the famed Dialtone. So we duded up – me in rumpled whites and hiking boots with calculated amounts of scuff; Sissy in po-mo Empire dress and PVC bolero jacket and a round bowler hat and plume – and we sauntered over the epoxy-resin cobbles to the Dialtone.

I played it for all it was worth, taking Sissy past the memorial crater arrondissements, along the echoing locks on the Seine where the sounds of distant small-arms fire ricocheted off the tile and whizzed over your head, past the eternal flame burning in the smashed storefront of the Burger King flagship store, and finally to the Dialtone.

Fat Eddie was bouncing that night, and I waggled my eyebrows at him surreptitiously, then at Sissy, and he caught on. "Mr. Rosen," he said, parting the crowd with a beefy forearm, "an unexpected pleasure. How have you been?"

Sissy's eyes lit up Christmas, and her grip on my elbow tightened. "You know, Edward: just the same, all the time. A little poorer with every passing day, a little older, a little uglier. Life goes on."

Fat Eddie smiled like the Buddha and waved aside my remarks with an expansive sweep of his arm. "You merely improve with age, my friend. This is Paree, monsieur, where we venerate our elder statesmen. Please, who is this lovely young woman with you?"

"Sissy Black, Edward Moreno. Sissy is my cousin, here for a visit."

Fat Eddie took Sissy's hand in his meaty paw and feinted a kiss at it. "A pleasure, mademoiselle. If there is anything we can do for you here at the Club Dialtone, anything at all, don't hesitate to ask."

Sissy flushed in the gaudy neon light, and shot a glance over her shoulder at the poor plebes stuck behind the velvet rope until Fat Eddie deigned to notice them. "Nice to meet you, Edward," she managed, after a brief stammer, and kissed him on both cheeks. This is a trustafarian thing, something she'd seen on the tube, but she did it gamely, standing on tiptoe. Not Fat Eddie's style at all, but he's a pro, and he took it like one.

He opened the door and swept her inside. I hung back. "Thanks, Eddie; I owe you one."

"You don't think I laid it on too thick?" he asked, rubbing at the lipstick on his cheeks with a steri-wipe.

I rolled my eyes. "Always. But Sissy impresses easily."

"Not like us, huh, Lee?"

"Not like us." I'd met Eddie playing dominoes on Montmartre with five frères, and he'd been winning. It could've gotten ugly, but I knew the frères' CO, and I sorted it, then took Eddie out and got him bombed on ouzo at a Greek place I knew, and he'd been a stand-up guy for me ever since.

"Everything cool tonight?"

"Lotsa uniforms, but nothing special. Have a good time."

I walked inside and paused in the doorway to light a stinking Gitane, something to run interference on the clouds of perfume. Sissy was waiting nervously by the entrance, staring around her while trying not to. The kids were all out, in trustafarian rags and finery, shaking their firm booties and knocking back stupid cocktails in between sets. "What you think?" I shouted into her ear.

"Lee, it's supe-dupe!" she shouted back.

"You want a drink?"

"Okay."

The bartender already had a Manhattan waiting for me. I held up two fingers, and he quickly built a second for Sissy, with a cherry. I unfolded some ringgits and passed them across the bar. He did a quick check on the scrolling currency exchange ticker beneath the bar, and passed me back a clattering handful of Communard francs. I pushed them back at him – who needed more play money?

I guided Sissy past a couple of stone-faced frères to an empty booth near the back, and took her jacket from her and put it on the bench next to me. She took a sip of her Manhattan and made a face. Good. If I kept feeding her booze she didn't like, she wouldn't knock back so much of it that I had to carry her out.

"It's *amazing*," she shouted.

"You like it?"

"Yeah! I can't believe I'm really *here!* God, Lee, you're the best!"

I don't take compliments well. "Sure, whatever. Why don't you dance?"

It was all she needed. She tossed her bowler down on the table and tore off to the dance floor. I lost sight of her after a moment, but didn't worry. The Dialtone was a pretty safe place, especially with Fat Eddie making sure no smooth-talking trustafarian tried to take her back to his flat.

I sipped my drink and looked around. There were a lot of uniforms, as Eddie had mentioned – and as many here at the back of the club as up near the door. Libertines didn't come up to the Boul' Disney often. Too busy being serious Communards, sharing and fighting and not washing enough for my taste. Still, it wasn't unheard of for a few of the frères to slum it up here where the richies played at bohemian.

These ones were hardcases, toughened streetfighters. One of them turned in profile, and I caught his earrings – these wackos wear 'em like medals – and was impressed. This Pierre was a major veteran, twenty confirmed kills and the battle of Versailles to boot. I began to think about leaving; my spideysense was tingling.

I shoulda left. I didn't. Sissy was having a wonderful time, kept skipping back, and after the second Manhattan, she switched to still water (no fizzy water for her; it makes cellulite, apparently). I was chewing on a tricky work problem and working on my reserve pack of Gitanes when it all went down.

The sound system died.

The lights came full up.

Fat Eddie came tumbling through the door, tossed like a rag doll, and he barely managed to roll with the fall.

A guy in power-armor followed Fat Eddie in, leaving dents in the floor as he went.

Throughout the club, the frères stood and folded their arms across their chests. I gave myself a mental kick. I shoulda seen it coming; normalement, the frères stick together in dour, puritanical clumps, but tonight they'd been spread throughout the place, and I'd been too wrapped up to notice the change in pattern. I tried to spot Fat Eddie out of the corner of my eye without taking my attention away from the frères. At first I couldn't see him at all; then he turned up, looking dazed, in front of the door to the Dialtone's aged, semifunctional kitchen. For a moment I turned to look at him. He gave me a worried smile, touched his finger to his nose and faded through the door. A second later a frère moved in to block the kitchen, standing in front of the door through which Fat Eddie had just vanished. I wished I knew how to roll with the punches the way Fat Eddie did.

The PA on the power-armor crackled to life, amplifying the voice of the Pierre inside to teeth-shaking booms: "Messieu'dames, your attention please." Power-Armor had a pretty good accent, just enough coq au vin to charm the ladies.

A trustafarian with a floppy red rooster's crest of hair made a break for the fire door, and a beefy frère casually backhanded him as he ran, sending him sprawling. He stayed down. Someone screamed, and then there was screaming all around me.

Power-Armor fired a round into the ceiling, sending plaster skittering over his suit. The screaming stopped. The PA thundered again. "Your attention, *please.* These premises are nationalized by order of the Pro-Tem Revolutionary Authority of the Sovereign Paris Commune. You are all required to present yourselves at the third precinct recruitment center, where your fitness for revolutionary service will be evaluated. As a convenience, the Pro-Tem Revolutionary Authority of the Sovereign Paris Commune has arranged for transport to the recruitment center. You will form an orderly single-file queue and proceed onto the buses waiting outside. Please form a queue now."

My mind was racing, my heart was in my throat, and my Gitane had rolled off the table and was cooking its way through the floor. I didn't dare make a grab for it, in case one of the frères got the idea that I was maybe going for a weapon. I managed to spot Sissy, frozen in place on the dance floor, but looking around, taking it in, thinking. The trustafarians milled toward the door in a rush. I took advantage of the confusion to make my way over to her, holding her hat and jacket. I grabbed her elbow and steered her toward Power-Armor.

"Monsieur," I said. "Please, a moment." I spoke in my best French, the stuff I keep in reserve for meetings with snooty Swiss bastards who are paying me too much money.

Power-Armor sized me up, thought about it, then unlatched the telephone handset from his chest plate. I brought it up to my ear.

"What is it?"

"Look, this girl, she's my mother's niece, she's only been here for a day. She's young, she's scared."

"They're all young. They're all scared."

"But she's not like these kids – she's just passing through. Has a ticket from Orly tomorrow morning. Let me take her home. I give you my word of honor that I'll present myself at the recruitment station" – the hell I would – "first thing in the morning. As soon as I see her off – "

I was interrupted by the frère's laughter, echoing weirdly in his armor. "Of course you will, monsieur, of course. No, I'm sorry, I really must insist."

"My name is Lee Rosen. I'm a personal friend of Commandant Ledoit. Radio him. He'll confirm that I'm telling the truth."

"If I radioed the Commandant at o-three hundred, it would go very hard on me, monsieur. My hands are tied. Perhaps in the morning, someone will arrange an appointment for you."

"I don't suppose you'd be interested in a bribe?"

"No, I don't really think so. My orders were very strict. Everyone in the club to the recruitment center. Don't worry, monsieur. It will be fine. It's a glorious time to be in Paree."

There was a click as he shut off the phone, and I racked it just as the PA reactivated, deafening me. "Quickly, my friends, quickly! The sooner you board the bus, the sooner it will all be sorted out."

Sissy was staring hard at the confusion with grave misgivings. She clutched my shoulder with white knuckles. "It'll be all right, don't worry!" I shouted at her. "It's a glorious time to be in Paree," I muttered to myself.

Best not to describe the bus ride to the recruitment center in too much detail. They packed us like cattle, and some of the more dosed trustafarians freaked out, and at least one tried to pick my pocket. I held Sissy tight to my chest, her hat and jacket squashed between us, and murmured soothing noises at her. Sissy had fallen silent, shaking into my chest.

A hundred years later, the bus rolled to a stop, and a hundred years after that, the doors hissed open and the trustafarians tumbled out. I waited until the rush was over, then led Sissy off the bus.

"What's going on, Lee?" she said, finally. She had a look that I recognized – it was the cogitation face I got when I started chewing on a work problem.

"Looks like the frères have decided to draft some new recruits. Don't worry. I'll get it sorted out. We'll be out of here before you know it."

A group of frères was herding the crowd through two doors: the women on one side, then men on the other. One of them moved to separate Sissy from me.

"Friend, please," I said. "She's scared. She's my mother's niece. I have to take care of her. Please. I'd like to see the CO. Commandant Ledoit is a friend of mine, he'll sort it out."

Pierre made like he didn't hear. I didn't bother offering him a bribe; a grunt like this would like as not take all your money and then pretend he'd never seen your face. The ones in the power-armor were the elite, with some shred of decency. These guys were retarded sadists.

He simply pulled Sissy by the arm until we were separated, then shoved her into the women's line. I sighed and comforted myself with the fact that at least he hadn't kicked me in the nuts for mouthing off. The women were marched around the corner – to what? They had their own entrance? Sissy vanished.

It took an effort of will to keep from smoking while I queued, but I had a sense that maybe I'd be here a long time and should hold on to my cigs. A shuffling eternity later, I was facing a sergeant in a crisp uniform, his jaw shaved blue, his manner professionally alert. *"Bonsoir,"* he said.

On impulse, I decided to pretend that I didn't speak French. I needed any leverage I could get. You learn that in my line of work. "Uh, hi."

"Your name, monsieur?" He had a wireless clipboard whose logo-marks told me it had been liberated from the Wal-Mart on the Champs Ellipses.

"Lee Rosen."

He scrawled quickly on the board. "Nationality?"

"Canadian."

"Residence?"

"Thirty, Rue Texas, number thirty-three."

The sergeant smiled. "The Trustafarian Quarter."

"Yes, that's right."

"And you, are you a trustafarian?"

I was wearing a white linen suit, my hair was short and neat, and I was in my early thirties. No point in insulting his intelligence. "No, sir."

"Ah," he said, as though I had made a particularly intelligent riposte.

The hint of a smile played over his lips. I decided that maybe I liked this guy. He had style.

"I'm a researcher. A freelance researcher."

"Jean-Marc, bring a chair," he said in French. I pretended to be surprised when the goon at the door dropped a beautiful chrome-inlaid oak chair beside me. The sergeant gestured and I sat. "A researcher? What sort of research do you do, Monsieur Rosen?"

"Corporate research."

"Ah," he said again. He smiled beneficently at me and picked up a pack of Marlboros from his desk, offered one to me.

I took it and puffed it alight, and pretended to be calm. "I haven't seen an American cigarette my whole time in Paris."

"There are certain . . . advantages to serving in the Pro-Tem Authority." He took a deep drag. He smiled again at me. Fatherly. Man, he was good.

"Tell me, what is it that you are called upon to research, in your duties as a freelance corporate researcher?"

What the hell. It was bound to come out eventually. "I work in competitive intelligence."

"Ah," he said. "I see. Espionage."

"Not really."

He raised an eyebrow dubiously.

"I mean it. I don't crouch in bushes with a camera or tap phones. I analyze patterns."

"Yes? Patterns? Please, go on."

I'd polished this speech on a million uncomprehending relatives, so I switched to autopilot. "Say I manufacture soap. Say you're my competition. Your head office is in Koniz, and your manufacturing is outsourced to a subcontractor in Azerbaijan. I want to stay on top of what you do, so I spend a certain amount of time every week looking at new listings in Koniz and its suburbs. I also check every change of address to Koniz. These names go into a pool that I cross-reference to the alumni registries of the top one hundred chemical engineering programs and the index of articles in chemical engineering trade journals. By keeping track of who you're hiring, and what their specialty is, I can keep an eye on what your upcoming projects are. When I see a load of new hires, I start paying very close attention, and then I branch out.

"Since you and I are in the same business, it wouldn't be extraordinary for me to call up your manufacturing subcontractor and ask them if they'd be interested in bidding on certain large jobs. I set these jobs up such that I can test the availability of each type of apparatus they use: dish detergent, hand soap, lotion, and so on. Likewise, I can invite your packaging suppliers and teamsters to bid on jobs.

"Once I determine that you are, for example, launching a line of laundry detergent in the next month or so, I am forearmed. I can go to the major retail outlets, offer them my competing laundry detergent below cost, on the condition that they sign a six-month exclusivity deal. A few weeks later, you roll out your new line but none of the retailers can put it on their shelves."

"Ah," the sergeant said. He stared pensively over my shoulder, out the door, where a queue of trustafarians waited in exhausted silence. "Ah," he said again. He turned to his clipboard, and I waited while his stylus scritched over its surface for several minutes. "You can take him now. Be gentle with him," he said in French. "Thank you, Monsieur Rosen. This has been educational."

Day 2: Bend Over and Say "Aaaah!"

They dumped me in a makeshift barracks, a locked office with four zonked-out trustafarians already sleeping on the industrial gray carpet. I rolled my jacket into a pillow, stuck my shoes underneath it, and eventually slept.

I was wakened by sleepy footfalls in the hallway, punctuated with the thudding steps of power-armor. I was waiting by the door when a frère in power-armor unlocked it and opened it.

He hit the spotlights on his shoulder and flooded the room with harsh light. I forced myself to keep my eyes open and stood still until my pupils adjusted. My roommates rolled over and groaned.

"Get up," Power-Armor said.

"Upyershithole," one of the trustafarians moaned. He pulled his jacket over his head. Power-Armor moved to him with mechanical swiftness, grabbed him by one shoulder, and hauled him upright. The trustafarian howled. "Motherfucker! I'll kick your ass! I'll *sue* your ass! Put me down!"

Power-Armor dropped him, then surveyed the others. They'd all struggled to their feet. The one with the potty mouth was rubbing his shoulder and glaring furiously.

"Vit'march," Power-Armor suggested, and followed us out into the corridor.

He wasn't kidding about the "vit" part, either. He moved us at a brisk trot up the stairs, easily pacing us. When I came to Paree, this office building had been a see-through, completely empty. A few years later, a developer had reclaimed it, renovated it, and gone bankrupt. Now it was finally tenanted. We finally emerged onto a roof easily six stories high, ringed with barbed wire, with a view of one of the cathedral domes and lots of crumbly little row houses. Other conscriptees were already on the roof, men and women, but I couldn't find Sissy.

Burly frères were in position around the roof, wearing sidearms. Some stood on cherry pickers raised several meters off the roof, with rifles on tripods. They swept the rooftop, then the street below, then the rooftop again. I wondered how they got the cherry pickers onto the roof in the first place, then spotted a cluster of power-armored frères, and figured it out. These boys would just each take a corner and *jump.* Beats the hell out of block-and-tackle.

"You will queue up to receive temporary uniforms," one of the Power-Armors broadcasted. I was right at the front of the line. A frère sized me up and pulled the zips open on several duffels, then tossed me a shirt and a pair of pants.

I hurried down the queue to a table laden with heavy, worn combat boots. They stank of their previous owners, and evoked a little shudder from me.

"Jesus-shit, are we supposed to fucking *wear* these?" The voice had a familiar Yankee twang. I didn't need to turn around to see that it was my roommate, Potty-Mouth. He was carrying his uniform under one arm, and holding the other one at his side, painfully.

The smile vanished from the frère's face. He picked up the smelliest, most worn pair, and passed it to him. "Put these on, friend. Now." His voice was low and dangerous, and his accent made the words almost unintelligible.

"I am *not* gonna 'poot zees ahn,' you fucking frog shit. Put 'em on yourself," Potty-Mouth looked to be about twenty, maybe a year older than Sissy, and he had a bull's neck and thick, muscular arms, and gave off a road-rage vibe that I associate with steroidal athletes. He dropped the uniform and picked up one of the boots, and pitched it straight into the frère's face, with a whistling snap that sliced the air.

The frère plucked it from the sky with chemically enhanced reflexes and shot it right back at Potty-Mouth. It nailed him square in the forehead.

Potty's head snapped back hard, and I winced in sympathy as he crumpled to the ground. I stepped away, hoping to melt back into the crowd. The sergeant from the night before blocked my way, along with the frère who'd thrown the boot. "Get him out of the way, Monsieur Rosen," the sergeant said.

"We can't move him," I extemporized. "He might have a spinal injury. Please."

The sergeant's smile stayed fixed, but it grew hard, and a little cruel. "Monsieur Rosen, you are a new recruit. New recruits don't question orders." The frère who'd thrown the boot cracked his knuckles.

I grabbed Potty-Mouth under his dripping armpits and hauled him over the gravel, trying to support his head and biting back the urge to retch as his sweat poured over my hands. At this rate, I'd be out of steri-wipes in a very short time.

I wiped my hands off on his shirt and crouched next to him. The trustafarians, shivering in the cold, reluctantly removed their clothes and put them into rip-stop shopping bags with Exxon logos. Women frères did the girls – still no sign of Sissy – and men did the boys, all nice and above-board. A frère came over to us, dropped two bags, and said, "Strip." I started to protest, but caught the eye of the sergeant, standing by one of the cherry pickers.

Resignedly, I stripped off my clothes and bagged them, then bagged my uniform along with them, and sealed it shut.

"This one, too," the frère said, kicking Potty-Mouth in the ribs.

Potty-Mouth jerked and grunted. His jaw lolled open. I began to mechanically strip Potty-Mouth of his stinking neoprene and spandex muscle-wear. I was beyond caring about microbes at this point.

The frère watched me, grinning all the while. I wondered how I ended up babysitting this spoiled roid-head, and stared at my feet.

Four frères in power-armor sailed onto the roof from the road below, carrying an ambulance bus at the corners. They set it down, popped the doors, and a cadre of white-coated medics poured out. The one who impersonally groped my balls for hernias and stuck me with several none-too-sterile needles needed a shower, and his white coat could've used a cleaning, too. When he bent over to check out Potty-Mouth, his pocket bulged open and I saw a collection of miniature bottles of Johnnie Walker Red. He popped me in the shoulder with some kind of mutant staple-gun that stung like filth. "What's wrong with this one?" he asked me, speaking for the first time.

"Maybe a concussion, maybe a spinal. I think his shoulder's dislocated."

The medic disappeared into the bus for a moment, then reemerged in a leaded apron and lugging a bulky apparatus. I realized with a start that it was a portable X-ray, and scrambled to get behind him. "No spinal, no concussion," he pronounced, after a long moment's staring into the apparatus's eyepiece.

"Okay," the medic said to himself, and made a tick on a wireless clipboard.

The medics bugged out the way they'd come in, and the frères withdrew, with rapid, military precision, up the cherry pickers.

I had a pretty good idea of what was coming next, but it still shocked a curse from my lips. The frères in the cherry pickers all harnessed up giant blowers and turned loose a stinging mist of sinus-burning disinfectant down on us. Trustafarians, male and female, screamed and ran for the barbed wire, then turned and ran back into the center. Above me, I heard the frères laughing. I stood my ground and let myself get soaked once, twice, a third time. I was about to make sure that Potty-Mouth was lying on his side when he groaned again and sat up. "Fuck!" he shouted.

He scrambled groggily to his feet, careered into me, righted himself, and wobbled uncertainly as the last of the spray settled over him. The disinfectant evaporated quickly, leaving my skin feeling tight and goose-pimply.

Potty-Mouth swung his head around with saurian sloth. He focused on me and grabbed my shoulder. "The fuck are you doing to me, fag?" His grip tightened, grinding my collarbone.

"Chill out," I said, placatingly. "We're in the same boat. We're drafted."

"Where are my clothes?"

"In that bag. We had to strip while they sprayed us. Look, could you let go of my shoulder?"

He did. "You may be drafted, bro, but not me. I'm leaving." He popped the seal on the bag and struggled into his civvies.

"Look, there's no percentage in this. Just keep calm, and let this thing sort itself out. You're gonna get yourself killed."

Potty-Mouth ignored me and took off toward the door we'd used to get onto the roof. He kicked it three times before it splintered and gave. I looked up at the frères in the cherry pickers. They were watching him calmly.

A small, wiry frère was waiting behind the door Potty-Mouth kicked in. He stepped out, grinning. Potty-Mouth threw a punch at the frère's solar plexus. The frère whoofed a little, but didn't lose his grin.

Potty-Mouth grappled with him, lifting the smaller man off his feet. The frère took the beating for what seemed like a long time, merely twisting to avoid the groin and face shots that Potty-Mouth aimed. The trustafarians on the roof were all silent, watching, shivering.

Finally, the frère had had enough. He broke free of Potty-Mouth's grip on his arms with ease, and as he dropped to the ground, smashed Potty-Mouth in both ears simultaneously. Potty-Mouth reeled, and the little frère aimed a series of hard, wicked-fast blows at his ribs. I heard cracking.

Potty-Mouth started to fall, but the frère caught him, picked him up over his head, then piledrivered him into the gravel. He lay unmoving there, head at an angle that suggested he wouldn't be getting up any time soon.

The frères in the cherry pickers scrambled down. One of them slung Potty-Mouth over his shoulder like a sack of potatoes and carried him down the stairs. The little frère who'd killed him stepped back into the doorway, pulling the broken door shut behind him.

"Get dressed," broadcasted a Power-Armor.

They herded us back downstairs without a word. The crowd moved with utter docility, and I could see the logic of the proceedings. Terrified, blood-sugar bottomed out, thirsty, we were completely without fight.

On the third floor, the cubicles and desks had all been piled in a corner, making one big space. A few long tables were set up with industrial-size pots of something that steamed and smelled bland and uninspired. My mouth filled with saliva.

"Form an orderly queue," said the sergeant from the night before, who was waiting behind one of the pots with an apron over his uniform, a ladle in his hand.

He looked each trustafarian over carefully as they passed through the line, clutching large bowls that were efficiently filled with limp vegetables, lumpy potatoes, and a brown, greasy gravy. Each of us was issued a stale baguette and a cup of orange drink and sent away.

We seated ourselves on the floor and ate greedily off our laps. Here in the mess, the frères relaxed and allowed the men and women to mingle.

Friends found each other and shared long hugs, then ate in silence. I ate alone, back to a wall, and watched the others.

Once everyone had passed through the line, the sergeant began walking through the clusters, stooping to talk and joke. He touched people's shoulders, handed out cigarettes, and was generally endearing and charming.

He made his way over to me.

"Monsieur Rosen."

"Sergeant."

He sat down beside me. "How is the food?"

"Oh, very good," I said, without irony. "Would you like some baguette?"

"No thank you."

I tore off a hunk of bread and sopped up some gravy.

"It is a shame about your friend, on the roof."

I grunted. Potty-Mouth had been no friend of mine – and in a situation like this one, I knew, you have to be discriminate in apportioning your loyalty.

"Ah." He stared thoughtfully at the trustafarians. "You understand, though, why it had to be?"

"I suppose."

"Ah?"

"Well, once he was taken care of, the rest saw that there was no point in struggling."

"Yes, I suppose that was part of it. The other part is that there in no place in a war for disobedience."

War. Huh.

The sergeant read my face. "Oh yes, Monsieur Rosen. War. We're still fighting street-to-street in the northern suburbs, and some say that the Americans are pushing for a UN 'Peacekeeping' mission. They're calling it Operation Havana. I'm afraid that your government takes a dim view of our nationalizing their stores and offices."

"Not my government, Sergeant . . ."

"Abalain. François Abalain. I apologize, I had forgotten that you are a Canadian. Where did you say you live?"

"I have a flat on Rue Texas."

"Yes, yes. Far from the fighting. You and the other *étrangers* behave as though our struggle here were nothing but an uninteresting television program. It couldn't last. You had pitched your tents on the side of a smoking volcano, and the lava has reached you."

"What does that mean?"

"It means that our army needs support staff: cooks, mechanics' assistants, supply clerks, janitors, office staff. Every loyal Parisian is already giving everything he can afford to the Cause. It is time that you, who have enjoyed Paris's splendor in comfort and without cost, pay for your stay."

"Sergeant, no offense, but I have rent receipts in my filing cabinet. I pay for groceries. I am paying for my stay."

The sergeant lit a cigarette and inhaled deeply. "Some bills can't be settled with money. When you fight for the freedom of the group, the group must pay for it."

"Freedom?"

"Ah." He looked out at the trustafarians, who were leaning against each other, eyes downcast, utterly dejected. "In the cause of freedom, it may be necessary to abridge the personal liberties of a few individuals. But this isn't slave labor: each of you will be paid in good Communard Francs, at the going rate. It won't hurt these spoiled children to do some honest work."

I decided that if the chance ever came, I'd kill Sergeant François Abalain.

I swallowed my anger. "My cousin, a young girl named Sissy, she was taken last night. She was just passing through, and asked me to take her out to the club. My aunt must be crazy with worry."

The sergeant pulled his clipboard out of his coat pocket and snapped it open. He scratched on it. "What is her last name?"

"Black. S-I-S-S-Y B-L-A-C-K."

He scritched more and scowled at the display. He scritched again. "Monsieur Rosen, I'm very sorry, but there is no record of any Sissy Black here. Could she have given us a false name?"

I thought about it. I hadn't seen Sissy for ten years before she emailed me that she was coming to Paree. She'd always struck me as a very straight, sheltered kid, though I'd been forced to revise my opinion of her upwards after she gutted out that long bus ride. Still, I couldn't imagine her having the cunning to make up a name on the spot. "I don't think so. What does that mean?"

"Probably a clerical error. You see, we're all so overworked; that is why you are here, really. I'll speak with Sergeant Dumont. She handled women's intake. I'm sure everything is fine."

Our "training" began the next morning. Like high-school gym class with heavily armed teachers – running, squats, jumping jacks. Even a rope climb. Getting us in shape was the furthest thing from their minds – this was all about dulling what little sense of initiative we might have left. I tried to stay focused on Sissy, on where she might have gone or what might have happened to her. For a few days my speculations got darker and darker until in my mind's eye I saw her being used as some sort of sex toy by the senior members of the Commune. I had no reason to believe this; the Communards were like the Victorians or the Maoists in their determination not to let sex get in the way of politics. But I was running out of even remotely acceptable possibilities. And then one afternoon I realized I hadn't thought about her at all since waking. The fatigue had fried my brain, and all I could think about was my next rest break.

Once we'd been thoroughly pacified, they started taking us out on work gangs of ten or fifteen, clearing rubble and repainting storefronts. On a particularly lucky day, I got to spend ten hours deep in rebuilt Communard Territory, laying down epoxy cobblestones.

We worked in a remote cul-de-sac, a power-armored frère blocking the only exit route, so motionless that I wondered if he were asleep. I worked alone, as was my habit – I had no urge to become war buddies with any of the precious tots I'd been conscripted with.

I'd never been this deep into the rebuilt zone before. It was horrible, a mixture of Nouveau and Deco perpetrated by someone who'd no understanding of either. The Communards had turned the narrow storefronts into 1930s movie sets, painted over their laserprinted signage in fanciful, curlicued Toulouse-Lautrec script. Cleverly concealed speakers piped out distant hot jazz with convincing Victrola hiss, clinking stemware, and Gallic laughter.

We arrived just after dawn, and within a very short time my knees were killing me. A few Parisians had trickled down the block: a baker who cranked out his awning and set baskets of baguettes in the window; a few femmes de ménage with sexy skirts, elaborate up-dos and catseye glasses clacked down the street; a gang of insouciant lads flicked their cigarette ends at us poor groveling conscriptees and swaggered on.

I managed to keep it together until the organ grinder arrived. It was the monkey that did it. Or maybe it was the Edith Piaf cylinder he had in his hurdy-gurdy. On balance, it was the way the monkey danced to Piaf – I started chuckling, then laughing, then roaring, so hysterical that I actually flopped over on my back and writhed on the same cobblestones I'd laid down.

The Parisians tried to ignore me, but I was making quite a spectacle of myself. Eventually, they all slunk away, looking embarrassed and resentful. I stared at the gray sky and held my belly and snorted as they departed, and then a patch of cobblestones beside me exploded, showering me with resinous shrapnel, bruising my ribs and my arm. The Power-Armor at the street's entrance lowered his PowerFist pistol and broadcasted a simple order: "Work."

It seemed less funny after that. Edith may have regretted nothing, but I started setting new records for self-pity.

I'm pretty sure I lost track of the time while we were trapped in that old office block. Maybe I was concussed – the frères weren't shy about slapping us around. I doubt it, though. More likely I just stopped thinking as a way to get through the days.

Until the evening they started dividing us into groups.

The frères said nothing as they culled people from the bloc in the mess hall. The smaller trustafarians had been clustered into two groups; no heavy labor for them, was my guess.

Unlike the scene when we were brought in, there was almost no noise. There was no sign of Sissy, but with our heads shaved I'm not sure I'd have recognized her.

I had just identified one group as being visually different when a pointing finger directed me into it, giving me opportunity to study its members close up.

We were a sullen-faced bunch, and I had this sudden, chilling feeling that wasn't helped in the slightest by the frère who grinned at us as he nudged us out the door of the mess hall. He's like a herdsman, I thought, and looking again at the faces of the trustafarians around me, I guessed that we were the group of troublemakers. We were being culled.

Day 9: Full Metal Baguette

The next morning I began to serve the Paris Commune in earnest. Our group had been taken out of the barracks and driven in the back of an old panel van to one of the outer arrondissements. The gunfire sounded a lot louder in the street than I was used to, though, and I felt a caffeine jag of fear when we were led into a dark, abandoned shop and taken to a bivouac in the cellar. We were given new clothes: Bangladeshi belts, the webbing of a weird fiber-plastic combo; and new T-shirts, the cotton still weirdly stiff, to wear under our good Communard uniform blouses.

In the anemic sunshine of an April morning they took us outside to put us to death.

Oh, that's not what they told us. "You are runners," a frère said as we stood in the street. He wore the badges of a lieutenant – though he bore just a single earring – and was using a loud-hailer to be heard above the gunfire that snapped like angry dogs at the buildings nearby. "We are still in the process of clearing the Blancs from this arrondissement," he continued. "It is a building-by-building job, and our ammunition consumption is high. We can't spare fighters to carry rounds to our positions, so that's what you will do. Follow me, monsieurs."

He took a step toward the corner. I started moving after him. I couldn't see any point in sticking around to be shot by one of the sour-faced guards.

At the end of the next block, a group of frères crouched behind a wrecked Citroën. Gunfire echoed from somewhere behind the building across the street from them. Our lieutenant reached the group behind the wreckage, and exchanged words.

"Here," the corporal said, throwing a hemp bag at me. I caught it, and had to stifle some very military language – the thing weighed a ton. It clattered like a cheap toy, which made sense when I looked inside and saw that the bag was filled with plastic magazines.

"Not him," our lieutenant said. He pointed to the last of the stragglers approaching the Citroën. "My friend, it's time to do your part." He gestured at me; I shrugged and tossed the bag to the laggard, a scrawny trustafarian whose cheeks still bore the remnants of semipermanent tattoos. He dropped the bag and didn't bother to restrain his opinion of its weight. "Pick it up," our lieutenant said. "Your life may depend on how well you carry that.

"We have a fire team in that building across the street. You will take this bag to them, and ask them if they've heard anything from the teams farther up the block. The damned Blancs are jamming our communications again." I looked along the line our lieutenant's finger had traced. It didn't seem that far to me. A couple of weeks ago, I wouldn't have thought twice about strolling across the street, even in the face of Parisian traffic.

The kid picked his way through the rubble to the edge of the farthest building on our side of the street. He peered across, reminding me of an old man I used to see on the Rue Texas from time to time, who took forever to work up the courage to brave the traffic on my narrow street. Dust had made the kid's face the same gray as the old man's. I guess I should have felt sick myself, but I don't remember feeling anything.

I saw movement across and up the street – that would be the fire team, calling its runner forward. The kid looked back at us, and I was impressed at how widely his eyes were open, and how white they looked. Our lieutenant casually waved the kid forward – though the gun in the lieutenant's hand lent a lot of weight to the gesture. The kid began to run.

Then he wasn't running anymore, and a dark red pool was spreading over the pavé from under his crumpled body. I hadn't heard a shot, and the kid hadn't made a sound, other than the dusty scuffling sound his body'd made when it hit the stones. Our lieutenant didn't seem that surprised, though. "Did you get it?" he asked the corporal. "Quickly!" The corporal nodded, simultaneously waving forward one of his companions, who gave him something too small for me to see, which the corporal plugged into a slot in a hardcover notebook. The new frère gave a thumbs-up, and picked up a wicked-looking, bloated rifle. Then he stepped out into the street, raised the gun, fired, and stepped back into the shelter offered by the pockmarked wall. Somewhere out of my line of vision, a building exploded.

It sounded like he'd blown up half the city. It was like being inside a thunderstorm, and I instinctively put my hands over my ears in a too-late attempt to protect them. The incredible noise was still rumbling when our lieutenant picked up another crudely woven bag, handed it to me and said, "Go."

I'd been numb up to that point, just watching what was happening without really seeing it. When my hand closed on the bag's handle and I felt the hemp fibers scratching my palm, it was as if I'd suddenly come to the surface of a warm lake and broken into clear, freezing air. That was the moment I realized that Sissy was dead. That we were all dead. No point in kidding myself; they'd probably killed her within a day of raiding the Dialtone. There were all sorts of ways it could have happened. None of them mattered to me. "Fuck the lot of you," I said quietly, and walked into the street.

I didn't run. What was the point? I walked as though I were just on my way to the corner to buy lunch. If I could have, I'd have whistled a jaunty tune, something from Maurice Chevalier or Boy George. My mouth was too dry to make a properly jaunty sound.

I passed the trustafarian, lying dusty and broken on the cobbles. I made a point of looking at the spot from which the killing shot must have come and was surprised to see that the building at the end of the block was mostly still there. That huge explosion, whose final basso still echoed, had come from the destruction of just one room. The chambre and its window – and, presumably, the Blanc sniper hiding there – had been plucked from the building's structure like a bad tooth. And now I was taking my little walk so that our lieutenant could see whether any more snipers waited. Now I realize that this is what it means to fight building to building, room to room. At the time, I thought nothing. Felt nothing. Just walked.

No shot came. No expanding round ripped open my back and spread my lungs out like wings behind me.

I reached the building that was my goal and discovered that the fire team was already moving through it, into its courtyard and beyond to the next block. A solitary, grimy frère waited for me. Grabbing the bag, he spat at my feet and hustled to join his comrades. I guess he didn't appreciate my sangfroid.

By the time our lieutenant and the others had caught up to me, I'd had a chance to do some thinking. I stripped off the stiff new T-shirt and web belt and buried them in some rubble. I didn't know what they represented, but I was pretty damned sure they had something to do with the way our lieutenant had been able to pinpoint the location of the sniper who'd killed Scrawny. The frères might kill me, but I was going to see that they didn't benefit in any way from it.

We were hustled through the ruined building in the wake of the fire team. Another body lying in the next street gave mute evidence to the existence of another Blanc sniper somewhere. Our lieutenant pointed to the ammo bag beside the body – which I now saw was that of the grimy frère I'd forced to play catch-up – and said to me, "No sense in letting that go to waste. Pick it up as you go."

I smiled broadly. "Glad to," I said. "You might as well keep your computer locked up, though." I spread my hands and shrugged. "No belt. No T-shirt. No service." I'm pretty sure I giggled; the whole scene had the surreality of a night in a trustafarian club.

Before our lieutenant could say or do anything, though, a frère wearing a headset stepped between us. "Lieutenant," he said, "Monsieur le sergeant Abalain wants to speak to you."

Just like that, our lieutenant's face had the same pallor as the dead trustafarian's. I was impressed; I hadn't thought an officer could be that scared of a noncom, even one as reptilian as Abalain. Our lieutenant took the headset and put it on. He closed his eyes as he listened.

"It was the shirt," Abalain said. We were sitting in his office, in a rebuilt nineteenth-century apartment building. Through the window I could see the office block that had been my barracks through the first few weeks of my nightmare. "They're made of a special cloth threaded with sensors. Developed to treat battlefield casualties; the sensors record the direction and velocity of anything that hits the cloth. We adapted it by stitching a small transmitter into the collar band. It's a very handy way of fixing a location on snipers, the more so since the Blancs and Penistes don't know that we can do this." He spread his hands and smiled. "Of course, it was a mistake that you were assigned to this duty."

I sipped from the Tigger glass Abalain had given to me. The wine was a good one – rich and full, tannins almost gone but still tasting a bit of blackberry. I guessed it had been in someone's cellar for a good few years before being called on to do its bit for the cause. Forcing myself to think about the wine was a deliberate attempt to keep my emotions in check. It had been nearly twenty-four hours since I'd been pulled from death duty, and I think I'd only stopped shaking just before being brought to Abalain's office. I have a vague memory of my fear and rage bursting from me as I was being led away from the carnage, of kicking the death-duty lieutenant in the balls. Of course, that could just be wishful thinking.

For some reason, it occurred to me as I sipped that it had been weeks since I'd had a cigarette. Not only did the wine taste better, I seemed to have been too busy or too frightened to go through withdrawal. "Does this mean that I'm free to go?"

Abalain laughed, the sound of a padlock rattling against a graveyard gate. "I admire your sense of humor, monsieur," he said. "Know that, if I could, I'd send you back to your place in the Rue Texas. My report on our little chat about your work has been read with interest by important people. Accordingly, I've been ordered to give you a new opportunity to serve the cause."

The next day I reported to the office next door to Abalain's. It wasn't furnished nearly as nicely, but it wasn't a cellar and there was nobody shooting at me, so I decided I was better off. I never saw either the lieutenant or any of my fellow targets again. I confess I didn't really worry about them either.

Abalain had told me to meet him in order to learn about my new assignment. I was pretty sure I already knew what it was, and while waiting for him to show I decided to investigate. I couldn't help myself; when presented with a mass of data I have to know what it is, and the battered metal desk that dominated the room was a pictorial definition of "mass of data." There were three distinct piles on top of the desk; the talus slopes of their near collapse pretty much covered the entire surface. Two of the piles were paper, the third was of various storage media: magneto-optical disks, a couple of ancient Zips, and even a holocube or two.

The paper pile nearest to me consisted of various official garbage: press releases, wire story printouts. The ones I looked at were all from either the UN or one of the three main Blanc organizations. The other pile was a series of virtually indecipherable French-language documents that I was eventually able to identify as field reports from Libertine officers and operatives.

"You can make some sense of that, yes?" Abalain stood in the doorway.

I looked him in the eye for a second, then returned to the reports. "What kind of sense do you want me to make?"

"You will do what you described to me when you were first – ah – recruited. I have need of information which I suspect is buried within these reports and press releases. You will use your skills to draw that information forth." He smiled at me with what he no doubt thought was encouragement. Maybe he'd been a management consultant before deciding that the revolution offered better opportunities to fuck with people. "You will work here, and send the information to me as you assemble it. You will use the clipboard and wearable that are in the upper right-hand drawer; they connect to a fiberoptic pipe linked directly to a secure folder on my desktop. You will, regrettably, have no outside access. But don't worry about that; I'll see that you get all of the information you need to do your work."

More than enough information, I told myself.

Day 30: The Revolution Will Not Be Franchised

"I gotta admit, I just don't understand this revolution."

"What's not to understand?" Abalain offered me a Marlie; I was somewhat surprised at the gesture, and even more surprised to find myself shaking my head. "We're not really revolutionaries, you know. We're trying to restore the glories of French civilization; in a way, that makes us conservatives."

I believe the accepted term is "reactionaries," I thought. "Which no doubt explains why so many of your slogans seem to have been drawn from fast-food advertising," I said, waving a flimsy at him. " 'La France: Have It Your Way'?"

"The fast-food philosophy is inherently French," Abalain said. "It's a peasant philosophy, not some tarted-up bourgeois haute-cuisine thing. It's like the epoxy cobbles you and your 'Old Paree Hands' are so dismissive about. They're perfectly in keeping with the scientific rationalism of the original revolution." He spoke in crisp, rapid French. He'd caught me listening too intently to one of his phone conversations the week before and confronted me with a barrage of French. When my facial expression made it clear that I understood every word, he'd nodded smartly and went back to his conversation, as though he'd suspected it all along.

"Unless they're laid down by Disney," I said.

"Then it's cultural imperialism," Abalain said. I'd have liked him just a little if he'd smiled, or showed any sign of having a sense of humor. But he was deadly serious, and I hated him even more for it.

"So what's your part in all this?" I asked. "You a spook?"

"I'm nothing of the sort, Monsieur Rosen. And if I was, I certainly wouldn't tell you." He blew a jet of smoke past my left ear; I smelled burning garbage. "I'm just a servant of the Commune," he said. "I do what I can to bring France back into the sunlight of scientific rationalism. Please know that we are all grateful for the assistance you have been providing."

And that you've been taking credit for, I thought. "I could do more," I said, "if I had access to more information." What I'd been given so far wouldn't have been enough to help a fundamentalist preacher track down sin. I had to be able to make a big score in order for my plan to work.

"I've been impressed with what you've given me to date," Abalain said. *Jesus*, I thought. *If they're impressed by that merde, this will be easier than I thought.* "Granted it hasn't had much direct tactical value. But already we've been able to wrong-foot the Penistes at least twice in the media. We've taken the lead in the propaganda campaign; in the long run that may be as important as anything our fighters do."

"At least let me see the uncensored field reports." I pulled a handful of crumpled flimsies from a pants pocket. Two-thirds of the text had been blacked or blanked. "I should be the judge of whether or not information is usable."

"I'll see what I can do," he said.

The next morning an unhappy-looking frère kicked a plastic box into my office. The papers, flimsies, and chips were chaos illustrated, but I didn't care. I always get a rush from a fresh source of data, and the rush was greater this time because the stakes were so much higher.

One of the first things I learned when I finally got down to analysis was that my old ami Commandant Ledoit was dead. The first reference was in a press release from a couple of weeks ago; he'd been killed, it was claimed, by the Blancs. But it didn't take much sleuthing to suss out that he had in fact been dusted by the Commune. I found a reference to a series of denunciations by Abalain's juniors, and while the accusations weren't detailed the result was still clear enough. If I hadn't already had my suspicions raised, that would have set my spideysense tingling.

As it was, I was more grimly satisfied than surprised. Every revolution eventually eats its young, someone once said. For the Paris Commune, the buffet had apparently begun. That was fine for me; in fact, my plan depended on it.

I worked hard over the next week. After what I'd been through, there was a deep, almost rich pleasure in being able to throw myself into investigation. Little by little I spun my web – making sure that I also took the time to generate some truly killer conclusions about what the Blancs and Penistes were up to. It was actually pretty easy. Compared with most corporations, governments are as complex as nap time at a daycare. And neither the Blancs nor the Penistes – nor the Commune, come to that – was even a government by any normal conception of that word. So it was only a few days after I started when Abalain brought me a bottle of really good Remy by way of congratulating me on my utter fabness. I'm more of a bourbon than a cognac type, but I accepted the bottle anyway. It was the least Abalain could do for me; I intended to make sure of that.

After he gave me the bottle, I didn't see the sergeant for two weeks. I took advantage of the break to wander around the building, and eventually even the neighborhood. It hadn't taken long for word to get out that Abalain had himself a pet spook, and nobody really paid any attention to the grubby guy in the soiled white suit. That dusted whatever doubts I may have had about Abalain's juice within the Commune; the man wore his sergeant's stripes like sheep's clothing.

Discovering the truth about Sissy's fate did not create my resolve to kill Abalain; it only deepened it. I'd hardly spared her a thought since the fresh lieutenant used me for a decoy, but in one raft of papers, I turned up an encoded list of inductees from the Dialtone. It was nicely divided by sex and nationality, though the names themselves were encrypted. Only one female Canadian appeared on the list. I realized then that it had been weeks since I'd thought of Sissy, and I felt myself poised atop a wall of anguish so high that I couldn't bear to look down. Instead, I went back to work, and turned up an encrypted list of bunk assignments – it was nearly identical to the list of inductees, but a number of the female names were missing, including the lone Canadian one.

Putting two and two together is what I do. I couldn't stop myself, then. Sissy and any number of young, carefree trustafarians had been conscripted for a very different kind of service to the Commune – the kind of service that required a boudoir rather than a bunk.

Up until then, I'd been trying to formulate a plan that would put paid to Abalain while I walked away scot-free. When I saw the second list, I felt a return of the unreal, uncaring fatalism I'd felt when I walked out into the street lugging the bag of ammunition. Abalain would die, and I would die, too.

The freedom to move around that Abalain's patronage afforded also gave me all the opportunity I needed to type in some new reports from a variety of unsecured terminals and wireless keypads, using the IDs I'd picked up from the uncensored reports Abalain had given me. There was nothing flamboyant or, God forbid, clumsy about these reports. I even managed to duplicate the horrible grammar some of the frère field agents had used. And most of the information I put into them could easily be verified, since it was just cribbed from other sources or from my own validated speculation on what the other side was doing. That's how you do it, you see: you put in so much truth that the few bits of fabulation go more or less unnoticed.

More or less, that is, until somebody decides that all those trees must mean something and makes a point of looking at the forest. I was pretty sure that, like all revolutions, this one had its share of tree counters.

I have to admit, though, that I was pretty nervous by the end of the second week. You like to think that you know your job, that the outcome of something you start is predictable within the limits of your experience. But every job carries with it the fear of complete catastrophe, and if this job went down in flames . . . It didn't bear thinking of.

So I was more than a little shocked when Abalain burst into my office late one afternoon, looking as though he'd just learned that capitalism really was the most effective economic philosophy.

"We have to go, you and I," Abalain said.

"Go where?" I asked. I hadn't expected to see him again; had, in fact, expected to read his obituary in the next batch of Commune press releases.

"I'll explain later. But take your notepad with you." He cut the pad free from its lock and cable and handed it to me. "We're going to need this to get through the lines."

"Through the lines?"

"Don't be dense, and just do as I say." Abalain seemed to be reverting to the bourgeois martinet I'd always suspected him of being. "I have some things to do. Meet me in the lobby in five minutes. Be there, Rosen, or I'll have you shot."

Normalement, I'm not so slow on the uptake. I guess that only the fact that I was so sure I'd done for Abalain had blinded me to what had really happened: the bastard had found out that he was going to be denounced and had decided to take his leave of his frères before they removed his head from his shoulders, or however it was that they dispatched those who no longer fit with the Commune's vision of the past-into-future.

I was only thrown off my game for a moment, though. My business forces you to think on your feet, and I was on mine in a second. I slipped into Abalain's office and started filling my pockets with whatever was lying about. I made sure that I grabbed his wearable; the computer was locked, of course, but I was rapidly formulating a plan for dealing with that.

My suit may have looked a little bit rumpled when I got to the lobby, but the frères were a pretty sartorially challenged bunch at the best of times, so I wasn't surprised that nobody noticed my bulging pockets.

"What's happened?" I asked Abalain as soon as we were outside and walking on the poly-resin cobbles. He'd headed us north, presumably toward the toney arrondissements of the northeast where the Blancs still held sway.

"A friend let slip that I was going to be denounced before the Central Committee," he said. "There's no justification for such a thing, of course."

"Of course," I said.

"But a man in a position such as mine inevitably seems to inspire jealousy, and justified or not I'm pretty sure things wouldn't go well for me if I let myself be called. So with regret I have to end my service to the revolution and the Commune. It's their misfortune."

"And me?" I stuffed my hands in my pockets in case Abalain got too curious about their shape.

"But I thought you were eager to return to your home." Abalain made a sympathetic little moue with his mouth, and it was all I could do to keep from kicking him in the balls. "You, Monsieur Rosen, are my ticket through the lines, of course."

"Of course."

As usual, Abalain was ahead of the curve on the whole denunciation thing. His casual wave was enough to get us through the various checkpoints and posts we encountered as we walked through the Communard zone; nobody'd been told yet that he was now an enemy of the revolution. I began to regret not spreading my disinformation a little more widely.

"Do you want to tell me how you plan to do this?" I asked him as we walked away from yet another group of fawning, too-serious-for-words frères. "I feel like someone being told to invest without seeing the prospectus."

"Capitalist humor. How droll," he said. "It's quite simple, really. We're headed toward a checkpoint in a comparatively stable part of the front. I'll talk us through our – the Commune's – lines. We're doing some field intelligence work, you and I. Once we're through our lines, we duck out of sight, approach the Blanc lines from a different angle, and then you provide me with my entree to the Blanc sector. Simple, no?"

"And how do I play my part in this clever plan?"

"Patience, my old. Patience. I'll explain when you need to know, and not before." I shrugged. It wasn't a question of whether Abalain intended to dust me, but when and how. I felt the weight of his wearable around my waist and hoped he'd at least wait until we reached the Blanc lines so that I could surprise him before he surprised me.

The checkpoint showed all the signs of a front that hadn't changed in weeks, possibly months. The smart-wire had accumulated a patina of grime and pigeonshit you just didn't see on the more active parts of the city. Dogs danced around the feet of the listlessly patrolling frères; there was no Power-Armor in sight. Someone had liberated a video lottery terminal from somewhere and set it up in the observation post Abalain dragged me into; the VLT's reader slot was stuffed with an override card that made play free but also eliminated any payout, and as Abalain drawled his lies to the lieutenant I joined a group of bored frères watching the symbols flash in pointless sequence across the terminal's screen. You'd never know, looking at the crap that had accreted around this corner, that there were parts of Paree where bits were being blown off bodies and buildings as the world's most pointless renovation project continued on its nasty way.

"We go now," Abalain said from behind me. "Do you think that you can tear yourself away from this excitement?" I bit back my reply and turned to follow. He hadn't even waited for me, and I had to jog for a moment to catch up with him. We ducked into a building, descended to the basement and spent a freaky few seconds in a dark, humid tunnel that brought back nightmares of my brief sojourn as a hot-wired guinea pig, before emerging into the wreckage of an old Metro station. In the distance, I thought I saw a flash of light – reflection from a sniper's scope?

I stopped, imagining the weight of the sniper's gaze on my chest, just below my sternum, and had a sudden vision of Sissy standing just as I was now. Who knew how many trustafarians had been sacrificed to flushing out the Blancs and then had their bunks reassigned. I felt a strange mixture of sorrow and relief – it had been quick then, for her; not the drawn-out nightmare of serial rape that had been slithering through my subconscious.

Abalain showed no hesitation; I'll give him that much. He grabbed my arm and pulled me out into the street. This close to freedom I found myself a lot less cold-blooded about being shot than I had been a couple of weeks before. Then we were safely across the road, and inside an abandoned block of flats sheltered from both Communard and Blanc eyes. We were able to traverse a couple of hundred meters of picturesque ruins without being exposed to any more than electronic surveillance. I figured we'd be nearly on top of a Blanc outpost before the frères finally copped to what Abalain was doing.

"So what are you going to do once you're out of Tomorrowland and back in the real world?" I asked him when he stopped us in what seemed to have once been a pretty nice courtyard. "How does a scientific revolutionary make his way in a bourgeois schematic?"

"I'll pretend that was a serious question and not just another pathetic attempt at snideness," he said. "Never try to out-sneer the French, monsieur. We're the masters." *You be expansive, you little shit*, I thought. *Expand away*; *it'll be more fun to watch you collapse.* "The fact is, Monsieur Rosen, I'm an extremely adaptable man. I won't have any trouble fitting into my new life. I'll probably have to move from Paris, and that will be a shame. But even if Bucharest or Buenos Aires isn't the City of Light, I can be comfortable."

He produced a small pistol and pointed it at me. "After all, competitive intelligence work can be done anywhere."

If he was expecting me to look shocked, I disappointed him. I hope I did, anyway. Frankly, I'd expected something a bit more clever. I was grateful, though, that an identity switch was the best he could come up with. After looking at me expectantly for a moment, he scowled and waved the pistol. "Let's go, Sergeant Abalain," he said.

The Blancs had seen us, of course, and a well-armed reception party was waiting when we emerged from the ruins and into the street across which their checkpoint sat. Abalain pushed me forward, then raised his hands above his head. A Blanc in stained coveralls gestured for me to do the same.

"I hope you guys can help me," Abalain said when we reached the Blancs. His English was almost completely unaccented, and I gave him points for that. A resourceful fellow, our sergeant. "I've been a prisoner of those bastards for months," he continued. "This is one of them. His name's Abalain. He's my gift to you if you'll call my embassy and get me out of here."

That set everyone to babbling. I smiled. "Thanks," I said to Abalain. "I always wanted to be famous." He didn't break character, not that I'd expected him to.

An officer showed up. His uniform was tailored, clean and crisply pressed. He wore aviator sunglasses and carried a swagger stick. *No wonder you guys can't retake the city*, I thought. "So this is the infamous Sergeant Abalain," he said to me.

" 'Fraid not," I told him. "But that is." I nodded at Abalain.

His face spasmed in pretty convincing outrage. "He lies!" he shouted. "He kidnapped me and killed my friends! You can't let him get away with this!"

"Oh, come on," I said. I turned to the officer. "Isn't there anyone here who's seen a picture of Abalain?" I already knew the answer to that – like many of his erstwhile companions, Abalain had been pretty thorough about avoiding cameras – but I was playing a role now myself.

The officer smiled, obviously pleased with himself. "Perhaps the thing to do is to try the both of you. You can't both be Abalain, but on the chance that one of you is . . ."

It was time. I unbuttoned my jacket. "We can settle this easily," I said, and unbuckled Abalain's wearable. Abalain's jaw dropped along with his new persona. I paused, savoring the moment. This was no substitute for Sissy, or even for the weeks he'd ripped from my life. But it was all I was likely to get, so I wanted it to last.

I showed the wearable to the officer. "Retinal lock," I said.

"If you want to see your cousin again, monsieur, stop now."

That pissed me off. "You pathetic son of a bitch," I said. I pulled the flimsies – the list of inductees and the bunk assignments – from my pocket. I held them up in his face. "Where's the Canadian female, François? Look," I stabbed the flimsy as though it were Abalain's heart. "She was inducted – now look here," I rattled the bunk assignments. "No bunk – what happened to her, Monsieur le sergeant? Sent to Montmarte? *Target practice?*" A note of hysteria crept into my voice. I swallowed, balled up the flimsies and tossed them against his chest.

"No," he said. "It wasn't like that – "

I didn't let him finish. Smacking the wearable up against my face, I thumbed the power switch. The computer farted its displeasure. "How sad," I said. "Sergeant Abalain's computer doesn't like the look in my eye." I turned it toward Abalain, who backed away. "Gentlemen?" I said to the Blancs. Two of them grabbed Abalain by the shoulders. He tried to twist his head away, but the wearable was more flexible than his neck was. A second later, the computer chirped and lit up all Christmas.

I dropped the wearable to the ground and emptied my pockets onto it. "You should be able to have some fun with all of this," I said. Abalain babbled something I didn't hear. The officer slapped him in the face – whether in response or just on general principle, I didn't care. Then they were all hitting him.

I used the last of my steri-wipes to get his blood off my hands.

Day 63: It'll All End in Tears

"France thanks you for the service you have rendered her, monsieur." I figured the Blanc general was speaking more for the benefit of the news weasels on the other side of the mirrorwall than he was for me, but I nodded my head with what I hoped looked like sagacity. "Bringing the beast Abalain to justice will show the world the true face that lies behind the mask of the Commune de Paris."

I tried to be blasé about it. But looking at this guy, I couldn't help but wonder about the arithmetic of Parec: how in the world did you add up the folks on my street, the ones I played baseball with, and the ones who sold me bread and sausage and wine – and end up with assholes like Abalain or this prat? What variable in the goddamn equation made people stop thinking and let their emotions do all the heavy lifting?

I'd hoped to feel cleansed at having done for Abalain, but I didn't.

"Good for you," I said, getting to my feet. "I'd love to stay and watch, but I have to go home now. I'm going to take a forty-eight-hour shower, and then I'm going to sleep for a week."

"I believe the people from your embassy want to talk to you, Monsieur Rosen," the general said warily.

"Have them call my service," I said. That's me: Mister How to Make Friends and Influence People.

"The photographers say they're not finished yet."

That's just great, I thought. Is there anybody in this city who isn't working an angle?

Sissy hadn't been working anything except maybe her hormones. I'd been able to store her carefully in the back of my mind while working up my escape plan. But she was clamoring to get out of my head now. Being away from the Commune didn't make me any more free than if I'd still been Abalain's pet ferret: I still had to face up to the fact that she was gone. How was I going to explain this to my aunt?

The door behind me slammed open.

"Lee!"

I turned around so fast I fell over. That's my story, anyway, and I'm sticking to it. Then she was down on the carpet with me and hugging me and crying and I guess I got kind of sloppy too. But I swear the first words out of my mouth were: "Where the fuck have you been?"

She slapped me, lightly. "I worried about you too."

"Jesus," I said, sitting up. "I was convinced you were – " I couldn't say it, not now. It seemed it could still happen; I might be imagining this. "What happened to you? How did you get away?"

"It was Eddie," she said.

"Not true, Lee." Eddie flowed into the room, graceful in spite of his bulk. "She's the one who did it. I just got her back across the lines."

"Will you two stop negotiating credits and just tell me what happened?"

"When they separated us when the bus stopped I was so scared," Sissy said. "Everyone was scared. But then I thought about what you'd said. You said not to worry. And you always looked after me, Lee." She smiled, and even though her eyes looked dead with fatigue I still felt better for seeing that. "I figured you knew what you were talking about. So I didn't worry. Instead, I tried to guess what you'd do, and I decided that you'd watch and wait for a chance to do something."

I looked at Sissy more closely. It wasn't just fatigue I was seeing in her eyes. There was something else, something sort of calm and understanding. This wasn't the girl I'd lost back at the Dialtone. Of course, being kidnapped can do that to a person.

"So I'm watching what happens, and what happens is that everybody's so scared that they all just stand there gibbering and crying all over one another," she said. "They must have been doing that all along, but I never noticed it. Until I sat back and made myself look. We were all just crying like babies. And the guards must have noticed too, because when I looked I saw that they weren't really paying any attention to us. They were all watching the guys being rounded up." We were the ones making the fuss, I remembered. Some of us, anyway. Some of us were still trying to think of a way of finessing ourselves out of that jam.

"So it was really pretty simple." Sissy smiled artlessly, and for a moment she was my kid cousin again. "I just kind of shuffled my feet and moved back without trying to move too much. And when I was at the back of the crowd I just sort of slipped out of it. It was dark and nobody noticed me. But you know, I don't think they were all that smart, Lee. We just let ourselves think they were 'cause we were all so scared. As soon as I started trying to think like you do, it was easy to get away." She hugged me fiercely. "I saw you trying to distract their attention from me, Lee." Now she was crying again. "What you did for me – I couldn't have done that for you." She dug her face into my shoulder and sobbed, and I felt like the stupidest idiot outside of a corporate boardroom. I had out-clevered myself into eight weeks or more of slavery, and she was smart enough to just walk away – and she was giving me the credit?

"And that's when Eddie saved me."

"I followed the bus," Eddie said with a shrug. "Probably not the smartest thing in the world, but hey. I should have seen it coming, and I didn't. I felt responsible, you know?" I knew. "Soon as I saw you all being off-loaded and sorted I figured I was screwed, and I was making my way back to the lines when I come across Sissy here. And damned if she didn't want to take me back and try to spring you. Took me ten minutes to persuade her we'd only get ourselves killed."

"You can always trust Fat Eddie," I said. "He knows three ways around every angle there is. Listening to him definitely saved your life." I decided then that I was never going to tell Sissy the full story of my service to the Commune. Even if it seemed that the Sissy who was smiling at me now wasn't the same kid who'd wanted to see the sights back in the great Before.

"She could have gone home, you know," Fat Eddie said. "Her mom sure as hell wanted her to. Instead, we've spent the last eight weeks nagging the shit out of anybody who'd listen, trying to find you. And now we have."

"And now I want a shower," I said. "I want some clean clothes."

"I want to go back to the Dialtone and finish my drink," Sissy said.

I stared at her. "You're joking, right?"

"Oh, you can shower and change first, if you want." She stood up, then grabbed my hands and pulled me to my feet. "Come on, Lee. It's a glorious time to be in Paree."

Paree – where snipers lurked in the high windows and unwashed thugs stared blindly at castrated video lottery terminals. Paree, where, on the pavé before a rusting Citroën, I had decided to die. The fatal anguish surged through me — and *out.*

I was a dead man, dead many times over in the past eight weeks, and yet, miraculously, *alive.* Alive, in Gay Paree, where famed Dialtone yet stood, where the bartender would mix me a Manhattan and my cousin Sissy would dance while I watched approvingly from a side table, chewing on my work problems and swapping ironic glances with Fat Eddie.

I extended an arm and Sissy took it at the elbow. Fat Eddie shouldered us a path through the crowd, over the epoxy cobblestones, and down the boulevard toward the Dialtone.

Arabesques of Eldritch Weirdness #8

❧

Jeffrey Ford

Inky night of live burial, gasping for dirt reeking with zombie blood wept from the eyes of a vampire bat into a flask in the hand of Doctor Imperius Fragturd, lab-coat clad, psychotic ex-Nobel laureate, who has his once-beloved wife encased in a block of ice in a walk-in freezer of his own brilliant design and who has gone off his rocker with surrogate lust for the innocent hips of Wendy Hartshine, cheerleader and glee club captain, IQ 40, the tasty piece of trim in the broken-down Thunderbird convertible on the side of the road outside the dilapidated mansion that, back in the monster-ridden days of yore, before radio and prohibition, was the site of the final battle, ending in a mutual expiration, of The Cat Faced Freak and The Stalking Brain Eater, who brutally ate corpus callosum with little remorse and less grace like an ordinary man carrying the transplanted soul of a lamprey that made the arcing electrical leap at the insistence of a thunderstorm's harnessed energy, and always too much radiation, way too much frigging radiation, causing ants to mutate into geniuses, themselves, so that all they want to do is crawl in the ears of sleeping children and burrow through their brains to nourish their aching, pinprick imaginations and in the process spark dreams of a shadow-clad figure skulking through alleys wielding a straight razor that once shaved the beard of the poor Lazarus, down but not out, though showing bone, whose rotting, yellow-nailed hands are clawing up through the soft earth over in the cemetery, birthing himself in order to once again seek the ancient mysteries of Hermes Trismegistus, the Egyptian adept with all the answers to all the questions, like how the town soda jerk, Jed Bleener, Wendy's wide-eyed, handsome beau, is going to save her screeching sweater meat from the clutches of Fragturd before he experiments on her flesh, turning it sour green and wrinkled in the act of implanting his own desire into her sacred, as yet undefiled, temple of God with a special formula of demon spittle, alien gaze, and ape sweat, making her love him the way he loves him, the way the Devil of insidious Science and all that is unknown, Heathen, Nazi, and anti-Christian insists that he do for the sake of the plot and the proliferation of pulp.

The Seven-Day Itch

ꕥ

Elise Moser

Paula's back had been itching for a couple of days. It was a strange itch, deep, persistent; unlike any other itch she ever remembered having. It was almost verging on pain, the kind you get when there's a boil on your back. That's what it felt like, a boil. But when she twisted her arm back and managed to just brush her fingertips at the edge of the spot she could tell there was nothing there.

Most of the time she didn't think about the itch, but occasionally it intruded into her consciousness. She felt it, suddenly, in the middle of a meeting at school, when the weenie from the staff association added six items to the agenda; she wiggled until she thought she could get at it with the corner of her chair, but she suddenly realized several people were staring at her. So she put it out of her mind. The next morning she tried to see it in the mirror, but no matter how she twisted she couldn't see anything but unblemished skin. In the shower she tried to scrub it with the loofah, but the loofah seemed to be getting caught on something – and anyway scrubbing didn't help, so she just backed into the hot water and forgot about the itch, again.

Now, lying in bed in the gray morning light, with Janet's warm breasts against her back and Janet's warm breath against her neck, Paula became aware that she could feel the itch again. This was perfect – Janet could scratch it for her. She reached a hand back and gently squeezed Janet's hip. "Janet." Janet hmmed. Paula shook the hip a little. "Janet," she said, a little louder, "can you scratch my back? It's been itching for days and I just can't reach it." Janet kissed Paula's back and then, lazily, propped her head up on her fist.

"Okay, honey bun. Where is it?"

Paula twisted her arm back and gestured toward the spot. "Kind of there. Give it a try, and I'll tell you when you get it." Janet started gently scratching and Paula directed her. "No, more to the left. No, my left. That's right. Almost there. A little higher. Higher. High – *yes, right there.* Is there something there?"

Janet paused and then scratched again. "Nope. Nothing."

"Scratch harder."

Janet scratched. "It feels funny."

"What do you mean 'funny'?"

"Well, kind of elastic, or something. Like I feel like I could push it in a little bit." Janet stopped scratching, and probed a little. The skin was almost like rubber, giving gently. Janet gave a little cry.

"What, Jan?"

"I don't know, Paul. It's so weird, but it feels almost like . . . like my fingertip is being . . . pulled."

Paula felt Janet pushing against her and then heard a kind of choking sound, as if Janet were struggling to swallow and breathe at the same time.

"Paula." Janet's voice was strangely pitched.

Paula was lying on her side, eyes closed but alert. "Yes?"

"Paula." There was a strange pause. Paula became aware that Janet was, well, almost panting. She gave a half-laugh, and turned her head part way around to look at Janet.

"Janet, what's the matter?"

Janet leaned over. Paula could hear her breathing fast. "What's the matter, Jan? What is it, babe?"

Janet inhaled, a great, ragged breath. "I don't know what's happening," she said, her voice wild, "this is too strange." She breathed again, deeply, deliberately. "Paula. One time, when I was in about grade five, I glued my eye shut."

Paula furrowed her eyebrows. What was Janet talking about?

"I glued my upper and lower right eyelids together with epoxy by accident while building a model plane." Paula waited while Janet paused. "I remember what that felt like, and it was *not* like this," she whispered.

"What is it, hon?" Paula asked, pushing down her impatience so her voice would come out calm and soothing.

"Part of my fingernail's gone, it's sunk into your back, it's gone."

Paula raised her eyebrows. Janet must be under more stress than she'd realized. What was she on about? Janet began to sob in a strangled way.

"Paula, you're going to think I'm crazy, even I think I'm crazy." She stopped and took a deep breath. "Paula, what does this feel like to you?"

Paula turned her head again. She shrugged. "I don't know. It feels fine. It doesn't really itch anymore. Maybe you could just stay there all day," she joked, and then laughed. The laugh died though; there was something about the quality of Janet's silence that was even more disturbing than the sobs had been. "Janet, what's wrong?" Still silence, except for a kind of bronchial rattling that must be Janet's breathing. Paula's voice rose. "What's wrong, babe?" No answer. "Come over here," she said, patting her side of the bed.

Paula could feel Janet pushing against her back with her other hand. Finally Janet stopped pushing and spoke, and when she spoke it was as if through gritted teeth. "I can't." she said in a hoarse whisper. "I can't. I don't know how to explain this, but" – and then her voice rose into a wail like a tidal wave – "I'm stuck in your back, my finger's stuck and I can't get it out!" Then Janet panicked. By the time she stopped flailing around both she and Paula had scratches, Janet on her hand and arm and Paula all over her back – and one long one across her cheek and the bridge of her nose, which she got when she tried to turn and face Janet and caught a wild arm on a sideswipe.

They both called in sick and then struggled to put on some clothes. Janet found a sleeveless cotton jumper someone had given her once which buttoned fortuitously up the left side. It was entirely unseasonal and it looked incongruous with Janet's hiking boots, but that didn't matter. Paula was more difficult to dress, until they finally found a black sequined evening jacket which was slit halfway up the back and had a deeply plunging neckline. It looked very eccentric over jeans and sneakers; any time Paula leaned to one side, one or both of her breasts would slip out of the exotic neckline like plump unruly fish. Paula put her hair in a ponytail and then stood in front of the hall mirror, head bowed so Janet could see over her, while Janet tried to pull a brush through her own hair. She was very nervous and wasn't really paying attention; the result was an unusually lopsided frizz, but Janet was too frustrated to keep trying.

They put Janet's giant coat over both their shoulders, Paula poking her forefinger accidentally into Janet's nostril as she tried to grab the lapel; then they tried to get into the car. Eventually they managed. They would have felt like a lesbian Laurel and Hardy if they hadn't been so freaked out already.

Paula drove them to Angie's office. Angie had been Paula's roommate when they were undergrads, and she had a thriving "woman-centered" medical practice. Paula and Janet had to sit in the waiting room, perched sideways on adjoining chairs, until some patient called in to cancel, and then Angie invited them in to the examining room. She started to make small talk but stopped when she noticed their strange clothes. She began to smile and then frowned when she saw Janet's finger stuck in Paula's back.

First Angie tried to just pull it out. This didn't work. Then she braced herself against Paula's back and yanked, hard, on Janet's hand, causing Janet to roar in pain. Then Angie examined them more closely. She tried to probe with a Q-tip, but the Q-tip got stuck and then, when she tentatively pushed at it, was pulled in, slowly, like a twig in quicksand, and disappeared. This made Janet whimper, and Angie sat down hard in the visitor's chair and got deeply red in the face. Paula kept trying to turn around and see them, saying, "What? What? WHAT!"

Finally Janet found her voice – a whispery, kind of choked version of her voice – "Oh Paul, you won't believe this, but Angie just pushed a Q-tip in there and it disappeared!" Paula rolled her eyes and looked over at Angie, tapping her temple and glancing meaningfully in Janet's direction – until she saw Angie's face. Angie looked like she'd just had an electrical shock. And she was shaking her head, slowly, as if trying to free herself of something.

They went home and tried to find a comfortable way to sit on the couch. Angie had said she'd do some research and call them, and to contact her if there was any change. In the meantime they had difficulty finding a way for Paula to pee, although it was no problem for Janet as long as Paula stood close enough, helped her push down her jeans, and ripped off the toilet paper for her. In the evening after they'd eaten – awkwardly, with Paula on Janet's lap, although Janet, bless her, said it was "kind of romantic" – Janet said that she could no longer see her fingernail at all. Paula felt Janet go rigid; then Janet shuddered, her whole body rippling as if a giant snake were flailing inside her. Finally, exhausted, they lay down together, in much the same spooning position in which they'd woken up. They lay stiffly, clutching hands, unable to sleep and somehow unable to talk to each other. They had no awareness of having fallen asleep until they woke up some time toward sunrise. Janet started to cry almost immediately, and shook Paula. "Paul," she whimpered, "Paul-A, my fingers, my fucking FINGERS!" When Paula got her calmed down enough to talk, Janet said that in her sleep, the two longest fingers, which had lain next to the disappearing forefinger at the spot, had been pulled in. All three forefingers were now inside. Paula began to feel queasy, and only wanted to get away and have some time to think about things, alone. This, of course, was the one thing she couldn't have.

By late afternoon Janet's fingers had all disappeared, the veins on the back of her hand seemingly growing out of Paula's skin. Paula still didn't feel anything, except for Janet's terrible hot panting and tears against her neck. She smelled Janet's fear-sweat; the whole house seemed filled with that smell now.

Angie had phoned in the morning, sounding grim. Then she came by in the evening and looked at them; her face curled in disgust and she said they'd better try an X-ray. She drove them back to the office and they tried to take X-rays but somehow they couldn't get a good picture. Around the spot where Janet's wrist bones penetrated Paula's back there was simply no image. Angie looked pale in the empty office and offered to amputate Janet's hand at the wrist. Janet vomited right there onto the lead apron. Paula shook her head.

That night, once again, they thought they wouldn't, but then they slept. This time though, the sleep came in small pockets, twenty or forty minutes at a time. Each time Janet woke up she cried and described for Paula the slim margin of hand that was missing that hadn't been missing before. She said she could feel the pull getting stronger now. By daylight it was up to her elbow and she couldn't stop sobbing; she was wracked by dry heaves and couldn't keep still. She had moments of panicked thrashing. She jerked Paula painfully as she flailed; her flesh, damp with fear-sweat, rubbing at the now-irritated skin of Paula's back. Paula desperately wanted her to be calm. She closed her eyes and imagined Janet in meditation, serene. It didn't help.

Around noon Janet broke one of the fingers on her right hand during a hysterical fit in the hallway on the way to the toilet. Paula called Angie who came over and taped it up, feeding Janet samples of a sedative so she could sleep. Paula still didn't feel anything at all except a little relief that Janet would be quiet for a while. She was beginning to realize that if they survived this Janet might lose a limb, or part of one – *if* they survived. She found herself imagining what it could be like to lose Janet; she forced herself to put it out of her mind. The tension was making her sick to her stomach. More and more she felt like a giant bird of prey, some kind of bizarre vulture, only instead of a huge pair of wings she had the bigger part of a woman attached to her back. Far from being able to fly, she felt ponderous, weighed down, grounded.

Janet slept through the night, but when she woke up she was jammed against Paula. Her speech still a little indistinct from the sedative, Janet told Paula that her shoulder was being sucked in, that the edges of the cotton jumper were starting to pull. She said that the more of her that was sucked in, the stronger the pull became. Over the course of the morning, as snow fell outside, Janet lost her shoulder and part of her left breast and she said her shoulder blades felt as if they had suction cups over them, or a wide flat vacuum cleaner. Paula's heart pounded against her ribs; she could hear the flat pain in Janet's voice, the dull agony. She suddenly felt panicky; she was trapped by Janet's body, Janet's sweaty skin pressed against her back and legs. Paula closed her eyes and pressed the panic down.

They were deeply regretting not having let Angie amputate, but it was definitely too late now. Paula felt alternately guilty, because she wasn't the one who was being sucked away (although who knew what would happen when Janet's whole body was gone), and disgusted, by the feeling of Janet's lump of a body attached to her. And then guilty again, for feeling disgusted. Did Siamese twins feel this way? Paula squeezed her eyes shut and felt every inch of Janet's twisted body pressed against her, wanting to preserve the feeling in her mind.

Late that night, with Janet's chin so hard up against Paula's back that her jawbone felt painfully like a vise against Paula's shoulder blade, Angie showed up with a van from the hospital; they were bundled into the back of it by two very large orderlies. It was weird, but it didn't occur to either Paula or Janet to ask what was happening. They were still thinking about how to survive through the next heartbeats, each in her own way.

They didn't go to a city hospital, but rather to some kind of base or installation out on the north shore. Once inside, they were examined by a number of people in white lab coats who poked, probed, and asked lots of questions in strange monotone clipboard voices. By the time the examinations and tests were finished, Janet's lower jaw was immobilized. They were given a sedative and immediately began to feel powerfully sleepy. Janet said, "Aula, I ove ou," which squeezed Paula's heart and pushed a great sob up through her constricted throat. Janet cried a little before slipping into unconsciousness; Paula heard her lover's breath become calm, almost like a baby's, before slipping under herself. In the morning Angie told her Janet's whole head was gone and then immediately administered a strong sedative which took effect even before Paula could really react. She woke up after two more days of strange mindless dreams, after, they said, the last tip of Janet's right big toe had disappeared between Paula's shoulder blades like a stone into a pool of water.

They kept Paula at the lab for over a week afterward, giving her every test under the sun. X-rays, CAT scans, blood work. They sedated her at night, and she dreamed of Janet's toe slipping into water, Janet's toe like the tip of an iceberg, Janet like a big fish swimming through her heart in a wash of blood and disappearing in a distance. While she slept they did exploratory surgery with lasers, looking into various parts of her body, although with no advance in their understanding. Finally they let her go home. Paula continued to see Angie on a weekly basis for months; there was never a sign of what had happened. Angie would ask Paula, "How do you feel?" and Paula would say, "Usual." She'd shake her head and sigh. By midsummer she could even laugh a little. She'd give Angie a wry smile, and she'd say, "At least that itch is gone."

The Scuttling or, *Down by the Sea with Marvin and Pamela*

ꕥ

William Sanders

The Bradshaws got back from their vacation late Friday evening and discovered right away that they were not alone.

Marvin Bradshaw was coming up the front walk, having gone across the road to pick up their accumulated mail from the neighbors, when he heard his wife scream. He ran up the stairs and into the house, cursing and wishing he had tried a little harder to get that pistol permit; but there were no intruders to be seen, only his wife standing white-faced and trembling in the kitchen, pointing in the direction of the sink. "Look," she said.

He looked, wondering what he was supposed to see. Everything was as he remembered, but then he had never given much attention to the kitchen area, which after all wasn't his department. He said, "What?" and then he saw something small and dark moving rapidly along the sink's rim. Now he saw another one, slightly larger, going up the wall behind the faucets.

"Son of a bitch," Marvin Bradshaw said. "Cockroaches."

"I came in here to get a drink of water." Pamela Bradshaw's voice was almost a whisper, as if that one scream had used up all her volume reserves. "I turned on the light and Marvin, they were *everywhere*. They went running in all directions." She shuddered. "I think one ran over my foot."

Marvin Bradshaw stepped toward the sink, but the cockroaches were too fast for him. The one on the sink dived off into space, hit the floor, and slipped into a barely visible crack beneath the baseboard. The one on the wall evaded Marvin's slapping hand and disappeared into the cupboard space above the sink. Marvin swore in frustration, but he felt a little relieved too; he hadn't really been eager to crush a cockroach with his bare hand.

"Cockroaches," he said. "Wonderful. Bust your ass for years, finally get out of the city, away from the dirt and the coloreds, into a three-quarter-mil house on one of the best pieces of ocean-front property on Long Island. And then you go away for a couple weeks, and when you get home you got cockroaches. Jesus."

He glared at his wife. "You know who's responsible, don't you? You had to go hire that God-damned Mexican maid."

"Inez is Guatemalan," Pamela protested. "And we don't know – "

"Mexican, Guatemalan, who gives a fuck?" Marvin had never seen the point of these picky-ass distinctions between people who said *sí* when they meant yes. Maybe you needed to know the difference between Japs and Chinamen and other slopes, since nowadays you had to do business with the yellow ass-holes; but spics were spics, whatever hell-hole country they came from.

"The fact remains," he said, "we never had cockroaches here, and then two months ago you hired her, and now we do. I'm telling you, you let those people in, you got roaches. Didn't I run that block of buildings in Spanish Harlem for your father, back before we got married? Cockroaches and Puerto Ricans, I saw enough of both. Don't tell *me*."

"I'll speak to her when she comes in tomorrow."

"No you won't." He took a sheet of folded paper from the stack of mail in his left hand. "That was what I was coming to tell you. Look what your precious Inez left us."

She took the paper and unfolded it. The message was printed in pencil, in large clumsy block capitals:

NO MAS. YOU NO PAY ME 5 WIKS NOW. GO LIV SISTER IN ARIZONA. PLES SEN MY MONY MARGARITA FLORES 72281 DEL MONTE TUCSON AZ 85707. INEZ

Marvin took the note back and wadded it up and hurled it at the kitchen wastebasket, missing. "Comes in here, turns our home into a roach motel, runs out on us when our backs are turned, then she expects to get paid. Lots of luck, you fat wetback bitch."

Pamela sighed. "I'll miss her, all the same. You know, I was working with her, trying to help her remember her past lives. I believe she was a Mayan princess – "

Marvin groaned. "Christ sake," he said, "not now, all right?"

He hadn't had much fun over the last two weeks. He hadn't liked Miami, which had been swarming with small brown people, and where there had been nothing to do but swim – which in his book was something you did only to keep from drowning – or lie around getting a tan, if you were asshole enough to want to look colored. The flight home had been delayed again and again. All in all, this was no time to have to listen to Pamela and her New Age crap.

"Okay," he told her, "we'll go out, get something to eat. Monday I'll call an exterminator. Antonio's okay? I could go for seafood."

Driving away from the house, he considered that at least there was one good side to the situation: eating out would give him a chance to have some real food, rather than that organic slop that Pamela tended to put on the table. He suspected this was merely a cover for her basic incompetence in the kitchen; chopping up a lot of raw vegetables was as close to real cooking as she could manage.

"Marvin," Pamela said suddenly, "you said an exterminator. You mean someone who'll kill the cockroaches?"

He glanced at her, wondering what the hell now. "What, you're worried about chemicals, poisons, like that?"

"Well, that too." Pamela paused, frowning. Marvin realized he'd just handed her something else to be a pain in the ass about. "But what I was going to say," she went on, "isn't there some other way? Besides killing them?"

"Christ." Marvin ground his teeth. "You want to get rid of the roaches but you don't want the poor little things hurt? What's that, more Oriental mumbo-jumbo? The roaches might be somebody's reincarnated souls?"

"I wish you wouldn't be so negative about reincarnation," she said stiffly. "I suppose it's not part of the religion you were brought up in."

Actually Marvin Bradshaw's parents had never shown any interest in any religion at all, and he had followed their lead; churches were places you went for funerals and weddings, and then only if you couldn't get out of it. All he had against reincarnation was that it was believed in by people from India – such as the one who collected fat payments for sitting around in a sheet spouting this shit to Pamela and a bunch of other goofy middle-aged women – and Hindus, after all, were just another variety of little brown bastards who ought to go back where they came from. (Which, in the case of the said Baba Lal Mahavishnu, Marvin suspected would be somewhere in New Jersey; but that was another matter.)

"In any case," Pamela added, "it's not true that human beings can be reborn as insects. That's a Western misconception."

"Then – "

"Still and all, Marvin." Pamela bashed right on over him, an avalanche-grade unstoppable force. "Babaji says it's always best to avoid harming any living creature. The karma accumulates. All those roaches, there must be hundreds, even thousands – disgusting to our eyes, of course, but so many lives. I can't imagine the karmic consequences of killing them all."

"Then what do you want me to do about the fucking things? Ask them nicely to leave? Get them their own place? How about you go talk to them," he said, enraged beyond control. "That would make any self-respecting insect hit the road."

She didn't answer. From the tone of her silence Marvin figured one of them would be sleeping in the guest bedroom tonight. Well, that was another bonus.

Pamela kept up the silent treatment almost all the way through dinner. Marvin knew it was too good to last. Sure enough, as he was finishing up his lobster, she started in again. "My God," he said, "couldn't you wait till we're out of here? Talking about roaches, what are you, trying to make me sick?"

He leaned back and looked at the remains of his meal. He didn't really like lobster all that well; he'd just ordered this one to jerk Pamela's chain. Antonio's was one of those places with live lobsters in a big glass tank, so you could pick yours out and have them boil his ass alive. Marvin had enjoyed saying "boil his ass alive" and watching Pamela cringe. She hadn't been too horrified, he noticed, to clean her own plate. Probably thought all those clams and scallops had died naturally. Ocean roadkill, maybe, run over by a submarine.

He got up, tossing his napkin on the table, and headed for the men's room. As he was coming back the proprietor stepped not quite into his path. "Mr. Bradshaw," Antonio said. "I hope your dinner was satisfactory."

Marvin nodded and tried to smile. Antonio was small and dark and his black hair was a little too glossy; but he came from a Portuguese family that had been in the area for a couple of centuries at least, and he ran a hell of a good restaurant. Marvin thought that Antonio was okay for, well, an Antonio.

"No offense," Antonio said, glancing around and lowering his voice, "but I couldn't help overhearing your conversation just now."

"You and everybody else in the place," Marvin said. "Sorry if she upset your customers, talking about cockroaches. She's been kind of weird, last year or so. Think she's getting change of life."

"Oh, that's all right." Antonio made a quick no-problem gesture. "No, what I was going to say, you're not the only one with roaches. I've heard a lot of people complaining, the last couple of weeks. It's like they just moved into the area." He made a face. "In my business it's something you worry about."

Marvin thought it over. So it wasn't just his house. Must be the new people moving in, bringing the pests with them. The standards had really gone to hell around here since that housing-discrimination lawsuit.

"Point is," Antonio went on, "it won't be easy getting an exterminator any time soon. You'll do well to get one by the end of next week."

"Shit!" Marvin said, louder than he meant to. "Hey, Antonio, I can't live with those things in the house for a week. You must know some people, guy in your line. You know anybody might be willing to make a special call? I'll make it worth their while."

Antonio shook his head. "Believe me, all the ones I know are already making 'special calls' and charging through the nose, too." He rubbed his chin. "Now there's one possibility, maybe . . . "

"Talk to me. Come on, Antonio. Help me out here."

"Well – one of my bus boys," Antonio said, "the one doing that table by the door, see? He's got this grandfather, supposed to be good at getting rid of roaches and rats and the like."

Marvin saw a short, chunky, very dark kid in a white apron. Coarse, badly cut black hair. Huge cheekbones, heavy eyebrows, big nose. "What's he," Marvin said, "Mexican?" Thinking, *no way.*

Antonio laughed. "Actually, he's an Indian."

"From India?" No way in *hell.* "Doesn't look it."

"No, no. American Indian. Some small tribe I can't even pronounce, got a reservation upstate."

"Huh." Marvin stared, amazed. As far as he knew he had never seen an Indian in these parts before. That was one thing you had to say for Indians, compared to other kinds of colored people: they kept to themselves, lived out in the sticks on reservations, didn't come pushing themselves in where they weren't wanted.

"I don't really know much about it," Antonio admitted. "Some people I know in Amityville, the old man did a job for them and they were very pleased. But they didn't tell me a lot of details."

"Huh," Marvin said again. "A redskin exterminator. Now I've heard everything."

"He's not an exterminator, strictly speaking." Antonio gave Marvin an odd grin. "This is the part your wife's going to like. He doesn't kill anything. He just makes the pests go away."

Marvin turned his stare onto Antonio. "This is a gag, right? You're going to tell me he blows a horn or something and they follow him away, like the Pied fucking Piper? Hey, Antonio, do I look like I'm in the mood for comedy?"

"No, this is for real." Antonio's face was serious. "I'm not sure how he does it – what I heard, he sort of smokes them out. Indian secret, I guess."

"I'll be damned." For a moment Marvin considered the idea. Indians did know a lot of tricks, everybody knew that. "Nah. Thanks, but I'll wait till Monday and hit the yellow pages. Hell, I can stand anything for a few more days."

But later that night, about to go to bed – in the guest bedroom, sure enough – he felt a sudden thirst, and went down to the kitchen to get himself a beer; and when he turned on the light, there they were.

Pamela hadn't been exaggerating. The cockroaches were everywhere. They swarmed over the sink and the counter and the dishwasher, the refrigerator and the walls and the floor: little flat brown oblongs that began running, all at once, when the light came on, so that the whole room appeared to squirm sickeningly for a moment. In almost no time most of the roaches had vanished, but a few remained, high on the walls or in other inaccessible places. Through the glass doors of the china cupboard Marvin could see a couple of them perched on top of a stack of antique bone-china dishes.

Then he glanced up and saw that there was a large roach on the ceiling directly above his head. Its long feelers waved gently as if in greeting. It seemed to be looking at him, considering a drop.

"Jesus Christ!" Marvin shouted, and ran from the kitchen without stopping to turn off the light.

His hands were shaking as he picked up the phone. The restaurant was closed for the night, and when he dialed Antonio's home phone he had to listen to a lot of rings before Antonio picked it up.

"Listen," Marvin said over Antonio's sleepy protest, "you know that old Indian you were telling me about? How fast do you think you could get hold of him?"

Next morning when Marvin went nervously into the kitchen for his coffee, there were no roaches to be seen. He knew they were still there, hiding during the daylight hours; still, it wasn't so bad as long as he couldn't see them.

He poured himself a cup of black coffee and went out through the sliding glass doors to the sun deck. The sun was well up above the eastern horizon and the light hurt his eyes; he wished he'd brought a pair of shades. He sat down at the little table at the north end of the sun deck, keeping his back to the sun.

The Bradshaws' house was built at the edge of a rocky bluff, sixty or seventy feet above the ocean. If Marvin cared to look straight down, through the cracks between the planks of the sun deck, he could see the white sand of what Pamela liked to call "our beach." It wasn't much of a beach, just a narrow strip of sand that sloped steeply to the water. At high tide it was almost entirely submerged.

He tested his coffee cautiously. As he had expected, it was horrible. Have to start interviewing replacement help; Pamela's efforts in the kitchen were going to be almost as hard to live with as the cockroaches.

Cockroaches. He made a disgusted face, not just at the bitter coffee. He had really lost it last night. Now, sitting in the bright morning sunlight with the cool clean wind coming off the sea, he couldn't believe he'd gone into such a panic over a few bugs. Calling Antonio up in the middle of the night, for God's sake, begging him to bring in some crazy old Indian. Going to be embarrassing as hell, eating at Antonio's, after this.

Marvin raised the cup again and took a mouthful of coffee. God, it tasted bad. Even more gruesome than Pamela's usual coffee-making efforts, which was saying something. There even seemed to be something solid –

He jerked suddenly back from the table, dropping the cup, spilling coffee over himself and not noticing. He raised his hand to his mouth and spat onto his palm the soggy cadaver of a drowned cockroach.

Marvin leaped to his feet and dashed for the railing and energetically emptied his stomach in the direction of the Atlantic Ocean. When the retching and heaving at last subsided he hung there for several minutes, clutching the rail to keep from collapsing to the deck, breathing noisily through his mouth.

It was then that Pamela appeared in the kitchen doorway. "Marvin," she said, "a couple of men are out front in a pickup truck. They say you sent for them."

The kid from Antonio's was standing on the front porch, hands jammed into his ass pockets. With him was a little old man – no more than five feet tall, not much over a hundred pounds – with a face like a sun-dried apple. They both wore faded jeans and cheap-looking checkered work shirts. The old man had on a mesh-backed cap with a Dolphins emblem on the front and some kind of feather dangling from the crown. Behind them in the driveway sat an old pickup truck, its paint so faded and scabbed with rust that it was impossible to tell what color it had originally been.

The kid said, "Mr. Bradshaw? Mr. Coelho said you had a roach problem."

The old man said something in a language that sounded like nothing Marvin had ever heard. The kid said, "My grandfather needs to have a look around before he can tell you anything."

Marvin nodded weakly. He still felt dizzy and sick. "Sure," he said, and led the way back to the kitchen.

Pamela came and stood in the kitchen doorway beside Marvin. They watched as the old Indian walked slowly about the kitchen, bending down and studying the baseboards, running his fingers under the edge of the counter and sniffing them, peering behind the refrigerator. Suddenly he squatted down and opened the access doors and reached up into the dark space beneath the sink. A moment later he was standing up again, holding something small and wiggly between his thumb and forefinger. His wrinkled dark face didn't really change expression – it hadn't been wearing any recognizable expression to begin with – but there was something like satisfaction in his eyes.

He spoke again in that strange-sounding language. The kid said, "He needed to know what kind of roaches you had. He says no problem. This kind is easy."

The old man went out on the sun deck and flipped the cockroach over the rail. He came back and said something brief. "He says one hundred dollars," the kid translated.

For once Marvin was in no mood to argue. He could still taste that coffee-logged cockroach. "When can he start?"

"Right now," the kid said. "If that's okay."

The kid went back up the hall – Marvin thought he should have had Pamela go along to make sure he didn't steal anything, but it was too late now – while the old man continued to study the kitchen. A few minutes later the kid was back with a pair of nylon carry-on bags, which he set on the counter beside the sink. The old man nodded, grunted, unzipped one of the bags, and began rummaging inside.

While he was rummaging the kid said, "Any animals in the house? Dogs, cats?"

Pamela shook her head. Marvin said, "Hell, no." That was something he couldn't understand, people keeping dirty hairy animals in the house. Maybe a good guard dog, but even he belonged outside, behind a fence.

"It would be better," the kid said, "if you could go somewhere, like out of the house, till this is over."

"Yeah?" Marvin grinned. "You'd like that, wouldn't you?"

Pamela kicked his ankle. To the Indian kid she said, "Is this going to involve any toxic chemicals?"

"No, no, nothing like that." The kid gestured at the pile of stuff the old man was taking out of the bag. "See, we don't even use respirators. No, it's just, well, better if you're not here."

"Uh huh," Marvin said. "Forget it, Geronimo. Nice try."

The kid shrugged. "Okay." He turned and began unzipping the other bag.

By now the old man had laid out several bundles of what looked like dried weeds. Now he selected four of these and twisted them together to form a single long bundle. From the bag he took a roll of ordinary white twine and began wrapping the bundle tightly from end to end, compressing it into a solid cylinder about the size and shape of a rolled-up newspaper. He put the rest of the stuff back into the bag and spoke to the kid.

The kid had taken out a small drum, like a big tambourine without the metal jingles, and a long thin stick with one end wrapped in what looked like rawhide. He gave the drum a tap and got a single sharp *poong* that filled the kitchen and floated off down the hallway.

The old man produced a throwaway butane lighter, which he lit and applied to one end of the herb bundle. Marvin expected a quick flare-up, but the stuff showed some reluctance to ignite. The old man turned the bundle in his fingers, blowing gently, until at last the end of the bundle was a solid glowing red coal.

By now smoke was pouring from the bundle in thick white clouds, billowing up to the ceiling and then rolling down to fog the whole room. Marvin started to protest, but then he decided that the smell wasn't bad at all. He recognized cedar in there – for an instant he recalled the time he had been allowed to burn the family tree after Christmas because his father was too drunk – and something that might be sage, and other things he couldn't guess at.

Hell, he thought, you could probably market this shit for some serious bucks. The old ladies in particular would go big for a new house scent.

Now the old Indian was turning this way and that, waving the smoldering bundle, getting the smoke into all the corners of the room. The kid started beating his drum, *poong poong poong poong,* and the old man commenced to sing. At least that was what he seemed to think he was doing, though for sure he was no Tony Bennett. It was a weird monotonous tune, maybe half a dozen notes repeated over and over, and the words didn't sound like words at all, just nonsense syllables such as a man might sing if he'd forgotten the lyrics.

Whatever it was, Marvin Bradshaw didn't like it a damn bit. He started to speak, to tell the old man to get on with the fumigating and never mind the musical production number. But the two Indians were already walking past him and up the hallway, trailing clouds of smoke and never missing a beat or a hey-ya. Marvin said, "Oh, fuck this," and turned to follow, to put a stop to this crap before it went any further.

Pamela, however, moved to block the doorway. "Marvin," she said, very quietly but in a voice like a handful of razor blades.

He recognized the tone, and the look in her eyes. There were times when you could jerk Pamela around, and then there were times when simple survival required you to back off. There was no doubt which kind of time this was.

"All right," Marvin said crankily, "let me go after them anyway, keep an eye on them. God knows what the redskin sons of bitches are liable to walk off with . . . is that liquor cabinet locked?"

The drumming and singing and smoking went on for the rest of the morning. The old man insisted on doing every room in the house, upstairs and down, as well as the basement, attic, and garage.

At one point Marvin paused on the stairs, hearing his wife on the hall phone: "No, really, Theresa, I swear, a real Native American shaman, and he's doing a smoke ceremony right here in our house. It's so exciting . . ."

There was a lengthy pause. Lengthy for Pamela, anyway. "Oh," she said at last, "I used to feel guilty about them, too. I mean, all the terrible things that were done to them. But you know, Babaji explained that really, the Native Americans who have it so hard nowadays – poverty and alcoholism and so on – they're the reincarnated spirits of white soldiers who killed Native people in earlier times, and that's how they're working off their karma."

Upstairs the kid was banging the drum and the old man was chanting and smoke was rolling back down the stairs, but Marvin stayed to listen a moment longer.

"I wish you'd been there," Pamela was saying. "Jessica told about giving some change to this poor homeless Negro she saw in the city, and Babaji said that giving was always good for one's own karma but after all, in a previous life, that man was probably a slave-ship captain."

There was a happy sigh. "It's just as Babaji says, Theresa. Once you understand how karma works, you realize that everything really *is* for the best."

Marvin snorted loudly and went on up the stairs. "Space," he mumbled, "the final fucking frontier."

A little before noon, having smoked up the garage until you could barely find the cars without feeling around, the old man stopped singing and held the smoke bundle up over his head. The kid quit drumming and said, "That's all."

"That's it?" Marvin folded his arms and stared at the kid. "And for this you expect me to cough up a hundred bucks?"

The old man was bent over, grinding the glowing end of the bundle against the floor to extinguish it. Without looking up he said something in Algonquin or whatever the hell language it was.

The kid said, "You don't have to pay now. We'll come back tomorrow. If you're not satisfied with the results by then, you don't have to pay at all."

Marvin started to tell him not to waste his time. But the old man turned and looked at Marvin with dark turtle eyes and Marvin heard himself say, "Okay. Sure. See you then."

When they were gone Marvin went back into the house and got out the key to the liquor cabinet. It wasn't often that he had a drink this early in the day but his nerves were just about shot.

The smoke had thinned a good deal inside the house, but the scent was still strong; he could even smell it out on the sun deck, where he took his drink. He leaned against the railing and looked out over the ocean, enjoying the salt breeze and the swishing mutter of small waves over the sand below. Saturday morning shot to hell, but at least it was over. Maybe there'd be a good game on TV in the afternoon, or a fight. Even a movie, as long as there weren't any Indians in it.

He became aware that his fingertips were tapping steadily on the railing, thumping out a medium-fast four-four beat that was, he realized then, the same rhythm the Indian kid had been beating on his drum.

"Jesus H. Christ," he said aloud. And downed his drink in one long shuddering gulp.

Pamela stayed on the phone for the rest of the afternoon, telling her big story to one cuckoo-clock friend after another. Since this kept her off Marvin's back, he figured the whole thing had almost been worth it.

He went into the kitchen and stuck a frozen dinner into the microwave. The smoke smell was still very pronounced, though the air looked clear and normal now. He took the cardboard tray out to the sun deck and ate his lunch, letting the sound of the ocean drown out the Indian music that kept running through his head.

Later, he tried without success to find a game on television. All the sports shows were taken up with silly crap like tennis. That would just about make it perfect, spend the afternoon watching a couple of bull dykes batting a stupid ball back and forth across a net. Finally he found a Bronson movie he hadn't seen before, and after that, over on PBS, Louis Rukeyser had some really interesting things to say about the stock market; and so Marvin made it through the afternoon, and most of the time he hardly noticed the smoke smell at all. And only a few times, maybe once or twice an hour, did he catch himself tapping a foot or finger to the beat of the Indian kid's drum.

When they went out to dinner that evening, Marvin drove clear to the next town up the coast, to a not particularly good and way to hell overpriced steak house, rather than eat at Antonio's. He was feeling particularly pissed off at Antonio, whom he suspected of setting the whole thing up as a practical joke. Ought to drown the grinning little greaseball, Marvin thought, in his own fucking lobster tank.

A little after eleven that night, Marvin was sitting in the living room, trying to read Rush Limbaugh's latest book, when Pamela called him from the head of the stairs.

He had the radio on, tuned to a New Jersey station that played country and western – which he hated, but he was trying to use one irritation against another; a bunch of Gomers singing through their noses might cancel out that God-damned Indian racket that wouldn't get out of his mind. Pamela had to call several times before he got up and came to the foot of the stairs. "What?"

"You'd better go out and have a look, Marvin," she said calmly. "There are people down on our beach."

"Oh, fuck." He'd always known it would happen sooner or later, but why did it have to happen now? "Get me my shotgun," he said, "and phone the cops."

Pamela didn't move. "Don't overreact, Marvin. I don't think there are more than two of them, and they don't seem to be doing anything. They're not even close to the house. Probably just walking along the beach in the moonlight."

"Sure." Marvin threw up his hands. "Right, I'll just go see if they'd like a complimentary bottle of *champagne*. Maybe a little violin music."

He went down the hallway and through the kitchen, muttering. Probably some gang of crack-head punks from the city, looking for white people to rob and rape and murder. Pamela wouldn't be so God-damned serene when they tied her up and took turns screwing her in the ass before they killed her. He hoped they'd let him watch.

The glass door slid silently open and Marvin stepped sock-footed out onto the deck. The tide was out and the sea was calm, and in the quiet he could definitely hear voices down on the beach.

He reached back through the door and flipped a switch. Suddenly the area beneath him was flooded with light, bright as day. One of the voices made a sound of surprise and Marvin grinned to himself. It hadn't cost much to have those big lights installed underneath the deck, and he'd known they'd come in handy some night like this.

He walked quickly across the deck and peered over the railing. It was almost painful to look down; the white sand reflected the light with dazzling intensity. He had no trouble, though, in seeing the two men standing on the beach, halfway between the house and the water. Or in recognizing the two brown faces that looked up at him.

"Hi, Mr. Bradshaw," the Indian kid called. "Hope we didn't disturb you."

The old man said something in Indian talk. The kid said, "My grandfather wants to apologize for coming around so late. But it was a busy night at the restaurant and Mr. Coelho wouldn't let me off any sooner."

"What the fuck," Marvin said, finally able to speak.

"You ought to come down here," the kid added. "You'll want to see this."

The logical thing to do at this point, of course, was to go back in the house and call the police and have these two arrested for trespassing. But then it would come out, how Marvin had gotten involved with the red bastards in the first place. The local cops didn't like Marvin, for various reasons, and would probably spread the story all over the area, how he had hired an Indian medicine man to get the cockroaches out of his home.

And if he simply shot the sons of bitches, he'd go to jail. There was no justice for a white man any more.

Marvin went back through the house. Pamela was still standing on the stairs. "It's those damn Indians," he told her as he passed. "If they scalp me you can call nine-one-one. No, you'll probably bring them in for tea and cookies."

He went out the front door and around the house and down the wooden stairway to the beach. The two Indians were still there. The old man was down in a funny crouch, while the kid was bent over with his hands on his knees. They seemed to be looking at something on the ground.

"Here, Mr. Bradshaw," the kid said without looking up. "Look at this."

Marvin walked toward them, feeling the sand crunch softly beneath his feet, realizing he had forgotten to put on any shoes. Socks full of sand, great. He came up between the old man and the kid and said, "All right, what's the – " and then in a totally different voice, "Jesus God Almighty!"

He had never seen so many cockroaches in all his life.

The sand at his feet was almost hidden by a dark carpet of flat scuttling bodies. The light from the floodlamps glinted off their shiny brown backs and picked out a forest of waving antennae.

Marvin leaped back and bumped into Pamela, who had followed him. "Look out, Marvin," she said crossly, and then she screamed and clutched at him.

The cockroaches, Marvin saw now, were not spreading out over the beach, or running in all directions in their usual way. They covered a narrow strip, maybe three feet wide, no more; and they were all moving together, a cockroach river that started somewhere in the shadow of the house and ran straight as Fifth Avenue across the sandy beach, to vanish into the darkness in the direction of the ocean. Marvin could hear a faint steady rustling, like wind through dry leaves.

"You wanted them out of your house," the kid said. "Well, there they go."

"How . . . " Pamela's voice trailed off weakly.

"They're going home," the kid said. "Or trying to."

Marvin barely heard the words; he was watching the cockroaches, unable to pull his eyes away from the scurrying horde. He walked toward the house, studying the roaches, until he came up against the base of the bluff. Sure enough, the roaches were pouring straight down the rock face in a brown cataract that seemed to be coming from up under the foundation of the house.

"See," the kid was saying, "the kind of roaches you got, the little brown cockroaches like you see in houses in this part of the country – they're not native. Book says they're German cockroaches, some say they came over with those Hessian mercenaries the King hired to fight Washington's guys. I don't know about that, but anyway the white people brought them over from Europe."

Marvin turned and stared at the kid for a moment. Then he looked down at the cockroaches again. "Fucking foreigners," he muttered. "I should have known."

"Now down in Florida and around the Gulf," the kid added, "you get these really big tropical roaches, they came over from Africa on slave ships. Then there's a kind that comes from Asia, very hard to kill."

Pamela said, "And your grandfather's, ah, medicine – ?"

"Makes them want to go back where they came from. Well, where their ancestors came from. Makes them *have* to. Look."

Marvin was tracking the cockroach stampede in the other direction now, out across the beach. The moon was up and full, and even beyond floodlight range it was easy to see the dark strip against the shiny damp low-tide sand.

At the water's edge the cockroaches did not hesitate. Steadily, without a single break in the flow, they scurried headlong into the sea. The calm water of the shallows was dotted with dark specks and clumps that had to be the bodies of hundreds, maybe thousands of roaches. Marvin found himself remembering something he'd heard, how you could line all the Chinamen up and march them into the ocean and they'd never stop coming because they bred so fast.

The old man spoke as Marvin came walking back across the sand. The kid said, "He says he'll leave it on the rest of the night, in case you got rats or mice."

"It works on them too?" Pamela asked.

"Sure." The kid nodded. "No extra charge."

"The hell," Marvin said, "you're going to claim you people didn't have rats or mice either, before Columbus?"

"Some kinds. Woods and field mice, water rats, sure. But your common house mouse, or your gray Norway rat, or those black rats you see in the city, they all came over on ships."

"I don't see any," Pamela observed.

"Oh, you wouldn't, not yet. The bigger the animal, the longer the medicine takes to work. Matter of body weight. You take a real big gray rat, he might not feel it for the rest of the night. Along about daybreak, though, he'll come down here and start trying to swim back to Norway or wherever."

The old man spoke again. "My grandfather says we'll come back tomorrow, so he can turn the medicine off. Can't leave it on too long. Things . . . happen."

At their feet the cockroaches streamed onward toward oblivion.

Marvin slept badly that night, tormented by a persistent dream in which he ran in terror across an endless empty plain beneath a dark sky. A band of Indians pursued him, whooping and waving tomahawks and beating drums, while ranks of man-sized cockroaches stood on their hind legs on either side, shouting at him in Spanish. Pamela appeared in front of him, naked. "It is your karma, Marvin!" she cried. He saw that she had long antennae growing from her head, and an extra set of arms where her breasts had been.

He sat up in bed, sweating and shaking. The smoke smell in the room was so strong he could hardly breathe. "Gah," he said aloud, and fought the tangled covers off him and got up, to stand on wobbly legs for a moment in the darkness.

On her side of the bed Pamela mumbled, "Marvin?" But she didn't turn over, and he knew she wasn't really awake.

He went downstairs, holding tight to the banister, and got a bottle of Johnny Walker from the liquor cabinet. In the darkened hallway he took a big drink, and then another, straight from the bottle. The first one almost came back up but the second felt a lot better.

He carried the bottle back upstairs, to the guest bedroom, where he cranked the windows wide open and turned on the big ceiling fan and stretched out on the bed. He could still smell the smoke, but another belt of Scotch helped that.

He lay there drinking for a long time, until finally the whiskey eased him off into a sodden sleep. He dreamed again, but this time there were no Indians or cockroaches; in fact it was a pleasant, restful dream, in which he found himself strolling across gently rolling pasture land. Big oak trees grew along the footpath where he walked, their branches heavy with spring-green leaves. Sheep grazed on a nearby hillside.

In the distance, at the crest of a high hill, rose the gray walls and battlements of an ancient-looking castle. A winding dirt road led up to the castle gate, and he saw now that a troop of soldiers in red coats were marching along it, headed in his direction. The *poong poong poong poong* of their drum carried across the fields to Marvin, and he could hear their voices raised in song:

hey ya hey yo hey ya
yo hey ya hey na wey
ah ho ha na yo
ho ho ho ho

He awoke again with the sun shining through the windows. He lay for a long time with a pillow over his face, knowing he wasn't going to enjoy getting up.

When he finally emerged from the guest bedroom, sweaty and unshaven, it was almost midday. Passing the main bathroom, he heard the shower running. Pamela would have been up for hours; she always got up ridiculously early, so she could do her silly meditation and yoga exercises on the deck as the sun came up.

Marvin was sitting in the living room drinking coffee when the doorbell rang. He lurched to his feet, said, "Shit!" and headed for the front door. Sunlight stabbed viciously at his eyes when he opened the door and he blinked against the pain. He opened his eyes again and saw the two Indians standing on his porch.

"Sorry if we're a little early," the kid said. "I have to be at work soon."

Marvin regarded them without warmth. "The fuck you want now?"

"Well, you know, Mr. Bradshaw. My grandfather did a job for you."

Marvin nodded. That was a mistake. When the agony in his head receded he said, "And now you want to get paid. Wait here a minute."

There was no way these two clowns could make a claim stick, but he didn't feel up to a nasty scene. His wallet was upstairs in the bedroom, but he knew Pamela kept a little cash in a vase on the mantlepiece, for paying delivery boys and the like. He dug out the roll and peeled off a twenty and went back to the front door. "There you are, Chief. Buy yourself a new feather."

The old man didn't touch the twenty. "One hundred dollars," he said. In English.

Marvin laughed sourly. "Dream on, Sitting Bull. I'm being a nice guy giving you anything, after you stank up my house. Take the twenty or forget it."

The old man jabbered at the kid. He didn't take his eyes off Marvin. The kid said, "You don't pay, he won't turn the medicine off."

"That's supposed to worry me? If I believed in this crap at all, I wouldn't want it 'turned off.' Leave it on, keep the roaches away forever."

"That's not how it works," the kid said. "It won't affect anything that wasn't in the house when the medicine was made."

Marvin thought of something. "Look, I tell you what I'll do. You give me some of that stuff you were burning yesterday, okay? And I'll write you out a check for a hundred bucks, right now."

After all, when you cut past the superstitious bullshit, there had to be something in that smoke that got rid of roaches better than anything on the market. Screwed up their brains, maybe, who knew? Take a sample to a lab, have it analyzed, there could be a multimillion-dollar product in there. It was worth gambling a hundred. Hell, he might not even stop payment on the check. Maybe.

But the old man shook his head and the kid said, "Sorry, Mr. Bradshaw. That's all secret. Anyway, it wouldn't work without the song."

Marvin's vision went even redder than it already was. "All right," he shouted, "get off my porch, get that rusty piece of shit out of my driveway, haul your red asses out of here." The kid opened his mouth. "You want trouble, Tonto? You got a license to run a pest-control business in this county? Go on, *move!*"

When the rattling blat of the old pickup's exhaust had died away, Marvin returned to the living room. Pamela was standing on the stairs in a white terry robe. Her hair was wet. She looked horribly cheerful.

"I thought I heard voices," she said. "Was it those Native Americans? I hope you paid them generously."

Marvin sank onto the couch. "I gave them what they had coming."

"I'm just disappointed I didn't get to see them again. Such an honor, having a real shaman in my house. Such an inspiring ceremony, too. Remember that lovely song he sang? I can still hear it in my mind, over and over, like a mantra. Isn't that wonderful?"

Singing happily to herself, *hey ya hey yo hey ya*, she trotted back up the stairs. And *poong poong poong poong* went the drum in Marvin's head.

He spent the rest of the day lying on the living room couch, mostly with his eyes closed, wishing he could sleep. He made no move toward the liquor supply. He would have loved a drink, but his stomach wouldn't have stood for it.

The hangover didn't get any better; at times it seemed the top of his skull must surely crack open like an overcooked egg. His whole body ached as if he'd fallen down a flight of stairs. Even the skin of his face felt too tight.

Worst of all, he was still hearing Indian music, louder and clearer and more insistent than ever. Up to now it had been no more than a nuisance, one of those maddening tricks the brain occasionally plays, like having the *Gilligan's Island* theme stuck in your mind all day. Now, it had become a relentless clamor that filled the inside of his head with the savage boom of the drum and the endless ululation of the old man's voice; and from time to time Marvin put his hands over his ears, though he knew it would do no good. He might even have screamed, but that would have hurt too much.

Pamela had vanished around noon; off to visit her crazy friends, Marvin thought dully, never mind her poor damn husband. But around four he tottered into the kitchen – not that he had any appetite, but maybe some food would settle his stomach – and happened to glance out through the glass doors, and there she was, down on the beach. She wore a long white dress and she appeared to be dancing, back and forth along the sand, just above the line of the incoming tide. Her hands were raised above her head, clapping. He couldn't hear the sound, but his eyes registered the rhythm: *clap clap clap clap,* in perfect synch with the drumming in his head and the boom of blood in his throbbing temples.

The sun went down at last. Marvin left the lights off, finding the darkness soothing. He wondered if Pamela was still down on the beach. "Pamela!" he called, and again; but there was no answer, and he decided he didn't give enough of a damn to go look for her.

But time went by and still no sign of her, and finally Marvin got to his feet and shuffled to the door. It wasn't safe, a white woman out alone on a beach at night. Besides, he needed some fresh air. The stink of smoke was so bad it seemed to stick to his skin; he itched all over.

He went slowly down the wooden steps to the little beach. The moon was up and full and the white sand fairly gleamed. He could see the whole beach, clear out to the silver line that marked the retreating edge of the sea.

He couldn't see Pamela anywhere.

He walked out across the sand, with no real idea what he expected to find. His feet seemed to move on their own, without consulting him, and he let them. His body no longer hurt; even his headache was gone. The drumming in his head was very loud now, a deafening POONG POONG POONG POONG, yet somehow it didn't bother him any more.

The damp sand below the high-tide mark held a line of small shoeless footprints, headed out toward the water. Marvin followed without haste or serious interest. He saw something ahead, whiter than the sand. When he got there he was not greatly surprised to recognize Pamela's dress.

The footprints ended at the water's edge. Marvin stood there for a while, looking out over the moonlit ocean. His eyes were focused on nothing nearer than the invisible horizon. His toes tapped out a crunchy rhythm on the wet sand.

He took a step forward.

Up at the top of the bluff, sitting on a big rock, the Indian kid from Antonio's said, "There he goes."

Beside him his grandfather grunted softly. "How long's it been?"

"Since she went in?" The kid checked his cheap digital watch. The little bulb was broken but the moonlight was plenty strong. "Hour and a half. About."

"Hm. Didn't think he was that much bigger than her."

"She had small bones."

"Uh huh." The old man grinned. "I saw you when she took off her dress. Thought you were going to fall off the bluff."

"She did have a good shape," the kid said. "For a woman her age."

They watched as Marvin Bradshaw walked steadily into the sea. By now the water was up to his waist, but he kept going.

"Guess he can't swim," the kid remarked.

"Wouldn't do him much good if he could. Come on, son. Time we were leaving."

As they walked back to the truck the kid said, "Will you teach me to make that medicine?"

"Some day. When you're ready."

"Does it have a name? You know, what we – you – did, back there. What do you call it?"

"A start."

The kid began laughing. A moment later the old man joined in with his dry wispy chuckle. They were still laughing as they drove away, up the coast road and toward the distant glow of the main highway.

Behind them the sea stretched away flat and shining in the moonlight, its surface broken only by the small dark spot that was the head and shoulders of Marvin Bradshaw, wading toward Europe.

A Halloween Like Any Other

ꕥ

Michael Arsenault

I was out on Halloween, as I always am, doing what I always do.

I was hunting vampires.

I'd waited until just after it grew dark, when the last rays of life-affirming sunshine had finally faded away, and then I'd headed out. No point in leaving before that, while they were still at home, sleeping their unholy sleep of the undead.

Those accursed creatures! How they'd pay!

I wandered the streets, searching and searching, knowing they were out there, knowing only I could find them, knowing only I could destroy them.

I paused under a streetlight, checked my weapons, rechecked my gear. I was ready. I'm always ready.

I smiled. Vampires get cocky around Halloween. They let their guard down. They think they can just blend in with us, that we won't notice them, that they won't be spotted. But they're wrong. They try to slip into the crowds, to hide among the trick-or-treaters, the costumed candy seekers, but they still stand out. I can spot them.

I was two hours into my patrol when I finally found one. He was nestled among a group of loud and obnoxious partyers, trying in vain to camouflage himself. But I saw through his disguise almost immediately. I approached the group from behind, careful not to make my presence known, and I followed and studied them until I was positive. They continued on their way down the block, oblivious to me, laughing and flinging empty beer cans, all the while unaware that a demon was among them.

I got sufficiently close and made my move.

"Freeze, hellspawn!" I shouted.

They all stopped then and turned, obviously wondering how to proceed. There was a pause as they tried to size me up. I wondered whether they could sense my righteous aura, or if they'd already fallen under the vampire's hypnotic influence. Either way, their lives would never be the same.

"Sorry," said a chubby man dressed as a clown. "But we don't have any change for you."

"I'm no beggar!" I said. "I'm out destroying evil. Donations welcome."

"Beat it," said the clown's transvestite friend. "You're creepin' us out."

They obviously had no idea that I was their only salvation. They were completely blind to the fact that I and only I could save their worthless necks. All save one. The demon, of course. He knew who I was. I could read it in his cold, cold eyes. I could also see fear settling in. I knew he'd be begging soon. I could hear it already, like music in my ears. The centuries-old game of hunter versus depraved satanic vermin would soon be played out.

"Don't you realize? That's no man! That's a vampire! Straight from the seventh level of Hell!"

"Yeah . . . and I'm Batman," the one in gray leotards replied, in what I felt was a rather Renfieldish sort of way.

"No." They were such blind fools. "I mean he's really a vampire. A real vampire. He'll drain you fools like a cheap bottle of wine!"

The cretins began to laugh then, laugh like the hand puppets of Lucifer that they had become. It was sad really, seeing them all bewitched so easily. I locked eyes with the beast, and he laughed too, thinking all too smugly that he was safe now.

I knew it was time to act. I reached into my coat for the vial in my pocket, brought it out, and removed the cork.

"This should make believers out of you," I said, holding my hand high. "It's holy water. The one true test for a vampire." I wound back my arm and let loose with the vial, flinging it in his direction.

Bullseye. It shattered against him, dousing his chest and sending droplets along his arms and across his face.

He laughed harder then, and the others joined him. They chuckled and slapped their knees. They kept doing it and doing it. Until, that is, the smoke started to rise.

The vampire's skin steamed and blistered and burned, and he let out a howl like the savage beast he was.

Panic ensued as the others broke out of the spell the vampire had woven.

The group began running about in circles, arms flailing and heads shaking, all in disbelief of what they were seeing. These people who only seconds before had considered this fiend to be a friend were now seeing him as he truly was. It was an awakening.

"Good God!" screamed the clown. "It's true! It's true! He's really a vampire!"

That's when it was my turn to laugh. Telling them it was "holy water" always made them let their guard down. Every good vampire hunter knows that that religious crap doesn't work for shit. For a proper reaction, you have to resort to a good undiluted dose of hydrochloric acid.

Understandably, none of them knew how to proceed. Luckily, I was there. They might have been falling into a state of shock, but I knew how to proceed. I knew how to end it.

I pulled the sharpened length of wood from under my coat and tossed it to the clown. "Stake him! Through the heart!"

He held the stake loosely in his hand, staring down at it, a look of horror on his face.

"Now!" I yelled. "It's our only chance!"

The clown raised his weapon, determination coming over his features, and he plunged forward. The stake met its mark, and a jet of preternatural blood spurted out of the creature's chest.

Chalk one up for the good guys.

My work done, I headed down the block before they started to lavish me with gratitude and praise. As an afterthought, I yelled back, "Remember to cut off the head and stuff it with garlic. Then burn it and the body separately!"

I turned the corner, leaving them to deal with the cleanup and the local authorities. I figured they owed me that much, after all I'd done for them. Besides, the night was still young, there were plenty of other unholy creatures to dispatch and plenty of candy around for the taking.

The Lights of Armageddon

ꕥ

William Browning Spencer

The light bulb died with a small *pop* that scared Mrs. Ward. She was sixty-seven years old, so it wasn't the first time a light bulb had died in her presence. But it was always an unsettling thing. At first, one was apt to think the pop and the world's sudden dimming were internal, as though a brain cell had overexerted itself and suddenly burst.

She was delighted to discover that she was not having a stroke, and, dropping her knitting into her lap, she shouted for her husband.

"What is it Marge?" he asked, coming up from the basement.

"This lamp blew out," she said.

Her husband walked over to the lamp, unscrewed the bulb, and walked off into the kitchen without saying a word. He returned with a new bulb. "Now we'll see if this sucker works," he said.

"Why shouldn't it work?" Marge asked. Her husband was an exasperating man.

"This is one of those light bulbs you made me buy from that odd fellow come round here yesterday. You remember. He said the money would go to good works and I said, 'What good works?' and he said – and not right away, but like he was making it up – he said, 'The blind.' "

"I remember that you were rude, Harry Ward, and that's why I had to make you buy a box. Sometimes you act like you were raised by apes."

"I couldn't help laughing," Harry said. " 'Light bulbs for the blind is kind of like earplugs for the deaf, ain't it?' I says. Now that was damned funny, but he didn't laugh. And I bought his box of light bulbs, didn't I? Two dozen to a box, Marge!" Harry held the light bulb up and regarded it with narrowed eyes. "Looks okay – which is more than you can say for that fellow hawking them. Here it is, maybe ninety degrees in the shade, and he's got on an overcoat, and his face is as white as plaster and his lips are red – that had to be lipstick, Marge – and he's got a scarf pulled up to his chin like he's freezing."

"The poor man was probably sick, Harry." Marge sighed. Her husband wasn't a sensitive man. He had his good points, of course, but sometimes she was hard pressed to say just what they were. Forty years ago, he had looked good with a mustache, and he had had a kind of haunted, poetic intensity. Now the mustache was gone, and the intensity was a sort of worried, pinched look, like a spinster who's convinced there is a gas leak on the premises.

"I need to get on with this knitting," Marge said.

"Okay," Harry said. "You always were an impatient woman."

Harry leaned over the lamp and screwed the bulb in. The room brightened.

"Well, it works," Harry said.

"Of course it works," Marge said.

Harry went back down into the basement, and Marge returned to her knitting. She dozed off for awhile, waking at around ten that evening when Harry came back upstairs.

"I'm going to bed," he said.

"I think I'll read a bit," Marge said. "I'm not the least bit sleepy."

She watched her husband march upstairs. She waited until the bedroom door closed, and then she went into the kitchen. She found the box of light bulbs in a cupboard. Then she got the stepladder out and placed it in the middle of the floor and climbed up and unscrewed the ceiling light fixture and replaced all three bulbs. She threw the old bulbs in the trash and moved on to the dining room.

By the time she had carried the stepladder upstairs and was unscrewing the light in the bathroom, she was worn out. You never gave a thought to how many light bulbs a house contained until you replaced the lot of them all at once.

And why – why do such a thing? If asked, if stopped by a concerned observer placing a hand on her shoulder, Marge would have said, "Why, I don't know. I can't really say just why." But there was no one to tender the question, and Marge's only thought was that it was a tiresome task. And the bedroom itself would have to wait until morning.

The odd fellow who had sold the light bulbs to the Wards was a magician named Ernest Jones. An accident while conjuring up certain demons had placed him in thrall to the Fair Ones, and he was now doing their bidding, distributing the light bulbs that would call them.

Despite the blazing Florida sun, he was freezing as he worked. He was cold right to the bone, cold clean through.

He was back at the caravan, packing a last light bulb into the box when his rival, a tall, smooth-talking magician named Blake, came into the trailer.

"I know what you are up to," Blake said. "You are lighting the world, so that the Fair Ones may find their way."

"Could be," Jones said. "I would advise you to mind your own business."

"Your advice comes too late," Blake said. "I followed you yesterday. I know what you are up to, and I'm not letting it happen."

"Look," Jones said, turning around. "I tell you what. I'll cut you in. You can be a Vanguard too. The Fair Ones can be quite generous to those who aid them."

Blake, a thin, haughty young man with an imperious air, chuckled. "I am afraid I have already negotiated a different contract. I have made a deal with the Immutable Abyss."

Blake produced a light bulb from his ample magician's pockets. "I have my own beacons," he said.

Jones growled low in his throat and rushed the taller man, who stumbled. The light bulb fell, smashing on the floor. A black, metallic lizardlike creature darted across the linoleum floor, barking sharply.

Jones and Blake wrestled on the floor. Blake suddenly went limp, and Jones stood up.

"You sonofabitch," Jones muttered. He began to intone the words that would summon the scavenger demons.

Blake, still lying on the floor, opened his eyes. He produced a small silver revolver and shot Jones in mid-incantation.

Blake summoned his own unholy crew to clean up the corpse. While they were munching on the mortal remains of his rival, Blake methodically destroyed the boxed light bulbs, crushing each spiderlike creature as it emerged from its shattered casing. Repacking the box with his Master's own beacons, he sang softly to himself. "That old black magic got me in its spell . . ."

Louise was new to country living, and she hated it. She was a young woman, twenty-two, in the prime of her life; she wasn't ready to retire to a screened-in porch, a rocking chair, and the conversation of about a jillion insects. Johnny had talked her into moving out here, saying, "I'll be the one who will have to drive fifty miles to work each day. All I'm asking is that you give it a try."

Where had her mind been? she wondered. "Louise Rivers," she said to the empty room, "a siren should go off in your mind when Johnny starts off, 'All I'm asking.' " *All I'm asking is you go to one movie with me. All I'm asking is one kiss. All I'm asking is you take off your pantyhose so I can admire your knees.* Yeah, sure.

So here she was stuck in the country and it was five miles to the miserable little fly-blown grocery store, and no car, and hot enough outside to melt the sunglasses she'd left on the lawn chair.

Louise walked up the dirt road to the Wards, feeling the midday sun breathing on the back of her neck like a rabid dog. The Wards lived in an old farmhouse squatting low in the Florida dust, palmettos flanking the door, a pickup truck under the single live oak tree.

Louise had the grocery list in her hand and the words in her mind: *If you are going to the store, I wonder could you pick up a few things for me.*

The Wards seemed nice enough, an old couple who had been married forever and even looked a bit alike, the way long-married couples will.

Louise knocked on the door. No one answered.

"Hello," Louise called. Maybe they were napping. The country inspired sleep.

Louise knocked louder. She turned the doorknob and pushed. The door swung inward, and an intense flickering light greeted her.

"Mrs. Ward?" Louise shouted. The living room was bathed in silver light that leeched color from the walls, the sofa, thc patterned chairs. Mrs. Ward rose from the sofa. The strobelike flashes made her movements jerky, image superimposed on image.

"Come in, my dear," Mrs. Ward said.

Mrs. Ward took Louise's arm and led her to the sofa.

The room was cold, like being inside a meat freezer. Mrs. Ward was wearing several sweaters, and a woolen cap was pulled down over her head, hiding her hair.

Mrs. Ward turned and shouted. "Harry, look who's here. It's our neighbor."

Louise looked to the top of the stairs where Mr. Ward stood. He began to move down the stairs, somewhat awkwardly for he was clasping a large box in his arms.

"Hello, hello!" Mr. Ward shouted. He was smiling and, like his wife, he was bundled up against the cold.

Louise had grown accustomed to the light. The brief moment of terror and dread had passed, and now the light seemed sweetly inquisitive, like the hands of children, shyly touching her face, sliding over her arms, gently stroking her mind.

"It's very bright," Louise said. She had forgotten why she had come.

Mrs. Ward leaned forward and patted Louise's blue-jeaned knee. "Not nearly enough," Mrs. Ward said. "There's not nearly enough light yet. It's still black as night as far as the Fair Ones are concerned. Harry and I do what we can, but we are only two people. You'll help, won't you?"

"Well, of course," said Louise.

Harry shuffled up to them and put the box on the floor. He reached into the box and pulled out a light bulb.

"My dear," Harry said, and he handed it to Louise with a courtly flourish as though presenting a rose.

Louise was charmed. "Why thank you," said Louise. The light bulb was cold and seemed to vibrate when she held it against her cheek.

"Please take a box with you when you go," Mrs. Ward said. "We've plenty."

Country people, thought Louise, *are so generous.*

It was already dark when Johnny took the exit to Polk Hill. He had had to stop once because love bugs had squashed up on the windshield in such numbers that he couldn't see. The Florida travel brochures were curiously silent on these little bastards, who haunted the highways in black clouds, always mating (hence, their name). The rotten insects had created an industry: love bug radiator grill guards, love bug solvent for the windshields, love bug joke bumper stickers.

Still, Johnny loved Florida, the way only a kid from Minnesota can love it. If he never saw another snowfall, another ice-laden tree, it would be okay. Louise had felt the same way. At first they had lived in Tampa but it was too big a city so he had talked Louise into moving out to Polk Hill, which was real country, filled with cows and cattle egrets and rednecks with dogs.

Johnny loved it, but Louise was still sort of down on the move. She missed Tampa.

Johnny turned on Waples Drive and slowed to accommodate the much-patched asphalt. Up ahead, light blazed from every window of the Wards' house. *What's the big occasion?* Johnny wondered.

Johnny drove around the curve and saw his own house, light pouring from every window. It was funny how, in the country, lights seemed brighter. He had noticed this before, but it was more pronounced on this moonless night.

Johnny stopped the car and cut the engine.

As he walked along the flagstone steps, he noticed how the light in the windows seemed to pulse. Odd. Looking down he saw that hundreds – thousands – of moths fluttered on the ground. Some of the insects were no bigger than a dime, others quite large with pale green or yellow wings.

Florida did have its share of bugs.

"I wouldn't go in there," a voice said.

Johnny turned to see a tall man wearing a tuxedo, complete with top hat and cape, and sporting a luxuriant handlebar mustache. Next to him was a girl in a sequined bathing suit and high heels.

The man stepped forward. "I'm afraid one of my employees was careless. Jones is a fair magician, but he's no match for any of the third-circle demons, and he was tricked, as easily as you or I might trick a child with a palmed card or a two-sided nickel. Now he has disappeared – consumed, I expect – but the damage has been done."

The man brushed a large moth from his lapel and continued. "I'm Maxwell Kerning, the Amazing Max, and this is my assistant, Doreen. You might have seen the flyers: *Amazing Max and His Traveling WonderRama*. No? Well, it doesn't matter of course. What does matter is that Jones seems to have recruited your wife and your neighbor in an attempt to summon some unpleasant entities."

"Louise isn't my wife," Johnny said. "We aren't married."

The Amazing Max shrugged his shoulders. "I believe that your precise marital status is incidental to the larger issue – which is the approaching end of civilization."

"I think that is too strong," Doreen said, moving to the magician's side. She had a soft lilting voice, and – Johnny noted – lovely kneecaps. "Probably only Florida would go."

"Disney World would fall," her comrade reminded her. "I believe the destruction of Disney World would pull the plug. Certainly the whole continental nexus would be sucked into that hole. Chaos would reign."

"That's true," Doreen said, her voice even more subdued.

"It's been nice meeting you folks, but I gotta be going," Johnny said. It wasn't good to humor crazy people beyond a certain point. Polite but firm, that was the ticket when interacting with nut cases.

Johnny opened the door to his house and walked into the cold light.

Every light in the house was on, the lot of them flickering like a defective neon sign, and Louise was sitting in the brown armchair. She was wearing an overcoat, wool gloves, and earmuffs.

Jesus, Johnny thought. It was colder than Minnesota, and the light reminded him of the curious, ambient glare that filled those northern skies right before a snowstorm. *I don't care for this*, Johnny thought, but even as he thought it some sly, cold hand reached in and stole the thought, scooped it up as though it were a chocolate-covered mint left unattended.

"Hey Louise," Johnny said. "It's sure bright in here."

"It's getting there," Louise said, standing up.

Suddenly Johnny felt his chest being squeezed. He toppled backward and was yanked off his feet. He was dragged out of the room, and the door slammed. The light – the blessed light – was gone and he tried to free his arms and scramble to his feet, his only thought to be reunited with the fierce, cold light.

"Better sit on him for a few minutes while his mind clears," Doreen said.

A terrible headache set in, and Johnny crawled over to a bush and vomited.

"He'll be all right now," he heard the magician say.

Johnny didn't feel like he was apt to rally. He rolled over on his back. A large beetle landed on his forehead, and he brushed it off and sat up. "Jesus." He blinked at Doreen's kneecaps, found some solace there, and asked, "What happened?"

The Amazing Max explained: "Doreen lassoed you. She's an artist with a rope, which I must say is fortunate for you. We almost lost you, you know. I am not a man who enjoys giving advice – let each man find his own path, I say – but you are out of your element here, young man, and I believe you should heed the advice of experienced elders."

Johnny looked at Doreen, who was demurely winding her rope.

"You saved my life," Johnny said.

Doreen looked up and smiled. She had blond, curly hair and black eyes, goggled with eye shadow so she looked a little raccoonian – but sweet.

"I didn't really save your life," Doreen said. "Just maybe your mind."

"Still," Johnny insisted, "I'm beholden."

Doreen fluttered her long eyelashes and looked away.

"I'm Johnny Harmon," Johnny said. "And I won't ever forget it."

The Amazing Max interrupted. "While I am delighted to hear that you will never forget your name, I believe the future in which you remember or forget anything may be brief if we do not address the immediate problem. We've got to pull the switch on all these lights before they attract the Fair Ones."

"Fair Ones?" Johnny asked.

"You don't want to know," the magician said. "Trust me, you don't want to meet them. They'll only have one chance to break through, so they'll wait until the Light is bright enough and then some. I think we've still got time. Where is the fuse box?"

"In the garage," Johnny said.

An investigation revealed the garage door to be down and electronically locked.

The magician questioned Johnny closely, then said, "We'll have to go through the kitchen to get into the garage. Johnny, you'll have to do it. You know the layout. Do you think you can walk through it with your eyes closed?"

"Sure," Johnny said. "The door to the garage is just to the right when you enter the back door."

The magician leaned forward and clutched both of Johnny's shoulders. Amazing Max smelled like cigarettes and Old Spice. "Okay. Now when you get into the garage, don't open your eyes. The light is on there too, I expect. With your eyes closed, can you find the switch for the carport door?" Johnny nodded. "Good. And don't open your eyes until I've said it's okay."

They slipped around to the back of the house, and Johnny unlocked the back door. "Good luck," the magician said, and Johnny, his eyes shut, pushed open the door and entered. He kept his arms out in front of him, and he slid his feet forward across the linoleum. He didn't feel the cold like he thought he would, but the darkness behind his eyelids wasn't complete. He could sense the strobe light of the room fluttering on his eyelids; rainbow-hued fragments drifted like ghostfish into his mind.

There were the shelves to his right. China plates, the Abraham Lincoln coffee mug, Louise's antique glass bottle collection . . . Whoops. A ceramic jug toppled forward and shattered on the floor. It made a loud noise, a sort of *whump-crash* that would have pleased a child. Johnny stood still. The rest of the house was silent.

Keep moving, he told himself. He found the door, felt along the frame until he discovered the doorknob, then turned it. The door swung open.

Woolen fingers touched the back of his neck.

"Ah," Johnny said. Miraculously, he did not open his eyes.

"Hey Johnny," Louise said from behind. "I didn't know what had become of you."

"Just going in the garage here," Johnny mumbled. "Just taking a look in the old garage."

"Well sure," Louise said. She didn't seem intent on stopping him. She wouldn't know that his eyes were closed. Not yet.

Johnny slid his feet across the concrete floor. A can of nails banged over. He almost fell over the extra tire, did in fact lurch forward, arms flaying the air. He regained his balance, found the opposite wall, and began moving toward the carport switch.

Louise spoke again. "What are you doing, Johnny?"

"Just give me a second," Johnny said. "I'll be right back. All I'm asking – "

"Ha!" Louise shouted. She slammed into him from behind, her arms encircling his, hurling him forward. His forehead banged against the wall. But his hand found the switch, and he hit it. He heard a clunk sound as the motor engaged, then the metallic rattle and clamor of the door ascending.

"Johnny Harmon!" Louise shouted, but he had turned to embrace her, and he held her tightly as she kicked and raged beneath him. Something exploded, followed by the tinkling sound of glass.

"You can open your eyes now, Johnny," the magician said. "And I might add – well done!"

Johnny opened his eyes in time to see the Amazing Max, a revolver in his hand, stride quickly into the middle of the garage, kick aside the shards of broken glass and, with a satisfied shout, slam a foot down firmly on something that screamed briefly and inhumanly.

It had looked, this now-silenced creature, like a spider, but with the black, shiny, chitinous exoskeleton of a beetle.

Johnny staggered to his feet and helped Louise up.

"What was that?" Johnny asked.

"One of the Fair One's minions. Not dangerous in themselves, but they are responsible for the light bulbs that call the Fair Ones." The Amazing Max pulled a flashlight from his pocket and turned it on. "Close the garage door again, please."

Johnny hit the switch. The door noisily descended.

They were in darkness now except for the beam of the flashlight.

"I assume that is the fuse box," the magician said. The beam of light played over the gray, rectangular box.

"Yes."

Amazing Max strode to the box, threw the two switches and then, methodically, unscrewed the half dozen fuses and put them in his pocket. "That should do it," he said.

They left the sealed-off garage and entered the now darkened house. The flashlight beam played over the kitchen floor, discovering fragments of the shattered jug.

The magician's voice sounded loud in the room. "We'll want to destroy all the light bulbs and look for the queen. She'll be laying more bulbs. Actually, I wouldn't be the least bit surprised if she were right – " The magician threw open the refrigerator door, stepped back, and fired into the refrigerator two blasts that mingled with another inhuman scream.

"Done then," the magician said. "So far so good."

"How you doing?" Johnny asked, putting an arm around Louise's waist.

"I been better," Louise said. "I'm freezing, for one thing."

They were following the Amazing Max from room to room as he destroyed light bulbs and the creatures within them. It was slow going in the dark, and the screams of the spider-creatures were a little unnerving.

"I reckon you'll warm up in awhile," Johnny said.

The magician, who overheard this remark, said, "No. I'm afraid not." He smashed another bulb, stomped another harbinger of doom.

"What?" Louise said.

The magician was already moving off toward the bedroom, but Louise ran after him, caught his arm, and turned him around. "What do you mean it won't wear off?"

The magician shrugged. "Nothing to wear off, actually. It's a bit of perception shuffling that the light does. The warmer the day, the colder you'll feel. The inverse is true too, so you might consider moving north."

The Amazing Max entered the bedroom and climbed up on the bed. "Hold the flashlight, Doreen," he said, and he began unscrewing the light fixture.

"Well, hell," Louise said. "Goddamn hell." She began to sob.

"It will be okay," Johnny said. "We'll keep the air on high or we can move back to Minnesota. We'll think of something."

"Doreen," the magician was saying. "I think that's the lot of them. Fetch those light bulbs from my truck, and we'll begin setting the world right again."

"What about the Wards?" Louise asked.

The Amazing Max walked across the living room and waved an arm at the picture window. "It was too late for the Wards," he said. "They'd gone too far. We had to torch them. We set the incendiary bombs before coming here." Out the window Johnny could see the guttering flames and an occasional garland of sparks floating into the starless night.

Amazing Max sighed. "I tell you, I'm ready for retirement. First Jones nearly destroys the world, then Blake disappears without a goodbye. I found this in his trailer." Amazing Max pulled a black object from his pocket and handed it to Johnny. It was a grotesque stone lizardlike carving about three inches long.

"What's this?" Johnny asked.

"It's one of the minions of the Immutable Abyss. De-animated now. The Fair Ones are no picnic, but it looks like Blake was in thrall to even worse news. The Immutable Abyss. Let me tell you" – the magician leaned forward – "you don't even want to think about the kind of things that dwell in the Immutable Abyss."

Max stood up. "Well, let's get going." Amazing Max took the box of light bulbs from Doreen and the tedious task of re-bulbing began.

Louise and Johnny drifted to a sofa.

"I feel awful about the Wards," Louise said. "Plus feeling generally awful."

Johnny nodded. "I guess we should look on the positive side, the end of the world being avoided, that sort of thing."

"I guess so," Louise said.

The magician came back into the living room and plopped into an armchair.

"Another crisis narrowly avoided," he said. He fished in his pocket, took out the fuses. "Doreen," he said. "Would you turn the electricity back on?"

Doreen took the fuses and left the room.

"How was this other magician going to call up the Immutable Abyss?" Johnny asked.

"I have no idea. I can't find him, so I can't ask him." Max shouted. "Hey Doreen! You didn't see Blake today, did you?"

Doreen's voice came back, far away.

"What?"

Max shouted the question again, louder.

"Sure," Doreen shouted back. "I told you. He's the one gave me these light bulbs."

The sun was beginning to come up. Oak trees, cabbage palms, and gaunt pine trees were surfacing in the dishwater dawn. Smoke from the Wards' home rose crookedly into the sky.

The magician was emptying his pockets of the last, unused bulbs. One fell, bursting on the coffee table, and a small, metallic lizard skittered over the mahogany surface, barking mournfully.

"Holy Jesus," the magician croaked. He stood up. "Doreen!" he screamed.

It was too late. The hum of the refrigerator, the thin voice of a radio announcer, the labored wheeze of the air conditioner – all these announced the return of electricity to the household. And, of course, the lights, the lights went on. They snuffed out the approaching dawn. They emitted a darkness thicker than tar, deeper than black plush velvet lining the inside of a coffin.

Johnny realized that he had never, in fact, encountered darkness. There was the darkness of a moonless night, the darkness of a windowless, midnight room, but this new darkness dwarfed them all. And already, although it could not have been anything but his imagination – many hours would pass before they came – Johnny thought he heard the first thundering footfall.

Doc Aggressive, Man of Tin #2

❦

Jeffrey Ford

From his Fortress of Solitude deep beneath a five-and-dime store in Newark, New Jersey, Doc Aggressive, that superior intellect, whose mind, an infernal combustion engine of mechanical imagination and brand-X Dupin ratiocination, fed on an elixir of masticated wax teeth and Fizzies, man of tin, with skin the color of a tarnished dime and resilient as the can around a cylinder of baked beans, man of vast adventures in his mission to rid the world of evil with his bulging muscles and wardrobe of torn shirts and frayed trousers, his widow's peaked hairdo like a skull cap of short shorn silver broom ends, his trademark grimace as if forever caught in the act of shitting rivets, puts the call out to his matchless posse of bizarre constituents – Ham Fist, a guy with a fist that is a big Easter ham able to serve a gathering of twenty, who pounds bad guys into submission and tightens his buddies up to slices of his smoked fatty goodness; Shyster, world renowned attorney and consummate ambulance chaser, who more than once extricated Doc's legal tin ass from nasty suits like the time Aggressive got a little too so with an innocent old codger he mistook for The Grim Hasbeen, slapping the old coot silly and putting the Tin Landslide on him; Jon Creep, creepiest guy in the world, who creeps out evildoers more often than they, themselves, are able to creep out Creep; Elastic Willie, rubber appendage specialist, wrapping up bandits with encompassing hugs, whose way with the lady villains is legendary and who consults Doc on matters of the heart, breaking down the whatsoever of birds and bees for his employer and recasting the intricacies of romance in the language of Tin; Deadeye, whose expertise is shooting guns, all kinds of guns, rifles, derringers, pistols, machine guns, staple guns, and killing people at long range so that nobody has to care too much or get messy – assembling his pentacle of associates in order to sally forth to Queasy Cay, and engage in battle against the Immortal Morgoloop, an ancient evil Neanderthal with the brain of an Isaac Newton, wrestling him under a red sun with a storm of bats flying crazy, machine-gun rounds spraying, tin biceps flexing, sweat like beads of mercury falling, so as to capture the craven caveman, giving Doc an opportunity to administer a good cheek fluffing and such a pinch in the name of Justice.

Bagged 'n' Tagged

ꕥ

Eugene Byrne

Call me stupid – I deserve it – but when Phyllis persuaded me to join what she called "the movement" I really thought she fancied me. I didn't realize how treacherous she was until it was too late. And no, we never did get to do the nasty. She saw to that.

They came for us all in the wee hours of a Sunday – a slack day for news, and with a general election due the Thursday after. I saw some of it at the Ealing branch of Cop-U-Like. Me and a few of the others were handcuffed to the bull bars of the vandal-proof Coke machine in the reception area when that oily bastard of a Home Secretary came onscreen to say a major terrorist group had been busted, that it was a great day for Law and Order, vote for us on Thursday, thank you and goodnight.

You'd swear The Margin were Sword of Allah, Angry Brigade, SNLA, and The Society for the Preservation of Hundred Acre Wood all mixed up. Those of us not preoccupied with irregular bowel movements managed an ironic titter.

I knew this wasn't about due process of law as we were each hauled into a little white-tiled room with a stout chair and some sinister looking equipment in the middle. It was like a dental surgeon had set up in a public toilet, only with more blood on the walls.

We were being tagged before we'd been tried.

My turn: A pair of mountainous rent-a-cops strapped me into the chair while the doc lit a cigarette and explained it was best not to struggle as it hurts more that way. He was at least seventy and didn't offer a general, but to smell the Tadjik Scotch on his breath you wouldn't need one. I got a local on the back of the neck, and one on the finger.

I'd heard that Phyllis had grassed us up. I didn't blame her; one of the guys had said they'd waved actual prison, or maybe the fruitcake tin, at her. So she sang. I'd have done the same. Wouldn't you?

The man in white lifted away most of the nail on my left index finger. I screwed my eyes shut and tried not to yelp. I failed.

Somewhere else, a few of the others sang a dirge about how they would overcome some day. This while a back-street Kildare on Minimum Wage was mutilating me in the name of the law.

Phyllis had been handing out leaflets on a street corner; from the way she talked I could tell she was a hot revolutionary babe – who fancied me!

So I went to a meeting of the Water Margin.

Someone said the name had been dreamed up by Iron John, the nearest thing this strictly nonhierarchical organization had to a leader. Someone said you got a Water Margin on high-quality writing paper, but I didn't buy that. "IJ" was, I would guess, in his fifties, a veteran of countless environmental and anticap campaigns who had spent too much of his leisure time with his head in the pharmaceutical cupboard, so he wasn't really capable of dealing with a 16MB concept like that.

There were about thirty of us scattered around London; punks, phreaks, tree-huggers, Earth mammas, elves, fairies, ravers, sociopaths, crusties, dolphin-fanciers, and at least twenty-eight different flavors of anarchist. And me. Each wanted something a little different from the next, and the only way they avoided long nights of futile ideological blether was to focus on nonviolent direct action.

That was hard enough; at the first meeting I'd been to, a damaged girl who lived in a black woolen sweater fifteen sizes too big for her suggested a kid might chase one of their flyers across a windy tube platform and fall on the electric rail. So the manifesto was changed to "relative nonviolence."

There is nothing relative about having all your property confiscated (no big deal in my case, but IJ would surely miss his Velvet Underground vinyl) and being tagged. Babylon and market forces can't handle relativism.

The Marginals I agreed with wanted to show people there was an alternative to junk consumerism, junk entertainment, and junk religion. That meant letting the corporations wither, creating sustainable communities, and ensuring that everyone who wants it gets some kind of real inner life, et cetera et yada and so forth. You know the deal.

I had no problem fitting in, but, for all that, I'd never have joined if not for the commotion Phyllis was causing in my underpants. I was sort of getting by; I still got occasional supply teaching jobs, though school budgets got smaller every year. I'd also do a bit of cash work here and there, cramming some rich kid, that kind of thing. And I had a half-decent bedsit that hadn't been burgled for eighteen months. No, it was simply that I was in between girlfriends, and Phyllis came along and . . .

"This will hurt," snarled the smaller of the two goons, his nose 2mm from mine.

At the back of the chair was the gizmo that sticks the chip in. It was just as well. If the drunken doctor had been using his hands, I'd be paralyzed or dead.

For a nanosecond, the pain was intense. The agony started in my back, went into my head, then shot on down through the rest of me.

Then it was gone again, before I'd had time to think about screaming.

Now the doc (I assume he was a doctor, although he'd probably been struck off at some stage) was in front of me with a little paintbrush in one hand and, in the other, a pair of tweezers holding my fingernail. Both his hands were shaking. Agonizingly slowly, his trembling fingers brought nail and brush together to paint on the magical glop that would hold it over the hole in my neck and stop it deteriorating.

Hacking off most of your fingernail is supposed to be humane; the chip is very sensitive to pressure to stop you trying to cut it out. So the nail gets grafted on as protection. But it doesn't take Sigmund Freud to figure out that mutilation is a way of impressing the full majesty of the law on the reprobate.

The hairs on the back of my neck stood to attention as the nail got stuck into place, and a Band-Aid got stuck on top of that.

(One other point of information, brethren and sistern; in the old days, the state used to beat the crap out of dissidents, imprison them, or kill them. Nowadays, instead of guns they have tasers and bean-bag guns or those sound systems that give you a massive pain in the goolies . . . The state doesn't kill or do anything headline-grabbingly horrible anymore. They have the technology to tackle dissent "humanely." And because of that they can be loads more repressive. Okay, sorry, I'll shut up now.)

"Next!" slurred the Finlay. In a flurry of strap-undoing and wire-disconnecting, the goons hauled me from the chair. I noticed the doc's hands were falling to pieces; he had eczema like Siberia has tree-stumps. And he wasn't wearing gloves. He had probably left a quarter of his healing hands in the root of my brain.

I was kept with some of the others – all men – in a bare cell with a couple of buckets, one for drinking water, the other for the bog.

We swapped notes; how much the implant hurt, what Babylon would do next, how long we'd all be sentenced for, how Amnesty International would save us. But after the first couple of hours, nobody said much. Some tried to sleep, some used various meditation techniques to chill. Some just stared at the wall. I tried to sleep as much as possible. I'd already figured that the local on my finger wasn't going to last and it'd get bloody sore. I was right.

In two days, they fed us once. A nice old duffer came in with a big box of Tesco sandwiches. There was lots of meat and fish, but as we were starving we just threw the animalstuff away. The butties were two or three days past sell-by. They were supposed to go to the roofless, the shanties, and other first quadranters – a charity handout. I guess the manager of this branch of Cops R Us had told the Sally Army he didn't have the budget to feed us.

A.M. on day three, we got sentenced. Our brief was a brisk young woman done up in pearls and navy pinstripe who said: "plead guilty or spend ten years on remand," i.e. in prison. Plead guilty, she said, and you'll be free in a few months.

The courtroom was empty apart from a few rent-a-cops and suits. The press and public galleries were empty. Since Babylon was marketing the bust as a major victory against terrorism and declining family values, they invoked state security to keep media, friends, and relatives away. My eloquent defense would impress no one. I pleaded guilty.

"Brian Harper," said His Honor consulting the terminal on the bench, "the grave offences to which you have pleaded guilty are in no way mitigated by the misguided, and if I may say so, intellectually sloppy ideology to which you and your co-defendants adhere. However, in view of your comparative maturity – you are . . . let me see . . . twenty-eight years old – and your hitherto clean record, I am prepared to be lenient in the hope that when you have served out your sentence, you can make something of yourself . . ."

This was good.

"I sentence you to three months reparative custody for criminal damage, three months reparative custody for conspiracy to commit criminal damage, and twelve months for being an accessory to trespass in an electronic communications system. The sentences will run consecutively."

Eighteen months! A year and a half! Aaaarrgh!

"The crimes were all committed against Southern Cable PLC," continued His Judgeship. "They will take custody of all defendants in this case . . ."

This might be good. Often the victims don't want their taggies, so they get privatized. You could end up breaking rocks, breaking the necks of chickens, assembling hardware . . . Working for a cable TV company didn't sound too dirty or dangerous. And we'd all be together.

In the past, Marginals had tied themselves to trees on development sites, thrown paint at objectionable edifices, graffed slogans on likely looking walls, injected sloe juice into supermarket TV dinners, and run around gridlocks stuffing Christmas pudding up the exhausts of petrol-driven cars.

Babylon knew this but didn't care. Babylon also knew of the Margin's greatest coup. A while before I joined they'd put Satan – Iron John's creation – into the stock system of Homeworld. Satan tumbled all the swipe numbers to one, the number for a gift-set of leatherex-bound novels by Jeffrey Archer – exactly the thing Mrs. Middle England would put in her front room to convince visitors she was a person of taste.

Homeworld had a just-in-time setup. Satan went live at 2:30 P.M. on a Sunday, and all over the country, stores – and the Homeworld Virtual Store – reordered nothing but these books from the merchandising bot, which automatically showed the supplier a legally binding contract. The Late Lord Archer's estate ended up a lot richer, and a printer somewhere ended up very rich indeed.

The Marginals never got busted for that. Homeworld was not a contributor to the funds of either of our two interchangeable ruling parties.

We were bagged and tagged for the Cable job. A couple of the zits had come up with the plan; wire is very vulnerable to elves and goblins and long-leggedy beasties. So they rigged up a van with a generator and all their magic boxes. My role was minimal – touring scrap yards picking up lengths of old coax cable. When everything was ready, they cut into all five of their porn channels at 3 A.M. with just a superimposed caption: "YOU'LL GO BLIND." The van injected from waste ground a mile from the borders of the nearest gated municipality while the rest of us watched at IJ's house.

It worked.

My trial lasted four minutes. Some of the others took longer to protest at what a travesty it was, but most pleaded guilty. Only a few were missing from the pen when they gave us some more vintage sandwiches and some bottled water and prodded us onto a bus.

We met the women on the bus. There was a lot of hugging and chatter and a sort of feeling of relief.

It amounted to: nobody was going to prison (excellent), we were going somewhere together (good), we were going to be given to a cable company (probably good), and they were all going to the West Country (there are worse places).

Mo sat down next to me, managing a smile. Mo was about my age, five and a bit feet tall with short, red hair and several layers of unkempt clothing.

"How're you doing?" she asked.

I shrugged. "How's your finger?"

"Fine. You can control physical pain easy enough. It's all this shit that's hard to deal with."

"Could be worse," I said fatuously.

The bus set off. Mo and I chatted. She, too, got eighteen months as she'd had little to do with the cable scam. Mo was no fundie, but distrusted technology. Man-stuff, she called it. Computers work by machine code, she said. Binary can only handle on or off, right or wrong, yes or no. Same thing with what they put up on screen; the only way to deal with a game-nasty or virtual enemy was to kill it. No room to be kind to it, no way to change it; machine code has no maybes, said Mo.

I wanted to tell her she was way behind the times, but I guessed it would be pointless. She'd only have argued that no amount of logical relativism in programming and no amount of games where you needed empathizing or negotiation skills changed the basic facts.

Instead I said, "Poor Phyllis," noticing she wasn't on the bus.

"Bitch," said Mo.

"Oh come on," I said, surprised. "They'd have given her a terrible time. You can't blame her for breaking under pressure."

Mo looked at me like slantwise. "Haven't you heard?"

"Heard what?"

"Phyllis was a plant. She works for Safe 'n' Sound Security. She was an infiltrator, a mole. Her job was to give us away in time for the election."

"Oh," I said, then said nothing for quite a while.

"Once we could freak around with the wire," Mo went on, "what were we going to do? Broadcast programs about whales and dolphins? Run meditation workshops? Tell people the government were liars? We'd not decided. We tried to cast a spell without visualizing the result."

Just beyond Chiswick, I realized I fancied Mo. It was no big deal; I used to fall in love at least twice a week (as I was only too painfully aware). Every time *I* felt it would be different.

This time I felt *it* would be different. Mo had strength and sense and, with all that witchstuff, she had an aura of serenity and mystery. I closed my eyes and in rushed this weird idea of her and me having babies. And I liked that.

This was very odd. At the time, I simply put it down to the stresses of events.

So I told her what I'd been thinking. It was clumsy, but there was no time for the usual etiquette. Besides, I'd tried this ploy before. ("Hi, my name's Brian and I've chosen you to have my babies.") Sometimes they hit me, or whistled up fifteen stone of muscle-bound drongo boyfriend. Usually they just laughed and ignored me.

Mo put her head on my shoulder. I put my arm around her, and we said nothing.

An hour later the bus was still bowling along the guide lane when a guy at the front, a tall, nervy bloke with a beard, stood up and speeched.

"Okay folks, listen up. My name is Daniel Organ, and I'm your probation officer. I'm not supposed to do this, but it's only fair to let you know what's going to happen . . ."

Everyone looked up.

"Southern Cable has accepted custody of you all. They'll be sacking some of their cleaning staff and junior technicians and replacing them with some of you . . . Most of you, though, will be assigned to the homes of individual members of the Board and to some senior managers."

We took this in silence. "Sounds like a roll of the dice to me," I said to Mo at last. "You might end up with a good family, or a bad one."

She snorted. “This isn’t justice.”

Tagging was the Law and Order magic bullet of the moment, a cost-effective way of dealing with convicts. If someone had mugged you, or burgled your house, they became your property for the term of sentence. You could use their labor to make some kind of restitution. A lot of people liked the idea because victim and perpetrator looked each other in the face; it helped them deal with it. In tests, it usually turned criminals into more useful people than being locked in a prison cell twenty-three hours a day. And if people didn’t want their own personal criminal, the taggie could be sold to some firm as a laborer for the term of sentence and his pay would go to the victim. Not that the pay ever amounted to much.

But this was wrong; we were being handed over like a basket of party favors to people we had not harmed directly.

“You want to put the big pink ribbons round our necks now or later?” said someone behind us.

Daniel Organ produced a small box with a keypad, like the remote control for a Drudge or a Hent System. “This is colloquially known as the Bastard Box, the Pain Pack, and several other things. This particular handset can control all of you, which is why there are no guards on this bus. I’m not going to demonstrate even the minimum extent of pain which can be inflicted via your implants, but what I will do is show you how it can be used to immobilize you. Please brace yourselves . . .”

He squeezed his thumb against the keypad, and everyone stiffened. Some of the others even stood to attention.

I couldn’t move. No matter how much I told my arms and legs to do something, anything dammit, they would not obey.

Daniel Organ squeezed the pad again. Instantly, my limbs resumed obeying orders.

“You are supposed to have certain rights, but forget them. We don’t have enough people to visit you even once during your term. If you’re lucky, you might get a visitor from the Howard League for Penal Reform, or a nice old lady from some charitable organization. If they do visit, and you have a problem with your owner, don’t bother complaining. You’ll only make things harder for yourself. You are the property of the person into whose custody you are transferred, and that's that. On the plus side, most of you are being assigned to private individuals. You're not being given to a hazardous waste cleaning company, or a quarrying firm. And I don't imagine any of these nice folks are going to try setting up gladiatorial combats between pairs of you . . .

"You are not permitted visits from family and friends. You can write to them once a month via the Probation Service. Your letters will be read by the censor, and any attempt to disclose your whereabouts will be removed from the letter . . ."

The censor needn't have worried about me. My mother died years ago, and I never got on with the old man. I hadn't seen him for years anyhow. And I didn't have any friends who'd be the sort to risk springing me.

"Don't imagine that you or any expert can tamper with either your box or the system," continued Organ. "The codes are immense, and they're changed every fifteen minutes. Britain's privatized penal set-up is now in the hands of global corporations who earn vast amounts of money, and you may be sure that their systems are very secure. They've not been cracked yet. And don't believe any stories you hear about people who can reconfigure the box to give you orgasms instead of pain. It's not true. Which is probably just as well.

"By the way, don't get too upset if nobody comes to release you on the exact date your time's up. That's just the way things are. Someone will remember you eventually."

When the bus left the motorway the signposts were for places like Bristol and Weston-Super-Mare. A short while later it pulled up at a well-lit gatehouse, with two heavily armed rent-a-cops dressed like New York's Finest (the more a private security goon's dress looks like something out of Hollywood, the less they get paid . . .), a robot dog, surveillance cameras, the lot. The sign said WELCOME TO HINTON LEA.

If none of us has heard of Hinton Lea it was because ten years ago it didn't exist. It was one of those gated villages that sprung up after the government scrapped the green belt, privatized the

Forestry Commission, and forced the National Trust to sell some of its landholdings for golf courses.

You, too, get away from city smog and crime and be just like the folks in *Country Lifestyle* mag for a down payment of 500K.

A few of us were to be dropped here, while the rest were to go to other burbforts hereabouts.

I was the first. I shook a few hands, slapped a few backs, and hugged Mo.

"See you on the other side," I smiled.

"Yeah," she said. "I'd like that. I'll send you any strength I've got to spare."

So, I'm on the step of this three-bed detached thing; a semi-detached parody of a Victorian Gothic Revival townhouse, the home of someone with no taste at all. My possessions amount to a prawnless prawn sandwich and a half-full bottle of Malvern Water, and Daniel Organ is reading my rights to the guy at the door who's looking at me like I'm a bowl of cold sick with a cherry on top.

It's ten at night, but it's spring and quite light and I can tell a lot about him.

He's about thirty-five. Not a lot older than me, but a universe apart.

His hair is too black not to be at least partly out of a bottle or implant. He is wearing shorts and a vest with the name of some poncey designer on it. This garment is almost not worth wearing as it's designed to reveal luxuriant expanses of depilated and roid-grown muscle.

". . . you will ensure that he is fed at least three adequate and nutritionally balanced meals a day," says Daniel, but my new owner is looking impatient.

He has a big moustache of the kind favored by Stalin and various other twentieth-century tyrants. Mum always said you should never trust a man with a moustache.

". . . you will provide access to adequate sanitation and washing facilities."

Oh goody.

". . . you will not physically or sexually abuse him."

A wolf has just appeared at his side. Correction, it's a very big dog, the sort that bites criminals. He pats the dog absently.

". . . you will ensure that he is provided with adequate warmth and shelter, you will . . ."

"Yeah, yeah, yeah," he says. "Just give me the zapper and the manual. I'm missing the golf . . ."

Organ hands over a bubble-wrapped remote. He also presents Mr. Universe with a glossy booklet on the cover of which is a cartoon of a man in a convict suit digging a garden, while in the foreground sits a sweet little old lady in a deckchair enjoying a cup of tea.

"You will ensure that the taggie's welfare is adequately . . ."

"Yes, yes," interrupts Mr. Impatient. "Where do I sign?"

My new owner speaks with the accentless, precise voice of somebody who spends a lot of time giving dictation to machines.

As soon as the bus has pulled away, he unwraps his handset, sets it to maximum, and tries it out.

I can feel the pain starting in my back and shooting down to my toes and across to my fingertips. I yell a lot.

It's set for a max five seconds before it cuts out automatically.

I collapse on the doorstep.

"Wow!" he says. "Nearly woke up the whole street! Let's make sure we understand each other, my friend. I don't like people like you. I don't like what you did to my company. You're scum. You fight against a system which has the best interests of everyone at heart, when you should be helping yourself and helping others by getting a job. But now you're here we're going to have to get along. Keep your nose clean, do as you're told, and we'll do just fine."

He leads me to the garage at the back of the house. In a corner is a tatty mattress and a few blankets. "This is where you'll sleep for now," he says. "My wife is nervous about having you indoors. Now, where are we . . ." He consults the manual, flips over a few pages as I stand around admiring his collection of power tools, wondering if it's possible to kill a man with a sander.

"Got it!" he says, pushing a few buttons on the box. "The immobilizer cuts in if you enter the house, or move more than twenty meters from this spot. Good night."

With that, he returns to the golf. He hasn't asked me my name, told me his name, or informed me where the bathroom is.

Later I slip out and piss on one of his flowerbeds.

Jeremy Henderson was not a member of the Southern Cable board, or even a senior manager. He wasn't clever enough. He was an area sales manager, though he'd avoid using the title outright and tried to give the impression he was more senior, more highly paid and more *in-dis-fuckin'-pensible* than that.

When the company found they had some of us left over after sacking the cleaners and giving us to senior management, they had a lottery. Jeremy Henderson won eighteen months of my life by racking up the highest score in a game of Bushido.

Jeremy Henderson had few paper books in his house except The Bible, a bound set of Jeffrey Archer novels (heh-heh!), a beginner's guide to Go, and a copy of Sun Tzu's *The Art of War*, which was presumably fashionable reading for proactive corporate pants at the time.

He worked in the weights room daily, and roided up as well. Mrs. (and she was a Mrs., you better believe) Henderson did not work. And the less work she had to do at home, the more proud Jeremy was.

For a while before he got married he flirted with that church that thinks Freddie Mercury is God and is coming back soon in a spaceship. Queen was JH's idea of classical music.

Now he was a Christian because everyone else who mattered was, and because deep in his soul he needed something to Total Quality Manage his moral superiority over first and second quadranters and anyone else who didn't live as he did. Jeremy's most primal fear was that someone might get one over on him.

In the SWOT Analysis he did on me, I guess I represented both an opportunity (status symbol, labor-saving gadget) and a threat (I might get one over on him).

Mrs. Henderson – Natasha; you know you can tell the age of trees by counting the rings? If I cared about fashion, I could have told the age of Natasha by studying the plastics and implants. I'd have bet my liberty that seventy percent of the women her age in Hinton Lea had the same hairstyle, same breasts, same nose, same lips, same dental work, same shaped arse, same flawless complexion . . .

Natasha looked like a soap bitch, but before her husband and master she was a self-effacing little mouse. She had met hubby seventeen years previously, had married two weeks after leaving school. She had never had a job, had probably never been out with any other guy. She wasn't the sort to cheat.

She had all the domestic electronics a decorative little hausfrau could desire, including a Moulinex Andy to do all the cleaning. She had no interests in life beyond watching soaps and talking about diets with her women friends over tea and cake.

She was also partial to the bottle.

For a week, I cleaned windows, did a bit of painting (Jeremy didn't trust me with anything tricky), cut the grass, and even got let out to do a bit of shopping. For almost every minute I was awake I thought about legging it. It would have been pointless; the tag has a beacon that the filth could home on from miles away, and cutting the tag out is a nonstarter, they say. And I wasn't about to try surgery on myself.

A week into my captivity, JH held one of his "famous barbecues."

Of course the most interesting piece of meat was not being cooked. Well, not literally anyhow.

Come seven, the garden was full of the cream of Hinton Lea society. Men in T-shirts and tight shorts contrived to show off their bottled muscles stood around drinking bottled Budvar and Sapporo and talked about cars, golf, suitplay, and management, all pretending they were more important than they really were. The women, mostly little wifeys who hadn't worked for years, or who maybe did work part-time but tried to hide it, talked about kids or cosmetic surgery, and pretended their husbands were more important than they really were. There were a few kids, half of them running around laughing and screaming, the other half standing around like clones of their parents, either perfectly behaved and polite, or affecting languid boredom.

My role was to swan around with the drinks and the nibbles wearing the white shirt, dicky-bow and brocade waistcoat Natasha had brought home for me the day before. I'd been dreading having to officiate over a heap of charred, stinking meat, but I'd forgotten that looking after the barbie is Real Man's Work.

My mission was to be seen by everyone. People would ask JH who I was, and he'd nonchalantly say, "You mean Brian? He's our taggie. A little present from Sir David."

Technically, this was true in the sense that the Chief Executive had raffled the remaining members of the Margin, but no way was Jeremy going to say he'd won me by pretending to be a Mangaflick hero.

The price of Hendersons hit an all-time high. His mates grinned and said he'd soon be too good to mix with them, then retired into little knots to bitch about him behind his back.

As the sun went down, most of the women drifted away to put kids to bed, or talk in the living room. The males huddled closer around the dying embers of the barbie to get maudlin and trade philosophy.

Maybe JH had stopped being the center of attention for a moment, but suddenly I felt a tingle down the back of my neck, turned and saw him holding the remote.

"Brian," he said, "c'mere."

I wandered over. The others stopped conversing and looked at me.

"There's one burger left on the barbie, Brian," he said. "Would you like it?"

"No thanks, JH," I said brightly. The others sniggered and dug one another in the ribs. They hadn't heard him called "JH" before.

"No, s'allright, you can have it," he said, slapping the lump of dead cow into a bun.

"I don't eat meat, JH," I said coolly. He knew it.

"Why's that, then, Brian? Think it's inhumane? Think you're better than the rest of us?"

"I don't like the thought of eating dead animal flesh," I said.

He slopped some relish into the bun, and held it out. "You want to overthrow our way of life, don't you? You and your weird mates want us all back in the Middle Ages, don't you? You'd rather we were all living in mud huts and eating grass."

I hadn't realized how drunk he was; it was unwise to challenge him, but I did. "All I want is a world in which the planet's resources are more evenly distributed and where everyone can achieve their full potential as a human being."

Don't forget I hadn't even heard of the Water Margin three months before this.

He sneered the last sentence back at me. "And what about us here? Aren't we striving towards our full potential as human beings?"

I didn't answer. Thought it best not to. "See!" he said to the others. "I told you he thinks he's better than the rest of us." To me again, "Eat the fucking burger. Do I have to make you?"

I took root. He thumbed the remote, and the pain shot through me.

The pain stopped. Some of his chums were laughing. Others looked at the ground uncomfortably. "You going to eat the nice burger, Brian?"

"No," I said as evenly as I could.

He turned it up. I fell to the ground, writhing around on the grass, trying not to cry out.

It stopped. I looked up. JH was simply raising a quizzical eyebrow and proffering the burger.

"No," I said.

"Anyone else want a go?" he sniggered, offering the remote around. Nobody did. He turned it up some more. Probably to maximum. This time I did yell.

It cut out. I managed to croak a "fuck you."

He went ballistic. "You pathetic bloody criminal! You come into my house like Lord God Almighty, sneering at the rest of us, thinking you're so damn superior. But who are you? What have you got? Nothing, you've got nothing. You *are* nothing. I'll fucking break you, you piece of shit!"

With that, he switched on again, leaving me yelling like an elephant with a toothache.

The pain went on for what seemed like hours, though it was only five seconds. When it stopped, a voice was saying, "Cool it, Jeremy. He's had enough. Forget it . . ."

"Fucking break him if it's the last thing I do," said JH, as someone popped another bottle for him.

Next day, JH stuck his head through the garage door at sparrowfart and said we were going to church. He gave me a suit, a shiny, bottle-green thing, then pushed me into the bathroom.

Again, I was being shown off. Having ascertained that I could drive he almost gave me the key until he thought better of entrusting his precious 4WD Lada Ostrovnik to me. Pity. I could have scared the bejeezus out of him by driving it recklessly; after all, he wouldn't dare use the remote to stop me.

Hinton Lea, population c. 2500, doesn't have a church. We went to some village nearby for a lowbrow evangelical service of the sort that validates your greed. None of that love-your-neighbor or Good Samaritan or turn-the-other-cheek nonsense for this crowd. The vicar, or pastor or whatever he was, told us how the Bible is God's User's Manual for Life.

It being sunny, we all hung out in the churchyard afterwards to network. JH chatted with his social betters and Natasha exchanged banalities with her friends.

Regular churchgoing was going to be wonderful.

IJ came up and clapped me on the back. I didn't recognize him for a minute as he, like me, had been washed and be-suited. He belonged to the Chief Exec himself and was living a tolerable existence in a room above Sir David's garage. Sir David had a huge paper and electronic library and allowed IJ the run of it when he wasn't tending two acres of garden.

Two of the others came over, also done up like rich men's dinners.

Then Mo appeared! She looked impossibly scrubbed and wholesome in a flowery print dress and straw boater.

We'd none of us recognized each other in the church and now frantically exchanged news. I told them how JH had tried to make me eat meat. Mo looked fit to murder him there and then.

"Has he a suit?" asked IJ.

"Must have," I said. "He won me in suitplay."

"Any idea what he uses to make it real?" asked IJ.

I didn't follow.

"Feelies, 'hancers . . . Drugs to heighten sensitivity," said Mo, smiling at IJ.

I shrugged.

"Doesn't matter," said IJ. "He's bound to use something. They all do. Try and make it to church next week. I'll have some black magic for you."

Mo and I chatted. She, too, was living in Hinton Lea, with the most junior owner of the lot. It turned out that Jeremy had actually won two of us, but his boss made him give the other one – Mo – to his assistant area sales manager, Wayne Roberts.

"He's an arsehole," she said, "but could be worse. He hasn't tried to rape me yet. I'm kept busy with . . ."

Three small girls and a boy, the eldest not above seven, rushed up to Mo and clustered around her legs, all chattering, all wanting to show her something or ask her questions.

"Meet the Roberts brood. I am their governess. My owners have too many kids and not enough money. Has Jezzer got a dog?" she asked, as the youngest tried to climb up her leg.

A man beckoned her and the kids away. "We go to the park every morning between ten and eleven," she said, waving.

JH graciously invited me to Sunday lunch, which I understand is an important ritual for people in regular well-paid work. Natasha slopped things from Marks & Sparks onto plates. They didn't bother trying to force meat on me. There was a bottle of Slovak plonk, too. JH was a member of the Skinfull of the Month Club, or something; he reckoned it was good stuff. It tasted like vinegar to me.

Afterwards, JH loosened buttons, draped his arms over the back of the chair, and got expansive. He lectured us about the innate idleness of the unemployed, how he pulled himself up by his bootstraps through a combination of hard work and back-to-basics morality. The jobless, the homeless, the hopeless were, you see, materially poor because they were morally poor – the mantra of smug idiots since time immemorial.

"Don't you wish you had all this Brian?" he said, waving his arm around, indicating the house, the car, the fridge, the wife . . . He didn't wait for a reply. "You can. If you've got the guts to work hard for it. In this life, you don't get anything for nothing. You're a bright bloke, there's still time, you should go for it."

I could have said it was all white noise. I actually said nothing.

He shrugged. "I will win," he said. "I'm a very bad loser. By the end of your time here, you will see everything my way."

IJ was right. After loading the plates into the dishwasher (his one domestic chore of the week), he took a little onyx box from a cupboard over the sink, popped two pills, and left the room.

He reappeared in a top-of-the-range suit, a combination of string vest and black plastic sense-pads. He carried one of those wooden Japanese practice swords.

In the garden, he stood in the middle of the lawn, clapped the visor down, and spent two hours doing battle with fresh air, looking like a very cross, oversized beetle.

The week passed quietly. Jezzer (as Mo had called him) did his nine-to-nines, Natasha watched television, went shopping and played bridge with her friends. Out of boredom I persuaded Jezzer to let me work on the garden. And each morning I took the wolf, whose name was King, for a walk.

In the park I'd meet Mo and the two of her charges who were too young for school. We talked and talked and talked. Usually about nothing in particular; neither of us wanted to focus too hard on our immediate situation. Naturally we had to be sort of discreet, so not so much as a handshake passed between us, but I really was falling in love. I liked to think she was, too.

On Sunday, we met IJ and some of the others at church again. He slipped me two small objects. "You'll know what to do with these," he said. "Don't take out the existing chip. Just plug this into the port next to it. I've called it Hieronymus."

I trousered his "black magic" and forgot about it until later in the day when Jezzer went out to the lawn with his sword. IJ had given me a small plastic bottle of pills and a gizmo with about two-dozen delicate little pins sticking out of it.

It was too late to try anything that day. Besides, although Jezzer deserved whatever nightmare that IJ had cooked up for him, it had been over a week since that incident, and I hadn't seen much of him since. I was in love, and aside from the fact that I could do little about it, life was almost tolerable.

My trouble is I get complacent too easily.

Another week passed and things still got better. I met Mo every weekday, and Natasha, who had the remote during office hours, but never once used it, took me shopping one afternoon. It was the first time we exchanged more than a few sentences, though I did most of the talking, prosing on about my favorite authors. I don't quite know what she made of all this; I think she saw a human being, rather than a criminal, for the first time. Maybe she felt my cultured and sensitive nature (ha!) was valuable. Anyway, she gave me the run of a bookshop on one of her cards.

Then came Saturday night . . .

I didn't know when or if Natasha was likely to make free with the plastic again, so I'd got her money's worth, and at midnight I was tucked up in the garage with some of my favorite sf classics.

Jezzer and Natasha were off at a dinner party and had left me with the immobilizer set at twenty yards, which meant that if the house caught fire or got burgled there was cock-all I could do about it. Shame.

I heard them come in after midnight and was about to sleep when I heard him shouting inside the house.

Then the side door to the garage burst open. There was Jezzer in his designer skivvies with the remote in one hand. With the other, he pushed Natasha through in front of him. She was wearing a silk nightdress.

"Here he is, then" he snarled at her. "Go on then. Get into the sack with him, bitch!"

"Jeremy, no!" she said, in tears.

He pushed her so hard she fell on top of me. “Go on then, get on with it. Go on Brian, give her a good seeing-to. It’s what you both want, isn’t it!”

She scrambled to her feet as Jeremy fumbled with the box, then turned it to maximum.

“What the hell’s going on?” I shouted through the pain.

“Don’t play the innocent with me!” he said. “I know your fucking game. Trying to get into my wife’s knickers so’s you’ll get an easier time of it here!”

“Rubbish!” was all I could manage. He turned the agony off. Natasha tried to leave, but he blocked her path.

“You think I’m completely stupid don’t you? I call up a credit card statement this afternoon and find she’s spent seventy Eeks in a *bookshop!* This ignorant cow hasn’t read a single book in the last ten years. And now, like every other Saturday night, she lies there like I’m raping her, never showing any sign of enjoyment. But she’s more than happy to spend my hard-earned money on some worthless bum because he talks to her about literature . . .”

“This is nonsense, JH,” I said. “I don’t fancy her. I’m sure she doesn’t fancy a scruff like me. She was only being . . .”

Jezzer wasn’t listening. “What’s your secret, then? Got a bigger cock than me, have you?”

I snorted.

“Come on, then!” he said. “Let’s both give her one! Maybe she’d like that, the frigid bitch!” He tore off her nightdress and, once more, pushed her onto me, pulling down his underpants as he did so.

“Come on then, Brian,” he said, “let’s see you in action.”

“Go to hell!”

He switched on the pain. I told him to screw himself, which of course is precisely what he would have loved to do.

“You’re one sick individual, you know that?” I said. “And even if I did want to get it up, it’d be difficult with your finger on the pain button.”

Natasha climbed off me again. “I’m sorry,” she said to me. “I’m sorry,” through her sobbing, gathering up her nightdress. I told her it wasn’t her fault. Jezzer let her through the door this time, then spent the next five minutes tearing up the books she'd bought me.

What he did to Natasha was terrible, but basically none of my business. I didn't know what was going on between them. What really angered me was that final act of vandalism. He was destroying knowledge, wisdom, and culture. He was a Nazi, a philistine. The fear that he and millions like him had of books was taking us all into a new age of barbarism.

Next morning, as we got ready for church, I popped IJ's pills into Jezzer's onyx box, and slipped upstairs to plug Hieronymus into the port on the visor of his suit.

As we were about to leave, Jezzer got an urgent call from the office. He drove off looking grim and determined. Natasha went back to bed.

I helped myself to some breakfast and spent half the morning sticking books together again. Then I did some work in the garden. I borrowed the antique-styled radio from the kitchen to listen while I worked. Right at the end of the lunchtime news I realized why Jeremy had left in a hurry. LBM, the huge electronics conglomerate, had mounted a bid for Southern Cable, promising new wire and all sorts of brilliant new services for domestic and commercial customers, not to mention bigger dividends.

We didn't see much of Jeremy for a while. He was busy going to meetings and helping with the hearts-and-minds campaign with shareholders. I didn't see much of Natasha either. Whenever I did, she looked sort of apologetic, as though the whole thing had been her fault.

In the park on Monday I told Mo everything that had happened. She listened in silence then looked me carefully in the eye, trying, I guess, to see if there really was anything between Natasha and me.

Finally, she said, "It's time to cast a spell. One that will change him forever." She glanced around to see that nobody was watching, kissed me furtively, called the kids together, and left.

Two days later she gave me a slip of paper with a London landline number on it and a woman's name. "Memorize the name and number," said Mo, "then lose the paper. Call it using one of Jezzer's phones anytime you know he's not at the office and ask for the woman. It doesn't matter if you don't get her. Just keep the line open for a minute or more."

"What is this, Mo?"

"The less you know, the less it can harm you," she said. "It's the philosopher's stone. It'll turn an arrogant shit into a sorry shit."

"Is this going to hurt anyone?"

"Not physically."

I took the paper, memorized name and number, and walked the dog home again.

When I got back, Natasha was waiting in the kitchen. She had made me some lunch. Also on the table were new copies of all the books Jezzer had destroyed. I thanked her lots, told her she didn't have to do this.

She shrugged. "It's his money."

"Aren't you frightened of him?"

"Not anymore. I'm leaving. I'm going to stay with my parents and get a divorce."

She explained how his behavior the other night was not exceptional. He beat her up every so often, had kinky sexual tastes, had been unfaithful. He kept pestering her to have sex with his friends while he watched. I didn't doubt a word of it.

She warned me (quite unnecessarily) that he'd be in a vile temper when he got home and found her note, and that it might be best to keep my head down and the books hidden.

"I would give you your remote control," she said, "so you can hide it or break it. But he's got it. He thinks I'd give it to you." She smiled weakly.

I carried her cases to the taxi for her.

JH got home at ten, found no supper and no wife waiting. He came into the garage, set the immobilizer and kicked me around a bit. He suspected I'd had a hand in Natasha's desertion. Perhaps I had.

He disappeared early next morning. The minute he did, I went into the house and punched up the number Mo had given me, making sure the system wasn't set to record.

A receptionist answered. I didn't get the company name, but it was a long one. I asked to speak to Elizabeth Colley.

I was put on hold; the screen filled with slo-mo pictures of waves and sea, but there was no company logo. This was obviously a line that prized discretion.

A young man came on. "I'm sorry," he said, "but Elizabeth is in a meeting. Can I take a message?"

"I don't think so," I said. "It's personal. Have you any idea what time she'll be free?"

"About an hour's time," he said. "Who shall I say called?"

"Henderson," I said, "Jeremy Henderson," and hung up, still no wiser as to what Mo's game was. I then went off to the bathroom to clean up the blood and bruises Jezzer had inflicted the night before.

Midmorning next day I was getting King ready for walkies when Jezzer arrived back home.

He was a zombie. I didn't ask what the problem was, especially as he went straight for the drinks cabinet. I said I was walking the dog. He ignored me.

In the park Mo and I sat at our favorite bench watching the kids chase each other around.

She nodded as I told her what had happened. "It worked then."

"The call I made?"

She nodded. "He's been fired."

"What?"

"Sacked, wasted, kicked out . . ."

"Mo, I'll say this in as many words, even though I'm sure I don't have to. I think I love you, and the only reason I can touch upon for why you're there in everything I think, dream, and do is your mystique, all the fabulous things that go on in your head. I want to spend ten lifetimes with you because I know you'll never become ordinary or boring to me . . ."

She smiled. I loved her smile, the brightness of her eyes.

". . . but just this once please stop being so enigmatic. Tell me what we've done to him."

"Let the dog off the lead," she said.

Despite my doubts about the wolf's suitability as a playmate, I did as ordered. King ran off with the kids.

"Jezzer has been sacked for disloyalty," she said. "Wayne told me Jezzer was a foot soldier on the anti-takeover committee. He knows the company's defense strategy. How would it be if he was caught making a call to the European Development Executive of LBM who's coordinating their takeover effort?"

"Would this senior executive of LBM be called Elizabeth Colley?"

Mo nodded slightly.

"And?"

"I got her name and number from FTNet. Wayne did the rest. At the tea table the other night, he was talking about the takeover. I mentioned how my Uncle Bernard was involved in something similar, but he'd been caught talking to the opposition when his firm looked at his itemized bill. I jokingly suggested Wayne might score a few points with the boss by suggesting that they quietly monitor everyone's linetime. After all, the firm pays their bills, so it's only fair."

Jeremy's bill had an LBM number on it, punched up from his home at a time he wasn't in the office. He had no recording to prove it wasn't him. He'd have had ten minutes to clear his desk. Every recruitment dbase in the world would now have DISLOYAL stamped over his name in big red letters. Unless he could find himself a very expensive forger to fry up a seamless new ident, and raise the money for new voice- and handprints and alter the records next to his iris-prints, he'd never have a management job again.

Three quarters of me was delighted the swine had got his due, the rest was apprehensive about what would happen to me.

"Do I become the property of Southern Cable?" I asked Mo.

"No," she said. "You're still Jezzer's. The law assigns you into the custody of a named individual for the duration of sentence. You can't be sold, though he can hire you out and keep your earnings."

I had this appalling vision of him undercutting the local paperboy . . .

"You're in a much more powerful position," said Mo. "If he needs you, he's got to start being nice. And Wayne needs to carry on being nice to me if he wants his kids looked after properly while his wife works to supplement the family budget. So in view of your declaration of your feelings, I can no longer see any objection to our performing a full-on Frenchie snog right here in broad daylight, but for the sake of the children I'll have no groping . . ."

I accepted her invitation with more speed than grace. We canoodled like teenagers for a blissful eternity, only coming up when we heard the dog barking in front of us and a child's voice saying, "Eurrrgh! What are they doing?"

Jezzer was talking to his solicitor when I got back: ". . . listen, even if I did want to talk to LBM – and I admit the thought had crossed my mind – I wouldn't dream of doing something as stupid and obvious as that . . ."

The man on the screen sighed and went on about how Industrial Tribunals had been abolished. He'd have to go for a civil action, and that'd cost.

I retired to the garage and my books. When I looked in again midevening, Jezzer was in a heap in an armchair, cradling a near-empty bottle of panther sweat.

I went to the kitchen, perched myself at the breakfast bar, and helped myself to bread and jam. It was hazardous, but I had to eat.

Jezzer stumbled in, red-eyed.

"It was Wayne, boring old useless old Wayne Roberts," he said to himself. "It must have been. He suggested Sir David look at everyone's bills. He fitted me up so's he'd get my job . . ."

He leaned heavily over the sink, turned on the cold tap and splashed water on his face. "What a state," he said. "What a bloody awful mess. Wife leaves me, kicked out of my job. Jeez, what a bloody mess . . ."

He turned to me. "I'm not as bad as you, though." He laughed a little. "No. I'm not a loser. Henderson is the best there is."

He opened the cupboard and took out his little onyx pillbox. Before I could decide whether or not to stop him, he had popped two of IJ's pills.

"Still the fucking best," he said, and crashed out of the room and up the stairs.

I didn't know what the pills were, but I knew he shouldn't be doing them in his loaded state.

I went to the bottom of the stairs. Before I could figure out how to stop him, he appeared on the landing, suited up. In his hand he held the remote, and into a silk sash around his waist was tucked a real samurai sword.

Oh bother.

"Out of my way, loser," he said, waving the remote. "Any trouble out of you and I'll immobilize you and cut your fucking balls off."

Oh well, I thought, standing aside as he thumped down the stairs, on your own head be it, Jezzer, mate.

I watched from the kitchen window as he stood on the lawn, pulled down the visor, drew the sword, and started swishing it around in the air, occasionally letting out some bloodthirsty yell as yet another phantom enemy fell to his cold steel.

Nothing weird happened through twenty minutes of this. I began hoping the pills were duds, and I'd plugged in Hieronymus the wrong way.

But no. Somewhere in Jezzer's head, his samurai opponents began to shape shift.

(IJ explained some days later. The pills were his own recipe, involving caffeine, a load of ketamine, a little acid, and a few other things. On arriving at Sir David's home, IJ immediately identified the man's twenty-four-year-old son as a feckless slacker and had discovered and ransacked his stash in exactly twenty-seven minutes. Hieronymus was IJ's own creation; he'd taken a couple of Bosch paintings and used one of Sir David's machines to assemble a plug that kicked into the Bushido game. At first, the images were subliminal, gradually accelerating into limited animation, until the point at which Jezzer, tanked up on a hallucinogen which can give you nightmares if you're not a happy bunny, found himself in hell.)

Jezzer was chasing next door's cat across the lawn with that sword, which no doubt had been lovingly sharpened.

I ran out, too late. The cat let out an astonished howl and cleared the fence in a single leap, leaving half its tail on the garden path.

"Stop, JH, stop!" I yelled. "Take the mask off!"

To my relief, he did, and looked around like he'd just beamed down from another planet. He threw the mask to the ground in disgust.

Then he walked to his 4WD. "It's Wayne, it's fucking Wayne Roberts who shafted me. They're all trying to destroy me. Wayne, Sir Frigging David, Natasha . . ." He looked at me. "And you!" He pointed the sword at me.

He opened the car door, threw the sword onto the passenger seat. "I'll sort you later," he said, starting the engine.

The Lada lurched out onto the road and sped away.

I gave chase. He quickly lost me, but I knew where he was going with that sword. To where Wayne Roberts, his wife, four kids – and Mo – were.

The Roberts house was ten minutes' walk away. I got there in two. It fronted onto the village green, a patch of grass about the size of a football field with a few park benches and flowerbeds and a venerable old oak in the middle.

Jezzer's Lada was smashed into the low brick wall at the front of Wayne's house.

In the car, Freddie Mercury was singing "We Are the Champions of the World" loud enough to drown an aero-engine, and Jezzer stood on the front lawn waving his sword, demanding Wayne come out to fight him like a man, and not cower like the treacherous piece of shit he actually was.

All the lights in the house were on, but I couldn't see anyone at the windows. I prayed that Mo and the kids, at least, had slipped out of the back door, or had barricaded themselves in securely.

"Jezz . . . Jeremy . . . JH, stop, for God's sake, stop," I yelled as I ran across the green towards him. He didn't even look at me, but in one smooth movement his left hand swept into the air and descended again to point at me.

I stumbled and fell. I couldn't get up again. He'd had the remote in his hand. I'd been immobilized.

I lay on the grass village green about thirty meters from Jezzer, utterly helpless, but I could see everything.

It was like this:

Another 4WD pulls up close by and out climb both the shift rent-a-cops. They look at one another as if to say "you tell me what to do so's you get the blame if we screw up."

These people protect the community from the barbarians outside; they don't have a freaking clue what to do with an actual resident who's gone harpic. They've not been trained in counseling skills. (Actually, they haven't been trained in anything.)

Jezzer sees them and is still having flashbacks about demons; he turns, lets out a ghastly scream, lifts the sword high above his head with both hands, and charges at them.

For one of those frozen moments, the goons can only gape. Then, cartoon characters, both turn and run. A moment longer and the nearest would have ended up with his head split neatly in two and with a sword lodged in his sternum.

Jezzer pulls up, stretches his arms out and bows, as though being applauded by an imaginary audience and sings along with the stereo.

"Weeeeeeeee are ther champions mah fre-hend . . . !"

As he turns, the tip of his sword touches the goons' 4WD. He stops, looks at me with a dastardly leer, and says, "I wonder . . . ?"

He pulls open the door on the passenger side and emerges with an assault rifle with a big tube running along the bottom of the barrel.

He laughs triumphantly, lays the gun on the bonnet of the car and oh-so-reverently sheathes his sword.

The gun has three magazines taped together. He pulls the first out and satisfies himself it's fully charged. He pushes it back in and cocks the gun. He reaches into the car again and brings out what looks like a weightlifter's belt with tin cans attached. He takes the first of the cans, pokes it into the rear end of the tube below the gun barrel, and slings the belt over his shoulder.

I could have told you someone would get hurt when the government allowed rent-a-cops to be armed. Business is business; you've got to control costs, so you hire people who'll bring their own tools friendless losers and fantasists who'll work double-shifts for a price of a tin of beans per hour, on the promise that one day they might – just might – get to lob rocket-propelled grenades (which they've paid for themselves) at a house-breaker or a twocker.

The main bedroom window in the Roberts house briefly glows orange, then the glass bursts out in millions of beautiful crystal fragments.

The curtains billow out after them. Only then is there any noise. It's quite loud.

"Put the gun down now!" shouts one of the goons from outside my field of view. Jezzer turns and fires the rifle on automatic.

He empties the whole magazine. Bullets ricochet, crack, and whine deafeningly from a stone wall close by.

He loads another grenade and fires it through a downstairs window of Wayne's house.

I have let Jesus into my heart; I am praying, really praying, for the first time since Mum told me that Jesus and Santa were two different people, praying that Mo and the kids and their parents are out of the house.

And Freddie Mercury is preening himself on the car sound system, something about having just killed a man, Mama . . .

There's a lot of noise else. Jezzer has alerted the whole village, and there's a deal of screaming and shouting all around.

He loads another grenade and fires it towards the far side of the green. I can't see where it goes, but the explosion is close.

There's this agonized creaking of wood and a sort of crump noise.

Jezzer has wasted the olde oak tree, pride of Hinton Lea.

Nothing happens for a while.

Now, we see that some resourceful member of the community has Done Something. From a side road emerges a drudge, a domestic robot with a happy smiling friendly helpful face-decal at the top. And a shotgun held in the arms that normally take the feather duster and the bog-brush.

Its owner must have rigged some kind of radio control, but it's academic. A well-aimed RPG from Jezzer turns Helpful Henry into a cloudburst of components.

Its happy face flops to the ground a few feet from mine.

What's that old movie where the two Americans end up surrounded by the whole Bolivian army? It's like that; there are suddenly dozens of people firing guns at Jezzer from three sides of the green, with more joining in all the time.

Several men and quite a few women have mustered like the stout yeomanry of old to save the town. They've formed a posse with their shotguns and licensed pistols, their .22s and even air rifles. They crouch behind garden walls and other cover to blast away at Jezzer.

As well as worrying about Mo and the Roberts household, I am now concerned about me. The sky is crowding with projectiles, and I can't even bat my eyelids for help, never mind crawl away. I suppose if anyone's noticed me lying here they think I'm dead.

Freddie Mercury assures us that he and his mates will rock us.

The Hinton Lea Home Guard are all lousy shots; most of the shotgun owners only use them occasionally for clay pigeons, and the pistol owners are firing from too far away.

So Jezzer stands there in full view, and looses four more RPGs in various directions.

This only stings his tormentors to redouble their efforts.

The 12-bores are making a real mess of his Lada.

Only when Freddie finally falls silent does Jezzer realize he's in a hostile environment. He steps back and disappears behind Wayne's garden wall.

A bullet furrows into the ground in front of me. Then another. And another, which I swear actually touches the tip of my nose.

I'm moving. Someone brave is dragging me towards the comparative shelter of a nearby garden.

"Are you all right?" says the voice I most love in all the world. Mo's face is right in front of mine.

I can't respond.

"Oh no!" she says to someone next to her. "He must be hurt. Where does it hurt? Have you been paralyzed my love . . . Oh. Paralyzed. Oh. That's all right then. Jezzer's immobilized him . . . Brian, darling. I'll have to leave you here for a moment. We have to get the children out. I'll come back to you in a minute . . ."

Someone shouts from the far side of the green, telling Jezzer to surrender before anyone gets seriously hurt.

Jezzer gets up and fires another grenade.

He doesn't dive back to cover immediately. He stands in full view and rests the butt of the gun on his hip and surveys the town contemptuously.

Although he's an easy target, everyone stops shooting. Maybe they're impressed, or want to savor this moment before the mad dog's last stand. I am certain that for most of the people here this is a game; there may be plenty of worried, terrified people elsewhere in the village, but the idea that guns and grenades maim and kill hasn't occurred to anyone who's come to play tonight. They've seen too many movies not to know that the good guy always lives in the end.

Suddenly, I am in pain.

I can move again.

I slowly, carefully, get to my knees.

Jezzer is holding the remote up high. "Brian, where are you? You're not much of a hostage, but you're all I've got. Come here, come to Uncle Jeremy."

I'm willing. Maybe I can talk him out of this lunacy. I get up to a crouch and wave my arms around in the air to show everyone where I am.

Someone lets off a shot at Jezzer from close by.

The remote held aloft in his hand disintegrates like a clay pigeon.

He looks at the hand where the zapper used to be, shaking his head in bemusement.

And that is all the chance I need. Like a jungle cat, I spring from my haunches over the wall and onto Jezzer before he can bring the gun to bear on me.

I get him on the ground. He is bigger than me, fitter than me, and more bonkers than me. But I am mad as hell, and to his K-addled brain, I look like the Lord of Darkness himself. So within moments, he's wailing in existential despair because he thinks that Satan himself is going to be kicking him in the bollocks like this for all eternity.

The citizens were all for hanging him from the remains of the olde oak tree, but it wasn't high enough, and then the police SWAT team helicoptered in to rescue him.

There were a few bruises and scratches, and lots of ringing ears, but no major injuries. Hinton Lea feted me as the hero of the hour, though you could tell a lot of them were a bit disappointed that the drama had not achieved a fitting conclusion.

You'd think they'd be sufficiently grateful to petition for my early release, or at least a few months' parole. But oh no. Fair and grateful people don't get to live in places like Hinton Lea.

The trial was straightforward enough. I'd got rid of the chip back on his suit visor in the garden, and everyone thought he'd just scored a bad batch of pills. So he was sentenced to tagging for life, but the legal squabbles over Jezzer and his property were another matter.

The judge made some very fine calculations according to all the people Jezzer had harmed. A big piece of him went to Wayne Roberts, another slice to Hinton Lea as a whole. Other individuals who had been injured or whose property had been damaged won minor portions.

Hundreds of others claimed his actions had stressed them so much they were on tranks or in counseling and entered claims for a morsel of Jezzer or his property. Also, Natasha filed for divorce, demanding half his stuff.

While the lawyers argue, Jezzer and I belong to Hinton Lea, our labors administered by the Community Council. I don't know who the official remote-holder is, but I've not seen one since that night.

Jezzer sleeps in the attic of the Parish Hall.

I'm sharing Wayne's family caravan with Mo.

Wayne wasn't keen on this arrangement, and still fears for the caravan's suspension. Mo quietly explained to him how complicated things might become if she were to tell the police about how she had been the one who got Jezzer sacked. Wayne might lose his nice, new, and better-paid job (the one that Jezzer used to have), and it would mean that Jezzer would have to have a retrial and . . .

Wayne saw that she spoke with great wisdom and caved in gracefully. On what we think of as our "wedding night," he left a half-bottle of Happy Shopper champagne by the bedside. See? A considerate gesture doesn't have to cost much, does it?

Wayne understands that you've got to meet people in the middle, even if they are taggies.

We've just been sweeping the streets. Jezzer's changed a bit.

"I've done a Pareto Analysis," he said. "I don't expect that'd mean much to you, but it's an extremely powerful business tool that helps you direct resources more productively. Now look at this graph I've drawn. It shows how there are slightly more sweet wrappers in Elm Close, but a considerably larger concentration of cigarette ends – but, interestingly, almost no cigar butts – down in the park. The cigar butts are more randomly scattered, though they tend to be . . ."

"Jezzer," I said (I'm on rather more familiar terms with him these days), "shut up."

"Anyway, I've designed these survey forms for us to record distribution of litter according to area, time of day, and season. As you can see I've already coded them up, so's we can borrow a spreadsheet and database package with a view to optimizing our . . ."

I walked away. Mo was waiting for me on a garden wall.

This is all still wrong. Us being here. But Mo makes it okay. We will get out of here one day. And we will win.

Amanda and the Alien

ꟾ

Robert Silverberg

Amanda spotted the alien late Friday afternoon outside the Video Center, on South Main. It was trying to look cool and laid-back, but it simply came across as bewildered and uneasy. The alien was disguised as a seventeen-year-old girl, maybe a Chicana, with olive-toned skin and hair so black it seemed almost blue, but Amanda, who was seventeen herself, knew a phony when she saw one. She studied the alien for some moments from the other side of the street to make absolutely certain. Then she walked over.

"You're doing it wrong," Amanda said. "Anybody with half a brain could tell what you really are."

"Bug off," the alien said.

"No. Listen to me. You want to stay out of the detention center, or don't you?"

The alien stared coldly at Amanda and said, "I don't know what the crap you're talking about."

"Sure you do. No sense trying to bluff me. Look, I want to help you," Amanda said. "I think you're getting a raw deal. You know what that means, a raw deal? Hey, look, come home with me, and I'll teach you a few things about passing for human. I've got the whole friggin' weekend now with nothing else to do anyway"

A flicker of interest came into the other girl's dark, chilly eyes. But it died quickly, and she said, "You some kind of lunatic?"

"Suit yourself, O thing from beyond the stars. *Let* them lock you up again. *Let* them stick electrodes up your ass. I tried to help. That's all I can do, is try," Amanda said, shrugging. She began to saunter away. She didn't look back. Three steps, four, five, hands in pockets, slowly heading for her car. Had she been wrong, she wondered? No. No. She could be wrong about some things, like Charley Taylor's interest in spending the weekend with her, maybe. But not this. That crinkly-haired chick was the missing alien for sure.

The whole county was buzzing about it: Deadly nonhuman life form has escaped from the detention center out by Tracy, might be anywhere, Walnut Creek, Livermore, even San Francisco, dangerous monster, capable of mimicking human forms, will engulf and digest you and disguise itself in your shape. And there it was, Amanda knew, standing outside the Video Center. Amanda kept walking.

"Wait," the alien said finally.

Amanda took another easy step or two. Then she looked back over her shoulder.

"Yeah?"

"How can you tell?"

Amanda grinned. "Easy. You've got a rain slicker on, and it's only September. Rainy season doesn't start around here for another month or two. Your pants are the old Spandex kind. People like you don't wear that stuff anymore. Your face paint is San Jose colors, but you've got the cheek chevrons put on in the Berkeley pattern. That's just the first three things I noticed. I could find plenty more. Nothing about you fits together with anything else. It's like you did a survey to see how you ought to appear and then tried a little of everything. The closer I study you, the more I see. Look, you're wearing your headphones, and the battery light is on, but there's no cassette in the slot. What are you listening to, the music of the spheres? That model doesn't have any FM tuner, you know.

"You see? You may think that you're perfectly camouflaged, but you aren't."

"I could destroy you," the alien said.

"What? Oh, sure. Sure you could. Engulf me right here on the street, all over in thirty seconds, little trail of slime by the door, and a new Amanda walks away. But what then? What good's that going to do you? You still won't know which end is up. So there's no logic in destroying me, unless you're a total dummy. I'm on your side. I'm not going to turn you in."

"Why should I trust you?"

"Because I've been talking to you for five minutes and I haven't yelled for the cops yet. Don't you know that half of California is out searching for you? Hey, can you read? Come over here a minute. Here." Amanda tugged the alien toward the newspaper vending box at the curb. The headline on the afternoon *Examiner* was:

BAY AREA ALIEN TERROR
MARINES TO JOIN NINE-COUNTY HUNT
MAYOR, GOVERNOR CAUTION AGAINST PANIC

"You understand that?" Amanda asked. "That's you they're talking about. They're out there with flame guns, tranquilizer darts, web snares, and God knows what else. There's been real hysteria for a day and a half. And you standing around here with the wrong chevrons on! Christ. Christ! What's your plan, anyway? Where are you trying to go?"

"Home," the alien said. "But first I have to rendezvous at the pickup point."

"Where's that?"

"You think I'm stupid?"

"Shit," Amanda said. "If I meant to turn you in, I'd have done it five minutes ago. But, okay, I don't give a damn where your rendezvous point is. I tell you, though, you wouldn't make it as far as San Francisco rigged up the way you are. It's a miracle you've avoided getting caught until now."

"And you'll help me?"

"I've been trying to. Come on. Let's get the hell out of here. I'll take you home and fix you up a little. My car's in the lot down on the next corner."

"Okay."

"Whew!" Amanda shook her head slowly. "Christ, some people sure can't take help when you try to offer it."

As she drove out of the center of town, Amanda glanced occasionally at the alien sitting tensely to her right. Basically the disguise was very convincing, Amanda thought. Maybe all the small details were wrong, the outer stuff, the anthropological stuff, but the alien *looked* human, it *sounded* human, it even *smelled* human. Possibly it could fool ninety-nine people out of a hundred, or maybe more than that. But Amanda had always had a good eye for detail. And at the particular moment she had spotted the alien on South Main she had been unusually alert, sensitive, all raw nerves, every antenna up.

Of course it wasn't aliens she was hunting for, but just a diversion, a little excitement, something to fill the great gaping emptiness that Charley Taylor had left in her weekend.

Amanda had been planning the weekend with Charley all month. Her parents were going to go off to Lake Tahoe for three days, her kid sister had wangled permission to accompany them, and Amanda was going to have the house to herself, just her and Macavity the cat. And Charley. He was going to move in on Friday afternoon, and they'd cook dinner together and get blasted on her stash of choice powder and watch five or six of her parents' X-rated cassettes, and Saturday they'd drive over to the city and cruise some of the kinky districts and go to that bathhouse on Folsom where everybody got naked and climbed into the giant Jacuzzi, and then on Sunday – Well, none of that was going to happen. Charley had called on Thursday to cancel. "Something big came up," he said, and Amanda had a pretty good idea what that was, his hot little cousin from New Orleans, who sometimes came flying out here on no notice at all, but the inconsiderate bastard seemed to be entirely unaware of how much Amanda had been looking forward to this weekend, how much it meant to her, how painful it was to be dumped like this. She had run through the planned events of the weekend in her mind so many times that she almost felt as if she had experienced them. It was that real to her. But overnight it had become unreal.

Three whole days on her own, the house to herself, and so early in the semester that there was no homework to think about, and Charley had stood her up! What was she supposed to do now, call desperately around town to scrounge up some old lover as a playmate? Or pick up some stranger downtown? Amanda hated to fool around with strangers. She was half-tempted to go over to the city and just let things happen, but they were all weirdoes and creeps over there, anyway, and she knew what she could expect from them. What a waste, not having Charley! She could kill him for robbing her of the weekend.

Now there was the alien, though. A dozen of these star people had come to Earth last year, not in a flying saucer as everybody had expected, but in little capsules that floated like milkweed seeds, and they had landed in a wide arc between San Diego and Salt Lake City.

Their natural form, so far as anyone could tell, was something like a huge jellyfish with a row of staring purple eyes down one wavy margin, but their usual tactic was to borrow any local body they found, digest it, and turn themselves into an accurate imitation of it. One of them had made the mistake of turning itself into a brown mountain bear and another into a bobcat – maybe they thought that those were the dominant life forms on Earth – but the others had taken on human bodies, at the cost of at least ten lives.

Then they went looking to make contact with government leaders, and naturally they were rounded up very swiftly and interned, some in mental hospitals and some in county jails, but eventually – as soon as the truth of what they really were sank in – they were all put in a special detention camp in Northern California.

Of course a tremendous fuss was made over them, endless stuff in the papers and on the tube, speculation by this heavy thinker and that about the significance of their mission, the nature of their biochemistry, a little wild talk about the possibility that more of their kind might be waiting undetected out there and plotting to do God knows what, and all sorts of that stuff. Then came a government clamp on the entire subject, no official announcements except that "discussions" with the visitors were continuing, and after a while the whole thing degenerated into dumb alien jokes

("Why did the alien cross the road?") and Halloween invader masks. Then it moved into the background of everyone's attention and was forgotten.

And remained forgotten until the announcement that one of the creatures had slipped out of the camp somehow and was loose within a hundred-mile zone around San Francisco. Preoccupied as she was with her anguish over Charley's heartlessness, even Amanda had managed to pick up *that* news item. And now the alien was in her very car. So there'd be some weekend amusement for her after all. Amanda was entirely unafraid of the alleged deadliness of the star being: Whatever else the alien might be, it was surely no dope, not if it had been picked to come halfway across the galaxy on a mission like this, and Amanda knew that the alien could see that harming her was not going to be in its own best interests. The alien had need of her, and the alien realized that. And Amanda, in some way that she was only just beginning to work out, had need of the alien.

She pulled up outside her house, a compact split-level at the western end of town. "This is the place," she said.

Heat shimmers danced in the air, and the hills in the back of the house, parched in the long dry summer, were the color of lions.

Macavity, Amanda's old tabby, sprawled in the shade of the bottlebrush tree on the ragged front lawn. As Amanda and the alien approached, the cat sat up warily, flattened his ears, and hissed. The alien immediately moved into a defensive posture, sniffing the air.

"Just a household pet," Amanda said. "You know what that is? He isn't dangerous. He's always a little suspicious of strangers."

Which was untrue. An earthquake couldn't have brought Macavity out of his nap, and a cotillion of mice dancing minuets on his tail wouldn't have drawn a reaction from him. Amanda calmed him with some fur ruffling, but he wanted nothing to do with the alien and went slinking sullenly into the underbrush. The alien watched him with care until he was out of sight.

"Do you have anything like cats back on your planet?" Amanda asked as they went inside.

"We had small wild animals once. They were unnecessary."

"Oh," Amanda said, losing interest. The house had a stuffy, stagnant air. She switched on the air conditioning. "Where is your planet, anyway?"

The alien pointedly ignored the question. It padded around the living room, very much like a prowling cat itself, studying the stereo, the television, the couches, the coffee table, and the vase of dried flowers.

"Is this a typical Earthian home?"

"More or less," said Amanda. "Typical for around here, at least. This is what we call a suburb. It's half an hour by freeway from here to San Francisco. That's a city. I'll take you over there tonight or tomorrow for a look, if you're interested." She got some music going, high volume. The alien didn't seem to mind; so she notched the volume up even more. "I'm going to take a shower. You could use one, too, actually."

"Shower? You mean rain?"

"I mean body-cleaning activities. We Earthlings like to wash a lot, to get rid of sweat and dirt and stuff. It's considered bad form to stink. Come on, I'll show you how to do it. You've got to do what I do if you want to keep from getting caught, you know." She led the alien to the bathroom. "Take your clothes off first."

The alien stripped. Underneath its rain slicker it wore a stained T-shirt that said FISHERMAN'S WHARF, with a picture of the San Francisco skyline, and a pair of unzipped jeans. Under that it was wearing a black brassiere, unfastened and with the cups over its shoulder blades, and a pair of black shiny panty-briefs with a red heart on the left buttock. The alien's body was that of a lean, tough-looking girl with a scar running down the inside of one arm.

"By the way, whose body is that?" Amanda asked. "Do you know?"

"She worked at the detention center. In the kitchen."

"You know her name?"

"Flores Concepcion."

"The other way around, probably. Concepcion Flores. I'll call you Connie, unless you want to give me your real name."

"Connie will do."

"All right, Connie. Pay attention. You turn the water on here, and you adjust the mix of hot and cold until you like it. Then you pull this knob and get underneath the spout here and wet your body and rub soap over it and wash the soap off. Afterward you dry yourself and put fresh clothes on. You have to clean your clothes from time to time, too, because otherwise *they* start to smell, and it upsets people. Watch me shower, and then you do it."

Amanda washed quickly, while plans hummed in her head. The alien wasn't going to last long wearing the body of Concepcion Flores. Sooner or later someone was going to notice that one of the kitchen girls was missing, and they'd get an all-points alarm out for her. Amanda wondered whether the alien had figured that out yet. The alien, Amanda thought, needs a different body in a hurry.

But not mine, she told herself. For sure, not mine.

"Your turn," she said casually, shutting the water off.

The alien, fumbling a little, turned the water back on and got under the spray. Clouds of steam rose, and its skin began to look boiled, but it didn't appear troubled. No sense of pain? "Hold it," Amanda said. "Step back." She adjusted the water. "You've got it too hot. You'll damage that body that way. Look, if you can't tell the difference between hot and cold, just take cold showers, okay? It's less dangerous. This is cold, on this side."

She left the alien under the shower and went to find some clean clothes. When she came back, the alien was still showering, under icy water. "Enough," Amanda said. "Here. Put these clothes on."

"I had more clothes than this before."

"A T-shirt and jeans are all you need in hot weather like this. With your kind of build you can skip the bra, and anyway I don't think you'll be able to fasten it the right way."

"Do we put the face paint on now?"

"We can skip it while we're home. It's just stupid kid stuff anyway, all that tribal crap. If we go out we'll do it, and we'll give you Walnut Creek colors, I think. Concepcion wore San Jose, but we want to throw people off the track. How about some dope?"

"What?"

"Grass. Marijuana. A drug widely used by local Earthians of our age."

"I don't need no drug."

"I don't, either. But I'd *like* some. You ought to learn how, just in case you find yourself in a social situation." Amanda reached for her pack of Filter Golds and pulled out a joint. Expertly she tweaked its lighter tip and took a deep hit. "Here," she said, passing it. "Hold it like I did. Put it to your mouth, breathe in, suck the smoke deep." The alien dragged the joint and began to cough. "Not so deep, maybe," Amanda said. "Take just a little. Hold it. Let it out. There, much better. Now give me back the joint. You've got to keep passing it back and forth. That part's important. You feel anything from it?"

"No."

"It can be subtle. Don't worry about it. Are you hungry?"

"Not yet," the alien said.

"I am. Come into the kitchen." As she assembled a sandwich – peanut butter and avocado on whole wheat, with tomato and onion – she asked, "What sort of things do you guys eat?"

"Life."

"Life?"

"We never eat dead things. Only things with life."

Amanda fought back a shudder. "I see. *Anything* with life?"

"We prefer animal life. We can absorb plants if necessary."

"Ah. Yes. And when are you going to be hungry again?"

"Maybe tonight," the alien said. "Or tomorrow. The hunger comes very suddenly, when it comes."

"There's not much around here that you could eat live. But I'll work on it."

"The small furry animal?"

"No. My cat is not available for dinner. Get that idea right out of your head. Likewise me. I'm your protector and guide. It wouldn't be sensible to eat me. You follow what I'm trying to tell you?"

"I said that I'm not hungry yet."

"Well, you let me know when you start feeling the pangs. I'll find you a meal." Amanda began to construct a second sandwich.

The alien prowled the kitchen, examining the appliances. Perhaps making mental records, Amanda thought, of sink and oven design, to copy on its home world. Amanda said, "Why did you people come here in the first place?"

"It was our mission."

"Yes. Sure. But for what purpose? What are you after? You want to take over the world? You want to steal our scientific secrets?" The alien, making no reply, began taking spices out of the spice rack. Delicately it licked its finger, touched it to the oregano, tasted it, tried the cumin. Amanda said, "Or is it that you want to keep us from going into space? You think we're a dangerous species, and so you're going to quarantine us on our own planet? Come on, you can tell me. I'm not a government spy." The alien sampled the tarragon, the basil, the sage. When it reached for the curry powder, its hand suddenly shook so violently that it knocked the open jars of oregano and tarragon over, making a mess. "Hey, are you all right?" Amanda asked.

The alien said, "I think I'm getting hungry. Are these things drugs, too?"

"Spices," Amanda said. "We put them in our foods to make them taste better." The alien was looking very strange, glassy-eyed, flushed, sweaty. "Are you feeling sick or something?"

"I feel excited. These powders – "

"They're turning you on? Which one?"

"This, I think." It pointed to the oregano. "It was either the first one or the second."

"Yeah," Amanda said. "Oregano. It can really make you fly." She wondered whether the alien would get violent when zonked. Or whether the oregano would stimulate its appetite. She had to watch out for its appetite. There are certain risks, Amanda reflected, in doing what I'm doing. Deftly she cleaned up the spilled oregano and tarragon and put the caps on the spice jars. "You ought to be careful," she said. "Your metabolism isn't used to this stuff. A little can go a long way."

"Give me some more."

"Later," Amanda said. "You don't want to overdo it too early in the day."

"More!"

"Calm down. I know this planet better than you, and I don't want to see you get in trouble. Trust me. I'll let you have more oregano when it's the right time. Look at the way you're shaking. And you're sweating like crazy." Pocketing the oregano jar, she led the alien back into the living room. "Sit down. Relax."

"More? Please?"

"I appreciate your politeness. But we have important things to talk about, and then I'll give you some. Okay?" Amanda opaqued the window, through which the hot late-afternoon sun was coming. Six o'clock on Friday, and if everything had gone the right way Charley would have been showing up just about now. Well, she'd found a different diversion. The weekend stretched before her like an open road leading to mysteryland. The alien offered all sorts of possibilities, and she might yet have some fun over the next few days, if she used her head. Amanda turned to the alien and said, "You calmer now? Yes. Good. Okay, first of all, you've got to get yourself another body."

"Why is that?"

"I've reasons. One is that the authorities are probably searching for the girl you absorbed. How you got as far as you did without anybody but me spotting you is hard to understand. Number two, a teen-aged girl traveling by herself is going to get hassled too much, and you don't know how to handle yourself in a tight situation. You know what I'm saying? You're going to want to hitchhike out to Nevada, Wyoming, Utah, wherever the hell your rendezvous place is, and all along the way people are going to be coming on to you. You don't need any of that. Besides, it's very tricky trying to pass for a girl. You've got to know how to put your face paint on, how to understand challenge codes, what the way you wear your clothing says, and like that. Boys have a much simpler subculture. You get yourself a male body, a big hunk of a body, and nobody'll bother you much on the way to where you're going. You just keep to yourself, don't make eye contact, don't smile, and everyone will leave you alone."

"Makes sense," said the alien. "All right. The hunger is becoming very bad now. Where do I get a male body?"

"San Francisco. It's full of men. We'll go over there tonight and find a nice brawny one for you. With any luck we might even find one who's not gay, and then we can have a little fun with him first. And then you take his body over – which incidentally solves your food problem for a while doesn't it? And we can have some more fun, a whole weekend of fun." Amanda winked. "Okay, Connie?"

"Okay." The alien winked, a clumsy imitation, first one eye, then the other. "You give me more oregano now?"

"Later. And when you wink, just wink *one* eye. Like this. Except I don't think you ought to do a lot of winking at people. It's a very intimate gesture that could get you in trouble. Understand?"

"There's so much to understand."

"You're on a strange planet, kid. Did you expect it to be just like home? Okay, to continue. The next thing I ought to point out is that when you leave here on Sunday, you'll have to – "

The telephone rang.

"What's that sound?" the alien asked.

"Communications device. I'll be right back." Amanda went to the hall extension, imagining the worst: her parents, say, calling to announce that they were on their way back from Tahoe tonight, some mix-up in the reservations or something.

But the voice that greeted her was Charley's. She could hardly believe it, after the casual way he had shafted her this weekend. She could hardly believe what he wanted, either. He had left half a dozen of his best cassettes at her place last week, Golden Age rock, Abbey Road and the Hendrix one and a Joplin and such, and now he was heading off to Monterey for the festival and wanted to have them for the drive. Did she mind if he stopped off in half an hour to pick them up?

The bastard, she thought. The absolute trashiness of him! First to torpedo her weekend without even an apology, and then to let her know that he and what's-her-name were scooting down to Monterey for some fun, and could he bother her for his cassettes? Didn't he think she had any feelings? She looked at the telephone as if it were emitting toads and scorpions. It was tempting to hang up on him.

She resisted the temptation. "As it happens," she said, "I'm just on my way out for the weekend myself. But I've got a friend who's staying here cat-sitting for me. I'll leave the cassettes with her, okay? Her name's Connie."

"Fine. That's great," Charley said. "I really appreciate that, Amanda."

"It's nothing," she said.

The alien was back in the kitchen, nosing around the spice rack. But Amanda had the oregano. She said, "I've arranged for delivery of your next body."

"You did?"

"A large healthy adolescent male. Exactly what you're looking for. He's going to be here in a little while. I'm going to go out for a drive. You take care of him before I get back. How long does it take for you to – engulf – somebody?"

"It's very fast."

"Good." Amanda found Charley's cassettes and stacked them on the living-room table. "He's coming over here to get these six little boxes, which are music-storage devices. When the doorbell rings, you let him in and introduce yourself as Connie and tell him his things are on this table. After that you're on your own. You think you can handle it?"

"Sure," the alien said.

"Tuck in your T-shirt better. When it's tight, it makes your boobs stick out, and that'll distract him. Maybe he'll even make a pass at you. What happens to the Connie body after you engulf him?"

"It won't be here. What happens is I merge with him and dissolve all the Connie characteristics and take on the new ones."

"Ah. Very nifty. You're a real nightmare thing, you know? You're a walking horror show. Here you are, have another little hit of oregano before I go."

She put a tiny pinch of spice in the alien's hand. "Just to warm up your engine a little. I'll give you more later, when you've done the job. See you in an hour, okay?"

She left the house. Macavity was sitting on the porch, scowling, whipping his tail from side to side. Amanda knelt beside him and scratched him behind the ears. The cat made a low, rough purring sound, not much like his usual purr.

Amanda said, "You aren't happy, are you, fella? Well, don't worry. I've told the alien to leave you alone, and I guarantee you'll be okay. This is Amanda's fun tonight. You don't mind if Amanda has a little fun, do you?" Macavity made a glum, snuffling sound. "Listen, maybe I can get the alien to create a nice little calico cutie for you, okay? Just going into heat and ready to howl. Would you like that, guy? Would you? I'll see what I can do when I get back. But I have to clear out of here now, before Charley shows up."

She got into her car and headed for the westbound freeway ramp. Half past six, Friday night, the sun still hanging high above the Bay. Traffic was thick in the eastbound lanes, the late commuters slogging toward home, and it was beginning to build up westbound, too, as people set out for dinner in San Francisco. Amanda drove through the tunnel and turned north into Berkeley to cruise city streets. Ten minutes to seven now. Charley must have arrived. She imagined Connie in her tight T-shirt, all stoned and sweaty on oregano, and Charley giving her the eye, getting ideas, thinking about grabbing a bonus quickie before taking off with his cassettes. And Connie leading him on, Charley making his moves, and then suddenly that electric moment of surprise as the alien struck and Charley found himself turning into dinner. It could be happening right this minute, Amanda thought placidly. No more than the bastard deserves, isn't it? She had felt for a long time that Charley was a big mistake in her life, and after what he had pulled yesterday, she was sure of it. No more than he deserves.

But, she wondered, what if Charley has brought his weekend date along? The thought chilled her. She hadn't considered that possibility at all. It could ruin everything.

Connie wasn't able to engulf two at once, was she? And suppose they recognized her as the missing alien and ran out screaming to call the cops?

No, she thought. Not even Charley would be so tacky as to bring his date over to Amanda's house tonight. And Charley never watched the news or read a paper.

He wouldn't have a clue as to what Connie really was until it was too late for him to run.

Seven o'clock. Time to head for home.

The sun was sinking behind her as she turned onto the freeway. By quarter past she was approaching her house. Charley's old red Honda was parked outside.

Amanda parked across the street and cautiously let herself in, pausing just inside the front door to listen.

Silence.

"Connie?"

"In here," said Charley's voice.

Amanda entered the living room. Charley was sprawled out comfortably on the couch. There was no sign of Connie.

"Well?" Amanda said. "How did it go?"

"Easiest thing in the world," the alien said. "He was sliding his hands under my T-shirt when I let him have the nullifier jolt."

"Ah. The nullifier jolt."

"And then I completed the engulfment and cleaned up the carpet. God, it feels good not to be hungry again. You can't imagine how tough it was to resist engulfing you, Amanda. For the past hour I kept thinking of food, food, food – "

"Very thoughtful of you to resist."

"I knew you were out to help me. It's logical not to engulf one's allies."

"That goes without saying. So you feel well fed now? He was good stuff?"

"Robust, healthy, nourishing – yes."

"I'm glad Charley turned out to be good for something. How long before you get hungry again?"

The alien shrugged. "A day or two. Maybe three. Give me more oregano, Amanda?"

"Sure," she said. "Sure." She felt a little let down. Not that she was remorseful about Charley, exactly, but it all seemed so casual, so offhanded – there was something anticlimactic about it, in a way. She suspected she should have stayed and watched while it was happening. Too late for that now, though.

She took the oregano from her purse and dangled the jar teasingly. “Here it is, babe. But you’ve got to earn it first.”

“What do you mean?”

“I mean that I was looking forward to a big weekend with Charley, and the weekend is here. Charley’s here, too, more or less, and I’m ready for fun. Come show me some fun, big boy.”

She slipped Charley’s Hendrix cassette into the tape deck and turned the volume all the way up.

The alien looked puzzled. Amanda began to peel off her clothes.

“You, too,” Amanda said. “Come on. You won’t have to dig deep into Charley’s mind to figure out what to do. You’re going to be my Charley for me this weekend, you follow? You and I are going to do all the things that he and I were going to do. Okay? Come on. Come on.” She beckoned.

The alien shrugged again and slipped out of Charley’s clothes, fumbling with the unfamiliarities of his zipper and buttons. Amanda, grinning, drew the alien close against her and down to the living-room floor. She took its hands and put them where she wanted them to be. She whispered instructions. The alien, docile, obedient, did what she wanted.

It felt like Charley. It smelled like Charley. And after her instructions, it even moved pretty much the way Charley moved.

But it wasn’t Charley, it wasn’t Charley at all, and after the first few seconds Amanda knew that she had goofed things up very badly. You couldn’t just ring in an imitation like this. Making love with this alien was like making love with a very clever machine, or with her own mirror image. It was empty and meaningless and dumb.

Grimly she went on to the finish. They rolled apart, panting, sweating.

“Well?” The alien said. “Did the earth move for you?”

“Yeah. Yeah. It was terrific – Charley.”

“Oregano?”

“Sure,” Amanda said. She handed the spice jar across. “I always keep my promises, babe. Go to it. Have yourself a blast. Just remember that that’s strong stuff for guys from your planet, okay? If you pass out, I’m going to leave you right there on the floor.”

"Don't worry about me."

"Okay. You have your fun. I'm going to clean up, and then maybe we'll go over to San Francisco for the nightlife. Does that interest you?"

"You bet, Amanda." The alien winked – one eye, then the other – and gulped a huge pinch of oregano. "That sounds terrific."

Amanda gathered up her clothes, went upstairs for a quick shower, and dressed. When she came down, the alien was more than half blown away on the oregano, goggle-eyed, loll-headed, propped up against the couch, and crooning to itself in a weird atonal way. Fine, Amanda thought. You just get yourself all spiced up, love. She took the portable phone from the kitchen, carried it with her into the bathroom, locked the door, and quietly dialed the police emergency number.

She was bored with the alien. The game had worn thin very quickly. And it was crazy, she thought, to spend the whole weekend cooped up with a dangerous extraterrestrial creature when there wasn't going to be any fun in it for her. She knew now that there couldn't be any fun at all. And besides, in a day or two the alien was going to get hungry again.

"I've got your alien," she said. "Sitting in my living room, stoned out of its head on oregano. Yes, I'm absolutely certain. It was disguised as a Chicana girl first, Conception Flores, but then it attacked my boyfriend, Charley Taylor, and – yes, yes, I'm safe. I'm locked in the john. Just get somebody over here fast – okay. I'll stay on the line – what happened was, I spotted it downtown outside the video center, and it insisted on coming home with me – "

The actual capture took only a few minutes. But there was no peace for hours after the police tactical squad hauled the alien away, because the media was in on the act right away, first a team from Channel 2 in Oakland, and then some of the network guys, and then the *Chronicle,* and finally a whole army of reporters from as far away as Sacramento, and phone calls from Los Angeles and San Diego and – about three that morning – New York.

Amanda told the story again and again until she was sick of it, and just as dawn was breaking, she threw the last of them out and barred the door.

She wasn't sleepy at all. She felt wired up, speedy and depressed all at once. The alien was gone, Charley was gone and she was all alone. She was going to be famous for the next couple of days, but that wouldn't help. She'd still be alone. For a time she wandered around the house, looking at it the way an alien might, as if she had never seen a stereo cassette before, or a television set, or a rack of spices. The smell of oregano was everywhere. There were little trails of it on the floor.

Amanda switched on the radio and there she was on the six A.M. news. " – the emergency is over, thanks to the courageous Walnut Creek High School girl who trapped and outsmarted the most dangerous life form in the known universe – "

She shook her head. "You think that's true?" she asked the cat. "Most dangerous life form in the universe? I don't think so, Macavity, I think I know of at least one that's a lot deadlier. Eh, kid?" She winked. "If they only knew, eh? If they only knew." She scooped the cat up and hugged it, and it began to purr. Maybe trying to get a little sleep would be a good idea. Then she had to figure out what she was going to do about the rest of the weekend.

Diary from an Empty Studio

ഋിര

Don Webb

Day 1. I couldn't paint when I took the medicine.

If I laid off for a few days the images would come and I could finish a canvas, but there was always the danger that I would forget who was doing the painting, or maybe even right and wrong. So I started this diary. I'll read it every day and write in it every day and that way I won't get in trouble like that other time. Yesterday I prepared a canvas. Today I put my medicine aside. Tomorrow I'll start my sketches.

Day 2. My name is Tyrone Watson. I am. I live in Austin, Texas. There, that seems pretty sane. I don't think it's a good idea to kill one's critics. Violence has no special beauty. If I want to get people, I'll just caricature them. I work for Roberta Sais.

I started today on *The Market of Values*, which will be a study in blues and grays of people at some sort of carnival buying and selling things of no value. Maybe I'll work in miniatures of Bessie Vollman's paintings.

Day 3. Ideas are getting really slippery today. It feels great. My sketchbook is filling up and *Market*'s coming along. Oh I forgot to do my focusing mantra.

My name is Tyrone Watson, MFA. I have had two one-man exhibitions. The last was five years ago.

There that's in control. In fact the only control problem I have is wanting to spend all my time up here painting instead of down in the shop, but that's normal. Artists want to do art. It's a pity that business hours coincide with the light being good.

Day 4. Depressed today.

Day 5. Depressed today. Did nothing. Got mad.

Day 6. My name is Tyrone Watson. I am thirty-eight. I live in Austin. I had a great day. A Mr. Simon Pound had a lot to ask me about my art. Maybe I'm in for a comeback. I started to take him upstairs and show him my work in progress, but a little voice told me not to. I don't mean a little voice like before, I just mean a hunch, that feeling of not letting people in on it until you're ready. I got a lot done today. *Market* should be finished tomorrow.

Day 7. Finished *Market*. Not as good as I had hoped, but still that's the essence of the artistic personality. Always dissatisfied. Like Faust. I'm starting something more freeform, a response to those people who caused me so much trouble. I'm going to call it *Exposed Heart*. I'm not sure how to start. Well, an idea suggests itself, but not a good one. My name is Tyrone Watson. I'm a thirty- something painter on the go.

Day 8. Busy.

Day 9. Spent several hours with my model.

Day 10. Mr. Pound came by today. I was disappointed to learn he wasn't an art critic. He is a retired cop. His life story seemed pretty interesting. Maybe I'll do him after *Exposed Heart* which is coming along nicely thank you. It's a little bit more gory than anything I've done in years.

Day 11. My name is Tyrone Watson. Today Mr. Pound came by and we discussed our life stories, which were amazingly similar. I want to get to know him because I'm going to do a picture of him called *The Multidimensional Blue Lines*.

He became a cop in the seventies. His big ambition from the first was to make detective. He studied every text on criminology, took every possible course and dedicated his life to that particular transformation, but various political forces downtown saw to it that he didn't make the grade.

I told him how critics had ruined my two shows, particularly the second show when Bessie Vollman's competing exhibition won such lavish praise. She had been the more "politically correct" artist. So her career took off and I managed a used bookstore for minimum wage and free studio space.

He asked if he could see my work in progress, and I told him no. I hate anyone to see something before I'm done with it. But I told him that I was interested in painting him. At first he seemed surprised, then readily agreed.

He asked me if I knew anything about the death of two art critics five years ago.

I asked him if he was still a cop.

He said that he quit the force a couple of years ago. He'd arrested too many criminals who got off on technicalities. So he quit. He was near enough retirement anyway and he had a few investments that had paid off well. He liked to keep his hand in. The police, he assured me, at least the good cops – the real force – still called him for advice.

I asked him how long he'd been interested in art. He said that every good cop is interested in art. The artistic mind and the criminal mind are very, very similar. Most criminals, he reasoned, were failed artists.

But criminals don't have critics, I told him.

"Of course they do," he said. "Cops, they catch inept criminals. The great criminals go free."

I had never thought of a cop as a critic for a criminal's art.

Day 12. Terrible dreams last night. I was too depressed to open the store.

Day 13. It's been almost two weeks and I'm doing fine. Maybe I'm over my trouble. My name is Tyrone Watson. Elementary, my dear Watson. Someone broke into the shop last night. They didn't take anything, but I think they may have been through my studio. Both the outside door and the studio door were open. Despite this I can't tell you how GREAT I feel. I started two different paintings this morning. I started to call the owner and tell her the shop had been broken into, but realized that would screw up my process. I painted like Picasso. I'll stay here at night. Maybe I'll catch my burglar and paint him. I'm ready. I'm ready for anything. I feel GREAT!

Day 14. I painted well into the night and finished my first painting; a riotous and much spangled study in purple and green called *The Water People Are Talking to Me*. I went out for a walk about 3 A.M. I needed inspiration for the second piece – a study in chrome yellow called *Voltman Discharges*. Oh what a wonderful great buzzy great picture! Zip zip, I say, zip zap.

Day 15. Mr. Pound came by with the news about Bessie Vollman. I felt really really bad for a moment as though it had something to do with me. I suppose that shows I have a great soul that I can feel sorry for a rival. I asked to see the obituary notice since he was carrying the paper. Sure enough although I was Bessie's greatest rival I wasn't mentioned. Maybe I should send a wreath or something, after all I would be remembered a hundred years hence and she will be forgotten. Maybe I should go to the funeral to do a second painting of her.

Mr. Pound told me that he was unable to find any references to my one-man show five years ago. He said he was hoping to see some photos of my previous work. He seemed genuinely sad when I told him that it had all been purchased by Japanese investors.

Did I have unsold pieces that I might consider parting with?

Of course I had to tell him that I sold everything a few years ago when devastating poverty took hold of my life.

We all have our ups and downs, he said. He is truly a wise man for a cop.

I asked him when he would come sit for me and he became agitated. I guess the thought of sitting for eternity is frightening to some. It brings out that fear that their flaws, that one tiny flaw that everybody has, might be magnified through the ages. After a while all they would be would be the flaw.

My name is Vincent van Gogh and I'm one-hundred-and-thirty-eight years old. Just kidding.

Day 16. I dreamt I was a child again. It must've been when I was in the sixth grade. We had an art teacher who we went to see twice a week. She gave us the assignment of drawing something on the schoolyard, so I drew the blue portable toilets that had been placed on the football field. I could see them from my desk if I craned my neck over. The bell rang and class was over and I was supposed to have the picture finished by the end of the period. Mrs. Elgood came over and told me to give it to her. That I could work on it Thursday. I said just a minute I could finish it and then it was done and I handed it to her, and she said, "Tyrone, there is nothing like this outside." I told her to look and she wouldn't look and I told her to look and she wouldn't look so I took hold of her head and tried to make her look and I pushed her face through the glass and she bled.

Then I woke up and all I can say is she should have looked.

I reread my entry for yesterday. I am really mad that the newspaper files have been tampered with. Maybe I'll go paint all of them. I'll paint every fucking critic into a corner. I was too mad to open the shop today. I heard some people knocking and the damn phone kept ringing. Ring a ding a ding until I took it off the hook. Probably the damn owner. I'll take care of her too. You shouldn't disturb a genius at work. There should be a law. I painted a bright red and orange painting today. *Angry Sun Bites Man*. I'll open up tomorrow.

Day 17. Depressed and mad.

Day 18. The police banged and banged on my door. Mr. Pound wasn't with them. They wanted to know if I knew that Ms. Roberta Sais, who owned the Book Cellar (and who in theory is my employer) had died. No, I said, I didn't know. Murdered, they said. No, I said, I didn't know. I was very busy. I had to work on my paintings. I thanked them for the news. She had heirs, they said. I said I always thought she put on airs. Heirs, they said, I should close the shop until the heirs came. And I said good. I made a "Closed on Account of Death" sign and hung it in the door.

In the afternoon Mr. Pound came by and pounded on my door until I answered it. I told him we were closed.

He said he was here to pose.

I let him in to do some sketches. He started to go upstairs to my studio. I told him I do my sketches in the shop. He wasn't easy to sketch because he kept talking. He hinted that he was a vigilante going after criminals the system might let off on some technicality – like no Miranda rights. Lots of stories of cars in the nights. For some reason I pictured them as moving silently and without headlights. "Dark of night doesn't stop you, eh?" I asked.

He reacted violently, then chuckled, and said, "No, dark of night doesn't stop me."

He talked a lot about criminals who made their confessions got off easily. With his pull down at the station he could help such a criminal. If the criminal doing the murders now were, say, to confess to him, he could make it very easy on the guy.

If on the other hand the current murderer were to try to weasel out – to escape from the long arm of the law – he would make it very difficult for him. He would track the murderer down and strike when the killer least expected it.

He didn't ask to see my sketches, which was good, because I wasn't pleased with them. When he left I tore them all up in little pieces.

I am going to sleep in the studio tonight – to protect my paintings. I am worried about them somehow.

Day 19. Today I painted *The Last Innocent Man*. The picture is full of big blue eyes looking everywhere. In the lower right corner is a single yellow square – representing a window. Inside an artist can be seen painting a flowery peaceful landscape. I may change the title to *This Is My Skull*.

Day 20. This morning I came to my senses and took my medicine. I realized I must have done some pretty bad things. I figured I'd wait for Mr. Pound, and when he came I'd confess to him. He could make it easy for me. He was my friend. I waited all day, but he didn't show.

About six I called the downtown police station. Mr. Pound had told me that he still had friends on the force. I figured I could ask around and they could put me in touch with him. It took forever to get in touch with homicide. While I waited I cursed myself for not having got his number. Then I got Detective Blick. I asked if he knew Mr. Pound.

"Mr. Clarence Pound?" he asked.

"I'm not sure of his first name. He is a retired policeman. He had told me he still had friends on the force."

"Let me guess, he told you that he tried to make detective but 'political forces' kept him from making the grade. He also said that he was a vigilante, bringing criminals to justice who had escaped their just desserts."

"Well, yes," I said.

"I am sorry to tell you this, sir, but Clarence Pound is a retired postal worker with some severe personality problems. Every few months he stops his medication for a while and gets to thinking he's some super-cop. If he's been bothering you, let me know and we'll pick him up and take him to his doctor."

"No. He hasn't been bothering me at all. Thank you."

I hung up as he was asking "Who are – "

Mr. Pound is some kind of nut. I'll have to be ready for him.

Day 21. I slept in the studio and he broke in. I woke up and saw him looking at my paintings. He had a gun in one hand and a flashlight in the other.

"They're blank," he said. "All of these canvasses just painted white."

"No," I said, "They're very subtle. You must study them carefully."

"They're blank. You're some kind of nut."

"No, you're the nut. You're an ex-postal employee. You're not a cop. You've never been a cop."

"That's not true." He pointed the gun at me.

"It is true. You're not a cop."

Suddenly he sat down. Just sort of collapsed. He didn't say anything for a long time. I thought about going over and taking his gun away.

Then he began to talk in a low monotone. He explained who he really was and everything became clear to me.

He is Mr. Carlos Pound, owner of a very important gallery in New York. Today we are putting my paintings into a U-Haul van. We will drive up to New York, where he'll host a one-man show for me.

I bet we make quite a splash.

Is That Hard Science, or Are You Just Happy to See Me?

ꕥ

Leslie What

Independence Day – Fourth Of July – Fireworks Begin

I was waiting in the hallway so I could be first to hear the doorbell, but Mother still beat me to the door. She held the spy clam gingerly, like finger cymbals, and its green light blinked to signal readiness. The spy clamshell was gray textured aluminum that looked both comical and scary; in fact, it was always that way at my house – you never knew whether to laugh or cry.

I said, "Oh, Mother!"

But she said, "Ginny, we have to know," and opened the door.

Jason took a step forward. He shrieked when the spy clam opened and its foot reached out, grabbing hold of his skin, to measure his temperature, blood pressure, and psychological profile. His freckles began to sweat – I never knew freckles could sweat – and though he stood as tall as the doorframe, he slouched enough that Mother looked bigger by comparison. He checked me out, as if trying to decide if I was worth dealing with *her*. I had already promised to make it worth his time, but I could tell he was having second thoughts.

Mother glanced at the readout, her eyes narrowing as the foot slowly retracted. The clam snapped shut, and a faint buzzing sounded. She already knew what Jason was thinking – she didn't need a spy clam for that. He was seventeen, same as me. He was thinking about things a seventeen-year-old thinks about and what would happen next. Mother was forty and was thinking about *then.* Her then, and all the trouble she'd gotten into.

She punched the ready button on my cattle-prod pants and said, "Okay. I guess you can go out with John."

"Jason," I said.

"Whatever," said Mother.

The prod pants fit like oven mitts, wired and preset to a maximum of stun. Wearing them made me feel huge, like I was a girl Michelin Tire Man. The pants had made Mother, their inventor, rich. Millions of units were in use across the globe, and so far there had only been five fatalities, from heart failure. Mother had used the profits to develop the Smart Twat and a lot of other weird surveillance technologies, most of which she tested on me.

It was the hot part of the afternoon, and I was boiling inside my pants. I could smell my own body odor above the sweet scent of deodorant and baby powder. Mother didn't care that it embarrassed me to sweat. God, she was crazy. No wonder the CIA had rejected her application.

I couldn't wait to get out of the house.

"Later," I said, clutching my purse and hoping she didn't search it.

"Nice to meet you, Mrs. Vuoto," said Jason.

"Ms.," Mother said.

"Whatever," said Jason, and I rushed him out the door and into his van.

The seats smelled a little sour, like summer sweat and brake fluid. I unrolled my window. The whoosh of air released the scented evergreen from Jason's paper tree air-freshener across the seat. We drove off.

"Did you get the tickets?" I asked.

Jason reached in his shirt pocket and fanned out two stubs.

Our alibi was going to the movies – a *Star Wars* marathon. That gave us time to fool around, eat, and even actually see a few episodes after, if we felt like it. Jason drove past the lumberyards, out of town, and onto the Mackenzie Highway. The thick trees shrouded the road, their shadow lowering the temperature enough that I stopped sweating. He passed the Leeburg Dam and drove over a narrow bridge. He turned left and eased the car onto a gravel road leading to the river. He parked. Once the engine was off, I heard the drone of flies and mosquitoes and I rolled up the window to keep them out. I began to sweat again.

Jason was all over me while I was still trying to figure out what to do in response. It wasn't easy knowing how far to take things. My pants emitted a warning beep, followed by a test buzz.

He pressed against me and thrust his tongue into my mouth. He reached beneath my shirt to fondle my breasts. In a minute I stopped caring that Mother was, no doubt at this very moment, watching the readouts that showed what we were up to. Jason pushed me back against the seat. As his hard crotch rocked against me and my breathing quickened to match his, I felt a tingling begin at the base of my spine and radiate outward. I thought I was having an orgasm, my first, but too late recognized that the tingling announced an impending discharge of electricity.

My pants came in a jolt of sparks and current and heat. I shrieked in shock as Jason shrieked in pain, then rolled away. Damn it! I could have dry-humped until morning!

"What the fuck?" he asked, drooling, his hair disheveled and eyes red and watery.

"I'm sorry," I said. "Really sorry."

He drove me home. We didn't speak. I never saw him again.

Merck Prescription Information, advertisement in the *Journal of the American Medical Association* (*JAMA*) – Brief Summary (for full prescribing information see professional information brochure):
S.M.A.R.T. utilizes technologies of lie detection, laboratory testing, and skin and mood sensors to detect the presence of HIV, STDs, and changes in EEG and cognitive abilities that suggest the presence of stress and deceitful behavior.

Indications and Usage

S.M.A.R.T. is available in a permeable chip designed to be implanted into subcutaneous fat, generally in the thigh, and is indicated for use in the prevention of sexual encounters. It may be used alone or in combination with other desensitizing agents.

Hiroshima Day – August 6 – The First Bomb Drops

I got off restriction and immediately got a date with some guy named Billy that I once met at the mall. Mother had retrofitted my cattle-prod pants with a tracking device, but I thought I had figured out a way to outwit her. Billy was my test drive. I couldn't wait to get out of my pants and hit the road.

I stocked my backpack with supplies and said I was going to the library. When I got there, I ducked into the bathroom, broke open the instant hot pack, and exchanged my cattle-prod pants for a pair of jeans. I duct-taped the hot pack an inch below the thermostat and GPS sensors in the crotch, carefully placed the pants in my backpack, then carried the backpack over to the information desk.

"Can you hold this for a while?" I said. "I forgot my library card and need to run back home and get it."

"Sure," said the librarian.

I gave her my pack, which she set under the counter, where it would be safe until I reclaimed it before the library closed.

Excerpt from the September 20 *Times Picayune* front page:

Republican Senator Hieronymus Bartholomew Bush of Jefferson Parish resigned yesterday after allegations that he had fathered three illegitimate children by three different women. Senator Bush's legislative career has been marred by controversy since it was revealed that his election was financed by the five-million-member Chastity Party, whose members helped to vault him from a relative unknown to a figure of national prominence. His campaign platform promised a return to family values, and he successfully sponsored several bills that provided tax waivers and tuition vouchers for teens who tested positive for virginity. Senator Bush recently spearheaded national legislation banning the sale of condoms without prescriptions. His attorney had no comment on the latest allegations.

Seretta checked the readouts soon after Ginny left the house and knew her daughter was up to something. The GPS seemed to be working okay, and Ginny appeared to be at the library. But the temperatures were too even, the location unwavering, and that scared her.

Ginny had never listened to her warnings. Seretta was doing everything she could think of to protect the girl but, evidently, that wasn't enough. What was the point of being a parent if you couldn't use your experiences to prevent those you loved from suffering hurt and pain? It was time to get serious, to take drastic action before Ginny did something she'd regret forever.

It was time to activate Ginny's S.M.A.R.T.

From *Get Your Hands Off My Body: The Ginny Vuoto Story*, by Ginny Vuoto as told to Kitty Kelly:

People have made fun of me since that first article in *Nature*, where my mom detailed how she invented the Smart Twat and how I was going to test it. Sure, I'm embarrassed, but I try to think about it like it's all happening to someone else and not me.

My mom doesn't mean to be a monster, but she is. Some things should be private. We all need the chance to make mistakes, just like we need the chance to succeed because of our own efforts. And that's why I think they should never have made the Smart Twat legal. Because even if it does "save" us from ourselves – and from guys – we don't learn from our experience. All we do is react to some mechanical device, and where's the lesson in that?

I know there are lots of problems in the world, and people feel like they have to do *something*. And I don't really have an answer to teen pregnancy or HIV. Maybe everyone just needs to lighten up. The world keeps changing. Morals change along with the times. Maybe we live in a world where every girl is just going to have a baby before she drives a car and that's that.

I really think the world is going to end because of war or global warming or some horrible disaster, so anything that happens to me doesn't really matter anyway.

"*Crisis in Feminist Values: The Smart Twat,*" excerpts from a paper presented by Lilith Miller-James, Ph.D., M.S.W., Department of Women's Studies, California State University, Fullerton:

There has been a vociferous outcry from the feminist press concerning issues of choice and how the ST encourages the perception that women are helpless and unable to choose appropriate courses of action. I would argue that the ST be seen as it was intended: as a stopgap measure to be used until another device is invented, approved, and distributed to assist abusers in changing behaviors and responding to the challenges of contemporary relationships.

> It is naive to ignore the reality of women's lives. Statistics show that one out of four women experiences some form of sexual abuse. Inaction is not an option. To paraphrase Hippocrates: Extreme Diseases require Extreme Remedies.

Hal slumped down in the passenger seat, waiting. His camera was fitted with a high-quality telephoto lens and loaded with a fast film. Fast times required fast film, as he liked to say. School had let out twenty minutes ago, and the kid should be here any second.

They were doing a special issue of the *Enquirer* on teenage pregnancy, and Hal's job was to spy on that Smart Twat kid, the one with the famous scientist mother, and to catch the girl in unflattering poses that would suggest tawdry caption ideas for the copywriter. He had wanted to cover the original court case, when the father failed to win custody before the device was implanted, but that was a big story, pitting parental rights against the rights of the individual, and his boss had given the assignment to someone with a little more experience. It took five years for the brouhaha to die down, and now here he was, covering yesterday's news. Sometimes he hated this job.

He noticed a teenager approaching the house.

He looked at the old press release and compared the picture to the girl now jogging down the walkway. It had to be her.

Jeez, he thought, she's just a kid. She was tall, wearing too much makeup. Her face was still chubby, her cheeks naturally pink, her legs spindly, like she hadn't quite grown into them. She reminded him of his youngest granddaughter.

He patted his equipment. No way, he said. She's just a kid. Let somebody else do the dirty work. He picked up his cell phone and was about to dial in, say he was sorry that he hadn't been able to arrange the shoot, when he noticed movement in the car parked in front of him. Morgan from *The Star.*

"Fuck it," Hal said. He popped the lens cap and focused. With his foot he honked the horn. The Smart Twat kid turned his way, exhibiting a look of surprise and maybe fear. He clicked the shutter, again and again, using up half a roll before she made eye contact with him and he felt too guilty about the whole thing to continue.

Transcript from the October 6 Episode of MTV's *The More Real World:*

(Camera pans the living room where twenty-somethings Jill, Mandy, and Tim sit on a futon couch.)

Jill (sipping a Diet Coke): Seretta said the Prozac made her gain weight, so she switched to an herbal antidepressant, but that didn't seem to help either. She said that it felt like a dark cape had been thrown over her, like the world was closing in, crushing her at its center.

Mandy: Yeah. We felt really bad for her. Her clothes didn't fit, and she thought she looked frumpy and a lot older than forty. (Giggling.) We tried to tell her she wasn't old, but of course she was; so she knew we were lying.

Tim: I don't think she cared much about her personal appearance, except that she was supposed to set an example for other women.

Mandy: It's so sad. That family is, like, so fucked up.

Jill: Oh, and, like, we're not?

Tim: Zing! I guess we all have to share a bite of that weenie.

(Jump-cut to kitchen, where Seretta sits at the breakfast table holding the sides of her mug.)

(Ginny enters. She is dressed in black and has a new piercing through her lip.)

Ginny: Mother.

Seretta: When you call me "Mother" instead of "Seretta," it usually means you want something

Ginny: I have to go to school, but I wanted to tell you something, so just listen, okay?

Seretta: Okay.

Ginny: I'm thinking that I'd like to go live with Dad.

Seretta: That ass!

Ginny: He's not an ass, Mother. He's my dad. Anyway, you said you would just listen.

Seretta: You can't mean this! We moved into this TV house because you said it would be good for us. You can't just abandon me to these morons.

Ginny: Guess I was wrong. I'm late. (She grabs a handful of Fruit Loops and hustles out the door.)

(Jump-cut to living room)

Mandy: Officially, it's called the Sensory Motivational Assessment and Response Test, though everyone in the world – except Ginny's mother, who invented the fucker – calls it the Smart Twat. Sometimes, I can't believe she did this – made Ginny go guinea pig. I can't believe it, but it's true.

(Jump-cut to kitchen, where Jill and Seretta sip herbal tea.)

Seretta: (wiping eyes with tissue) Nothing prepares you for parenting. Sometimes you don't know what to do.

Jill: I never really thought about what it was like for my mom. Not that she thinks about what it's like for me.

Seretta: I tell myself I've got to snap out of this, but it's not that easy. (Swallowing herbal uppers and chasing them with half a box of fat-free chocolate bars.) I haven't felt especially suicidal, but one thing still terrifies me. Too often, it feels as if it would be just as easy to be there instead of here.

Richard's attorney said, "Of course the decisions in cases like these usually go with the mother, but since the child wishes you to have custody, we can hope."

So much drama and publicity surrounded the entire court case. The phone rang constantly, even in the middle of the night. Reporters waited at Richard's door like hungry dogs wanting to be let in. Thankfully, all his legal expenses were being paid by Male Rights (MR), an organization founded by men who had been denied custody of their children.

"The one thing that could hurt us," the attorney said, "is if she brings up that accusation of date rape. I know it isn't true; I'm just worried about how it will sound in court."

The way Richard remembered events, Seretta had been as willing as he had. But she had since tried to poison his relationship with their daughter with some crap about him forcing himself upon her. He remembered that first night in detail, the way Seretta had dressed (a black lace shirt, tight jeans, heels), the delicate scent of spice at the base of her neck, how she had used her tongue in ways his wife had long since forgotten.

There was no force involved. He had gone over it enough times in his mind to be sure. It was only after – when her period was late, when Seretta realized, finally, that he was not going to leave his wife for her – that she began to accuse him of taking advantage of her. Not that he had ever promised anything. She knew he was married from the start, but never thought twice about the immorality until later.

They were close in age, and he was no worldlier than she was. Why did she blame him because she had gotten pregnant? He'd naturally assumed that she had taken precautions – if *he* had been the one at risk for an unwanted child he certainly would have. So maybe he had pressed a bit too hard for the abortion, but it had seemed like the best course at the time. When Seretta changed her mind, she accused him of wanting to murder their baby.

Should he have tried harder to be sensitive to Seretta's needs? Probably. He could see that now, just not then. She blamed him for everything that had gone wrong. So did his ex-wife, who had legitimate cause. Thank god Ginny didn't hate him. His marriage had dissolved years ago, and he was racked with guilt for causing everyone so much pain. His daughter meant the world to him.

Transcript excerpts from the *Jerry Springer Show:*

Jerry: Richard Derringer's very public relationship with Seretta Vuoto has left him vulnerable to the label of "woman hater," but Richard says this isn't true. It's only Seretta that he hates.

Richard: Mr. Springer . . .

Jerry: Call me Jer.

Richard: Mr. Springer. . . .

Jerry: Okay, call me Jerry. You look nervous. What's the matter? You never watch the show?

Richard: Once or twice. I saw the one with the Siamese twins.

Jerry: My finest hour. So tell me about your ex-wife.

Richard: She's not my ex-wife. We weren't married.

Jerry: Whatever. I bet she was hot. Or was your wife the cold fish?

Richard: Look, I'm not going to answer that.

Jerry: She's some sort of scientist, right?

Richard: Her degree is in psychology. It's a soft science. Not hard like physics, but she sure acts like she knows everything.

Jerry: I like this hard and soft stuff. Can we talk a little more about that?

Richard: I worry that my daughter might be watching.

Jerry: (laughing) You let your daughter watch a show like this?

Richard: It's not up to me. She lives with her mother.

Jerry: But not for long, eh?

Richard: I think it's better not to talk about this on camera. Did you hear talk of a planned school shooting in Minneapolis?

Jerry: Got my guys on it already.

A letter to *JAMA:*

Recently, the adult guardians of a teenage patient demanded I prescribe a Smart Twat on the child's behalf. This raised several issues of consent, as well as a general question of accountability on the part of the OB-GYN toward the psychosexual health of her/his patients.

1) If I fail to follow the guardian's directive, and my patient suffers from abusive relationships as a result – perhaps contracts diseases ranging from genital warts to HIV – will I be liable for monetary damages?

2) If I prescribe the device, and the child is prevented from consummating relationships that prove harmful and, as a result of this, experiences diminished creative capacity due to "lack of suffering," will I be liable for interfering with her right to autonomy?

3) And finally, does prescribing the Smart Twat indicate that I have abandoned my religious belief that sex is a sacred act, which should not be consummated before marriage? Or does it enforce that belief through a scientific interventionist approach?

While on the surface these questions may seem frivolous, I believe these to be complex issues that must be addressed. The conscientious physician will consult not only his attorney but also a competent ethicist.
L. Smith, M.D.
New York, NY 10029

An excerpt from *Get S.M.A.R.T.* by Seretta Vuoto:

It's not the fun I want to take away. You have to believe that.

I want to spare you from an unwanted pregnancy and the emotional pain and the risk of contracting an incurable illness, all of which are potential consequences to every sexual union. Just hoping it won't happen to you can't protect you. Look around. None of *those* girls thought it would happen to them, either.

What S.M.A.R.T. will do: Sense when a potential partner is lying to you. Measure his (or, in the case of a lesbian partner, her) degree of affection and loyalty.

What S.M.A.R.T. won't do: Find your perfect mate. Protect you from the emotional hurt of loving someone who refuses to return your love.

From the Introduction to *It's All My Fault: My Love Affair with Seretta Vuoto* by Richard Derringer:

I'm not telling the most intimate details of my life for the money, but to set the record straight.

I thought I loved Seretta. It was only when I learned what kind of person she truly was that I learned to despise her.

An excerpt from Seretta Vuoto's letter to the *New York Review of Books* (*NYRB*):

So, why didn't Richard Derringer (*It's All My Fault* Review, *NYRB,* April 23) wait to pork me till he learned what kind of person I "truly" was?

Seretta was a failure as a mother. A public failure. Her daughter's "As Told To" book was on its twentieth week on the amazon.com bestseller list and had sold more copies than her own book. Who knew what had possessed Seretta to agree to appear on *The More Real World?*

Ginny had left a note on the kitchen table: "Gone to Daddy's for the weekend." She had also left out a half-gallon of milk, now spoiled, and a sink full of dirty dishes. Seretta began to tidy up, a habit.

The phone rang – that cute sociologist she had met at her last lecture.

"I was wondering," he said, "if you'd have time for coffee?"

She had liked him; he had asked intelligent questions and seemed thoughtful, the kind of man who might be considerate.

"I don't drink coffee," Seretta said.

"Well, how about tea?"

Her heart was racing, she broke out in a sweat. Either her S.M.A.R.T. chip was psychic, and he was a jerk, or she was having an old-fashioned anxiety attack.

"Maybe a drink?" he prompted.

Be brave, she told herself. You have protection.

"Okay," she said. "When?"

"Would tonight be convenient?"

"Can I meet you somewhere?" she asked.

"How about the Tea Bar at the Hilton?" he suggested.

She hung up the phone.

Even if her S.M.A.R.T. gave her the green light, she doubted she could sleep with him. She didn't deserve a good relationship. It had been difficult, really difficult, being alone all these years, trying to raise a daughter by herself. Seretta loved Ginny more than she could say. How could she forgive herself for wondering, still, what her life would have been like had she gone through with the abortion?

Deposition from the *Derringer v. Vuoto* Custody Hearing:

Lewis Webster, Attorney for the Plaintiff, Richard Derringer: Whom would you like to live with?

Ginny Vuoto: My father. I think he'd be a lot less strict.

Lewis Webster: Do you ever think your mother doesn't love you?

Ginny Vuoto: Sure. I mean, I have to. Because of everything. It's like, what would have happened if my mother had used a Smart Twat before she got pregnant? I mean, from everything she's ever said to me or written about my dad, I'm pretty sure that she wouldn't have had that affair with him if she'd "only known better." And if she hadn't, like, you know, done it, then I wouldn't have been born. So, like, maybe she'd be happier, more fulfilled, but I'd still be an egg and that's why I want to go and live with my dad.

It wasn't intentional. Seretta hadn't meant to spy.

She had gone into Ginny's room to open the windows and air out the house. She scooped up a bundle of clothes for the wash and, in the laundry room, sorted Ginny's things by color. That was when she found the packet of birth control pills in Ginny's pocket.

Seretta's first impulse was to flush the pills down the toilet, but something made her stop. Her hands trembled as she slipped the package back into the jeans jacket. She brought all of Ginny's clothes back into her room and left them in a pile.

She picked up the phone and dialed Richard's number from memory.

"Hello," she said.

"Hello," he answered coldly, still furious because of the custody hearing. He had the right. Having her attorney expose Richard's arrest for an old charge regarding his unsuccessful solicitation of a prostitute was a low blow. But a mother fought for her child, and, lucky for her, the judge had been a prudish and conservative appointee.

"Is Ginny there?"

An uncomfortable pause followed. "I haven't heard from her in a coupla days," he said. "Anything wrong?"

"No," she said. "Nothing." She hung up the phone.

She had broken up his marriage, and he hated her. His ex-wife hated her. Ginny hated her. Sometimes it was a struggle for her not to hate herself.

She decided to cancel her date, stay home, and watch TV.

From above her she heard a whirring sound as a camera clicked on automatically. Seretta threw a book at the lens and managed to dislodge the whole thing. "Show's over," Seretta said. She sat on the process couch, her head in her hands, self-conscious despite the broken camera. God, Seretta thought, why won't Ginny let me help? Why is she so stubborn?

Labor Day – September 3 – Back To Work

Big date was tonight. I tried cutting out my chip with a blade, but it was deeper than I thought and the blood was so gross I had to stop.

The boy's name was Eric Something. I met him in a chat room. He had promised me dinner, but before we got there we stopped to park in an empty furniture store lot. We went to the back of his van, on top of pillows on the floor where the seats should have been.

I took my pants all the way off, but he left his scrunched down around his ankles, like there wasn't enough time to remove his shoes. I knew he didn't love me, which was fine. I didn't even know him and didn't much like him.

What I wanted to do had no relation to love.

My Smart Twat allowed me to kiss him and get in a few gropes before sounding its electronic alarm. I managed to temporarily disable it by cutting off the circulation with my arm, but, as things progressed, the device sensed that a threat still loomed and it mounted a full-scale attack. First, it released chemical scavengers in my bloodstream and made me breathe out some nitrous compound that effectively constricted the blood supply to the arteries feeding Eric's penis. His erection wilted; he pushed away from me.

"Fuck," I said, "Sorry."

I could have given him a better explanation. Mom has told me often enough, in graphic detail and with diagrams and anatomically correct language, exactly how the chip operated; she's made me take sex education classes from the age of two.

Eric looked embarrassed, maybe angry.

"It's not your fault," I said to make him feel better. Male ego. You know. I tried to give him a blowjob so he wouldn't be angry. He had hair there, but it didn't seem all that gross compared to everything else. It got me hot to know I could get him so excited, to feel I had such power over him.

Too bad the Smart Twat was smarter and more persistent than I anticipated. It attacked my immune system. My nose ran, my eyes teared, my throat closed, and I had to pull my mouth away from his penis to catch my breath. I broke out into hives and started to swell like a basted turkey.

"Fuck!" I said. "I'm really sorry."

Eric jerked upright and grabbed at his pants.

"No, wait!" I said. "I'm okay. We can still do it!" I could not stop crying or stop the hacking cough and nonstop snot drip.

"Later," he said. He scooted over to unlock the door and push me out.

I stuffed my bra and underpants in my pocket. It was a fifteen-minute walk home.

Mom was still awake, reciting a speech for some conference. She had either not seen the monitors or was in denial. I sneezed and coughed and let my underwear fall to the floor. It felt good not to even try to hide what had happened.

Mom stared, her eyes and mouth open wide, as if she'd just eaten a bowling ball and was having second thoughts.

I had to laugh. It was almost better this way than if I had actually gone through with it and gone all the way.

And she'd never even know I was still a virgin.

Six Gun Loner of the High Butte #6

ꕥ

Jeffrey Ford

Under a red sun, vultures circling like wagons against the Comanche, dry wind rising from the south laced with a hint of starvation and thirst, like the aroma of Miss Pearl's perfume in a cramped room over the Four Fingers Saloon on a night in August after a blazing gun battle when bullets flew, passersby ducked behind rain barrels, horses pranced sideways, deputies slammed shots of rot gut at the bar, whores giggled, propositioned by Death just passing through, and the school marm clutched her parcel of gingham meant to be sewn into a dress for her Eastern beau who would not arrive by stage that night or any other in this life, Six Gun Loner, AKA Gristled Thunder, better known as Scrap Morrow, who had ushered more arrogant curs to boot hill than a mule has fleas, man of the lightning hand, the eagle eye, the quick wit, and prodigious tobacco spit, scourge of desperadoes, friend to children and brother of the giant red man known as Muskingtoluckok, Indian prince of the lost tribe of Israel with the sign of the coyote carved in his left cheek, the feather of a Thunderbird dangling from one long knotted hank of hair, and a hatchet that once cleaved the skull of the Skunk Ape of Briar Canyon, sat on his trusty steed, Old Parsimony, surveying, from the high butte, the desert where he would soon ride, like a bat out of hell back to Sorrow Gulch for a last kiss from Miss Pearl, a last piss from a bottle of rye, before meeting Doc Holiday's tubercular ghost in a gun duel in the dark that would decide the fate of the West and be remembered forever as the only shootout he ever lost, the one that transformed him from Six Gun Loner into Kid Skeleton, fleshless, fiery, lacking all social graces, with a cackle that could start a stampede, insatiable seeker of gold and murderer of murderers throughout the territory then and now and forever, in perpetuity, until the doggies retire and the stars fall on Alabama.

Encounter of Another Kind

༻༺

David Langford

At the time it seemed a good night for our work. A thin watery fuzz, half mist and half rain, was blurring the moon and had made haloes round the lights of the main road. This dark lane was still puddled from afternoon showers, so that when our van tilted and bumped along it the headlight reflections rose in silent luminous bubbles through the trees. Even I took a long moment to identify them. The right frame of mind is so important.

This was a high-activity area of Wiltshire, where sightings came regularly with the seasons. It was crop circle country, too, but I had always been uneasy about that work: it's too showy and physical, and too many fanciful hoaxers had spoiled the impact of our own real, authorized creations. But the fertile location was just happenstance. The man Glass lived close at hand and was known to take this lane from Pewsey village to his house. Tonight he had been delivering one of his lying, offensive lectures, and the driving time from London . . .

I checked my watch. Perhaps Glass's wife would be doing the same, and laying out coffee-cups. Would she believe his incredible, incoherent story a few hours hence? We were ready by the roadside, in a field muddy and trampled enough that our own traces could make no difference.

The stage was set in the bubble-tent. Mackay had long finished stringing his cables and was hunched over his little panel of lights, rapt like a boy playing trains. Sometimes I wondered about Mackay. It was easy to imagine him working with anyone, even the IRA, grinning all over that fat face and soldering his fussy circuits for sheer love of gadgetry. He never seemed to absorb the idea that we were evangelists laboring in the service of a great truth.

One amber light blinked and double-blinked in the box. Ten-minute test. The coast was clear and the kid hadn't yet gone to sleep at his post up the dark lane, at the junction. We were as ready as we would ever be.

The kid's role was relatively minor, but I still worried about him getting it right. You never know what to make of these teenage agglomerations of hair, leather, and studs. But he'd asked sensible questions about the reports of Visitors in this and that country: sometimes putty-faced midgets with enormous eyes, sometimes six or seven feet tall. I dare say they can take what form they like, I'd told him, and he seemed satisfied. Now Mackay was deeply indifferent to that kind of speculation, and Glass would naturally have made it a basis for mockery.

Yes. Peter Glass was a man long overdue for the attention of the skies. Whenever some hint of the mysterious and wonderful came creeping shyly into the world, it was always he who'd rush to be interviewed and turn everything to mud with his touch. It was the planet Venus, it was a low-flying plane, the witnesses imagined it all, he was just lying, she is mentally disturbed, who can believe in little green men anyway?

(A cheap newspaper phrase, that last. In the classic accounts They are never green.)

It is particularly maddening when an encounter we *know* to have been physically real is explained away as hallucination. People who ought to be fighting at our side are seduced by talk of visitations and abductions being all a matter of strange psychological states blah blah blah which if properly studied might give new insight into the mind and blah blah blah. What is this stuff but a fancy version of "he's barmy and she made it all up"? Of course it must be said that some people do make it up. I loathe a hoaxer.

The large oblong indicator at dead center of Mackay's panel went red and a low buzz sounded. I keep my distance from electronics hobbyism, but that one was obvious enough. The kid had clocked what was presumably the right car going by. Now he should be hauling out that big DIVERSION sign from the sodden undergrowth. A quiet country lane was about to become quieter.

I always kept the pallid mask off until the last minute: it's hot and uncomfortable. Lights were flickering in the distance, approaching. Glass himself would be seeing those eerie reflections rise up the wet trees. Perhaps they would take on a new significance for him, now or in retrospect, because Mackay had flicked the first of his switches. Could the tiny hiss even be heard over the engine noise? A receptive frame of mind was needed.

In the classic UFO encounter by road and by night, an unidentifiable light is seen above and the car ignition mysteriously fails. This will often be the preliminary to a "missing time" or even an "alien abduction" experience. We were certainly going to see to that. At the second click from Mackay's board the quartz-halogen cluster blazed intolerably from the sky (in fact from a cable slung precariously between tall trees on either side of the lane), and at the third Glass's ignition mysteriously failed.

The sky-gods command powers beyond our scope, of course, and their servants down here must resort to earthly expedients. I think a priest might feel the same when he doles out the bread and wine and is sure it represents a truth, while doubting that the miracle of blood ever really comes to pass as it had in scriptural days. Mackay's opposite number in London had done his part well enough: the relay in the HT circuit and the tiny cylinder with its servo-operated valve just under the driver's seat. Of course it is the signal from the first switch that releases the gas.

Longstead 42 is a transparent and almost odorless psychotropic agent, used to ensure the properly receptive frame of mind. Its effects do not last long, but Glass was still trembling and almost helpless in his stalled Volvo when we adjusted our bulging masks and came to him. The sequence of events, colored and exaggerated by the mild hallucinogen, must already have been etching itself deep into his memory . . . all the more so for its theoretical familiarity. His own scoffing researches would reinforce the impact of what happened now. I tried to be gentle with the hypodermic, but there was no need to conceal this injection. Unexplained scars and puncture marks are all part of the classic abduction experience.

The kid's lightless motorbike was coughing at the gate as we helped Glass towards our mother ship. Mackay fingered his pocket controller, and the great inflated igloo pulsed in a riot of colored lights. A bubble marquee is perfect for this work despite the faint roar of the compressor: it even has an airlock. I myself found it a deeply moving sight. If only . . .

He did not resist as we stripped him and settled him on an examination table of a design as unearthly as our resources could arrange. For him this would be a place of stabbing supernatural light, thanks to a few drops of atropine that dilated each eye to the full; and strange small Beings would hover around. The kid, who had changed into his own mask and white leotards before joining us now, was already short enough: but the deceptively high table made midgets of us all, while dry-ice fog confused the issue of how far down our legs might actually go. Truth is all a matter of presentation. Our putty-complexioned masks swelled at the top into mighty domes of intellect, and we peered through huge eyes of empty black glass.

So we set to work, following the guidelines laid down by a myriad published cases. This is a hugely documented phenomenon. Mackay and I had had plenty of practice with communicants of both sexes, and we worked well together. Biopsies, minute incisions. Needles in Glass's navel, liquid drooling into his ear, surreal alien mechanisms blinking as they diagnosed and recorded nothing at all. Intermittent chemical blackouts helped break up the stream of his memory (partial amnesia is highly characteristic). There was a star map ready to show him, a patternless scattergram on which he could later impose any meaning he cared.

He gaped. I knew we had him. Why should he be so loud in his filthy skepticism if he were not already close to belief, just waiting for the sign? Recorded messages of peace and millennial warning washed over him, the voices digitally processed into eerie tones appropriate to the farther stars. Never again would he be able to say with sincerity that it was all ridiculous, that in all probability the quote UFO abductees unquote are merely drawing attention to themselves with lurid fantasies.

The culmination is the terrible Probe, the thing that bulks large in the encounter/abduction story which I believe has sold more copies than any other. It is a huge ugly object, like a phallus designed by H. R. Giger in a bilious mood: thirteen inches long, vaguely triangular in cross-section, gray and scaly, tipped with a jagged cage of wires. (The shaft is actually painted fiberglass.)

It is a necessary part of the experience that the victim should feel himself anally penetrated by this probe. Of course we relied on suggestion: after showing him the thing, and turning him over to obstruct his vision, I would actually insert a finger. The greased rubber glove was already on my hand.

But there was a hitch before the Probe came into play. The head-masks do not make it all that easy to see to the left or right. We had blacked Glass out again to allow a quick breather and a cup of tea from the thermos . . . and there was a confused sound. I fumbled impatiently with the mask and at the same time felt a small sharp pain in my thigh, some stinging insect, perhaps.

When I'd finally pulled the stifling thing off my head I saw that Mackay had fallen over. The fog lapped around him. I thought at first he must have had an accidental whiff of the blackout agent. Everything was blurring and the tent walls shimmered. The kid smiled at me. It is not possible that the mask could smile.

I told him to take that stupid thing off. I do not know whether I meant the mask or the smile. He invited me to remove it for him, and though I first reached out in blind anger at his playing around, I was suddenly afraid that if I touched it the great head would be built of living flesh. No. I said something loud, perhaps not an actual word. Was Glass's body melting and oozing off the table? No.

There is a gap here. Partial amnesia is highly characteristic. Things tilted heavily in and out of focus. I remember the feel of another insect and knew this time it was a needle. By then I was pressed into the cold soggy fabric of the tent floor, choking in our artificial fog. Insistent fingers tugged at my tight white alien costume.

Everything inside my skull was whirling in tight, chaotic patterns, led by a silly persistent worry about whether the syringe had been properly sterilized (I was always very conscientious about this). What did I know about the kid? It was his first outing. I had barely seen him before. They can take what form they like.

Those eyes.

He said . . .

I do not recall all the words. That scopolamine cocktail is meant to be disorienting. The thin voice conveyed that we were playing a dangerous game. More than once he said: “My sister.” I thought of sister worlds, sister craft gleaming silver as they made their inertialess turns and danced mockingly off the radar screens. He said: “In an institution.” Would that have been the Institute of UFO Studies? At another point he said: “You bastards” and “did all this to her” and “waiting a long time for this . . .” The words of the sky-gods are always enigmatic, and perhaps we are only their bastard offspring.

It was so hard to think. All this is confused in a red blur of pain, because to impress his seriousness upon me he then made scientific use of the Probe. Nor was there any reliance on suggestion or on a greased and rubber-sheathed finger. “This is for her. You hear me? This is for her.” Did I hear that? At the time I could not begin to appreciate it as an exalting, a transcendent experience. I am sure that no chemical agents assisted the loss of consciousness which duly followed, although not soon enough.

Waking up on chill plastic stretched over mud, racked with cramps and another, deeper ache . . . is not an experience to be recommended. The “kid” was long gone. I never knew his name, if on Earth he ever went under a name. I tried not to be consoled by the discovery that Mackay too had been warned, every bit as emphatically as myself.

Under a dismal gray moon we limped somehow through the clear-up procedure and left Glass to sleep it off in his wretched Volvo, itself now stripped of our London man's gadgetry. When he uncoiled himself in the small hours, he would be awakening to his new membership in the ranks of abductees, the sufferers from "missing time." Would he proclaim it or would he lie by silence? Who cared? Glass was no longer important.

The truth is what's important. After a longish period of convalescence and keeping a low profile (even my once-friendly family doctor was terrifyingly unsympathetic about the injury), I now see myself in the position of a worldly priest who has at last received his own sign. But it's a sign like the miraculous appearance of the face of the Virgin Mary in one's toilet bowl. The kind of thing that will do to win peasants: meaning so much to the recipient, but just another tawdry, commonplace sensation to the world at large. For this muddying of the waters I blame the people who have made up garish UFO encounter tales without ever having a genuine experience like the one we gave to Glass. Oh, I do loathe and despise these hoaxers, almost as much as the narrow-minded skeptics themselves.

Meanwhile, how can I hope to publish *this* truth and have its very special status believed? How can it help me to my rightful position among the elect when They finally beam down in glory from the stars, with all their wonderful cargo? How?

Tales from the Breast

ഇന്ദ

Hiromi Goto

The questions that were never asked may be the most important. You don't think of this. You never do. When you were little, your mother used to tell you that asking too many questions could get you into trouble. You realize now that not asking enough has landed you in the same boat, in the same river of shit without the same paddle. You phone your mother long distance to tell her this, and she says, "Well, two wrongs don't make a right, dear," and gives you a dessert recipe that is quoted as being Prince Charles's favorite in the September issue of *Royalty* magazine.

> *Your success in breastfeeding depends greatly on your desire to nurse as well as the encouragement you receive from those around you.*
> – Brinkley, Goldberg and Kukar, *Your Child's First Journey* (copyright © 1988, 2nd Edition, page 173)

"Is there anything coming out?" He peers curiously, at the baby's head, my covered breast.

"I don't know, I can't tell," I wince.

"What do you mean, you can't tell? It's your body, isn't it? I mean, you must be able to feel something," scratching his head.

"Nope, only pain."

"Oh." Blinks twice. "I'm sorry. I'm very proud of you, you know."

* * *

The placenta slips out from between your legs like the hugest blood clot of your life. The still-wet baby is strong enough to nurse but cannot stagger to her feet like a fawn or a colt. You will have to carry her in your arms for a long time. You console yourself with the fact that at least you are not an elephant who would be pregnant for close to another year. This is the first and last time she will nurse for the next twelve hours.

"Nurse, could you please come help me wake her up? She hasn't breastfed for five hours now."

The nurse has a mole with a hair on it. You can't help but look at it a little too long each time you glance up at her face. The nurse undresses the baby but keeps the toque on. The infant is red and squirmy, and you hope no one who visits says she looks just like you.

"Baby's just too comfortable," the nurse chirps. "And sometimes they're just extra tired after the delivery. It's hard work for them too you know!"

"Yeah, I suppose you're right."

"Of course. Oh, and when you go to the washroom, I wouldn't leave Baby by herself. Especially if the door is open." The nurse briskly rubs the red baby until she starts squirming, eyes still closed in determined sleep.

"What do you mean?"

"Well, we have security, but, really, anyone could just waltz in and leave with Baby," the nurse smiles, like she's joking.

"Are you serious!"

"Oh, yes. And you shouldn't leave valuables around either. We've been having problems with theft, and I know you people have nice cameras."

You have just gone through twelve hours of labor and gone without sleep for twenty-eight. You do not have the energy to tell the nurse of the inappropriateness of her comment. The baby does not wake up.

Your mother-in-law, from Japan, has come to visit. She is staying for a month to help with the older child. She gazes at the sleeping infant you hold to your chest. You tell your mother-in-law that the baby won't feed properly and that you are getting a little worried. "Your nipples are too flat and she's not very good at breastfeeding," she says, and angry tears fill your eyes.

"Are you people from Tibet?" the nurse asks.

Breastmilk is raw and fresh.
– *Your Child's First Journey* (page 174)

You are at home. You had asked if you could stay longer in the hospital if you paid, but they just laughed and said no. Your mother-in-law makes lunch for herself and the firstborn but does not make any for you because she does not know if you will like it. You eat shredded wheat with NutraSweet and try breastfeeding again.

The pain is raw and fresh.

She breastfeeds for three hours straight, and, when you burp her, there is a pinkish froth in the corners of her lips that looks like strawberry milkshake. You realize your breastmilk is blood-flavored and wonder if it is okay for her to drink. Secretly, you hope that it is bad for her so that you will have to quit breastfeeding her. When you call a friend and tell her about the pain and blood and your concerns for her health, you learn, to your dismay, that the blood will not hurt her. That your friend had problems too, that she even had blood blisters on her nipples, but she kept right on breastfeeding through it, the doctor okayed it and ohhhh the blood, the pain, when those blood blisters popped, but she went right on breastfeeding until the child was four years old.

When you hang up, you are even more depressed. Because the blood is not a problem and your friend suffered even more than you do now. You don't come in first on the nipple tragic story. You don't even come close.

"This isn't going very well," I try smiling, but give up the effort.

"Just give it some time. Things'll get better." He snaps off the reading light at the head of the bed. I snap it back on.

"I don't think so. I don't think *things* are going to get better at all."

"Don't be so pessimistic," he smiles, trying not to offend me.

"Have you read the pamphlet for fathers of breastfed babies?"

"Uhm, no. Not yet." Shrugs his shoulders and tries reaching for the lamp again. I swing out my hand to catch his wrist in midair.

"Well read the damn thing, and you might have some idea of what I'm going through."

"Women have been breastfeeding since there have been women."

"What!"

"You know what I mean. It's natural. Women have been breastfeeding ever since their existence, ever since ever having a baby," he lectures, glancing down once at my tortured breasts.

"That doesn't mean they've all been enjoying it, ever since existing and having done it since their existence! Natural isn't the same as liking it or being good at it," I hiss.

"Why do you have to be so complicated?"

"Why don't you just marry someone who isn't, then?"

"Are you hungry?" My mother-in-law whispers from the other side of the closed bedroom door. "I could fix you something if you're hungry."

Engorgement
– (page 183)

The baby breastfeeds for hours on end. This is not the way it is supposed to work. You phone the emergency breastfeeding number they gave to you at the hospital. The breastfeeder professionals tell you that Baby is doing what is only natural. That the more she sucks, the more breastmilk you will produce, how it works on a supply and demand system and how everything will be better when the milk comes in. On what kind of truck, you wonder.

They tell you that, if you are experiencing pain of the nipples, it's because Baby isn't latched on properly. How the latch has to be just right for proper breastfeeding. You don't like the sounds of that. You don't like how *latch* sounds like something that's suctioned on and might never come off again. You think of lamprey eels and leeches. Notice how everything starts with an "l."

When the milk comes in, it comes in on a semitrailer. There are even marbles of milk under the surface of skin in your armpits, hard as glass and painful to the touch. Your breasts are as solid as concrete balls, and the pressure of milk is so great that the veins around the nipple are swollen, bulging. Like the stuff of horror movies, they are ridged, expanded to the point of blood-splatter explosion.

"Feel this, feel how hard my breasts are," I grit my teeth.

"Oh my god!"

"It hurts," I whisper.

"Oh my god." He is horrified. Not with me, but at me.

"Can you suck them a little, so they're not so full? I can't go to sleep."

"What!" He looks at me like I've asked him to suck from a vial of cobra venom.

"Could you please suck some out? It doesn't taste bad. I tried some. It's like sugar water or something."

"Uh, I don't think so. It's so . . . incestuous."

"We're not blood relations, we're married, for god's sake. How can it be incestuous? Don't be so weird about it. Please! It's very painful."

"I'm sorry. I just can't." Clicks off the lamp and turns over to sleep.

> *Advantages also exist for you, the nursing mother . . . it is easy for you to lose weight without dieting* ***and regain your shape sooner.***
> – (page 176)

"You look like you're still pregnant," he jokes. "Are you sure there isn't another one still in there?"

"Just fuck off, okay?"

Your belly has a loose fold of skin and fat that impedes your vision of your pubic hair. You have a beauty mark on your lower abdomen you haven't seen for five years. You wonder if you would have had a better chance at being slimmer if you had breastfed the first child. There is a dark stain that runs vertically over the skin of your belly, from the pubic mound, over the belly button and almost in line with the bottom of your breasts. Perversely, you imagined it to be the marker for the doctor to slice if the delivery had gone bad. The stain isn't going away and you don't really care because, what with the flab and all, it doesn't much make a difference. You are hungry all the time from producing breastmilk and eat three times as much as you normally would; therefore, you don't lose weight at all, you just don't gain on top of the residual fat you have already achieved.

"You should eat as much as you want," your mother-in-law says. She spoons another eggplant on to your plate and your partner spoons his over as well. The baby starts to wail from the bedroom, and your mother-in-law rushes to pick her up.

"Don't cry," you hear her say, "Breastmilk is coming right away."

You want to yell down the hall, that you have a name and that it isn't Breastmilk.

You eat the eggplants.

The hormone prolactin, which causes the secretion of milk, helps you to feel "motherly."
– (page 176)

Just how long can the pain last, you ask yourself. It is the eleventh day of nipple torture and maternal hell. You phone a friend and complain about the pain, the endless pain. Your friend says that some people experience so much pleasure from breastfeeding that they have orgasms. You tell your friend that if that was the case, you would breastfeed until the kid was big enough to run away from you.

The middle-of-the-night feed is the longest and most painful part of the breastfeeding day. It lasts from two to six hours. You alternate from breast to breast, from an hour at each nipple to dwindling half hour, fifteen minutes, eight minutes, two, one, as your nipples get so sore that even the soft brush of the baby's bundling cloth is enough to make the toes of your feet squeeze up into fists of pain, tears streaming down your cheeks. You try thinking about orgasms as the slow tick tick of the clock prolongs your misery. You try thinking of S & M. The pain is so intense, so slicing real, that you are unable to think of it as pleasurable. You realize that you are not a masochist.

> *Because you must sit down or lie down to nurse, you are assured of getting the rest you need postpartum.*
> – (page 176)

You can no longer sit to breastfeed. You try lying down, to nurse her like a puppy, but the shape of your breasts are not suitable for this method. You prop her up on the back of the easy chair and feed her while standing. Her legs dangle, but she is able to suck on your sore nipples. You consider hanging a sign on your back. The Milk Stand.

Your ass is killing you. You take a warm sitz bath because it helps for a little while, and you touch yourself in the water as carefully as you can. You feel several new nubs of flesh between your vagina and your rectum and hopefully imagine that you are growing a second, third, fourth clitoris. When you visit your doctor, you find out that they're only hemorrhoids.

"I'm quitting. I hate this."

"You've only been at it for two weeks. This is the worst part, and it'll only get better from here on," he encourages. Smiles gently and tries to kiss me on my nose.

"I quit, I tell you. If I keep on doing this, I'll start hating the baby."

"You're only thinking about yourself," he accuses, pointing a finger at my chest. "Breastfeeding is the best for her, and you're giving up, just like that. I thought you were tougher."

"Don't you guilt me! It's my goddamn body and I make my own decisions on what I will and will not do with it!"

"You always have to do what's best for yourself! What about my input? Don't I have a say on how we raise our baby?" he shouts, Mr. Sensible and let's-talk-about-it-like-two-adults.

"Is everything alright?" his mother whispers from outside the closed bedroom door. "Is anybody hun – "

"We're fine! Just go to bed!" he yells.

The baby snorts, hiccups into an incredible wail. Nasal and distressed.

"Listen, it's me who has to breastfeed her, me who's getting up every two hours to have my nipples lacerated and sucked on 'til they bleed while you just snore away. You haven't even got up once in the middle of the night to change her goddamn diaper even as a token fucking gesture of support, so don't you tell me what I should do with my breasts. There's nothing wrong with formula. I was raised on formula. You were raised on formula. Our whole generation was raised on formula, and we're fine. So just shut up about it. Just shut up. Because this isn't about you. This is me!"

"If I could breastfeed, I would do it gladly!" he hisses. Flings the blankets back and stomps to the crib.

And I laugh. I laugh because the sucker said the words out loud.

It is 3:27 A.M. The baby has woken up. Your breasts are heavy with milk, but you supplement her with formula. 5:15. You supplement her again, and your breasts are so full, so tight, that they lie like marble on your chest. They are ready.

You change the baby's diapers and put her into the crib. In the low glow of the baby light, you can see her lips pursed around an imaginary nipple. She even sucks in her sleep. You sit on the bed, beside your partner, and unsnap the catches of the nursing bra. The pads are soaked, and, once the nipples are exposed, they spurt with sweet milk. The skin around your breasts are stretched tighter than a drum, so tight that all you need is one little slice for the skin to part. Like a pressured zipper, it tears, spreading across the surface of your chest, directed by your fingers, it tears in a complete circle around the entire breast. There is no blood.

You lean slightly forward, and the breast falls gently into your cupped hands. The flesh is a deep red, and you wonder at its beauty, how flesh becomes food without you asking or even wanting it. You set the breast on your lap and slice your other breast. Two pulsing orbs still spurting breastmilk. You gently tug the blankets down from the softly clenched fingers of your partner's sleep, unbutton his pajamas and fold them back so his chest is exposed. You stroke the hairless skin then lift one breast, then the other, to lie on top of his flat penny nipples. The flesh of your breasts seeps into his skin, soft whisper of cells joining cells, your skin into his, tissue to tissue, the intimate melding before your eyes, your mouth an O of wonder and delight.

The unfamiliar weight of engorged breasts makes him stir, restless, a soft moan between parted lips. They are no longer spurting with milk, but they drip evenly, runnels down his sides. The cooling wet becomes uncomfortable, and his eyelids flutter. Open. He focuses on my face peering down and blinks rapidly.

"What's wrong?" he asks, voice dry with sleep.

"Nothing. Not a thing. How do you feel?"

"Funny," he answers, perplexed. "My chest feels funny. I feel all achy. Maybe I'm coming down with something. My chest is wet! I'm bleeding!"

"Shhhhh. You'll wake the baby," I caution. Gently press my forefinger over his lips.

He was groggy with sleep, but he is wide-awake now. Sitting up. Looks down at his chest, his two engorged breasts. He looks at my face. Then back at his breasts.

"Oh my god," he moans.

"It's okay," I nurture him. "Don't worry. Everything is fine. Just do what comes naturally."

A sudden look of shock slams into his face, and he reaches, panicked, with his hands to touch himself between his legs. When he feels himself intact, relief flits his eyes to be permanently replaced by bewilderment.

I smile. Beam in the dim glow of light. Turn on to my side and sleep sweetly, soundly.

Science Fiction

ꕥ

Paul Di Filippo

Pissing warily but with immense somatic relief in one of the ill-maintained and rather frightening restrooms at Penn Station. And Corso Fairfield blissfully directs his golden urine into the commodious porcelain basin. Distilled from several cups of tedious Amtrak coffee. While trying not to eyeball the spectacle around him. Motivated not by antihomosexual anxiety. Certainly not a prejudice found in Corso's liberal soul. But rather a discretionary maneuver directed at the homeless men. Who throng the room, with its scatter of smudged wet paper towels across the tiled floor. Washing their feet in the sink. And other even less savory parts.

Corso finishes his own noisy voiding. And replackets his penis. Certainly nothing special, and in no wise superior to the members of the surrounding indigents. But indisputably all his own. Yet regrettably not likely to be shared with any female. Since his wife Jenny left him. Running away with his exceptional car mechanic. Jack Spanner. A double loss. And hard to quantify the ratio of injury between bedroom and garage.

But his lonely penis is now safe. Behind the sturdy zipper of his best pants. Donned this morning back home, several hundred miles northward. With a white shirt and camphor-smelling wool jacket suitable for meeting editors. And agents. And bosom pal Malachi

Stiltjack. That rich bastard. And also an ensemble entitling one to enter fine restaurants. For expense-account meals. Moreover and finally, pride-enhancing when encountering with unfeigned glee any of one's public. Adoring public. Who should chance to recognize one from dustjacket photos. However unlikely. Granted his small and undemonstrative readership. Which, one must forever believe, is always just on the verge of growing exponentially.

The problem of washing one's hands. When bums barricade the sinks. Corso hesitates, shifting his soft modern satchel from hand to socially unsanctioned postmicturating hand. When one of the mendicants departs. Leaving the taps running. So that one does not even have to touch them. Saving one from contact with numerous New York mutated germs too vile to mention.

At the sink. Satchel secured between pincered knees. Pumping some opalescent soap the shade of cheap rosé wine into a palm. Lathering up. While one's elflock-bearded, multishirted neighbor to the right is balanced on one bare foot. The other unshod appendage embasined. Caked absolutely black with street grime. Causing Corso to flinch inwardly. But his initial reaction is mild. Compared to the emotions that flood him as the foot comes clean. For the foot is not human. By any stretch of even Corso's trained imagination.

Putrid water runnels down the trap. Depriving the scrubbed foot, like a fish stick denuded of crust, of its concealing coating. Revealing something that looks like an ostrich's appendage. Hard yellow ringed bony digits. Terminating in claws. That could disembowel with a kick. And a spur above the ankle. Also potentially lethal.

Falling back from the sink. Dripping soapy water on one's best pants. Knock-kneed as one strives valiantly to prevent the satchel from dropping to the contaminated floor. And now the bum with the avian foot taking umbrage. At such evident revulsion. So ungentlemanly expressed.

"Hey dude what's your problem."

Corso seeking suitable words for a polite response. But unable to link any placatory syllables together in his confusion. So as finally to mutter bluntly only, "Your foot."

The bum regarding his elevated foot, sunk still below Corso's new line of sight in the fount. So recently laved of its dirt disguise.

To reveal the underlying otherness. “Okay, so it ain’t pretty. But Jesus you’d think I was some kinda alien, way you jumped.”

Which of course is the exact dilemma. Only it is no longer. A dilemma.

For the homeless stranger has removed his foot from its bath. And now the instrument of Corso’s disconcertment is revealed to be fully anthropomorphic. Scabbed, cracked, and horny-nailed, yes. But otherwise unremarkable.

Corso recovers. As best as possible. “I am exceedingly sorry. Please accept this donation toward the future care and refreshment of your foot.”

Corso tenders a five-dollar bill. Retrieved from pants pocket. The retrieval having somewhat dried at least one hand. In a manner most unbecoming to his best pants. Which now exhibit a damp stain. Much too close to the groin.

“Gee thanks pal.”

“Think nothing of it.”

Paper towels from the dispenser complete Corso’s ablutions. Although some slight stickiness of soap remains. Not wholly rinsed in the confusion. He turns to depart. Cannot resist one last backward glance. And sees the bum redonning a tattered sock. Which piece of clothing features a hole strategically placed. To allow a spur to protrude.

Corso shakes his head. He should have expected some visitation of this nature. For this is not the first time reality has played the deceitful trull with him.

And when he’s asked again
what his problem is
he will lay all blame
squarely yet perhaps unfairly
on his profession
of science fiction.

Twenty years now. Two decades of writing science fiction. And before that, naturally. Two prior decades. Of reading it. Subsisting in youth on an exclusive diet. Of pulp adventures.

Sophisticated extrapolations. Space operas, dystopias, and technological fantasies. Millions of words that shaped his worldview. Ineluctably. Like so many hands molding raw clay into an awkward shape. And baked him. In a kiln fueled with paraliterature. So that ever afterwards no other kind of fiction would make any real impression. On the pottery of his mind.

Then came the adolescent dream. Forgotten circumstances of its birth. Lost in the mists of his SF-besotted youth. But quickly becoming an omnipresent urge. To write what he loved. Despite no one inviting him to do so. In fact barring the gates. With shotguns cradled across the chests of the genre guardians. The hard years of apprenticeship. Hundreds of thousands of words. Laboriously composed. Read and rejected. By hard-hearted editors. Who emitted the mustard gas of their dreadful intelligence. To paraphrase Ginsberg. And proving Corso Fairfield could quote. From someone other than Asimov, Bradbury, or Clarke. The ABCs of the genre. Superseded by newer names, surely. Yet still talismanic to ignorant outsiders.

Improvement by microdegrees. Understanding himself better. And what made a story. Tools honed. Finally his first sale. Ecstasy soon replaced by despair. At the realization of how hard this path was going to be. Yet not relenting. Further sales. To better markets. Then a book contract. For a novel titled *Cosmocopia.* Which allowed him to leave the day job. Managing an independent bookstore-cum-Bavarian-beercellar. Named with dire whimsy. CHAPTER AND WURST.

And Jenny so supportive throughout. Married straight out of college. Ever faithful. Rejoicing in his eventual success. Even attending various conventions. Unlike most SF spouses. Who would all rather undergo tracheotomies with spoons. Than meet the odd-shaped and weirdly intelligent readers whose necessary and even lovable support underpinned the books. Not to mention encountering disgruntled and jaded peers. Deep in their cups. Looking up from below the liquor with the hapless expressions of drowning victims.

And a future that seemed to stretch ahead fairly brightly, albeit labor intensively. Until Corso's recent blockage. Due to massive failure of suspension of authorial disbelief. In one's own conceptions. And vision. And even chosen medium. And the advance for the overdue project already long spent. On septic tank replacement, a trip to Bermuda, and a new transmission. Putting some of Corso's unearned future royalties for *The Black Hole Gun* directly into the pockets of the treacherous Jack Spanner. Who had been eagerly present to rescue Jenny when she jumped the *Federation Starship Corso Fairfield.* When it was beset by the mind-parasites of Dementia VII.

The first hallucination occurred at the supermarket. A watermelon developed a face. A jolly face, but nonetheless unnerving. And began talking to Corso. Who failed to heed the import of the melon's speech. So fixated was he on the way that parallel rows of black seeds formed the teeth in the pulpy mouth. Doubtlessly the melon had had much to say. Words that might have given Corso some guidance. During future outbreaks.

Needless to say, Corso did not share this vision with Jenny. But subsequent manifestations proved less easy to conceal. Since Jenny was present. Staring in shock. As Corso attempted to open a door that wasn't there. In the sidewalk. In front of the local multiplex theater. On a busy Saturday night. And other peculiar delusions at other times as well. Until she reached her breaking point. And fled.

Corso felt curiously unfearful of these eruptions. Of surrealism. And dire whimsy. Granted, they were momentarily shocking at times. When he was taken by surprise. His mind elsewhere. As with the bird-foot man. But once engaged with each new derangement, for however long it persisted, Corso felt a decided sense of liberation. From duties and expectation. From his own persona. From consensus reality.

And what more
after all
did any reader
of science fiction
demand.

The offices of *Ruslan's Science Fiction Magazine.* Low-rent quarters on lower Broadway, parsimoniously leased by the parent corporation. Klackto Press. And shared with the publishing chain's stablemates. *Fishbreeder's Monthly*, *Acrostic Fiend's Friend*, *Tatting Journal.* One receptionist for all the wildly incompatible magazines. A bored young woman with a scatter of freckles. Across acres of exposed cleavage. A vista that stirs Corso's penis in its hermitage. But like any solitary's spasm, the moment inevitably passes without relief.

"Um, Corso Fairfield for Sharon Walpole. She's expecting me."

"Hold on a minute please. I'm right in the middle of printing."

Corso sits perforce. Resting his satchel across his damp lap. In case of renewed lust attack. As the woman dances her enameled fingertips noisily across her keyboard. Generating finally some activity in the printer beside her. Corso painfully reminded of his own vain attempts recently to coerce output magically from his own printer. The buffers of which hold not the unborn chapters of *The Black Hole Gun.* But only pain.

Picking up the phone. Reaching Sharon Walpole. Humiliatingly, from the receptionist: "What did you say your name was." Name conveyed to receptionist again and thence to Walpole. Grudging admittance secured.

Through a busy bullpen of interns and editorial assistants and graphic designers. Photos of loved ones on the desks. Free donuts by the coffee urn. Happy chatter. All workers earning a regular paycheck. With regular health-coverage deductions, unthinkingly groused over. Yet so willingly would they be assumed by Corso. In exchange for some stability.

The view from Walpole's cluttered corner office. A rooftop water tank. A ghost sign for Nehi Soda. A sliver of one stalwart tower of the Brooklyn Bridge. Walpole behind her desk. Hugo Awards on a shelf behind her. Trim and blonde. Dressed in a mustard-colored pantsuit. Chunky gold necklace and earrings and bracelets. Fixing Corso with a beam of bright-eyed welcome. Behind which is the message. *Don't waste my time.*

"Corso it's always a pleasure." Air kisses. Floral-vanilla scent of perfume. "What brings you into the city."

"Oh, mainly meeting with my editor at Butte Books."

"That would be Roger Wankel."

"Yes, Wankel." Inwardly, Corso winces. At the memory. Of the recent reaming-out endured over the phone. As Wankel screamed about missed deadlines. And penalties incurred at the printing plant. Which would accrue to Corso's accounts. If not literally, then karmically.

"And of course I need to touch base with my agent."

"Clive Multrum."

"Still, yes. And it's very likely I'll have dinner with Malachi."

No need for a last name. Since everyone in science fiction knew Malachi Stiltjack. Fixture on the bestseller lists. And at many conventions. And on a number of committees. Of the Science Fiction Writers of America. And PEN. Not to mention adjudging many awards. Or making media appearances. As SF's unofficial ambassador to the mundane world. To discuss cloning. Or the internet. Or virtual sex. And by God where did he find the time to write.

Walpole positively frisking at the mention of Stiltjack. Disconcertingly girlish timbre to her voice now. "Oh please give Malachi my best. Ask him when he'll have something new for us. We haven't seen anything from him since he had the cover story two months ago."

"Ah certainly Sharon. Two whole months. Imagine." Corso's last appearance in *Ruslan's* so long ago the millennium has since rolled over. "Happy to act as go-between, ha-ha. Which actually brings me to the reason for my visit. I was hoping you might take something from me."

Walpole begins fidgeting with a bracelet on her left wrist. "Well, of course we're always happy to look at any story of yours Corso. After all, our readers are still talking about 'The Cambrian Exodus.' But I didn't think you were currently working at shorter lengths. Do you have the manuscript with you."

"Ah, but that's the rub. I don't. Damnable oversight. Dashing from the house to catch my train. In fact, the story's only just begun. It's a winner, though. I'm certain of it." Corso's fugitive mind has blanked on the impressive title he earlier prepared to woo Walpole. Now he has to fashion one out of thin air. He looks desperately out the window. " 'The Towers – The Towers of Nehilyn.' "

Walpole spins one bracelet on her left wrist. Evident excess of impatience. Corso finds it hard to focus. On her unsympathetic face. The golden motion around her wrist is seductive. The bracelet a blur of uncanny energy. He feels the beginning of a fugue. Onset of one of his sciencefictional hallucinations. But the prospect of visiting an unreal world is seductive. More enticing than this humiliating begging ritual.

Walpole speaking schoolmarmishly. "Well, you know we hardly ever commission anything, or buy from an outline. You do have an outline to show me at least, don't you."

"An outline. Not with me, alas. How foolish. Forgotten likewise at home. But if you could signal your faith with, um, a contract, or even a check perhaps, I'd email the whole project folder on Monday. Very extensive notes. World-building, in fact. Equal to Anderson or Clement."

Sharon Walpole stands up now. And is plainly unscrewing her hand. Corso fully embracing the revelation. Of Walpole's cyborg nature. The bracelet revealed not as jewelry but as the rim of some prosthetic fixture. And now the threaded extension is disclosed. Shiny metal. Reminding one of such familiar terms as "plastalloy" and "durasteel." And the corresponding threaded hole into her forearm. And Corso is fixated by the dismantling. Overly intimate dismantling. His lower jaw drops further. For now the hand is detached. And the editor lays it upon the desk. Like a fleshy paperweight. And reaches into a drawer. To come up with a substitute hand. A giant lobster claw. Bright red. Which she starts to attach.

And all the while talking. "Corso I'm afraid I can't help you. Your lateness with your novel for Butte is already a scandal. And such a track record does not inspire confidence. There's no way I can advance the good money of Klackto Press on such a tenuous project."

The lobster claw is firmly seated now. And waving. From the incongruous end of a feminine arm. To illustrate editorial hardheartedness. And business savvy. Which Corso should acknowledge. Except how can he honor in others the commonsensical standards which he never upheld in his own life.

Walpole's voice. Descending into a droning alien monotone. Now Corso's calm begins to dissipate. The fantasy no longer an alluring alternative to his problems. But rather menacing, in fact.

"Send me the story. Send me the story. Then we'll see. Then we'll see." And the claw looming larger and larger. Audibly clattering. Directly in Corso's wide-eyed blood-drained face.

And then he's scuttling backward
out of the office,
the building,
into the streets,
thinking only
of the giant pot one would need
to boil a crustacean that big.

Lines of office workers at hot-dog and falafel and gyro carts. With nothing on their mundane minds. Save mortgage payments, love affairs, television shows, shopping sprees, and ferrying hordes of overindulged children from event to event. No obsessions with intergalactic ambassadors. Or fifth-dimensional invaders. Or the paradoxes of time travel. Only solid sensible quotidian activities concern them. The eternal verities. Home and family. Sex and status. Untainted with abnormal speculations derived from technological angst. Of sense of wonder. They know naught. They flip the wall switch for the overhead light. And never think. About the infrastructure behind the scene. And why should they really. That's what engineers are for.

Corso's stomach rumbling. Yet he turns reluctantly from the line of vendors. Why purchase a cheap lunch. If Clive Multrum will stand him to a meal. And doesn't his agent owe him that much. For the monies earned by *Cosmocopia.* Which was a Featured Selection. Of the Science Fiction Book Club. And optioned by a Hollywood studio. Named Fizz Boys Productions. Which proved to be two ex-parking-lot attendants from L.A. Temporarily flush with profits from an exceedingly large Ecstasy deal. And with no more realistic chance of actually making a film. Than two orangutans fresh from the jungles of Kalimantan. And by the time their option expired. Interest in *Cosmocopia* was dead. And another flavor of the week was all the rage. Probably something by Stiltjack.

Multrum's building on Park Avenue South. Classier by far than the Ruslan quarters. Concierge in a Ruritanian uniform. Your name sir. May we inspect your briefcase sir. Multrum and his peers here obviously a prime target. For enraged terrorists. Eager perhaps to avenge injustices against disenfranchised writers. Of whom Corso is certainly one. But he manages to disguise his true affiliations from the vigilant guardian. A fat sixtyish man with a dandruff-flecked comb-over. Who directs Corso to the elevators.

Eleventh floor. Corridor with doors to numerous suites. Into Number 1103, anticipatorily unlocked upon notification by the admiral downstairs. Impeccable furnishings. Rugs from Araby and Persia. Paintings by artists as yet unknown outside New York. Yet inevitably destined for fame and fortune. Such is Multrum's unerring taste. Leather couch. Wet bar. Bookshelves holding hundreds of titles by Multrum's clients. Looking like some Hollywood set-designer coordinated them. *Cosmocopia* on the lowermost shelf, partly shadowed.

Multrum's personal assistant emerging from in back. Well known by Corso. And likewise. An imperturbable Korean woman. Soberly dressed in black linen. Flat face and hair so jet-dark it should be sprinkled with stars. Named most improbably Kichi Koo. And Corso has always longed to ask her. Did you assume this cognomen deliberately. In some kind of madcap Greenwich Village fit of bohemianism. Or were your parents so blithely cruel. But he never has or will. Since Koo has never once so much as cracked a smile in his presence.

"Mr. Fairfield, hello. Mr. Multrum is on the phone presently. But he will see you soon."

"Thank you, ah, Ms. Koo. I believe I will help myself to a drink then. To ease the wait."

Koo's wall-like face assumes an even sterner mien. "As you wish."

Corso pours himself some of Multrum's finest single malt. Often dreamed of, seldom tasted. By writers. Of Corso's stratum. Sipping it with pleasure. Letting his eyes rove over the shelves. Where they encounter a long row of books by Malachi Stiltjack. Stiltjack being Corso's entry point into Multrum's aegis. Not the only debt Corso owes the man. And the rightmost title not familiar. *Gods of the Event Horizon.* Taking it down. Published last month. And probably already in a second printing. Reading spottily in the text. Yes, yes, transparent style, stirring action, big ideas. That's the winning formula. To be applied to *The Black Hole Gun.* As soon as one returns home. With a face-saving check in pocket. To stave off the bill collectors. And stock the fridge. With beer and jugged herring.

"Corso you bastard are you drinking up my entire bar."

Multrum slapping Corso jovially on the back. Causing expensive liquor to slosh. Onto Corso's shirt.

"Ah but no, of course not, Clive. Just a small tot. To enliven the humors. And prime the digestive track. For lunch."

Multrum has Corso by the elbow. A large fragrant cigar projects from Multrum's face. His agent steering him away from the bar. A silver-haired man of middling height. Clean-shaven and smelling not only of Cuban tobacco but also of expensive aftershave. Available only to literary agents above a certain income level. No doubt. His face engraved with lines that oddly map both a habit of smiling and one of sneering. Not plump but layered with a generous amount of self-satisfied tissue. As if to say, *I am insulated by my success.*

"So you haven't eaten yet. Surprise, surprise. Well, me neither. Let's go to Papoon Skloot's. I have something important to discuss with you."

"And is this, um, Skloot's a pricey establishment."

Another slap rattles Corso's bones. Hail fellow well met. We're all adults here. Don't give your shameful poverty a thought. Old bean.

"Don't sweat it my friend it's all on me."

"So very kind of you Clive."

"Can the shit and let's move."

A taxi ferries them to Papoon Skloot's. During the ride Corso can ponder only Multrum's mysterious words. Something important to discuss. One senses the axe about to fall. Ass meeting sidewalk. Creditors gnawing on one's bones. Unjust fate for a simple soul. Who never asked for much. And since youth dreamed only of traveling the starlanes in prose. And who deserves some slack. Now that he is temporarily stymied. By a lack of belief in his own fictions. While at the same time beset. By those very sciencefictional conceits made real.

Corso nearly gives way to self-pitying tears by the end of the ride. But manfully stifles them. Instead adopting an eager air of gaiety. Commensurate with the atmosphere inside the posh restaurant. Where various literati and glitterati clink flutes of champagne. Amidst expensive fabrics, elaborate chandeliers, and servile attendants. And consume tiny portions of elaborately mangled foodstuffs. From plates big as the shields of warriors. In a bad fantasy trilogy.

Buck up. In the face of elitist pretensions. One must go out in style. This Corso's vow. Despite liquor-sticky shirt, soapy trousers, and satchel containing only a return Amtrak ticket, a toothbrush, and a recent issue of *Fantascience Journal.* With a picture of Hugo Gernsback on the cover.

"What'll you have Corso. Can't decide, huh. Used to ordering through the drive-up window, hey. Okay, let me get us started." Multrum rattles off a litany of dishes. The server brings their drinks. Corso allowed one sip. Before Multrum launches into business.

"Now listen to me Corso. You and I both know you're in deep shit with Wankel and Butte Books. But I've negotiated you one final extension. However, the grace period hinges on you going over there in person and kissing some ass."

"Exactly my own strategy Clive. Of course, Kowtow and touch cap. Not too proud to beg. Yes, certainly. I already have an appointment later this afternoon with Roger."

"Excellent! Then back home to dig into *Neutron Cannon.*"

"Ah, *The Black Hole Gun.*"

"Sure, whatever. But before then, you're going to do both of us a big favor. You're going to knock out a tie-in novel. Vestine Opdycke from Shuman and Shyster called me, desperate for a last-minute replacement for Jerome Arizona. Arizona bailed on this project, and they need it yesterday."

His second drink of the day is inflating Corso's brain. Leery of visionary states. But no immediate untoward incidents. No smerps or thoats rampaging through the restaurant. As they once did in the Wal-Mart. Where the beasts received no cheerful hello. From the oblivious store greeter.

Allowing a drift of mellowness to overtake his anxiety-plagued day. "But Arizona is usually so reliable. Never misses a deadline."

"True. But that was before he was caught by the local cops in bed with two sixteen-year-olds."

"Oh."

"So, are you onboard."

"But what's the nature of the project."

"A novelization of the *Starmaker* movie."

Corso misbelieves his ears. "The Stapledon classic."

"I think that's the guy's name."

"But there's already a book. Hundreds of pages of impeccable speculative text. They must have used that as a source of the script. Can't they just reissue the original."

"The movie doesn't exactly follow the original anymore. Just the new love interests and space battles alone demand a different version. C'mon, it's easy money. No royalties though. Strictly work for hire."

Corso is bewildered. Lowering his glance to his immaculate napkin in his lap. How to answer. Traducing one's youthful idol. But quick cash. And a foot in the door at Schuman and Shyster. Maybe a good way to dissolve one's block. Crib from a master. What choice does one have.

Corso raises his eyes to Multrum's face.

The agent's brow is mutating to a jutting ledge. Features thickening. Facial pelt growing. Stained horsey teeth protruding. Multrum has devolved. To Neanderthal status. And so have the other diners. And staff. Walking awkwardly with curved backs and bowed legs. Their neckties cinching their enlarged necks. Like barbed wire overgrown by a tree.

Multrum grows impatient. His voice remains unchanged. Thankfully. No primordial grunts to misinterpret. "Well Corso what's your answer."

Even as Corso rummages for his own voice, Multrum continues to devolve. Scales. Fangs. Horns. Spiked tail. Multrum now an anthropomorphic saurian. A dinosaur in Hugo Boss. And the rest of the patrons. Similarly antediluvian. One female dinosaur. Categorized by her dress. Picks up her steak with disproportionately small forelimbs. And pops it entire into her slavering, razor-toothed mouth.

Sweat soaks Corso's shirt. Reptilian stench emanates from his table partner. Must phrase one's acceptance of the odious assignment in the most genial terms. Lest agent take offense. And disembowel one with a casual kick.

For Corso sincerely doubts
Multrum would stop
after only fifteen percent
of his client
was eaten.

One's third female gatekeeper of the day. The receptionist at Butte Books. Cheeks still hamstery with adolescent avoirdupois. Purple nail polish. Gingery hair secured in two outjutting tails on either side. Of a face both too wise and utterly naive. A recent graduate, no doubt. Of a prestigious school. That should be ashamed of itself. For culturing and feeding innumerable such starry-eyed hapless romantics. Into publishing's voracious low-wage maw.

"Ah, Mr. Fairfield to see Mr. Wankel."

"Go right in please."

Corso expected to wait. The easy access discommodes him. For he needs to utilize a jakes.

"Is there, um, a restroom I could avail myself of first."

"Certainly. Here's the key. Left down that corridor."

Carrying the sacred key. Almost as if he works here. At the firm which ignored all his suggestions. For the cover of *Cosmocopia.* And instead of Whelan or Eggleton. He got the defiantly pastel work of Murrell Peurifoy. Whose *oeuvre* consists almost entirely of covers for humorous fantasy novels. And the image Peurifoy supplied for the eponymous device of Corso's book. Looked like a hybrid of a juicer, the postmodern VW Bug, and a penile extension pump.

Through the limited-access door. Into the uttermost stall. Hanging satchel from a coat hook. Gratefully dropping one's trousers and boxers. Taking a seat. Peristaltic relief. Still blessedly easy to obtain. Unlike the mental variety.

Additional patrons entering noisily. A familiar voice and an unknown one. Wankel himself the former. Jovial banter above hardy plashing of piss.

"So you're meeting with Corso Fairly Fried. What's his story these days."

"Pathetic case. Fair amount of talent. But he's gotten too deep into this whole mythos of the genre thing. Thinks SF is some kind of mystical calling. Instead of just another job. Imagines he's writing for a fraternity of supermen. Instead of a bunch of dorky, over-intelligent fifteen-year-olds."

Laughter from the unidentified interlocutor. "Jesus! Can't he see it's all interchangeable. Mysteries, technothrillers, westerns. Just a load of identical crap. Well, I know one thing. I won't make *that* mistake. I'm not getting trapped in this dead-end field. Another year or two and I'm outta here. I've already got some feelers out at *Maxim.*"

Zippers laddering upward. *"Maxim,* huh. Must meet a lot of beautiful women there."

"You bet."

Sounds of hand-washing. Departure. And a sob betokening black desolation in the farthermost stall.

Corso Fairly Fried. His public image. Known to everyone but oneself. Passion and dedication to one's chosen field. Derided and cast aside. One's motivation laughable. If not predicated strictly on commercialism. Not to mention exclusion of any artistic striving. To build upon the work of past heroes. Giants of the medium. Who no doubt received similar treatment. From their own traitorous editors.

And when he faces Wankel. The temptation will be there. To spit in his eye. Or punch same. But he of course cannot. For

Multrum would rend his impetuous and violent client into bite-sized pieces. To be shared with the other velociraptors. Corso's only choice. To swallow his shame. And carry on.

Back to the receptionist. Return the key. Into Wankel's sanctum.

Roger Wankel standing by a table near the window. View of steel and glass canyons. Assaultive in their uncaring facades. Birds in flight. Boyish shock of tawny hair angling across the editor's wide brow. Close-set eyes. Nose and lips chosen from a child's catalog of facial features then misplaced in an adult facial template. Sorting through a stack of cover proofs. Perhaps Peurifoy already engaged to limn *The Black Hole Gun.* If so, one has only a dual question. Is that window shatterproof. And how far to the ground.

"Corso! A real pleasure to see you! How's Ginny doing."

"You must mean Jenny. She's fine." Unspoken of course. That she is fine with someone else.

"Great, great. Now I assume you're here to talk about the extension. Never thought it would get approved. But Multrum's one tough negotiator. You're lucky to have him on your team."

"Yes. He has a thick hide."

"True, true. Now what can you share with me to convince me you've got a handle on this project."

Restraining oneself from "sharing" venomous accusations. Of venality and double-dealing. Instead babbling in a stream-of-consciousness fashion. About likely plot developments. Which might occur. To Corso's protagonist. Russ Radikans. Owner of the Black Hole Gun. Ancient artifact of a vanished race. The Acheropyte. And Russ's lover. Zulma Nautch. Starship pilot. Of the *Growler.* Zulma's evil clone sister. Zinza, deadly assassin. And so forth. With Wankel taking it all in. And nodding sagely. The hypocritical bastard.

A knock at the office door. Which Wankel ignores. But a workman enters regardless. Mustache, dirty brown coveralls, hammer hanging from a loop, work gloves tucked in a back pocket. And without a word. The man begins to dismantle one of the office walls. Using a putty knife. To peel sheets of thin substance away. Not plaster or particleboard, but a resinous veneer. To reveal not girders and joists. But rather the raw blue air several dozen stories up. A breeze strokes Corso's cheek.

Corso flummoxed into silence. Wankel confused. But only by his author's hesitation. "Go on, I'm listening." So that Corso realizes. This is another hallucination. And he tries to continue. Tries to embrace the unpredictable unreality of his senses.

Now several more workmen arrive. All twins to the first. A busy horde of disassemblers. They fall to aiding the original in deconstructing the walls. Until soon Corso and Wankel sit at the top of a lofty naked pillar. A few square feet of carpeted floor. Exposed on all sides. To Manhattan's brutal scrutiny. Since the rest of the office has inexplicably vanished. A stage set struck. By the Hidden Puppet Masters. Who intend to decimate. Corso's solipsistic self.

Breezes riffle Corso's hair. He cannot go on. Because of the actions of one workman. Who has stepped confidently off the pillar. And now climbs the sky itself. As if the air were a gentle blue slope. He heads for the "sun." And as he approaches the orb he does not shrink. But rather puts the sun into its true scale. A disk as big as a hubcap. And donning his gloves. The workman begins to unscrew the sun.

At the same time the other workmen have shut down Wankel. Employing a switch at the back of his neck. Corso's enduring suspicions of the existence of some such switch now validated. And they pick up the editor's chair with him in it. And tip it upside down. But Wankel remains attached. Grinning moronically.

And then as the sun is finally completely unthreaded from its socket descends the ultimate darkness.

As if Russ Radikans
just employed his
Black Hole Gun
on his very Creator.

"Corso my boy. Wake up!"

That plummy voice. Steeped in all the luxuries of a cozy life. So familiar. From a credit-card commercial. And one for Saturn automobiles. And many a convention panel. Not to mention the occasional phone conversation. In the nighted hours. When despair crept up. On the protégé. And he dialed the mentor's home phone. A number millions of fans would have killed for. One such being the vanished younger Corso himself. And even now when one is accorded one's own small professional stature. Still half-disbelieving. One has been granted such a high privilege.

Corso unshutters his eyes. He is recumbent. Half naked. Atop a wheeled stretcher. Shielded by dirty curtains on rings. From the pitiful and pitying gazes of fellow sufferers. Evidently in a hospital emergency room. And by his side sits Malachi Stiltjack.

Stiltjack wears an expensive charcoal suit. Many yards of Italian fabric girdling his extensive acreage. Of a finer cut even than Multrum's. Vest. Watch chain. Other dandyish accoutrements. Silver hair razor-cut and styled to perfection. His middle-aged shiny pontifical face beaming. Presumably at Corso's reattainment of consciousness.

"What – what happened to me?"

"You passed out in your editor's office. Bad show my boy. Many of us have longed for such an escape, but it's pure cowardice to make such a melodramatic exit. Reflects poorly on your endurance and stamina. How could you handle a multicity book tour if one little bout of tedium causes you to crumple like an empty potato-chip packet. So they'll ask. In any case, an ambulance rushed you here. I tracked you down when you failed to meet me."

"Oh Christ, Wankel will put me at the top of his shit list now for sure."

Wry expression on Stiltjack's face. "And you weren't there already."

Corso chagrined. "You know then about me missing my deadlines."

"But who doesn't. *Locus* even did a sidebar on your predicament in the December issue. Didn't you see it then."

"I let my subscription lapse. Money was tight. And reading *Locus* just makes me nervous. All those big-money deals, all those brilliant, joyous, glad-handing *professionals.* How does it all relate to the actual dreaming – "

"Come now Corso you should know better than to believe all that printed hyperbole. None of us is ever really secure. Most writers just put up a good front."

An ungenerous feeling of anger and envy at his friend. "Easy enough for you to say Malachi with your castle and contracts and – and concubines!"

The padrone unoffended by the peon's eruption. Magnanimous and solicitous from on high. "Now, now Corso such resentment ill becomes you. But I understand completely that it's your creative blockage talking. That's the crux of your trouble. Not your material circumstances. Or your wife's desertion."

A wail of despair. "My God has *Locus* run a sidebar on that too!"

"Not at all. But the grapevine – "

"Do my goddamn peers ever stop gossiping long enough to collect their awards."

"Let's put aside the all-too-human deficiencies of our comrades for the moment Corso and consider my diagnosis. Think a minute. If *I* were the one suffering the blockage, would all my money and possessions make me feel one whit happier. Of course not. Same thing with one's physical health. Psychological or somatic, an easy and natural functioning is the one essential to your peace of mind. Clear up your creative logjam, and you'll be back on top of the world."

"An easy prescription. But hard to administer to oneself."

"Let's work on it together a little longer. It's not that late in the evening. We can still have dinner. But first we need to get you discharged."

Doctor summoned. Corso reluctantly given a clean bill of health. Possibly a small case of food poisoning adduced. From Papoon Skloot's. Spoiled coelacanth in the prehistoric kitchen. Which would serve all the egregiously wealthy diners right. Bidden by a surly yet attractive red-haired nurse to dress oneself. Nurse not lingering to peek at Corso's neglected manhood. As half-fantasized. By a lonely and too-little-of-late-fondled professional daydreamer. And soon out on the twilit streets.

Stiltjack swinging a cane with a golden grip. Casting a radiant appreciative gaze at the whole wide world. Scurrying business drones. Sweaty delivery persons. Idling teenagers. A cherry for his picking. Or kicking. Should any viciously magisterial whim overtake him. *Droit du seigneur.* My mundane subjects. Corso striding silently alongside. Certain that if any pigeon shits. The excrement will hit the one who presents the most abject target.

"Now then tell me about your problems lad."

Corso complies. Recounts his disenchantment with the work. Displacement of tropes into real life. And the fugue states. And even as he describes his disease. He nervously awaits another strike. But nothing. Yet Corso's sigh of relief is undone. By Stiltjack's next words.

"So you've got the dicky fits. I thought they wouldn't have hit you for another few years yet. But they do occur in direct proportion to one's talents. So I shouldn't be surprised."

Corso simultaneously flattered and alarmed. "The dicky fits."

"Named after you-know-who of course. Our patron saint."

"But you mean to say – "

"That I've had them too. But of course! Every cold-stone writer of science fiction goes through them at one point or another. Most come out the other side. But of course a few don't. With luck you won't be numbered among the latter."

"It's an occupational disease then."

"Oh it's not a disease. It's a privileged glimpse of reality."

Corso stops. "What are you saying Malachi."

"Aren't you listening to me. You've been vouchsafed a vision. Of the plastic, unstable nature of reality. The illusory character of the entire cosmos. It's the god's-eye perspective. Conceptual breakthrough time."

Corso's tone sneering. "And I suppose then that you've benefited immensely from these visions. Maybe even learned how to become a deity yourself. Maybe I'm just a character in one of your fictions."

"Well, yes, I have become rather a demigod. As to who created whom, or whether we're both figments of some larger entity – well, the jury is still out."

"I would appreciate some disproof of your insanity."

"Naturally. How's this."

The surging pedestrian crowd freezes in place. And the traffic too. On the sidewalk appear Sharon Walpole, Clive Multrum, and Roger Wankel. In their standard configurations. But then each morphs to his or her abnormal state. Walpole's prosthetic lobster claw. Multrum's reptilian guise. Wankel's android fixity. Corso approaches the marmoreal figures. Pokes them. Turns to Stiltjack.

"Satisfied now. Or shall I trot out Jenny and her new beau. I believe they're attending a car show in Duluth at the moment. I could bring onstage that derelict from Penn Station as well. His name by the way is Arthur Pearty. A fascinating fellow once you really get to know him."

"No. Not necessary. Just send these – these specters away."

The editors and agent vanish. Life resumes. Stiltjack moves blithely onward. Corso numbly following. The world's deceptive insubstantiality now confirmed. A thin shambles. A picture painted on rice paper. Corso sick to his stomach.

"It's best not to cause such large-scale disruptions. The universe, whatever it is, is not our toy. We did not create it. We do not run the hourly shadow show. We are unaware of the ultimate rationale for its existence. But a small tweak here and there. Aimed a personal betterment. Such little perquisites are permitted those of us who have come out the other side of the dicky fits."

"But, but – but even if you decide to go on living, how can you continue to write science fiction! In the face of such knowledge."

Malachi pausing. To signal importance of his words. "Well, as to motivation now Corso it's all a question of whose imagination is superior, isn't it. Weird as the universe is when you finally comprehend it, a trained mind such as yours or mine demands that our own imagination be even more potent in its conceptions.

If you're a real science-fiction writer, that is. Now why don't we go enjoy a fine meal. I can guarantee that we won't be interrupted."

And Corso laughs
loud enough to cause strangers
to gape
for his appetite
is suddenly prodigious
and not just for food.

– For Horselover Fat, Jonathan Herovit and, of course, the Ginger Man.

Mother's Milt

ℬ℘

Pat Cadigan

Milt appeared at breakfast, about as unsavory a sight as you could ever see at 7:30 on a summer morning: long stringy hair threatening to dip into the bowl of cereal, old faded sweatshirt with the sleeves hacked off, showing wiry arms with a river of tattoos flowing up and down them, even older jeans faded to baby blue overlaid with a sheen of brown.

"Say hi to Milt, Lynn," my mother told me, planting a quart of milk on the table next to his technicolor elbow. "I bailed him out of jail last night instead of your father."

"Hi, Milt," I said.

His head moved slightly; I saw one watery hazel eye peering at me between the strands of hair and I could tell he was amused by the wary tone in my voice. I might have been amused, too, if I'd been in his position, but I wasn't. I looked at my mother. As usual, the creases in her crisp, white coverall seemed sharp enough to cut flesh. My mother never failed to do mornings extremely well, even if she'd been up very late the night before.

"Drunk driving," she said. Sitting down at Milt's left with her own bowl of cereal. "We can't go on like that."

"Drunk driving isn't funny, Ma," I said. Milt sat up straight. He looked like a knife-murderer.

"I meant your father," she said, "not Milt. Milt was in on a shoplifting charge."

"I know who you meant."

Milt glanced at my mother. She patted his arm. "*Don't worry.* I said you could stay, so you can stay. If you want to."

"And if I don't," he said, turning that psycho face to me, "ain't you afraid of forfeiting the bail?"

"My mother isn't afraid of anything," I said. "Haven't you figured that out yet?"

Before my mother left for work at Busy Hands, she presented Milt with a complete list of his chores for the day, reading it aloud to him just in case he was, in her words, literate-embarrassed. "Do the dishes, tidy the living room, vacuum all the rugs, dust all the downstairs furniture, change the linens on the beds upstairs – there are three bedrooms, including the one you're staying in – and clean both bathrooms. Do a good job and I'll give you a treat when I get home from Busy Hands."

He took the list from her in what I thought of as Standard Dumb Amazement, blinking when she stood on tiptoe to pat him on the head, and then stared after her as she bustled out the door leading to the garage. Bustled was the only word for the way my mother moved; once you'd seen her do it, you understood exactly what it looked like. He went to the window over the sink and watched her drive away.

Finally, he turned back to me, holding the list the way I'd seen people hold bills from auto repair shops. "Is she kidding?" he asked me.

I spread a thin layer of cream cheese on the other half of my pumpernickel bagel. "Are you in jail?"

He laughed, crumpled the list, and tossed it over his shoulder into the sink. "What I am is outta here."

I got up, went to the junk drawer, and pulled out the gun. "I don't think so."

Those watery hazel eyes got very large. "Holy shit, girl! What are you doing?"

"Come on, *Milt*, what do *you* think?"

His gaze went from the gun to me, back to the gun and back to me.

"Give up?" I said. He started to raise his hands, just the way people did on TV. "The dishes. I'm helping you do the dishes."

He took at step toward me and I aimed at his crotch. Most people make the mistake of aiming a gun at a man's head or chest, but believe me, setting your sights lower will get their attention much better.

"Do I have to persuade you that I can and will use this on you? Do you think this is the first time I've had breakfast with a convicted felon on my mother's sufferance?"

He squinted at me. "Who *are* you people? *What* are you?"

"Conscientious citizens," I said.

"Listen, I don't want you here any more than you want to be here. But here we are." I jerked my head at the table. "Stack 'em and rack 'em. I'll plead self-defense."

"Are you gonna keep that gun on me all day? That's what you'll have to do."

"We all gotta do what we gotta do, Milt," I said. "And you gotta get busy."

"How old are you?" he said suspiciously.

"Sixteen."

"My God." He didn't believe me, of course; I'm built like a linebacker, hostage to genetics.

"The house is a mess, Milt," I said. "Okay?"

He folded those skinny arms. "What if I just refuse to move?"

"Then it's going to be a boring day for both of us," I said. "And you'll go back to jail at the end of it."

That finally reached him. "I can't do that. And I can't stay here," he said. "Please, honey – Lynn – give a guy a break, will ya?"

"You got a break. You're out of jail."

He was staring at the gun again.

"Well, sort of," I added. "Look, my mother's eccentric even by your standards – "

"I heard *that.*"

" – but don't get the idea she isn't serious. My mother doesn't kid around. She doesn't know how." I gestured at the dishes waiting on the table. "Come on, Milt. Is it going to kill you to do a dish?"

He got the point, but I could tell even he was surprised to find himself gathering up bowls and silverware and plates and taking them to the sink. The whole time he was rinsing things off and putting them in the dishwasher, I could practically hear the wheels turning in his head: when he could get a good opening to try to overpower this big, crazy bruiser of a girl, how far could he run and how fast, and what the hell was he doing, why had he accepted his release to a total stranger in the first place? My mother always chose well, though. Old Milt had obviously spent more than a few nights sleeping rough and the prospect of spending at least one night indoors before he made off with anything that wasn't nailed down with a value of over five dollars had been too tempting to resist. Going along with the crazy little gray-haired lady who had chosen to foot bail for him over her husband had been a pretty good idea in the middle of the night.

The phone rang just after he'd gotten the vacuum cleaner out of the hall closet. My mother, of course; she was pleased to hear that Milt was on schedule, but dismayed that I still had to hold the gun on him. As if that were unusual. Anyone would think she'd have learned by now – they spend at least one whole day working under the gun. My mother, the eternal optimist, always hoping that she'd get a quick study.

Just before lunch, he made a break for the front door. I let him yank on it and try to break the windows. Then I made him finish vacuuming the runner in the hall before I gave him his lunch. He kept muttering *I don't believe this* over and over while he spooned up tomato soup.

Dusting is when they usually try for the phone. I left the room briefly, just so he could get it over with. He was dabbing it with the feather duster when I came back. I wouldn't have brought it up, but he felt compelled to.

"How come you can get calls when the phone's dead?" he asked accusingly.

"The phone's not dead," I told him. "You just don't know how to use it."

"Jesus Christ." He threw down the feather duster. "I want to know what's going on here. Your mother said I could stay *if I wanted to.* Well, what if I don't want to?"

I hefted the gun slightly. "I think you want to."

He picked up the feather duster and finished doing the end tables and the bookcases.

There was another fuss about changing the beds. He didn't think he had to change his, since he'd just spent one night in it, and then he tried to tell me his back was too weak for him to turn the mattresses, a charade he insisted on playing out with all three of them, so it was a slow, clumsy process. But it got done. I let him have a snack break in front of the TV before I told him to set the kitchen table for dinner.

"That wasn't on the list," he said, unable to tear his eyes away from that skinny little game show hostess who waves her arms in front of washer-dryers as if they were miracles.

"My mother would want you to fill out the day with something useful," I told him.

"But really," he said, punching the couch cushion behind him, "I think I hurt my back with those damned mattresses. No fooling. I ought to get in a hot tub." He looked up at me and smiled for the first time. "God, a hot bath would be heaven right now. You could even stay there and keep the gun on me, I wouldn't mind."

I just bet he wouldn't. But he wasn't the only one who'd seen *The Beguiled.* Still, if you don't let them try everything, they don't believe. Seduction occurred to some of them sooner, and some of them later, and the second group usually try it on my mother rather than me.

"What did you have in mind?" I said. "A bubble bath?"

His smile got bigger and more enthusiastic. "You got something sweet smelling? I bet you have. Something you like for your boyfriends to smell on you."

"I wear Obsession," I told him. "Only Obsession. It wouldn't smell right on you. There's Obsession *pour Homme,* but we don't have any."

"Obsession, eh?" His smile shrank a bit. He was looking at the barrel of the gun again and didn't realize I knew what he was staring at. "You obsessed with guns?"

"No. Cleanliness, actually."

He threw back his head and laughed. The studio audience coincidentally laughed right along with him and he used the remote control to turn down the volume. "I can see that. All the more reason for me to take a bath before your mother gets home. So I can be as clean as the house when she comes in."

"This house isn't clean," I said. "The windows are filthy. You do those tomorrow."

He laughed again. "How's the old saying go? I don't do windows?"

"Yeah, sure, Milt. But it's just a saying. You change the drapes, too, and you vacuum upstairs and you clean the cellar and I don't know what all. My mother'll leave you a list, of course."

He slumped against the back of the couch. "Oh, come on, little lady Lynn. Are you gonna spend another whole day holding that gun on me?"

"If I have to."

"What about tonight? You and your mom gonna take turns guarding me?"

"We lock you in your room. You were locked in last night, but I guess you didn't know it."

He combed his fingers through that stringy hair. "Look . . . all this has been, you know, kinda weird and kinky and interesting, but it's gotten old. I gotta tell you, I was really wondering about your mom last might when she bypassed your old man and took me out instead. It seemed like one of those great opportunities, too good to be true. See, I know sooner or later my prints are gonna turn up with my real name and then I'm in the soup for sure. So I thought, well, I'll go with this Good Samaritan – Good Samaritanness?" He gave a little nervous laugh. "Well, whatever, I'll go with her, and I'll have a little something to eat and a good night's sleep and then I'm off to Mexico, Canada, parts unknown – " he shrugged. "Then I get dishpan hands at gunpoint."

"You don't have dishpan hands," I said. "Dishwashers have made dishpan hands obsolete. You've got busy hands."

"Yeah, right. What is that. 'Busy Hands' where your mother works – maid service?"

"You're exactly right. It's a maid service. My mother cleans houses for a living. But it's that old story – who shaves the barber? In this case, you do."

He stared at me, baffled. Apparently, he'd never heard that old chestnut about the village where every man who didn't shave himself was shaved by the barber, so who shaved the barber. I guess they don't get much parlor philosophy in jail.

"Never mind," I said. "Break-time's over. Set the table."

He hesitated, ready to argue further, and then thought better of it. "You'll have to talk me through this," he said, leading the way into the kitchen. "I can never remember which fork goes on the right."

"That's easy," I said, "you never put forks on the right. You don't want to risk accidentally piercing a dinner companion."

He looked over his shoulder at me. "Really?"

I just shook my head. "Oh, dammit. We forgot to run the dishwasher. Well, you'll have to wash a few dishes by hand. There isn't time for a complete cycle before my mother comes home." I had to poke him in the ribs with the gun a few times to get him in the right frame of mind. "See, now I am gonna get dishpan hands," he said grumpily as he stood at the sink.

"Not with Softi-Bubbles," I said, sitting at the table. "It's specially formulated to leave your skin sweetly soft while it cuts the grease. You can also wash your fine linens in it and even use if for a bubble bath."

He snorted. "Yeah. The bubble bath I'm never gonna get."

I was really tired of his whining. "You can take a bath after dinner if you really want to."

He stacked the dishes in the rack and let them drain. "You can make me clean, but I gotta tell you, I can't cook, even with that gun to my head. You can blow my brains out if you want, but there's nothing I can do."

"That's okay. My mother will be bringing dinner home with her. She's got a friend in the catering business."

"Great. Rubber chicken."

"You could always go on a diet." As I'd figured, that shut him up fast. After experiencing bail my mother's way, he didn't want to know what her idea of a diet would be. He was stubborn, but he was learning.

When he finished setting the table, I decided to let him go back to watching TV in the living room until my mother came home, rest his weary back. I was pretty sure my mother would be pleased with the job he'd done on the house, so she wouldn't mind my giving him a little extra relaxing time.

And I was right. My mother walked through the house beaming with pleasure, while Milt and I trailed behind her in a little parade. I still had the gun on him, of course – there was no telling if he'd be stupid enough to try attacking my mother. But her effusive praise caught him off guard. After a day with me, he'd been expecting almost anything but that.

"I especially like the way you made the beds," she told him as we trooped back downstairs to the kitchen. "Is that how they do it in prison?"

"How'd you know I'd been in prison?" he asked

"Get real, Milt," I said.

"Well, jail, yeah, but just about everybody's been in jail – "

My mother laughed. "Good heavens, where did you come by that idea? Young man, there are people who go their whole lives and never see the inside of a *jail.* Let alone the big house. Lynn's father was in the big house. We've learned to tell ex-cons by body language. And tattoos, of course." She ran a finger up his left arm as she ushered him into the kitchen. "Some of those are jailhouse tattoos. You really ought to have them worked on, covered over with better designs if you don't want to have them removed altogether."

All he could do was stare at her as she sat him at the table and took her place to his left.

"Lynn, you may serve now," she said, waving a hand at the white bags she had set on the counter. "And then afterwards, it'll be time for your treat," she added to Milt, wiggling her index finger in his stupefied face.

Tonight's offering was a stroganoff. I'd rather not eat so much red meat – in fact, I'd often thought of going vegetarian – but my mother wanted to keep me big. I worried about what the insides of my arteries looked like, even though my mother insisted that was no worry at all at my age.

"Jesus!" Milt said as the aroma hit him in the face. "I'm starved! Your daughter didn't give me much for lunch."

"Eating heavily in the middle of the day would have made you sleepy," my mother told him. "Now, chow down. You've earned it."

He'd finished half his plate before it occurred to him that I wasn't holding the gun on him anymore. But I did have it in my lap, and it was pointing at him before he could make so much as a twitch in my mother's direction. She frowned at me and then gave Milt a look.

"Let's not fight at the table, you two." She turned back to me. "Okay?"

I shrugged. "He started it."

Milt's fork plopped in his food as he buried his face in his hands. "My God, my God," he moaned. "How did I get here? What's happening? What kinda crazy deal is this?"

My mother gave his forearm a small push. "Elbows off the table, Milt."

He peeked at her from between his fingers. "Lady, I don't know what's going on here with your locked doors and your unbreakable windows and your dead phones and your gun-toting daughter, but I think I wanna go back to jail."

"Oh, no, you wouldn't like that," my mother said. "Jail's so risky. My friend Carol the caterer might bail you out then, and you'd like that a lot less than this, believe-you-me. She bailed out Lynn's father around lunch-time." My mother shook her head, going *tch-tch-tch.* "She'll forfeit the bail, of course, but it was a last-minute thing, this dinner she had to do, and they insisted on stroganoff. The Royal Lodge of the Mooses said they'd pay one-

and-a-half times the normal fee for it, so even minus the lost bail money, Carol still makes out like a bandit."

"Carol *always* makes out like a bandit," I said. "She's the Robin Hood of the testimonial set."

"Yes, but catering is *so messy*," said my mother. "I much prefer to clean up a mess than make one." She paused, contemplating a noodle on the end of her fork. "You know, I also think I prefer weather that's too cold to too hot. What about you, Milt?"

Milt's expression was completely despairing. "Huh?"

"Do you prefer your weather too cold or too hot? Or, let's put it this way – if you could, would you go to Canada or Mexico?"

"Why?" he asked tonelessly.

"This is just *dinner conversation*," she said, a little exasperation creeping into her voice. "Everyone should know how to make small talk. Small talk's got a bad rap. If you could see the way some of the more bashful guests suffer sitting next to each other at one of the banquets my friend Carol caters, you'd understand the virtues of being capable of superficial conversation." She put down her fork and wiped her fingers on her napkin before laying a hand on Milt's arm. "Milt, this is *your* civilization, the one *you* have to live in and you have *got* to get civilized."

"Okay," he said, "okay, okay, anything you say, whatever you like, lady. Just take me back to jail so I can plead guilty, pay my debt to society, and when I get out, I'll go get civilized."

"Well, *that's* the *good* news," my mother said brightly. "I was going to save it for after dinner, but I'm really impressed with those beds. The shoplifting charges have been dropped."

His mouth fell open. A very unoriginal reaction, but at least it was harmless. "How?"

My mother spread her arms. "How do you think?" She leaned toward him, beaming like mad. "You have a job! With Busy Hands!" She grabbed both his hands in hers and gave them a little shake. "You passed the audition! You aced the try-out! You made the team! But you know, I really thought you would." She turned to me without letting go of him. "Lynn? Dissenting opinion? Comments?"

I was still holding the gun on him while I ate. "You know me, Ma. I bow to your superior judgment. Do you have a uniform that will fit him?"

"No," he said, snatching his hands away. "I won't do it. Blow my brains all over this kitchen if you want, but I won't do it. I won't be no crazy lady's slave. You can chain me up in the cellar, you can lock me in your attic, you can kill me. But I know my rights and you're violating them. Ain't no way you can kidnap somebody from jail and make them be a slave for you.

"How do you kidnap somebody from jail?" I said. "Ma, do you know?"

"No, I don't." She chuckled. "Kidnapping's illegal. I've got all the official papers and everything – they signed him over to me, and he went of his own free will. What' s the matter, Milt, housework got you down? I know you won't believe this, but it's actually easier to clean somebody else's house than your own.

"That's why this place looked the way it did, before you went to work on it. Tomorrow, you can do the windows and take care of the draperies, there' s the laundry – "

"No! Didn't you hear me, lady? I said *no!* That's capital N, capital O, N-O, *no!*" He gave me a frightened look, as if he expected me to shoot him for that.

"You're just tired," my mother said, picking up her fork again. "You'll feel better after a good night's sleep. Always works for me – I used to feel this way after slaving all day for Lynn's father, and then he'd come home drunk, mess everything up – " she tucked some stroganoff into her mouth and chewed thoughtfully. "I just had to get a system, you know. Work with a system and you can conquer the world. And I really thought Lynn's father had finally gotten his mind right at last. You know, we did have to chain him in the cellar for a while. That was awful, even with the soundproofing. But he was doing so well and then – " she shrugged. "Well, we salvaged what we could and there's no use crying over spilled stroganoff. Such as he is. I must say he's not half as gamy as I thought he'd be for the age he was." My mother twiddled her fork in the noodles. "You're much younger. You've got a chance now. Go with it, hon. I really would cry over spilled Milt."

He looked down at the stroganoff and turned almost as white as my mother's uniform.

"May I be excused?" I said, wiping my mouth. I've got some stuff I'd like to do and obviously I haven't been able to get it done today."

"Go ahead. Milt will clean up. A week's training here," she added to him, "and then you can wear the uniform. Have a good six-month probationary period, and I'll let you ride up front with me in the van, where Lynn's father used to sit. *Lynn!*"

I paused in the doorway. "What?"

She held out her hand and snapped her fingers. "The *gun*, silly."

I'd carried it off without thinking. And of course, that was when Milt finally made his move. But he wasn't thinking either; he just lunged at my mother and she smacked him right in the mouth with the heel of her other hand, knocking him off the chair onto the floor. When I left, she was dabbing at his split lip with a napkin, holding the barrel of the gun under his chin. I resisted a joke about crying over split Milt.

Upstairs in my room, I fired up the computer, turned on the modem and got into the police computer. That was one of the few things I had learned that my mother hadn't taught me – in fact, I think it was the only thing she herself couldn't actually do. I tried to show her how once, but she just couldn't get it. Couldn't *hack* it was the way she put it, and she didn't even understand why I laughed when she said it.

Fortunately, the police still hadn't run Milt's prints, so I jiggered some stuff around to fix it so that they never would. In a town of this size, there's very little urgency to run someone's prints – nobody expects someone on the ten most wanted list to turn up on a shoplifting charge. My mother would say they were just lazy, good thing for us. Perhaps she was right, but I preferred to think that it was more like maybe the police were closing one eye and working with the Busy Hands system. There are lots of police families on my mother's client list, and you can practically eat off their floors.

I suppose it was cold, but I couldn't bring myself to feel particularly bad about my father. He'd never been a very good father; if he had, my mother would have given him a lot more latitude. I took care of his records while I was in the police computer – Carol would appreciate the favor – and then downloaded the arrest reports for the day. My mother wouldn't be going out to the jail again for a while, but it's always good to keep current. And who knew but that Carol might have another rush job to fulfill? She would appreciate that favor, too.

And she'd remember all these little favors I did her, so when I turned eighteen, she'd back me up when I finally went to my mother and told her how I felt. I mean, Busy Hands is a wonderful service and I'm very proud of the way my mother started it with nothing and built it into the fine operation it is today. But the fact is, I really, *really* hate housework, even when someone else is doing it. It's just so boring.

But I think I've developed a real taste for the catering business.

Deep Space Adventure #32

Jeffrey Ford

On the second giant planet in orbit around the star that defines the stinger of the Scorpion constellation, at a spot along its vast equator, in the mazelike crystal gardens, where sharp shards of clear-as-water atomic lattice structures thrust into absolute night, some smaller than the width of a pencil, some taller than skyscrapers, Colonel Rasuka, famous explorer and two-fisted astronaut of the Deep Space Corps, donned in bubble helmet and sporting his jet pack that allowed him to float among the formations like a goldfish through coral holes in the deep sea of the Far Tortuga, turned his lantern slightly to the right, and unbeknownst to him, awakened a dormant, ineffable entity that latched onto that stream of a beam of illumination only to ride its reflection back into the eye of Rasuka, who later that day returned with the alien presence percolating in his gray matter back to his ship, *The Empress*, where he moved among the crew, becoming more and more bizarre in his proclamations and twitching movements, until, all of a sudden, *pop*, out of the top of his head shot a brainiac thing with pulsing cerebellum and a dozen long tentacles, two of which sported the obligatory bug eyes, searching out other crew members in order to feed off their energy by slipping a tentacle up their nose and draining out their bodily essence until finally the creature was stopped by the Robot Friend of Man, Executor 1000, looking for all the world like a metal scarecrow with twinkling Christmas-light eyes and a screw for a nose, who zapped the thing with a ray gun, disintegrating it into a pile of wet ash, but not before all of the humans had been killed, leaving the robot alone in space, lost in space, to whisper in his voice like the whir of an electric can opener, "Good riddance, " to one and all.

The Wild Girls

ℬℭ

Pat Murphy

I was thirteen years old when I met the queen of the foxes.

My family had just moved from Connecticut to California. It was a hot summer day, and the air conditioner in the new house wasn't working. My father was at his new job, and my mother was unpacking boxes while she waited for the air conditioner repairman to come. I helped my mother unpack a box of dishes, but when I dropped a china plate (one of a set of twelve), my mother suggested that I go out and play. There was an edge in her voice.

I didn't argue; I went outside. The backyard wasn't much: an expanse of tired-looking grass bordered by dusty shrubs and flowers. A high wooden fence blocked my view in all directions.

I opened the gate in the back fence and looked out at a dirt road that ran alongside a rusting set of railroad tracks. Our new house was on the very edge of a development on the very edge of town. On the far side of the railroad tracks, was a walnut orchard – rows of trees with dark rough trunks and smooth pale branches.

If I turned right, the dirt road would lead into town. If I turned left, it would lead away from town, into unknown territory.

I turned left.

For a hundred yards or so, the dirt road ran parallel to our neighbors' back fences, then it left the housing development behind. To my right were the railroad tracks and the walnut orchard; to my left, another orchard and an open field. Farther along, the dirt road and the railroad tracks passed near a small creek. I clambered down the embankment to walk along the creek.

It was cooler by the water. Soft-leafed green trees shaded the gully. Moss grew on the rocks and jays shrieked at me from the trees. The creek turned, and a tiny path led up the bank through a tangle of bushes and vines. I climbed the path and entered an overgrown woody area, where gnarled old trees shaded the weedy ground. Through the trees, I caught a glimpse of something orange – a brilliant, unnatural, day-glo color. I followed the path toward the color and found a small clearing where the underbrush had been cut down. A large armchair, upholstered in fabric that was a riot of orange daisies on green and turquoise paisley patterns, sat under a twisted tree. In front of the chair was a large, flat-topped boulder; on the boulder was a teapot with a broken spout. Boards had been wedged among the branches of the tree to make shelves. Haphazard and not quite level, the shelves supported an assortment of odd items: a jar of peanut butter, a battered metal tin, a china cup with a broken handle, two chipped plates, a dingy teddy bear.

"What the hell are you doing here?" a girl's voice asked.

I looked toward the voice, startled. A girl about my age, dressed in ragged jeans and a dirty T-shirt, sat on a low branch of the tree to my left. Her face was streaked with red-brown clay – vertical stripes on her forehead, horizontal stripes on her cheeks. Her hair was a tangle of reddish curls, held back with a rubber band and decorated with a blue jay feather.

"I . . . I was just looking around," I stammered.

"Who said you could come here?" she asked, her voice rising. "This is private property."

I felt my face getting hot. "Sorry. I just. . . ."

"You think you can come poking around anywhere?"

"I said I was sorry. . . ."

"You kids from the development think you own everything."

"I didn't mean. . . ."

"Why don't you just go back where you came from?"

"That would be fine with me," I managed to say, just before my voice broke. I turned away, feeling tears on my face, and immediately tripped over a rock and fell hard, catching myself on my hands and one knee. When I scrambled to my feet, the girl was standing beside me.

"Who the hell do you think you are, anyway?" I snarled at her, trying to cover my tears with anger. "I wasn't doing anything wrong."

She was studying me, her head cocked to one side. "You haven't been here before, have you?" she asked, her voice calmer.

I shook my head. "My family just moved to this lousy neighborhood."

"Your knee is bleeding," she said. "So's your hand. Come on and sit down. I've got band-aids."

I sat in the armchair, and she washed my cuts with water from the creek, carried in the china cup. She took a box of band-aids from one of her shelves. While she dabbed at my scraped knee with a wet bandana, she explained that some kids had been there a few days back and messed with all her stuff, pulling down the shelves and tipping over the chair. "There are some really mean kids around here," she said. "You're lucky I didn't just start throwing rocks at you. I can hide in the trees and nail a kid with a rock from thirty feet away."

She sat back on her heels, studying my bandaged knee. "Well, I guess you'll be okay now." She met my eyes with a steady gaze. "You asked who I am, so I guess I better tell you. I'm the queen of the foxes."

"The queen of the foxes," I repeated.

"That's right – the queen of all the foxes." Suddenly she was on her feet. "Come on. I'll show you something cool."

No time for any more questions. She was running away through the trees, and I followed.

She led me to a place by the creek where you could catch orange and black newts with thoughtful eyes. The queen of the foxes caught one and handed it to me. It felt like cold rubber on my hand. It didn't struggle to escape. Instead, it blinked at me and then started walking with high, slow steps, as if it were still moving through water.

At first, I stayed on the bank of the creek. When I said I'd be in trouble if I got my clothes dirty, the queen of the foxes pointed out that my bleeding hand had already left smears of blood and mud on my shorts. Since I was already in trouble, I might as well have all the fun I could. So I got into the creek too, freed the newt that she had caught for me, and caught another.

Then we sat on the bank and dried out. While we were there, she painted my face with clay from the bank. War paint, she called it. She showed me how to make a squawking noise with a blade of grass. A couple of blue jays sat in the tree and scolded us for making such a racket.

"Hey, what's your name, anyway?" I asked her.

"My name? She leaned back and looked up at the branches of the trees. "You can call me Fox."

"That's not a name."

She shrugged. "Why not?"

"I can't tell my mother that your name is Fox. She won't believe it."

"Why do you have to tell her anything?"

"She'll ask."

She shrugged. "So make up something she'll like better. You call me Fox, and I'll call you Mouse."

"No you won't."

"Then what should I call you?"

"Call me Newt," I said, thinking of the slow-moving amphibians with their thoughtful eyes. "That would be good."

Somehow or other, the afternoon went away, and I realized that I was hungry and the sun was low in the sky. "Hey, I've got to get going," I said. "My mother will be really pissed."

"Ah," she said, lying back in the grass. "I don't have to worry about that. I don't have a mother."

"Yeah?" I squinted at her, but her eyes were closed and she didn't notice. As I tried to figure out what to say, I heard a man's voice calling in the distance. "Sarah! Sarah, are you there?"

She frowned. "That's my dad," she muttered. "I better go talk to him." She ran off through the trees toward the voice. After a minute, I followed.

The path led to an old white house on the edge of the woods. It wasn't like any house I'd ever seen before – there was no driveway, no yard. A dirt road ended in front of the house, where a battered old sedan was parked beside an enormous motorcycle. Weeds grew in the flowerbed beside the front steps, and there was all kinds of junk near the door: a cast-iron bathtub half filled with water, a barbecue built from an oil drum, a pile of hubcaps. The paint on the house was peeling.

Fox stood on the front porch, talking to a burly man wearing blue jeans and a black T-shirt with the sleeves torn off. They looked up and saw me standing on the edge of the woods. "This is Newt," Fox said. "Newt, this is Gus. He's my dad."

He didn't look like anybody's father. He didn't have a beard, but he needed a shave. He had three silver studs in his left ear. His dark hair was tied back with a rubber band. On his right arm, there was a tattoo, an elaborate pattern of spiraling black lines.

"How's it going, Newt?" Gus didn't seem at all startled at my strange new name. "Where did you come from?"

"My family just moved here, mister uh. . . ."

"Just call me Gus," he said. "I don't answer to mister."

I nodded uncomfortably. He didn't look like anyone's dad, but it still seemed strange to call him by his first name.

"I found her in the woods," Fox said. "Showed her where the newts live."

"That's good. I'm glad you found your way here." He seemed genuinely pleased. "Be nice for Sarah to have some company."

I kept looking at the tattoo. I had never met anyone with a tattoo before.

He walked down from the porch and sat on the bottom step. "You interested in tattoos? Take a look." I studied his arm. "You can touch it if you like. It's okay."

Gingerly, I traced one of the spiraling lines with a finger.

"Got it in New Zealand from a Maori fellow. It's supposed to attract good fortune. Seems to work. Right after I got it, I sold my first short story."

There was a little too much implied by all that for me to absorb, but I nodded as if I understood.

After a minute, he stood up and said, "You want to join us for dinner? Nothing fancy – just canned chili."

"No, thanks," I said. "I'd better go home."

"Don't forget to wash your face," he suggested.

Fox and I washed up with the hose outside the house, and then I headed home.

I got home just when my father got back from work. He was telling my brother that he shouldn't just be sitting around watching trash on TV. My mother was complaining about the cost of fixing the air conditioner. I snuck up to my room and changed before anyone noticed my muddy clothes and wet shoes.

When I got downstairs, I set the table, and we had dinner.

My mother and father did not like one another much. Dinner was just about the only time they sat down together. A vague sense of tension hung over the table, centering on my father. He was always angry – not about anything in particular, but about everything, all the time. But he pretended he wasn't angry. He was always joking, but the jokes weren't very funny.

"I see you've decided that meat is better if it's black around the edges," he said to my mother that night. The London broil was well-done, though far from black. "That's an interesting theory."

My mother laughed at my father's comment, pretending that he was just joking.

He glanced at me. "Your mother thinks that charcoal is good for the digestion," he said.

I smiled and didn't say anything. My own strategy for dealing with my father was to say as little as possible.

My father turned to my brother. "What educational shows did you watch on TV today? I'm sure you can learn a great deal from watching 'The Price is Right.' "

"I didn't watch TV all day," my brother said sullenly.

"Mark explored the neighborhood this afternoon," my mother said.

"I see – out looking for trouble. I'm sure there are just as many young hoodlums in this town as there were in Connecticut. I'm confident you'll find them." Once, in Connecticut, the police had brought Mark home; he'd been with some boys who had been caught shoplifting.

"I met some kids down the block," Mark said. "They all belong to the country club. Can we join the country club so I can go swimming with them?" This last question was directed to my mother.

"Swimming at the country club?" my father said. "Now isn't that nice? Maybe we need to get you a job so that you don't have so much time weighing heavy on your hands."

Mark didn't say anything. My father was talking about how young he had been when he had his first job. I noticed that Mark was staring at me, and I could feel it coming. He was going to say something to get my father off his case and onto mine. When my father paused, Mark said, "Hey, Joan, how come you always hold onto your glass when you eat? It looks really stupid."

I looked down at my hands. My left hand was gripping my glass of milk tightly.

"You look like you're afraid that someone's going to try to steal your milk from you," my father said, chuckling. "Just relax. You're not living in a den of wild animals."

The next day, I went back to Fox's place in the woods. When my mother asked where I was going, I told her that I was going to play with a girl I had met. I told her I was going to have lunch with my new friend. Just when my mother was starting to ask a bunch of questions I didn't want to answer, the phone rang. It was one of my mother's friends from the city. I stood there for a minute, like I was waiting for my mother's attention, until she impatiently waved me out the door – which is what I had really been waiting for.

I found Fox curled up in the armchair under the trees, reading a book. "It's too bad there aren't any hedgehogs around here," she said, as if she were continuing a conversation that we'd begun much earlier. "They have hedgehogs in England." She tapped her finger on the book, and I looked over her shoulder at the picture.

"It's cute," I said hesitantly.

"Foxes eat 'em," she said, grinning.

I gave her a dubious look.

"Let's go." She was out of the chair and leading me off into the woods to show me where a branch of the stream ran into a culvert, a concrete tunnel that was so big that when I was standing in the stream I could barely reach the top with my outstretched arm. We waded in the stream and went into the culvert, walking through the algae-scented darkness until the mouth of the tunnel was a tiny spot of light in the distance.

"Isn't this great?" Fox's voice echoed from the culvert walls. "Even in the middle of the afternoon, it's cool in here. It's a great place to hide."

I looked into the darkness, black and velvety, silent except for the delicate music of trickling water. It was simultaneously terrifying and inviting.

"I wonder where it goes," Fox said. "One of these days, I'm going to bring a flashlight and keep going."

I glanced toward the glimmer of light at the mouth of the culvert, then stared into the darkness again and shivered. "Okay," I said. "We could do that."

"Great. Come on – I'll show you some secrets." She splashed in the direction of the opening, and I followed, returning to the heat and the light of the day.

She showed me a maze of tiny paths that ran through the underbrush around the clearing. They were just big enough for us, no bigger. She had stacked stones at places where the paths intersected – "for throwing at intruders," she told me. Then she touched my arm. "Tag," she said, "you're it."

She ran away into the maze, and I chased her, ducking under a branch, running around a corner, always staying on the path because plunging through the underbrush was painful and scratchy. I tagged her, and then she chased me, whooping and shouting as she ran. Around and around, up this path and down that. Sometimes, I caught a glimpse of the clearing with the armchair, the place I had started thinking of as Fox's living room. And sometimes I was deep in the bushes, concealed from the world. Around and around until I knew that the path by the broken branch led back to the living room and that the one by a pile of rocks led back to the place where the newts lived and so on.

Fox was chasing me, and she had fallen silent. I didn't know where she was. I crept quietly back toward the living room. I was almost there when I heard a sound behind me. Fox dropped from the branch of a walnut tree and tagged me from behind. "You're it," she said. "Let's have lunch."

We went back to her living room in the clearing for lunch – it seemed like the most natural thing in the world to eat peanut butter on crackers under the trees.

"Are there really foxes around here?" I asked her.

"Sure," she said. "But you never see them during the day."

"How did you get to be queen of the foxes?"

She was sitting in the armchair and the light shining through the leaves of the walnut trees dappled her hair. I squinted my eyes in the lazy afternoon heat, and the bright spots of sunlight looked like jewels; the battered chair, like a throne. She tipped her head back regally, looking up into the leaves. "It started a long time ago," she said slowly. "Back when I was a little girl."

Then she told me this story.

> Once there was a woman who did not like who she was. She felt uneasy with herself, as if she did not fit inside her own body. When she looked in the mirror, she did not recognize herself. Was that her nose? Were those her eyes? They didn't seem quite right, though she could not have told you what the right nose or eyes would be.
>
> The woman lived with her husband in a house on the edge of the woods, not far from a small town. She had a little girl who was just barely old enough to go to school.
>
> One day, when the woman's little girl was at school and her husband was at work, the woman left the key to the house on the kitchen table and walked out, leaving the door wide open behind her. She walked along the trail that led into the woods. When she was deep in the woods, she left the trail and walked between the trees where there was no trail.

She was far from the trail when it started to rain – gently at first, and then harder, raindrops hammering against her and soaking her shirt and her jeans. She looked for a place to take shelter and found a hollow log that was large enough to crawl inside.

She crawled in on her belly. It was dry inside the log – snug and warm. She waited for the rain to stop, closing her eyes and listening to the water rattle against the leaves overhead, drip to the forest floor, and trickle through dead leaves. Listening to the rain, she fell asleep.

When she woke, she had changed. For the first time, she felt at home in her body. The smells around her were intense and inviting – the delicious scent of rotten leaves and grubs; the warm smell of the squirrel that lived in the tree overhead. As she listened to the squirrel in the branches, she could feel her ears moving to follow the sound. When she looked down at herself, she saw that her body was covered with fur. She nuzzled the long, bushy tail that curled around her paws.

Somehow, as she slept, she had changed into a fox.

Fox shifted in the armchair, looking at me for the first time since she started telling the story. "That was my mother," she said. "I was the little girl."

I was lying on the ground, drowsing as I listened to Fox's voice. Listening to the story, I had forgotten why Fox was telling it. I sat up, staring at Fox.

"You're saying your mother turned into a fox?"

She nodded. The sunlight still dappled her hair, but it no longer looked like jewels. She was a ragged girl sitting on a battered armchair, watching me with a strange intensity.

I hesitated. Maybe she was joking. Maybe she was crazy. "That can't happen."

She shrugged. "It did. I left one day to go to school. When I came back, my mother was gone."

"Maybe she just went off somewhere. Why do you figure she turned into a fox?"

Fox leaned her head against the frayed back of the chair. "The night she disappeared, my dad and I were sitting on the porch, and I saw a fox sneaking around the edge of the yard. I knew it was my mother."

"How did you know?"

"By the look in her eyes. I just knew. I asked my dad and he said that it was as good an explanation as any." She frowned, looking down at her hands. "Things weren't so great then. Dad was drinking and stuff." She looked up. "He's quit that since."

I hesitated. Crazy story. Maybe talking about her dad was safer than talking about her mother. "What does your dad do, anyway. How come he's at home in the middle of the day?"

"He writes stories and books. Mostly science fiction. Stuff with rockets on the cover, even when there aren't any rockets in the story. Sometimes . . ." Her voice dropped lower. "Sometimes he writes pornography. Real sexy stuff. He doesn't show me that, but I know the drawer where he keeps it. I've heard him say it pays better than science fiction."

I was trying to absorb this information when Fox sat upright. "Listen," she said, her voice suddenly urgent.

In the distance, I could hear voices – some boys talking and laughing. "We got to hide," Fox said, jumping out of the chair. I followed without question.

From a hiding place in the bushes, I could see three boys – my brother and two strangers – walking down the path.

"Most of the teachers are assholes," one of the strangers was saying. He was a stocky, blonde boy. "Get Miss Jackson for English, if you can. She's an easy grader."

"Fuck, don't talk about it. I can't believe it's only two weeks until school starts," said the other boy. He was tall, and his brown hair was greasy. "Let's stop and smoke already."

The blonde boy had just reached the edge of the clearing. "Hey, look at this." The blonde boy collapsed in the armchair. He pulled a plastic bag and papers out of his pocket and started rolling a joint. My brother was looking around at the shelves, the teapot, the dolls. "It looks like a little kid's fort."

"Looks like a great place to party," said the dark-haired boy, sitting on the ground. "Bring some girls." He grinned. "No one would bother us out here."

The blonde boy lit up and took a deep drag. From my hiding place, I could smell the dope. He passed the joint to the dark-haired boy.

"The girls around here like to party?" my brother asked.

The blonde boy laughed. "Some of them are stuck up, but some are okay."

The dark-haired boy passed the joint to my brother who inhaled deeply.

I wondered where Fox was. The dark-haired guy was describing Christina, a girl who liked to party. "She's hot," he was saying. "Got a great body, and she knows how to use it."

The blonde boy laughed. "Like you ever got close enough to find out."

It was weird, crouching in the bushes watching the boys smoke and talk about school and girls. I felt invisible and strangely powerful. The boys didn't know I was there. My brother didn't know I was watching him smoke dope. They didn't know I was listening to them.

"I gotta take a leak," the dark-haired boy said. Taking a step in my direction, he started to tug at his fly.

"Hey, this is private property." On the other side of the clearing, Fox had stepped out of the trees. "You're trespassing."

The boys all stared at her. The blonde boy grinned and the dark-haired boy laughed, his hand still on his fly. "Yeah, right. Well, I gotta pee, so I guess I'm going to keep on trespassing. Stick around, and you'll see something you've never seen before."

Fox disappeared down the trail. The blonde boy was laughing now too. "I don't think she wants to see that, Jerry."

"Shut up, Andrew."

I backed off down the trail.

"Hey, what's that," Jerry said, peering in my direction. "I think someone else is in there."

A rock flew out of nowhere and smacked Jerry on the shoulder. Then I ran down the trail, remembering what Fox had said when I met her. "I can hide in the trees and nail a kid with a rock from thirty feet away."

I heard Jerry crash into the bushes. I think he was chasing me, but I'm fast when I need to be. And he was too big to fit easily down the path. Somewhere Fox was whooping, and I heard my brother and the blonde boy cursing. The path I was on ran away from the living room, then back toward it. I scooped up some rocks from a pile by the trail. When I reached a spot close to the living room, I lobbed one at my brother. I think I hit him, but I didn't stay to watch – I was running again and there were crashing sounds in the bushes, then a sudden burst of cursing. Another rock had hit home.

Fox was silent now. But I could hear crashing and cursing in the clearing. I slipped closer, moving quietly along the path. Through the bushes, I could see the boys. My brother's face and arms were covered with scratches; he was picking brambles out of his T-shirt. Andrew, the blonde boy, was bleeding from a cut on his head where a rock had hit. Jerry was pulling down the shelves in the tree. The teapot was shattered on the ground. That must have been the crash I had heard. "Fuck you, assholes," he was yelling at the trees. "Fuck you all."

I heard footsteps behind me, and I shrank back into the bushes. Gus was coming down the path from the house.

"Fuck," said Andrew. "Now you've done it." He started to run away, but Gus was fast. He had one hand on the back of Andrew's T-shirt and the other on my brother's shoulder. Jerry was gone, running down the path and into the woods.

"Hey, let go," Andrew whined. "We weren't doing anything."

Gus had looked scary when I met him, and he had been smiling then. He wasn't smiling now. He was looking at the shelves on the ground, the broken teapot, the plates and cups scattered in the weeds. "The evidence is against you, kid. Looks like you've been fucking with my daughter's stuff."

"That was Jerry," Andrew said. "We didn't do anything."

"I don't like kids fucking around on my property," Gus continued, as if Andrew hadn't said anything. "I think the cops might be interested to know about all this." His eyes were on the baggy of dope, abandoned on the armchair. "Maybe calling them would be the best way to make sure this doesn't happen again."

The blonde boy was saying something else about how they hadn't been doing anything. I've never seen my brother look so pale and miserable, not even when my father was ragging on him.

Reluctantly, I left the safety of the woods and returned to the clearing. "Hey, Gus," I said hesitantly.

"You all right, Newt?"

"Yeah. Um . . ." I jerked my head at Mark. "That's my brother Mark. Um . . ." I frowned, looking at Mark and then at Gus and then at the ground. "Maybe you could let him go?"

"Your brother, huh?" He stared at Mark and then at Andrew. "Sarah, will you get your ass out here?" His tone had softened a little.

Fox stepped out of the trees on the far side of the clearing.

"What happened here?" Gus asked.

"They were trespassing. When I told them to leave, that other kid said he was going to pee on my stuff. So I started throwing rocks at them."

"We didn't know we were trespassing," Andrew said. "We were just taking a shortcut and . . ."

"Do yourself a favor and shut up," Gus said.

Andrew stopped talking. Mark didn't say anything.

"That's better," Gus said in a conversational tone. "I don't like kids fucking with my daughter's stuff, and I don't like being lied to. I'd like to figure out how I can be sure that this won't ever happen again."

"I won't ever come here again," Mark said.

Gus nodded. "That sounds good. Your sister is all right, and that speaks well for you." He turned to Andrew. "How about you?"

"We weren't doing anything really," he started saying. "We just . . ."

I saw Gus's hand tighten its grip on Andrew's T-shirt, and Andrew stopped.

"I won't ever come back here," he said.

"All right," Gus said. "I believe you. Now before you leave, you're going to help me put these shelves back in the tree, okay?"

Mark and Andrew nodded. Gus let them go. For a minute, I thought they were going to run, then my brother turned toward the tree. They helped Gus put the shelves back while Fox and I stayed at the edge of the clearing, watching.

"All right," Gus said when they were done. "Now get the hell out of here."

The boys walked to the edge of the clearing and then started running. Fox walked across the clearing to her dad's side; I stayed where I was, waiting for him to start the lecture that I knew was coming. We shouldn't have started trouble, we shouldn't have been throwing rocks. Everything we did was wrong.

He didn't say anything for a moment, then he looked down at Fox. "If I'm not around, just let trespassers be," he suggested mildly.

"Okay," Fox said. "I guess so."

He put his hand on her shoulder for a second. "You okay?"

"Yeah. I'm fine."

He nodded. "Well, I needed a break anyway. But I'd better get back to work."

He headed for the house, having never delivered the lecture. I stared after him, then looked at Fox. "You know, your dad's not like anyone else I've ever met."

She grinned and nodded. "Yeah, I know." Then she glanced in the direction the boys had run. "I think he's right – they won't be back."

"Yeah."

"You've got a good arm," she said. "You hit your brother good. How come you asked my dad to let him go?"

I shrugged, feeling uncomfortable. "He was already scared enough. And if the cops had brought him home, my father . . ." I stopped, unable to describe how awful that would be. "It would be really bad."

Fox frowned, studying my face. "Okay – it's cool."

My brother was waiting for me in the backyard when I got home. He was sitting on one of the patio chairs, not doing anything. I stopped, just inside the gate.

"I ought to clobber you for throwing rocks at me," he said.

I stayed by the gate, ready to run. I shrugged nervously. "I got Gus to let you go."

"Yeah." He kept staring at me. "So how do you know that guy?"

"He's my friend's dad."

"Andrew says he's some kind of crazed biker. Says he's dangerous and we should report him to the cops."

I thought about the tattoo and the motorcycle in the yard. "He writes books," I said. "He's really an okay guy." I started for the back door.

"Hey, Joan?" he said. He was leaning forward in the chair, and his hands were in fists.

"Yeah?" I stopped.

"Thanks for asking him to let me go."

I stared at him. My brother never thanked me for anything. "Yeah. Okay."

"You won't tell about any of this, right?"

"I'm not saying anything."

"Okay." Looking relieved, he leaned back in his chair. "You know, Andrew says that girl is nuts. Everyone at school makes fun of her."

I bit my lip. I could imagine Fox at school. She wouldn't fit in at all. She didn't look right, didn't act right. She belonged in the woods.

"You hang out with her, and everyone will figure you for a dweeb too. 'Course, there's nothing new there." His voice was relaxing as he made fun of me. I turned away and went inside to wash up for dinner.

The next couple of weeks were great. My mother was busy unpacking, and she seemed just as glad that I spent every afternoon with my friend.

But on the Saturday just before school started, my mother announced that we were going over to the neighbors for a barbecue at their pool. "Cindy Gordon is just your age," she told me. "And Mrs. Gordon is leader for the local senior Girl Scout troop. I talked with her about being the assistant troop leader."

I must have frowned, because she asked, "Why are you making such a terrible face?"

"I . . . uh . . . I don't know if I want to be a senior Girl Scout," I said hesitantly. "I mean, being a Girl Scout was fine when I was a little kid, but I don't think . . ."

"Don't be silly," my mother interrupted. "You love being a Girl Scout."

I didn't love being a Girl Scout. My mother liked being a Girl Scout leader.

"I can't go to a barbecue this afternoon," I said. "I'm going to Sarah's house. She's expecting me."

"Do you want me to call her mother and tell her that you can't come? I'm sure she'll understand."

"I don't have her phone number, and she doesn't have a mother. I have to go to her house."

My mother's frown deepened, and I could see her wondering about Sarah's family. I shouldn't have said anything about Sarah's mother. It had slipped out.

But my mother was losing interest in my problem. "There's no time for that. You have to help me make some potato salad." She headed for the kitchen.

"But I have to go to Sarah's house and tell her I can't play this afternoon."

My father was in the kitchen, getting a beer from the refrigerator. He frowned at me. "Your mother has arranged this barbecue, and it's a command performance," he said. "We all have to be there. Isn't that right?" The last comment was to my mother.

"It'll be fun," she said brightly. "You'll like the Gordons." It wasn't clear whether she was talking to me or to my father. Neither one of us responded. My father turned away, taking his beer to the living room where he could read the paper.

There was no escaping it. I went to the barbecue at the Gordons' house. Cindy Gordon was a slender girl with braces and short blonde hair. Her brother Andrew was the blonde boy I had seen in the woods.

Cindy and I sat together on lawn chairs. Andrew and Mark were swimming; our parents were on the other side of the pool.

"Do you miss your friends in Connecticut?" she asked me. "I'd hate to move."

"It's been okay." I didn't tell her that I didn't have any really good friends in Connecticut. I had some kids I hung out with, but no real friends. I liked to read, and I did well in school. Both those things made me suspect.

"What have you been doing since you moved?"

"Reading. Hanging out. Not much." I didn't mention Fox. It seemed unlikely that Cindy knew Fox. I studied the ice in my glass of soda.

"My mom says you're going to be joining the Girl Scout troop."

I glanced at Cindy. She was working hard to be friendly, and she had the look of a smart kid herself. "Yeah. That's what my mom says too."

"It's not so bad. We went white-water rafting last year."

She told me about the raft trip down the Stanislaus River, and it sounded all right. Better than gluing macaroni on cigar boxes, which was mostly what we did in Connecticut.

We left the Gordons' house at around five. I wanted to go to Fox's then, but my mother said I couldn't. She was in one of her family togetherness moods, and I had to stay home, even though my father was sitting in the living room reading the paper and my brother was watching TV and she was doing a crossword puzzle. "Spending a little time with your own family won't kill you," she said.

When I went to bed, I couldn't fall asleep. I heard my parents arguing downstairs – my mother was talking about how she wanted to spend more time with the Gordons and my dad was sneering at the idea. That went on for a while, then they went to bed. The house was quiet, but I lay awake, wondering whether Fox had missed me that afternoon.

I felt itchy and restless, and finally I couldn't stay in bed any longer. I got up quietly, got dressed, and snuck downstairs. I followed the dirt road toward Fox's. Some light spilled over the fences from people's backyards, and it wasn't too dark. Then I turned off the road into the woods, where it was really dark. There was a half moon, but only a little light filtered through the trees.

The woods were different at night. I kept hearing things rustling in the bushes. Even though I knew the way, I kept thinking I was lost. I kept thinking about zombies and high-school students out looking for trouble. The two seemed equally threatening.

I went to Fox's clearing. It was strange being there in the middle of the night. I saw something move in the shadows, and I stopped where I was.

A fox stepped from the shadow of the chair. In the moonlight, her fur was silvery gray and her eyes were golden. She sat down and neatly curled her tail around herself, studying me as if she were coming to some sort of decision. Then she stood up and trotted toward Fox's house.

I hesitated, then followed. The light in the kitchen window was on, and I could see Gus sitting at the kitchen table. His head was resting on his hand, and he was writing in a notebook. In the light of the bare bulb in the kitchen ceiling, I could see dark shadows under his eyes, lines of unhappiness around his mouth.

I hesitated, staring in. I thought for a minute about turning around and going home, but I couldn't face going through the dark woods alone. I knocked lightly on the door and watched through the window as Gus got up to let me in.

I hadn't been in the house before. The kitchen sink was filled with dirty dishes, but that wasn't what caught my attention. There were bookshelves on every wall – some crammed with books, others with papers. It seemed so weird: bookshelves in the kitchen.

"Newt," Gus said softly. He didn't ask me why I was out so late, like any other grownup would have. "Good to see you." He really did seem glad to see me.

"Is Fox asleep?"

"I'm afraid so."

"Oh. I wanted to talk to her. Is she . . . is she mad at me?"

Gus frowned, sitting down at the kitchen table and gesturing toward a chair where I could sit. "She was upset that you didn't come by."

"My mother made me go to a barbecue at Cindy Gordon's house. Cindy's mother is the leader of the Girl Scout troop, and my mother wants to be assistant leader, so I'm going to have to be in the troop. But I came out here, even though I was scared." I don't know exactly why, but I was starting to cry as I talked – because I was thinking about Fox being mad, because I had been really scared in the woods and now I felt safe, because Gus was being nice to me and suddenly I had to cry. Gus held up a hand, stopping me before I really got started.

"Relax, Newt. Take a deep breath." He watched me for a moment. "You know, you don't really want to tell me all this. You want to tell Sarah – I mean, Fox." Without getting up, he reached over to a bookcase and grabbed a spiral bound notebook and a pencil. "Write it down. Write a note that explains what happened. I'll make sure Fox gets it."

"Why can't you just tell her?"

He leaned back in his chair. "If I told her, I'd say it in my words. You should say it in your own words. Tell your own truth. That's important."

I sat at the kitchen table and wrote a long note to Fox about how I couldn't call because I didn't know the phone number and about how my mother wouldn't let me go and about sneaking out after dark and about seeing the fox in the clearing. I wrote about how sorry I was that I couldn't come. Then I tore out the pages and gave them to Gus.

"Could you give that to Fox?"

"I sure will."

I handed him the notebook too. He opened it to the first page, where he wrote down a phone number. "There's our number," he said, handing me the notebook. "You keep that. Use the notebook to write other stuff down."

"What kind of stuff?"

He shrugged. "Stuff that happens. Stuff that you're scared of. Stuff that you make up. Sometimes it helps to write stuff down. Come on – I'll walk you home."

With Gus there, the woods weren't scary. The shadows were just shadows. The noises were just birds and mice and distant cars on the freeway. He left me at the gate to our backyard.

The next day, I found Fox in the clearing, sitting in the armchair. "Hey, Fox," I said. "I'm sorry I had to go to that stupid barbecue yesterday."

"My dad gave me your note."

"He said you were mad at me."

She shrugged. "I was. But he said that not all parents are as understanding as he is. Some parents push their kids around."

"He got that right."

"So it's okay. Let's go to the tunnel."

The tunnel was the culvert. Sometimes, we walked deep into the darkness, and Fox made up stories: we were the first explorers in the world's deepest cave; we were rebels, hiding in the sewers of Paris; we were traveling to the center of the Earth, where there were still dinosaurs.

That day, Fox didn't make up a story. We just walked into the darkness, the cold water squishing in our sneakers. We were deep in the culvert when Fox said, "You saw the fox last night. What did you think of her?"

"She was beautiful."

"What did her eyes look like?" I wished I could see Fox's face. She sounded strange – her voice tight and strained.

I remembered the fox's golden eyes. "Like . . . like she knew what I was thinking," I said.

For a moment, Fox was silent. Then she said, "My mom was beautiful. I remember she had really small hands. And her hair was the color of fox fur. Kind of rusty red-brown."

I hesitated. "Do you really think she became a fox?" I asked cautiously.

Fox stopped walking. In the darkness, I could hear her breathing; I could hear water trickling somewhere. "Sometimes, you gotta believe something crazy," she whispered in the darkness. "Because all the other things you could believe hurt too much. I mean, I could try to believe something else. Like she just ditched my dad and me and went off with some other guy. But I think it would be really cool to turn into a fox. I could see why she'd want to do that. I like thinking of her as a fox, living out in the woods. So that's what I believe."

"I can see that," I said. It did make a kind of crazy sense. I groped in the darkness and took her hand. "Okay – then I'll believe it too."

"Hey, let's go and see the newts," Fox said, leading the way out of the darkness.

* * *

The next week, school started. The teacher was calling roll in my English class when I saw Fox in the back row. Her face was clean, and she was wearing a clean shirt and corduroy pants that weren't dirty or torn. I kept glancing her way, but she didn't look back.

The teacher, Ms. Parsons, was a fluttery woman with wispy hair and a high, breathless voice. That first day, she read us a poem about daffodils and asked us what we thought of it. I didn't think much of it, but I didn't say that.

When class was over, I hurried to catch Fox on her way out. "Hey, Fox. How's it going?"

She glanced at me, her face carefully expressionless. "Around here, my name's Sarah."

"Okay. And mine's Joan."

"Look – I gotta go," she said. She was walking quickly, and I had to hurry to keep up. She seemed smaller than she did in the woods. She hugged her books to her chest as if she were cold. She didn't smile.

"What's the matter?" I said. "Where are you going?"

She didn't slow down. "I've got some stuff to do."

"Hey, Joan!" I turned and saw Cindy Gordon and another girl, standing at a nearby locker.

I touched Fox's arm. "That's Cindy Gordon," I said. "I know her. Let's go say hi." I walked toward them, but when I got there, Fox wasn't with me. I saw her back as she headed away down the corridor.

"Hi, Cindy," I said.

"Hi, Joan." Her friend was staring after Fox. "This is Sue. Sue, this is Joan."

"Do you know that girl?" Sue asked me.

"Yeah. Why?"

She glanced at Cindy but didn't answer my question.

Cindy closed her locker and said, "Joan just moved here from Connecticut. She lives right near me." She looked at me. "We're going to the cafeteria to get some lunch. Want to come?"

Fox was no longer in sight. I shrugged uncomfortably. "Sure. I guess so."

I ate a hamburger from the cafeteria at a table with Cindy and Sue and a couple of their friends. They asked me a few questions about Connecticut, but mostly they talked about the classes they were in and what their teachers were like.

I walked to science class with Cindy and Sue. The teacher, Mr. McFarland, was a tall, skinny guy wearing plaid pants and a shirt with a pocket protector. He talked for a while then asked us to pair up with lab partners. When everyone was milling around, trying to find a partner, I saw Fox at the back of the class, standing alone. I left Cindy and Sue, who had paired up immediately.

"Hey," I said to her. "Want to be partners?"

She looked at me, frowning a little. "Don't do me any favors."

I frowned back. "What's with you, Fox?" I said, very quietly. "Why are you acting so weird?"

"Didn't your new friends tell you? I am weird."

I followed her gaze. Cindy and Sue carefully looked away when I glanced at them. Then I looked back at Fox. "Look – do you want to be lab partners or not?"

She bit her lip and shrugged. "I guess."

For the rest of class, Mr. McFarland had us examine flowers and look for all the parts: the sepals, the petals, the stamen, the pistil. Fox worked with me, but she wasn't the same person that she was in the woods. She was quieter, more subdued. In the woods, she was in charge; she knew what she was doing. Here, she was out of place. At the end of class, Fox vanished into the crowd of students before I could catch up with her.

After school, as I walked home with Cindy and Sue, Sue asked me about Fox. "How do you know Sarah?"

"I met her when I was walking along the railroad tracks," I said, feeling uncomfortable. I knew that Cindy and Sue would never go wandering in the woods by themselves.

"I heard that she and her father live in this junked-out house in the woods. Her father's really scary. He rides this big Harley, and he has all these tattoos."

"I've been to her house," I said slowly. "It wasn't so bad. And I met her dad. He's a nice guy."

Sue was looking at me like I'd said that I'd been to Mars in a UFO. "You've been to her house?"

"Yeah, I've been to her house," I said, with a bit of an edge in my voice.

"Hey," Cindy said, "what did you think of Mr. McFarland's pants. Weren't those wild?"

So we talked about Mr. McFarland and how weird he was. I was grateful that Cindy had changed the subject. I got the feeling that she didn't like the way that Sue was trashing Fox. She asked if Sue and I wanted to come over for a swim, but I said I couldn't. "Gotta do some stuff at home for my mom."

I went home, changed into jeans, and headed for the clearing in the woods. Fox wasn't there. I went to her house, and Gus said she hadn't gotten home yet. I checked down by the stream where the newts lived, then I went to the culvert.

I listened at the opening. "Fox?" I called. No answer. The water was low now, just a trickle running down the center. I saw a couple of muddy footprints on the dry cement beside the water; they looked about the right size for Fox's feet. "Fox?" I called again.

I headed into the darkness, walking on the curving cement side of the culvert, staying out of the trickle of water. My footsteps echoed the length of the tunnel.

Every other time I'd been there, Fox had been leading the way. It seemed darker than it had ever been before. "Fox?"

"Yeah?" Her voice was soft. She was just a little bit farther in.

"I was looking for you."

"Well, you found me."

I bumped into her. She was sitting on the side of the culvert with her feet in the water. I sat down beside her.

"You didn't wait for me after class."

"I figured you wanted to hang out with those other girls."

"You could have walked home with us," I said.

"No, I couldn't. They don't like me."

"They just don't know you," I said, knowing even as I said it that she was right. Cindy might accept her, but Sue wouldn't.

She didn't say anything.

"My mom's going to make me join that Girl Scout troop. If you joined the Girl Scouts, then . . ."

"No thanks," she said. "Not interested. That wouldn't change a thing."

I sat with her in the darkness, knowing she was right

"Forget school," she said suddenly. "Let's see how far we can go in the tunnel."

"Right now? We don't have flashlights or anything." The light of the entrance was very far away.

"Come on," she said. "I think I know where it comes out."

I followed her into the darkness, splashing through the water. She kept hurrying on ahead, in charge again. "Wouldn't this be a great place to hide a treasure if you had one," she was saying. "No one would ever find it in here."

The light of the entrance disappeared behind us. The air smelled stale and muddy. We couldn't get lost – there was only one tunnel, and to get out all we had to do was turn back – but my heart beat faster and it was hard to breathe. At last, after what seemed like hours, I saw a pinprick of light ahead of us, getting bigger as we approached.

When we emerged into the sunlight, Fox was grinning. We were on the far side of the orchard; we had walked almost a mile underground. "Wasn't that cool?" she said.

I lay on the ground in a patch of sunshine, so glad to be back in the light of day. She sat beside me, hugging her knees.

"Yeah," I admitted. "That was kind of cool. I couldn't have done it without you."

She nodded, acknowledging her position and authority. She was, once again, the queen of the foxes.

That fall, my life was divided into two worlds.

After school and on weekends, I spent as much time as I could with Fox in the woods. At school, I walked a narrow line. Sometimes I hung out with Cindy and her friends, and sometimes I hung out with Fox.

One day, I walked into science class and found a glass aquarium tank filled with big green frogs. Mr. McFarland held a squirming frog and demonstrated how to stick the needle in the back of the frog's neck and sever the spine. "Now you'll all do the same," he said. "Each pair of lab partners will dissect a frog."

When he asked if there were any questions, Fox raised her hand and said she wouldn't do it

He nodded, and said that he would kill the frog for any teams that couldn't do it themselves.

"No," Fox said. "I won't cut up a frog if you kill it. I won't have anything to do with this." She was almost shouting at him.

Mr. McFarland got a little red in the face. "I guess you'll have to talk about that with the dean of girls," he said stiffly. "Joan, why don't you join one of the other groups?"

"I won't do it either," I said quietly. "I guess I'd better go see the dean of girls too."

Mr. McFarland looked surprised. I was, after all, a good student. But I couldn't abandon Fox, so we both went off to see the dean of girls. She looked at Fox sadly and at me with surprise. "Sarah, I'm sorry to see you here again – and Joan, I'm surprised to see you here at all."

While Fox sat with her arms folded, looking miserable and stubborn, I did a lot of talking about cruelty to animals and respect for life. In the end, the dean of girls was sympathetic about what she called our "squeamishness." I suggested that Fox and I go to the library, do research on this type of frog, and write up a paper. The dean of girls and Mr. McFarland agreed on that.

In English class, I wrote poetry that I knew Ms. Parsons would like. Stuff about clouds and rain and sad feelings. I'd always been good at figuring out what teachers liked and giving it to them.

Fox just couldn't get the knack of that, although I explained it to her. "It's not honest, Newt," she told me once, when we were sitting out in the clearing. "You're writing stuff that will make her happy rather than writing stuff that you like. Why waste your time?"

I shrugged. "I get good grades. It keeps my parents off my back."

I thought Fox's poems were more interesting than mine, but they weren't about the sort of things that Ms. Parsons liked. Fox wrote about the peeling paint on her house, about the stink of the mud in the culvert, about the graffiti on the wall by the schoolyard. Fox wouldn't take the time to make sure that everything was spelled right, and she wouldn't bother to copy a poem over so that there weren't any cross-outs. Her handwriting was awful. Ms. Parsons took points off for spelling and neatness, but I think the real reason that Fox got Cs was because her poems made Ms. Parsons nervous.

When Ms. Parsons got entry forms for a short-story contest sponsored by an organization of women writers, she gave me one. "They want imaginative stories from girls like you," she told me. "Why don't you write a story and show it to me. Then I'll send it in."

At lunch that day, Cindy told me that Ms. Parsons had given her an entry form too. "I'm going to write about going rafting," she told me earnestly. "We found litter in the river and that made me think about nature." I nodded politely, though I couldn't imagine anything duller.

After school, I told Fox about the contest. "Are you going to write a story about puppies and kittens for Ms. Parsons?" she asked me.

I shrugged, feeling uncomfortable. Ever since Gus had given me the notebook, I'd been writing down stuff that I wouldn't show to Ms. Parsons, stuff I wouldn't show anyone.

"You ought to write about something you really care about," Fox said. "My dad says that's where the best writing comes from."

I shrugged again. "If I did that, I wouldn't want to show it to Ms. Parsons."

"You don't have to show it to her. You've got the entry form. You can just send it in yourself."

"Maybe you should write something," I suggested.

Fox shook her head. "Yeah, right. Like those people would want to read anything I wrote."

"Maybe we should write something together," I said. "What could we write about?"

"Wild girls," Fox said, without hesitation. "The wild girls who live in the woods."

"How did they get there?"

She was sitting in the big chair, looking up at the leaves of the tree and squinting a little against the sun. "One of them grew up there."

"Her mother was a fox," I said, "and her father was a wizard. The wizard loved the fox and turned her into a woman, but she was never happy so she went back to being a fox."

"I guess the other one came along later," Fox said slowly. "She's a princess, the daughter of an evil king and a beautiful but stupid queen. She's traveling through the forest on her way to get married to a wicked duke. But she runs away and finds the wild girl in the forest."

"Then they team up, and it's like Robin Hood," I said. "They steal from the rich and give to the poor."

"And all the animals in the forest are their friends."

We decided to write a story. I didn't tell Ms. Parsons; I didn't tell my mother. We told Gus, but he was the only one. He showed us where he kept his dictionary so that we could look up words. Otherwise he left us alone.

A few weeks after we'd started working on the story my mother asked me about the contest. "Cindy's mother tells me she's writing a story for a teen writers contest. You do very well in English. Don't you want to write a story?"

"I don't think so," I mumbled. "I'm really busy with school."

"It seems like you have plenty of time to play in the woods every day," she said.

"Sarah and I are working on a project for biology class. We're studying newts. Maybe we'll enter it in the science fair." The phone rang then, and I got away.

After Fox and I had been working on the story for a month, Gus let us use his typewriter to type it up. He gave us stamps and a big envelope so we could mail the story in.

For a couple of days after we sent it in, we didn't know what to do with ourselves. We knew that the story couldn't even have reached the contest judges yet, but we kept checking the mail anyway.

In the clearing, we sometimes practiced reading the story aloud – because the contest winners would get to read their stories aloud. We figured out who would read which parts, how we would alternate lines of dialog.

A couple of months later, Ms. Parsons asked Fox and me to stay after class. She had the strangest expression on her face – her eyes were angry, but her mouth was smiling a tight little smile. "You girls didn't tell me you were entering the teen writers contest," she said.

I glanced at Fox and then back at Ms. Parsons. "Oh. Well, we did."

"Your mother didn't even know you had entered, Joan. I called to tell her the news."

I nodded, trying to smile. "I thought it would be a surprise."

"Oh, she was very surprised. And happy, of course. Your story won first prize in your age group. That's quite an honor. The contest organizers want you to come to San Francisco to read the story aloud at a ceremony; they'll be printing it in an anthology of stories for girls."

I looked at Fox, and she was grinning. "We won," she said. I wanted to jump up and down and hug her, but Ms. Parsons was still talking.

"I'm looking forward to reading the story," she said. "The judges thought it was extremely imaginative and well-crafted."

Ms. Parsons got the contest organizers to send her a copy of the story, after I lied and said we didn't have a copy. She gave a copy to my mother, and they both read it.

They had to like it, since it had won the contest, but I don't think they understood it at all. "It's very imaginative," my mother said. "How ever did you and your friend think of all those clever names?"

"Your metaphors are very nice," said Ms. Parsons. She was always talking about metaphors in class. "But I do wish you had shown it to me before you sent it in. I think I could have helped you tone it down just a little."

We gave a copy to Gus. "It's got the raw power of adolescence," he said. "Great stuff." When I was heading home that afternoon, he said, "Give my regards to the evil king."

Of course my mother started making plans. She insisted I give her Fox's phone number, and she talked to Gus on the phone. "I thought I'd take the girls shopping for some clothes to wear to the ceremony," she told him brightly. "It's such a special occasion, and I know they'll want to look nice."

Fox didn't want to go, and Gus wouldn't make her. After talking to Gus and Fox on the phone, my mother said that she was very proud that I had had the patience to work with that girl and that maybe I should write my next story without her.

She took me shopping and made me try on dozens of dresses that she thought would be appropriate. I hated them all, but she finally settled on a plain red jumper with a black turtleneck underneath. "Not too dressy," she said. "But very cute."

On the evening of the ceremony, we drove to San Francisco, which was only about an hour from where we lived. My father was away on a business trip, so he couldn't be there. My mother had arranged for Gus and Fox to come with us.

Fox was wearing a dark blue dress. Gus was wearing a gray suit, but his belt had a big Harley Davidson buckle and that helped a little.

Gus kept talking to Fox and me about how we'd be great, but I felt a little sick. The story had been ours, ours alone. Now my mother thought it was hers and Ms. Parsons thought it was hers, and for all I knew the contest people thought it was theirs. Everyone thought they owned a piece of us. We were whittled away to nothing.

Fox and I waited backstage at a big theater with all the other kids who were reading their stories. Four high-school students were in one corner of the room, pretending to talk about what books they had read but actually proving to each other how cool they were. The elementary school kids were in another corner – they were reading first. A young woman sat by the door – a college student, I'd guess. As I watched, she pulled a makeup case from the pocket of her coat and put on lipstick. She looked, I thought, so cool and perfect. My mother wanted me to look like that.

We waited with the others for a minute, feeling uncomfortable and stupid. "Let's just leave," Fox said softly.

"What?"

"Let's sneak out of here. This is no good. It isn't our story anymore."

I glanced at the door. "We can't do that."

"Sure we can." There was a note of pleading in her voice. "Who's going to stop us? We're the wild girls." She looked down at her hands. She wasn't Fox anymore. She was Sarah, and she was unhappy. "It's all gone wrong."

"It's the clothes," I said. "How can we be wild girls, dressed like this? It just doesn't work."

"They don't want us to be wild," she said sadly. "Wild girls have dirt on their faces."

"Or war paint," I said.

As I watched, the college student stood up and walked down the hall to the ladies room, leaving her coat draped over the arm of the chair. I hesitated for a moment, then stood up. "Come on," I said to Fox. She followed me to the coat. I quickly dipped my hand into the pocket, grabbed the makeup case, and kept walking until I found a spot backstage where no one would bother us.

The lipstick was a lovely shade of red. Fox closed her eyes while I painted her forehead with wavy lines and spots, drew jagged lightning bolts on her cheeks and streaks on her chin. The lipstick felt cool and smooth on my face as she drew circles on my cheeks, lines on my forehead, a streak down my nose. I unbraided my hair—my mother had braided it tightly and neatly. It frizzed around my face like a cloud.

"We're ready now," Fox said. She was grinning.

As the elementary school students were walking off, a woman announced our names. At that moment, I grabbed Fox's hand and we walked to the microphone together. The woman at the podium stared at us, but I did not hesitate. I took the microphone from the woman's hand and stood still for a moment, staring out at the audience. Then I said the first line of the story, which I'd memorized months ago.

"We are the wild girls who live in the woods. You are afraid of us. You are afraid because you don't know what we might do."

"We didn't always live in the woods," Fox said, picking up the next line. "Once we lived in the village, like all of you. But we gave that up and left it all behind."

That is the moment I remember. The hot lights on my face; the sweet greasy scent of lipstick; the startled faces in the audience.

The feeling of power and freedom as my voice rolled from the microphone, booming over the hall.

I looked out at the sea of faces – so many people, all watching us. I could see Gus – he was grinning. Beside him, Ms. Parsons sat with her mouth open; my mother was scowling. They were shocked. They were angry. They were afraid.

We were the wild girls who lived in the woods. We had won a contest, we had put on our war paint, and nothing would ever be the same again. We were the wild girls, and they did not know what we might do.

Jumping

ꝏ

Ray Vukcevich

We stood waist-deep in the muddy green cattle pond. Seven of us. Boys, girls. None of us more than eleven. All of us standing perfectly still.

"Leeches," Carly had said at breakfast. "Leeches are the way out."

"Who wants out?" I'd wanted to know, because I always felt fine in the morning when the sun had not yet cooked the juices from the day, and my belly was full of pancakes and new milk, and the long night was a fading memory. Not so bad, not so bad. Ask me how it's going. Okay, so how's it going? Not so bad.

Carly had given me her china blue okay for you, buster brown bozo look. In fact, she'd swept the mess hall with the look. She could say a lot with a look like that, like sure you've got your pancakes and you've got your milk but how long do you think it really is until dark? Not to mention the cows. Oh, forget it. Just forget it. I don't care what you do.

I could feel the leeches on my legs. My head felt light and tight and I'm thinking maybe it's nap time, slappy happy nappy time. Maybe just sink under the surface and fluff up a big mud pillow and pull the green slime up to my chin and drift off and wake up somewhere else. Was that the way it was supposed to work?

"Hey, Carly," I called, "just how the heck is this supposed to work?"

"The leeches," she said "transport you from the inside out, interdimensionally, if you know what that means, piece by piece to another world. Over there, first you're blood and then you get your muscles and your bones and your skin and stuff and then you're you, and you're not here any more."

"Bleed me up, Scotty," I said, but no one laughed. "Are we there yet?" Still nothing. We had sunk so low we were just heads in a pea-green sea.

"This looks like a painting of Hell," I said.

"They don't send kids to Hell," someone said.

"They send them to camp," Carly said.

Where before they'll let you ride the ponies for five stinking minutes, they make you follow the cows around all day with super pooper-scoopers. Look at us. Dozens of little butt munchkins dotting the fields as we move in on the cows with our dark green garbage sacks.

How you do, Buckeroo?

Okey dokey skinny-dipping with Carly, leech lazy and taking it easy.

But here it comes. The moment of transport.

Or not. Because next I know I'm on my back and on the bank and naked Carly is sitting on my stomach picking leeches off my legs. Shc looks back over her shoulder at me. "You idiot," she says.

I'm looking at her bottom but I'm seeing the future. Eaney meany jelly beanie the clouds open up, the angels sing, and I see us dancing, eating linguini, drinking white wine, and checking out Paris.

Or maybe it was Rome. What did I know about faraway cities that summer?

"So, if I decide to go jump off a cliff," she says, "will you just stupidly follow right along?"

She doesn't know I can see the future. She doesn't know that she will have the power to drain the blood from my brain any time she wants; a sidelong glance, a crooked smile, a feather-light touch to my arm, and one time she'll drop her keys and bend over to pick them up and I'll know she's doing it on purpose, but it won't matter.

"Yes," I say, "I'll jump after you, Carly."

Kapuzine and the Wolf: A Hortatory Tale

ℵ

Laurent McAllister

Don't be scared, children. We live in a world where all stories end happily. So listen now and listen close.

In the Suburbs: An Exemplary Life

Once upon a time, not long ago, outside a city that was a forest, two sisters lived in an abandoned housing project. The older sister was called Mareen Rotritter, the other Kapuzine. The older sister ran a praiseworthy household, spotlessly clean and unfailingly sterile. The younger sister was only twelve. She spent her time playing with the ancient machines, running down the long corridors or exploring the suburbs.

For Kapuzine, nothing was more beautiful than the view from their kitchen window – the streets lined with rusting hulks of gas-guzzlers, the jagged skyline of crumbling factories, the endless brick facades of the other housing projects, the handful of windows that remained suffused with a golden light, burning like campfires when twilight fell. It gladdened her heart, as it should gladden ours, to find herself in a human-made landscape where people were the measure of everything.

However, she avoided leaning too far out the window, since, to her left, a mass of green-enshrouded buildings marred the neat and angular skyline like a verdant, cancerous sore: the looming mass of Hundred-Waters City . . . It was as if she knew what dreadful fate awaited her there, though it was only the normal repugnance of a daughter of the suburbs faced with unbridled nature.

She was a dear little girl, beloved by all the other dissidents who had hidden out among the concrete plazas, burnt-out malls, and shabby bungalows after the Revolution, when the Gardeners had come to gather all of the greater city's inhabitants within the straitened confines of the Ring, where streams ran in the streets, trees grew out of windows, and people lived enslaved to nature. Most of all Kapuzine enjoyed, every Sonntag, being driven around the suburbs by her sister, aboard an old electricab Mareen spent the week charging with amps drawn from scraps of the old power grid. It reminded the young girl of the stories her sister told her, of the good old times when one would drive to a corner store to obtain groceries wrapped in silky smooth plastic or encased in colorfully decorated tins and boxes.

It sounded so much nicer than having to scrounge for dented cans in the ruins or barter with the farmers who trekked to the outskirts of the suburbs and offered dirt-encrusted produce. In her heart of hearts, Kapuzine truly and faithfully yearned for the marvelous days when unrestrained consumption had been the rule.

Now, it so happened Mareen's lover was one of the valiant Woodcutters in Hundred-Waters City, fighting the ever-crafty Wolves who stalked the streets inside the Ring. Whether Mareen loved the cause more than the man or the man more than the cause, this story does not tell, but we may choose to believe she loved the man because of his devotion to the cause.

In any case, her love was great enough to encompass both and she vowed to aid him in his struggle. Using the resources of a vacated factory, she created for the Woodcutters a batch of explosive putty, something they could hardly do within the Ring at the City's heart, where the scarce supplies of useful chemicals were grudgingly doled out for household use by the Hounds and Foxes.

To get some of the explosives to the Woodcutters without excessive risk of detection, Mareen resolved to enroll Kapuzine. Her little sister was just the right age: old enough to be trusted for the mission, but young enough not to be suspected of anything worse than mischief. Mareen explained to her what she must do.

"See here, Kapuzine," she said. "You will carry this basket into the City. To cross the Ring, you will say you have gone to see our grandmother Kunigunde, that you are bringing her some food we have baked ourselves."

Do not be mistaken: Kapuzine was a brave little girl. Still, she was terrified of the City. She refused: let her older sister go herself; she went often enough, more than twice a month, to lie in the arms of her lover. Why couldn't she go this time as well?

Mareen explained patiently that she was already under surveillance. The Wolves grew her face on the leaves of their file-trees, and they suspected her of involvement with the Woodcutters. Should they see her carrying a package, they would search it, discover the plastique in her possession, and arrest her. Kapuzine, on the other hand, had never been within the Ring, and she was young enough to relax the Wolves' vigilance. A single trip would be enough; she would bring the Woodcutters a sample of the new plastique, and, once they were convinced of its effectiveness, they would make other arrangements to smuggle the rest inside the City.

"But the City . . ." protested Kapuzine. "It's all so dark, and all those trees and green things . . ."

"You're too old now to be afraid of greenery," said Mareen in a stern voice. "Remember: under all the grass and the earth, there is concrete and asphalt and cobblestones, safe as houses, just like here. Once, before the Gardeners came to power, the City was exactly like the suburbs: pure and clean and hard. It still is underneath. You must remember this always."

"And what if the Wolves get me?"

Mareen bit her tongue in frustration, then said wheedlingly: "Look, Kapuzine, I swear you'll be perfectly fine so don't worry. And if you do this for me . . . Well, you know I've always said I wouldn't let you smoke before you're thirteen?"

"Yes," said Kapuzine, anticipation rising in her voice.

"If you do this for me, then you can have your first cigarette when you come home."

"Oh, Mareen! Really?"

And so in the end Kapuzine let herself be convinced. Her sister plied her with admonitions and advice far into the evening, then sent her to bed for the few hours that remained before she must leave.

Into the City: A Perilous Passage

Kapuzine had set out before the day became too hot. She traveled along the cracked asphalt road that led to the City. The rusted carcasses of destroyed vehicles littered the embankments, but the road itself had been kept clear. She swung her basket from her hand, trying to look cheerful and innocent, as her sister had advised.

She had been told so many things her head spun. Mareen had warned her about the Hawks and the Hounds keeping watch along the Ring, about the Foxes and the Wolves who might stop and question her once she was inside the Ring. Her older sister had explained how to answer politely without seeming scared or showing too plainly her dislike of the regime, how to choose the correct side streets, how to avoid getting lost in the maze of shrubbery-draped buildings, all alike in their Revolutionary verdure . . . Kapuzine hoped she would remember everything.

By mid-morning she had reached the City. Other travelers came and went from the suburbs constantly, crowding into the encampments of semi-permanent structures set all about the periphery of the Ring. Here people traded, gambled, and conducted barely licit activities far from the stern gaze of the Hounds. Kapuzine was so enchanted by this (never forget that she was still a little girl) that she tarried for nearly an hour, going from tent to tent and peering inside to discover what each held.

Finally she recollected her mission and hurried toward the Ring, overcome by guilt.

Her disquiet returned in full force as she approached the core of the City. Across the loop in the river, the buildings and the trees they supported rose toward the sky. Even from this remove, she could make out the trees growing out the windows of high-rises. She shuddered, as if struck by an obscenity. Though it was growing close to noon, the center of the City was sunk in viridian gloom under the leafy canopy.

To cross the Ring, she had a choice of three bridges. These were heavily manned by Hawks and Hounds. And each bridge had barracks built at both ends, holding shock troops of Bulls.

Kapuzine trudged over to the nearest bridge, one eye on the City's fervid foliage to her left. At the checkpoint, she was interrogated by a Hound, who asked for her name and place of residence. He pointed a stubby-fingered hand at her: "Where are you going?"

"To see my grandmother. She lives on the Sonnenfelsgasse."

"What are you carrying?"

"Just some food and drink."

"Show me. Empty your basket."

Mareen had been crafty: when Kapuzine laid the contents of her basket onto the table, what the Hound noticed was the bottle of aged wine, rescued from an old cellar in a deserted quarter. He didn't bother to examine the fragrant loaf of gingerbread that enclosed the lump of plastique and masked its scent. The brave messenger girl trembled inwardly, for this was a Hound whose flaring nostrils bespoke a modified olfactory system, able to sense the most subtle odors.

"That's illegal contraband, little girl," said the Hound in a hard voice, pointing with a theatrical frown at the bottle. "You can't bring that inside."

"Oh please, sir, don't punish me!" Kapuzine's voice quavered piteously: Mareen had coached her for half an hour to get it just right. "I didn't know it was wrong! I found it in a basement, and I just thought she'd like it."

"Well now, it's not your fault," said the Hound, allowing himself to be mollified. "You're too young to know all the ramifications of the law. Don't worry, I won't punish you. I'll just confiscate the contraband," said he, slipping the bottle into his private locker, "and let you off with a warning: never ever do this again! Do you understand?"

"Yes sir. Thank you for being so nice."

"That's all right. Now go on. Go visit your grandmother."

Kapuzine repacked her basket with the gingerbread, the container of butter, and the cookies, and made her way across the bridge, her heart pounding so hard in her chest she was sure one of the Foxes would hear it with the sound-amplifiers at the base of their funnel-shaped ears. Yet no one else bothered to stop her. Before she knew it, she had passed across the bridge and was inside the Ring.

Within the Ring: A Heroic Journey

It was like crossing into an enchantment. The world changed so suddenly the young girl could hardly believe her eyes themselves were not deceiving her, as in the old tales of virtually realistic games . . .

There was less traffic within the Ring than Kapuzine had expected. It was hard to tell how many people were abroad, since sight was obstructed in all directions: someone might have been stalking her from ten paces away, and she would never have known it. The courageous little girl progressed farther along the city streets, transformed into the gloomy lanes of a dark forest as if by a villainous spell, until she had completely lost sight of the Ring and of the daylight beyond its moats.

Kapuzine kept tripping on the roots that carpeted the narrow streets. Boughs and trunks erupted from the windows of buildings, to meet and interlace above the street. Nowhere was open sky visible: when she raised her head, all that met her gaze were a hundred different shades of poisonous green. The sun struggled in vain to pierce through the canopy; the streets and alleys were enwebbed in shadows.

Water fell from the eaves of the tallest buildings, silvery cascades splashing passers-by and feeding the rivulets that meandered through the grass and humus.

The smells were the worst part: the rich tang of decaying leaves, the spicy aroma of mosses and flowers, and, underlying it all the reek of loam, earth so thick all around her she could almost feel it insinuating itself beneath her fingernails, soiling her skin under her garments. If you wish to envision it, my friends, imagine being forced to wear clothes stained with your own excrement.

Kapuzine, overwhelmed by these sensations, paused and shivered with disgust.

Unthinkingly, she went to the wall of a nearby building, choosing a spot where a patch of the ubiquitous vines had died off. Desiccated, dark red stalks were left clinging to the stone, tiny filaments sprouting in threes along their length, each terminating in a tiny disk that adhered to the brick. Kapuzine plucked off these filaments, loosening a dead stalk's hold on the wall, finally broke it off altogether. She laid her hand on a red-orange brick, now free of vegetable infestation. The rough contact of the porous baked clay under her fingers brought her away from panic and back to herself.

She stood up straight then, took a step away from the wall. She must not be seen damaging vegetation! She would be placed under immediate suspicion, if not apprehended directly. Mareen would be terribly angry with her. She was unwilling to leave the wall and its lovely bricks, yet she must. She had no choice.

She recollected Mareen's directions. She was to follow this alley until it intersected with the Sonnenfelsgasse, then turn left . . .

Kapuzine set off once more, tightly clutching the plastic handle of her basket. Certainly, she could not have suspected that, from the shadows among the trees, a Wolf watched her go.

Kapuzine walked and walked, came at last to an intersection. It wasn't the right one, for there were no signs for Sonnenfelsgasse. She decided to continue along this same alley, then stopped in dread. There was a gorilla across the intersection. He was a true beast – the smell of his pelt reminded the young girl of a stray dog she had once very carefully petted in the street.

The huge dark-haired form, leaning on its knuckles, was inspecting its surroundings with quick movements of its head. Kapuzine remained rooted to the spot. The gorilla moved, approached her. She looked about, seeking help, but she saw no one.

The giant ape passed by her, less than two meters distant. It gave her a single incurious glance from its liquid brown eyes, grunted once in warning, but otherwise ignored her. When it had gone, Kapuzine took the small cloth out of her basket to wipe her forehead.

It had been one of the ancient inmates of the prison, the Tiergarten; all had been freed when the Gardeners had come to power, left to roam the city as they would. She remembered the tapes she had viewed as a child: gorillas were gentle and retiring, they posed no danger unless they felt threatened.

She forced her legs into motion again. This deep within the Ring, she began to pass groups of people: Ants laboring to bring down a wall, in order to give an oak more room to expand, Pigs rooting through the soil, mulching it with human droppings, Hedgehogs removing parasitical vines from small copses to let the trees breathe. The smell of manure was overpowering and almost made her retch. Yet she did not turn back.

A long-legged Messenger Pigeon ran by, his legs moving inhumanly fast. Kapuzine's gaze followed him longingly. He at least seemed to know where he was going.

She came to another intersection, but again she could find no sign announcing the Sonnenfelsgasse. At this she grew even more worried. Mareen had said, "You will come to an intersection, then you must head left along the Sonnenfelsgasse . . ." If she was meant to pass straight through two intersections, why hadn't Mareen told her? Or had Kapuzine forgotten, her head filled so full of advice it had crowded out other facts?

She looked all around her indecisively: should she go back the way she had come? Probably she should simply ask a passerby for information . . .

And then the Wolf stepped out of hiding.

Sonnenfelsgasse 263: An Unexpected Betrayal

She was a tall woman, with a way of keeping her head slightly tilted to the side, as if favoring a weak ear. She wore her black uniform in a style so jaunty – carefree, even – one might believe she was merely putting up good-humoredly with a slightly inane dress code. What the young girl could see of her face, mostly hidden by a large pair of mirrorshades, seemed pleasant.

Yet, seeing her approach, Kapuzine felt an instant of terror – true terror this time, for she knew what danger this woman represented. The Wolf smiled as she approached, and she spoke in a musical voice.

"Hello there. You seem lost."

What bright, well-kept teeth she had! No doubt the entirely vegetarian diet made up for the lack of proper dental-care equipment.

Kapuzine forcibly banished all stray thoughts from her head. She looked demurely at her feet, then up at the woman, in a rehearsed gesture of innocent bashfulness, as she answered: "Well . . . Yes, ma'am, I am. At least I think I am. I'm looking for the Sonnenfelsgasse. Have I gone too far in?"

"Where are you going on the Sonnenfelsgasse?" asked the Wolf.

Was this really as wicked a creature as Mareen had said? Kapuzine felt so hopelessly lost she gave the real address, though she stuck to her cover story:

"Number 263. I'm going to see my Grandma Kunigunde. I've never been there so I don't know if I'm going the right way."

"Hmm. You're sure it's 263?"

"Yes, ma'am."

"You came in by the Aspernbrücke, yes? In that case you've passed the intersection already. You should have turned left just after the big flame-tree."

"Oh, thank you!" exclaimed Kapuzine, and turned to go.

"No, don't leave yet, girl," said the Wolf in a caressing voice. "You don't have to walk back all that way. The Sonnenfelsgasse curves around, you see, and number 263 will in fact be fairly close to here. What you must do is keep on walking in the direction you were going, until you come to a big fountain. There's a side street to your immediate left, heading back north, more or less. If you follow that, you'll come onto the Sonnenfelsgasse around number 230, then you can go left and you'll get there faster. All right?"

Restless and in a hurry to be on her way, Kapuzine was shifting her weight from foot to foot.

"Yes," said the young girl, lulled by the Wolf's kindness and cheer, not thinking for a moment to question the woman's truthfulness. "Thank you very much!"

"My pleasure. We live to serve."

As she travelled even deeper within the Ring, the gloom thickened around Kapuzine, but her spirits had been lifted. Wending her way through the underbrush, the little girl came at last to the fountain, wondered idly at the moss-covered statuary, and then entered the side street that led to the Sonnenfelsgasse. For the first time, Kapuzine noticed songbirds warbling in the trees. There were flowers blooming here and there; as she bent down to peer at them she realized some were in fact quite pretty. This forest was not so hateful after all. Her heart beat happily as she walked, and she daydreamed about the taste of her first cigarette.

Her eyes had grown attuned to the patterns of the greenery surrounding her. So, when she came to the next intersection, she realized that the tiny purple flowers of a clinging vine near the corner spelled out the name of the street. Sonnenfelsgasse! The street names had been there all along, but she had been looking for printed signs. *What a silly girl I am!* she thought. Mareen had forgotten to explain this trick of the Gardeners to her, but she should have understood right away.

Now that she knew what she was looking for, she quickly spotted house numbers amid the ivy screening the facades down the Sonnenfelsgasse. They were limned by yellow blossoms, and she counted off the numbers as she walked, until she found Sonnenfelsgasse 263.

The doorway, behind a curtain of hanging vines, was flanked by a metallic box she recognized with a thrill of pleasure: an intercom. So, the Gardeners hadn't yet expunged all signs of civilization from the City!

She approached the door, glanced around guiltily, then murmured into the box: "It's me, grandmother. I am bringing cake and wine. Open the door."

"Lift the latch," replied a scratchy, tinny voice. "I am too weak, and cannot get up."

This made no sense, but it was the expected countersign, so Kapuzine trustingly waited for Mareen's contact to unlock the door. The lock clicked open and the muffled voice added:

"Just come up the stairs to the first landing. I'll be there."

Inside the stairwell, the air was dank and smoky, with brands picked from flame-trees burning slowly in the darkness. The wooden steps creaked as Kapuzine climbed swiftly. All her fears had left her – she was too young to know that to be unafraid is to blunder blindly into the walls of life.

When little Kapuzine reached the first landing, she pushed open a half-closed door, discovering an empty room, rank with the smell of disuse. A scarred tree trunk filled the windowframe. What little light slipped around it only served to emphasize the room's squalor. Sitting on an overturned crate, a woman wrapped in a long cloak turned her head when Kapuzine came in.

The young girl froze, surprised to feel so uneasy when she'd reached her goal at last. For a moment, she stood transfixed by the gaze of the woman's unnaturally wide eyes, almost owl-like in the flatness of their corneas.

"Oh, grandmother, what big eyes you have," Kapuzine whispered.

"The better to see you with, my dear," answered the woman affably.

Somewhat reassured by the Woodcutter's tone and by the axe she could now see in the room's corner, Kapuzine sidled closer. But when the woman nodded approvingly, a strand of her hair parted and the young girl stopped moving, struck by the sudden glimpse.

"Oh, grandma," she said disbelievingly, "what big ears you have . . ."

"The better to hear you with, my child," replied the woman, who was no longer smiling.

Kapuzine saw then the weapon lying on the crate beside the seated woman, and she backed away abruptly, until the back of her legs bumped against the large earth-filled bin from which the room's tree was growing.

"Oh, what a big gun you have," she said, her voice tearing with despair.

The young girl tightened her grip on the basket's handle, but it was too late. It had been too late when she had entered the room. The false Woodcutter rose to her feet, throwing back her cloak to show the black uniform beneath.

"The better to arrest you with," the Wolf said coldly.

The injustice of it all filled Kapuzine to bursting. "But I did everything the way I was supposed to!" she cried out.

"Sometimes, that simply isn't enough," said the Wolf, as she levelled her gun upon the trembling girl in front of her. "You mentioned Sonnenfelsgasse 263 to my colleague. It so happens that only yesterday, we rooted out this particular nest of Woodcutting vermin. My colleague sent a Swallow by another route to warn me; he got here even faster than a Messenger Pigeon. We had already learned the countersigns . . . And here you are."

The Wolf motioned with the gun, "Now, come with me."

Kapuzine shook her head. Mareen's instructions had not covered such a turn of events. She no longer knew what to do.

"Where are you taking me?" she asked, not needing to fake the quaver in her voice.

"To the Tiergarten."

The little girl's determination crumbled. Her hand opened, and the basket rolled onto the grimy floor. The Wolf did not bother picking it up. Kapuzine knew then that, even if she was still far from the pits of the Tiergarten, still breathing free air, still dressed in the worn synthetic fabrics of the suburbs, she had in fact been gulped whole by a force too powerful too resist. Though she had not yet passed the gates of the Tiergarten, she had already entered the belly of the Wolf.

Yet, though she may have thought herself forsaken by all, she was soon to join the legendary heroes we still sing today.

Inside the Tiergarten: An Indomitable Courage

The Tiergarten was surrounded by a thick hedge of thorn trees, so no one could climb in or out. Atop the living wall, Hawks kept watch, their huge, binocular-like eyes scanning every arrival and departure. Little did they know that the approaching prisoner would be the first to defeat their ceaseless vigilance.

A small pack of Wolves escorted Kapuzine inside the prison, the tall shapes of multiply modified men and women dwarfing the child in their midst. Once they had passed through the gates, guarded by lounging Bulls in their vests of human leather, the young girl blinked in surprise.

Behind the leafy walls, the Tiergarten had been preserved exactly as it once had been. The grassy swards were kept cropped by freely roving goats. The sandy paths shone whitely in the sun, and soon the boots of the Wolves crunched along one of the winding lanes.

They walked by some of the animal pits. Kapuzine thought of the gorilla that had come from here, pity and envy welling in her heart. The Wolves were no doubt endowed with a grim sense of irony, for the young girl saw naked concrete again for the first time since she'd entered the Ring. The cement enclosures and cages had been kept free from the taint of greenery. The only change brought about by the Gardeners was the presence of people inside them, while the former tenants were free to roam the leafy streets.

The stench of manure, human or animal, rose above the maze of pits, moats, and fences, a fetor so thick it seemed to the young girl that it should be visible as a tangible cloud under the hot summer sun.

At last, they came to the barracks housing the central den of the City's Wolves. Though she still held herself bravely, Kapuzine ached all over with fear, her muscles cramping so tightly she sometimes stumbled. Though she was terrified, she was intent on holding back her tears. Show no fear, Mareen had told her once. And she thought Mareen would not be afraid in her place, so she had to be brave, too. *Even if they slap me, I won't cry*, she promised herself. *Even if they . . . if they . . .* But her imagination failed to picture anything worse.

One Wolf shoved her into cell IB4, making her lie down on a bed that had a mattress but no sheets. He knelt to manacle her wrists to the bunk's headboard.

"What is going to happen to me?" she squeaked out, in spite of her resolve.

The Wolf did not answer, leaving once he was done. Kapuzine closed her eyes, willed herself to sleep, but sunlight still entered through the barred window. It was too bright, and too early in the day, for her usual nap.

Another Wolf came in. With a start, Kapuzine recognized the woman she had met in the City, the one who had directed her to the Sonnenfelsgasse. She had seemed so nice, and yet she had been so treacherous. What would she do to the little girl now in her power? Those questions and many others must have nearly choked Kapuzine as she waited.

The Wolf turned to a man standing at the door, waving him inside. He also wore the black uniform of the Wolves, but he seemed as young as Mareen, his features still unmarred by the blemishes of adulthood. He waited, standing at attention, while the Wolf resumed looking at Kapuzine, her head slightly tilted to a side.

"The dear girl . . ." she whispered, as her dark eyes sized the small figure stretched out on the bunk. "This is going to call for the utmost delicacy. Do you feel up to it, fellow Wolf?"

"Yes, I do," barked the Wolfling.

The Wolf surely thought to herself, *What a tender young creature! What a nice plump morsel she would make!* But she was unwilling to risk killing Kapuzine during questioning, thereby displeasing her masters. She chose instead to leave the young girl in the care of her assistant, who would bear the penalty if he slipped up.

Kapuzine understood nothing of this, for Mareen had told her little of the Tiergarten. Once a Woodcutter or a sympathizer entered the Tiergarten, there was nothing else to hope for than a quick death. The little girl had only grasped something of the prison's dreadful aura from the stories cut short when she had wandered in on Mareen and her friends, from the way Mareen's throat tightened when she spoke of the old zoo, from so many cues that were no less telling for being unspoken. She was sure of only one thing. She would say nothing, would never betray Mareen, would force her captors to let her go in the end.

And when the Wolf she knew added, "Remember, be gentle with her," before she left, Kapuzine could only think it was a kindness. All her life in the suburbs, she had known nothing else. Perhaps it was a fatal weakness in her, but it is ever the mark of the civilized to be judged weak by the true savage.

Into Cell IB4: A Virtuous End

Imagine, if you will, all that a human body can suffer without being brought past the brink of death. Imagine it, for you will not be told by this teller. Imagine a mind losing track of day and night, as it is slowly twisted further and further, until its sense of time crystallizes around the comings and goings of Wolflings, their sharp instruments and their blunt ones, their wild laughs of pleasure as they take their fun with an ever-compliant flesh poppet. Imagine the places a mind will go to forget what is happening to the rest of the body. Imagine trying to breathe without stirring the ribcage, to spare cracked ribs and bruises left by sand-filled socks. Imagine waiting (minutes? hours?) for a bowl of thin broth to cool because to sip it hot would bring agony to teeth snapped in half.

Imagine, if you can, that after all this you still have told your tormentors nothing. Nothing.

How much longer do you think you would be able to remain silent? Once, Kapuzine's young mind had worked in absolutes; but absolutes were for children. One believed in good and evil in the way one believed in black and white. Her sister Mareen was good. The Gardeners, Mareen's enemies, were therefore evil.

But evil, she now knew, was not the mere opposite of good; it was a stranger sort of thing, possessed of infinite variety, whereas good only boasted a few distinct strains. Unexpectedly, evil was not synonymous with pain: it brought its own kind of pleasures with it, for to be free of torment, even for an instant, was an ecstasy beyond compare. And more than once she caught herself thinking how lucky she was to have experienced in cell IB4 joys so intense as to wipe out all her other memories . . .

In her delirium, these thoughts passed her lips, though she only half-believed them, when a man entered her cell. While the door was open, distant moans and muffled cries crept through. Kapuzine no longer noticed them; they were part of the soundtrack now.

Automatically, she flinched and shut her eyes, even though he was wearing the red uniform of a lowly Ant. Did she wonder if he had been listening? When time had passed (a minute? a second?) and she did not feel his hands upon her body, she was gripped by fear: what new torture could be taking so much time to prepare? Sometimes it was better to know beforehand, to lay eyes on the implements in advance, to envision the full dimensions of the coming pain; for sometimes the Wolflings were not as harsh as they might be, and the torture did not hurt as much as she'd feared. Hoping to wrest this meager relief from the encounter, Kapuzine opened her eyes and took a second look.

She grew aware that it was night, though she had forgotten exactly what night was. Flame-trees were burning in the yard outside, and the flickering light, coming through the barred window, made shadows dance across the squatting man's face.

"Kapuzine, can you hear me?" he asked when she opened her eyes.

The red uniform finally registered, and the little girl relaxed slightly, with a raspy sigh of relief. Her visitor was only a caretaker, like those who came in regularly to replace the soiled mattress or clean the vomit-spattered floor. Those never brought pain with them. Yet, she did not answer him. It was too painful to speak, and she had nothing important enough to say.

"I'm a Woodcutter," he whispered then. "Your sister told me to give you this."

He took out a pack of cigarettes.

"Oh," said Kapuzine, remembering her wish – it seemed so far away, a childish whim that the whole world should have forgotten. She smiled – her lip split anew and a trickle of blood wet the corner of her mouth. "It's true then!" she whispered. "Mareen has sent you to rescue me."

The effort to say so much left her exhausted. Her breathing became labored, and she grew dizzy.

"Yes," the man said, his face still hidden by shadows. He waited for her to catch her breath a bit, then asked: "Do you want me to light you one?"

"Oh, please," whispered Kapuzine. She was still dizzied, yet she must have felt she was dreaming a wonderful dream.

The divine smell of burning tobacco leaves soon swirled around her. She grasped the small tube between her two unmangled fingers, brought it to her lips, and puffed delightedly. She had practiced smoking already, unbeknownst to Mareen, though only with cigarette butts retrieved from the gutter. This was infinitely better . . .

It took only two puffs for her throat – scraped raw by the pumps they'd used to clear her lungs after she'd been drowned in animal feces – to react to the fragrant smoke. She started coughing; her lungs felt aflame and her entire rib cage was being hammered to pieces. She desperately tried sitting up and sharp pains shot through parts of her body she had never paid attention to before coming to the Tiergarten. After a time the coughs eased and the pain ebbed.

The burning cigarette had dropped to the floor, where it still smoldered; Kapuzine ineffectively stretched out her fettered hands towards it. The Woodcutter retrieved it for her, brought it back to her lips. She inhaled again, once only. This time she did not cough. She felt her mind clear somewhat and a trickle of new energy course through her veins.

"How . . ." she started to ask; the Woodcutter guessed the question on her lips.

"We cannot smuggle you out of the prison," he stated. "Anyway, you're in no shape for a breakout. The Hawks would be on us in the twinkling of an eye."

"Oh, I see . . ." said Kapuzine, though in fact she did not see. The man continued.

"And the Woodcutters cannot risk you talking. They could risk sending me, because I know nothing. I just met Mareen outside the Ring, in the tents of the tinkers and ragmen."

"I don't understand," said the young girl, her eyes blinking.

"I've come to stop the pain," he said. "I'll make it so you won't hurt anymore."

"That would be very nice," she said slowly, still confused. "Are you a doctor then?"

He did not answer. In the shifting gloom, the girl saw the Woodcutter's left hand sneak behind his broad back. When it reappeared, it was no longer empty. Kapuzine understood his meaning at last.

"What a big gun you have . . ." she whispered, her voice breaking, for it could not be doubted this man had been sent by Mareen, Mareen who was the only one who knew about the cigarettes, Mareen who loved her and whose envoy would have rescued her, if rescue was at all possible. She wanted to wail, to cry out to Mareen, but her voice was gone, her lungs felt full of blood and leftover shit, no wind remained to her, and now not even a second of time . . .

The Woodcutter had lied. For while there still dwelled a mind within her skull to feel things, that mind hurt with a fear so intense this final pain was beyond comprehension. And when the shattered scraps of her brain settled within her blasted skull, there was no one left to feel anything anymore – so how can it be said that she had felt the pain stop?

The execution was meant to be quiet, thus the silencer that almost doubled the length of the gun barrel. It did muffle the sound of the shot, but when the bullet exited the girl's skull, it ricocheted upon the concrete wall with a loud crack.

As the Woodcutter opened the door of cell IB4, pistol reloaded and held at the ready, he could only hope that the unexpected noise had not been noticed, even by the sensitive ears of the Wolves and Foxes, else he was doomed in turn. It turned out that the noise had indeed gone unnoticed, blocked by the thick door and lost in the general low-level din. And so the Woodcutter was able to make his way out of the cellblock, out of the Tiergarten, back to his people, to report on the success of his mission.

Now, some might say his successful flight was a stroke of luck; but we who tell this tale and you who hear it know better. It was the hand of destiny, weaving her old miracles, helping us take the first step on the path of our ultimate redemption.

And this is why we celebrate Kapuzine's memory, blasting her molded plastique effigies to bits on her feast day (formerly

St. Barbara's), hearing in the repeated detonations like an echo of the first crack in the tyranny of the Gardeners. For though the tale of Kapuzine and the Wolf may appear unendurably sad, it is full of a holy joy. This little girl did not stray from her path; she did not fall prey to the lure of the green woods; she was not conquered by the Wolves she feared. She remained undefeated to the very end and endured a noble death, a martyr to our cause.

Thus must her example ceaselessly inspire us in our fight. Through her sacrifice she makes it all possible. One day we shall chase the Gardeners out and retake our birthplace. One day we shall uproot the trees of the City, scrub out the encroaching earth, defoliate the bushes, and char the flowers to ashes. One day we shall walk again upon clean stone, asphalt, and concrete.

And live happily ever after.

Meet the Witpunks

❧

Michael Arsenault is the author of over one hundred and eighty other short stories, twenty-six novels, and nine screenplays. Tragically, "A Halloween Like Any Other" is his only surviving short story, after a fire consumed all copies of his other short fiction. His novels, while kept safe from the blaze, were soon after stolen by a vengeful ex-girlfriend who published them all under her own name and is suspected to be involved in the aforementioned arson. Despite these setbacks, Mr. Arsenault has tried to remain optimistic, but his ex's recent Academy Award nomination for best screenplay has come as a bit of a blow.

Eugene Byrne (www.eugenebyrne.co.uk) was born in Waterford in the Irish Republic, but grew up in Somerset in the U.K., where he went to school with his great mate and occasional collaborator Kim Newman. Eugene lives in Bristol with his wife and two children and works as a journalist. His published work includes novels *Back in the USSA* (with Kim Newman), *ThiGMOO*, and *Things Unborn*, and a handful of short stories. He would have written a lot more by now if he hated his day job and didn't have to spend so much time talking rubbish in pubs.

Pat Cadigan (users.wmin.ac.uk/~fowlerc/patcadigan.html) made her first professional fiction sale in 1980, and since then her work has appeared in the field's top print and online magazines. Many of these stories are collected in *Patterns* and *Dirty Work*. Her novels include *Synners* and *Fools* – both winners of the Arthur C. Clarke Award – as well as *Mindplayers*, *Tea from an Empty Cup*, and *Dervish is Digital*. She has taught writing workshops and was for a time a Visiting Fellow at the Cybernetic Culture Research Centre at Warwick University. Pat moved to England in 1996 and now lives in North London with her husband Chris Fowler and their cat Calgary.

Bradley Denton is the author of novels *Wrack & Roll, Buddy Holly Is Alive and Well on Ganymede, Blackburn,* and *Lunatics.* He is also the author of numerous short stories, some of which are collected in *One Day Closer to Death* and in the World Fantasy Award-winning two-volume set *A Conflagration Artist* and *The Calvin Coolidge Home for Dead Comedians.* Born in Wichita, Kansas, he now lives in self-imposed exile in Austin, Texas. His favorite color is blue; his favorite novel is *Adventures of Huckleberry Finn*; his favorite enchilada is "cheese"; his favorite movie is *Blazing Saddles*; his favorite U. S. president is Truman (because he was the best cusser); and his favorite album is *Let It Bleed.*

Paul Di Filippo is a native Rhode Islander. He managed to turn a four-year college education into three full-time years and three part-time years, all without ever actually obtaining a degree. So far, this has not stopped him from selling well over one hundred stories, many of which are collected in several books. He lives in Providence with his mate of some twenty-seven years, Deborah Newton, a cocker spaniel named Ginger, and two cats named Mab and Penny Century. Someday he hopes to own a house with room enough to display his 10,000 books in some fashion other than vertical stacks three deep.

Cory Doctorow (www.craphound.com) will have three new books out in 2003: the novels *Down and Out in the Magic*

Kingdom and *Eastern Standard Tribe*, both from Tor Books, and the collection *A Place So Foreign and Eight More*, from Four Walls Eight Windows. He is also the coauthor of *The Complete Idiot's Guide to Publishing Science Fiction* (with Karl Schroeder). Cory won the John W. Campbell Award for Best New SF Writer in 2000. He coedits the popular weblog *Boing Boing* (boingboing.net) and works for the civil liberties group the Electronic Frontier Foundation in San Francisco.

Jeffrey Ford is the author of the trilogy of novels comprising *The Physiognomy* (winner of the 1988 World Fantasy Award), *Memoranda*, and *The Beyond*. His most recent books are the novel *The Portrait of Mrs. Charbuque* and the collection *The Fantasy Writer's Assistant and Other Stories*. His short fiction has appeared in the field's top print and online magazines, as well as in numerous anthologies, including *The Year's Best Fantasy and Horror, Volumes 13* and *15*. He lives in South Jersey with his wife and two sons and teaches Composition, Research Writing, and Early American Literature at Brookdale Community College.

Hiromi Goto (www.eciad.bc.ca/~amathur/hiromi_goto) was born in Japan and moved to Canada with her family at the age of three. Her most recent novel, *The Kappa Child,* was the recipient of the 2001 James Tiptree Jr. Memorial Award and was short-listed for the 2002 Sunburst Award. Her first novel, *Chorus of Mushrooms,* was awarded the Regional Commonwealth Writer's Prize for Best First Book. She has also written a fantasy novel for children called *The Water of Possibility.* Hiromi is a creative writing instructor, editor, and the mother of two children.

Marty Halpern has been an editor for Golden Gryphon Press since the summer of 1999. In addition to acquiring new works of fiction and working with authors and artists, he also manages the goldengryphon.com web site. Along with Golden Gryphon Press publisher Gary Turner, Marty was a finalist for the 2001 World Fantasy Award/Special Award, Professional. He has a second anthology to be published in 2003: *The Silver Gryphon,* coedited with Gary Turner. To earn a few extra bucks, Marty occasionally works as a corporate business systems analyst, specializing in security configurations and authorizations for SAP software. He lives in Silicon Valley.

Nina Kiriki Hoffman has had a variety of mini-careers, including piano teacher, janitor, guitar teacher, English tutor, secretary-receptionist to a psychologist, fiddle teacher, café lunch singer, and movie extra. Her current jobs are writer, magazine production worker, and copyeditor. She has sold more than 200 stories and a number of middle school and media tie-ins. Her novels include *The Silent Strength of Stones, A Red Heart of Memories, Past the Size of Dreaming,* and *A Fistful of Sky.* Nina lives in Eugene, Oregon, with cats and a mannequin. Her anime collection keeps growing.

Ernest Hogan is a six-foot-tall Aztec Leprechaun. His novels, *Cortez on Jupiter, High Aztech,* and *Smoking Mirror Blues,* have an international cult following. He has published a variety of short fiction, nonfiction articles, essays, reviews, illustrations, and cartoons. This is all because visions keep forming in his brain and won't leave him alone until he puts them on paper. But he can't seem to take it seriously. Currently, he is completing *Walter Quixote,* a "mainstream" novel that is as funny and weird as anything else he has done. A toothless coyote skull named Huehuecoyotl keeps watch over him.

Claude Lalumière (www.lostpages.net) was born to a unilingual francophone family, but it didn't take. He taught himself to speak English by the age of three and now lives and writes in his chosen language. He was a bookseller for thirteen years; during most of that time, he owned Nebula, a Montreal bookshop devoted to "the fantastic, the imaginative, and the weird." His criticism appears frequently in numerous print and online venues. He's a columnist for *Black Gate*, *Locus Online*, and *The Montreal Gazette*. His fiction has been published in *Interzone*, *Other Dimension*, *The Book of More Flesh*, and others. He lives in Montreal.

David Langford (www.ansible.demon.co.uk) is a twenty-two-time winner of science fiction's Hugo Award – sixteen times as "fan writer" for humorous and critical commentary on SF, five times for his SF newsletter *Ansible,* and once for best short story with "Different Kinds of Darkness." After taking a physics degree from Brasenose College, Oxford, he spent five years as a nuclear weapons physicist for the British Ministry of Defence before escaping to freelance bliss and poverty in 1980. Langford has published some twenty-five books since collaborating on a 1978 "reconstruction" of *The Necronomicon.* His latest, as compiler/editor, is *Maps: The Uncollected John Sladek.*

Laurent McAllister is the symbionym chosen by Yves Meynard and Jean-Louis Trudel for their collaborative efforts, which have so far yielded one young adult book and eight published stories. Another book is in the works, while their first book together has been honored with the 2002 Prix Boréal. Meynard and Trudel hold degrees in fields ranging from mathematics and computer science to physics and astronomy. Their individual writing in French and in English totals over one hundred stories, more than twenty young adult books, three novels, one award-winning collection, and two short novels. Meynard has published the fantasy novel *The Book of Knights,* and Trudel has translated Joël Champetier's *The Dragon's Eye,* both from Tor Books. Meynard coedited the fifth volume of the Canadian anthology *Tesseracts,* while Trudel coedited the seventh volume. Both have won the Prix Boréal, Prix Solaris, and Aurora Awards for their individual work.

James Morrow (www.sff.net/people/Jim.Morrow) was born in Philadelphia and spent much of his adolescence in a cemetery, making 8mm horror films with his friends. He also drew comic books, dabbled in live theater, and wrote short stories. His skepticism concerning the God hypothesis resulted from reading Voltaire, Ibsen, Camus, and other "honest atheists" in his tenth-grade world literature class. In 1979 Morrow tried his hand at novel-writing and soon found himself addicted. His efforts included the nuclear-war comedy *This Is the Way the World Ends,* the religious satire *Only Begotten Daughter,* and the Nietzschean sea saga *Towing Jehovah.* He has won the Nebula Award twice, the World Fantasy Award twice, and the Grand Prix de l'Imaginaire once.

Elise Moser lives in Montreal. Her last lover disappeared without a trace.

Pat Murphy (www.brazenhussies.net/murphy) has won numerous awards for her science fiction and fantasy writing, including the Nebula Award for best novel and best novelette (both in the same year), the Philip K. Dick Award for best paperback original, and the World Fantasy Award. Her novels include *The Falling Woman, Adventures in Time and Space with Max Merriwell, Wild Angel, There and Back Again,* and *Nadya.* She lives in San Francisco, where she works for the Exploratorium, a museum of science, art, and human perception. Her favorite color is ultraviolet.

William Sanders (www.sff.net/people/sanders) graduated from Arkansas A&M College, and served in the U. S. Army Security Agency from 1963 through 1966. He has at various times worked as a musician, shipping clerk, construction laborer, encyclopedia salesman, traveling preacher, and dishwasher at the New York Stock Exchange cafeteria. In 1973, having fulfilled the statutory odd-occupations requirement, he took up writing, first as a sports and outdoor writer and then, in 1988, turning to speculative fiction. His stories have appeared in numerous magazines and anthologies and have been nominated for various awards, including the Hugo and the Nebula; in 1998 his short story "The Undiscovered" received the Sidewise Award for Alternate History. He is also the author of twenty published books, including his latest novel, *J.* He lives in Tahlequah, Oklahoma, with his wife and his cat and his old motorcycle.

Robert Silverberg (www.owmyhead.com/silverberg) is the award-winning author of *Dying Inside, The Book of Skulls, Lord Valentine's Castle,* and many other celebrated science-fiction novels and stories. He lives in the San Francisco Bay Area. "Amanda and the Alien" was filmed in 1995 by IRS Productions under the direction of Jon Kroll.

Michael Skeet is a writer and broadcaster based in Toronto. A long-time film critic for CBC Radio, Michael is also a two-time winner of Canada's Aurora Award for science fiction. He was a cofounder of the writers' organization SF Canada and served as its first vice-president.

William Browning Spencer published his first novel, *Maybe I'll Call Anna,* in 1990, the year he moved to Austin, Texas. Since moving to Austin, he has published novels *Résumé with Monsters, Zod Wallop,* and *Irrational Fears,* and a collection of short fiction, *The Return of Count Electric & Other Stories. Résumé with Monsters* was voted Best Novel in 1995 by The International Horror Critics Guild. His stories have appeared in Dozois's *The Year's Best Science Fiction,* Hartwell's *The Year's Best SF,* and in Datlow and Windling's *The Year's Best Fantasy and Horror.*

Allen M. Steele (www.sfwa.org/members/steele) was born in Nashville, Tennessee. He holds a B.A. in Communications and an M.A. in Journalism. He became a full-time science fiction writer in 1988, following the publication in *Asimov's* of his first short story, "Live from the Mars Hotel." He has since published more than a dozen novels and collections and has twice won the Hugo Award for best novella. Before turning to SF, he worked as a newspaper staff writer, freelanced for business and general-interest magazines, and spent a short tenure as a Washington correspondent, covering politics on Capitol Hill. He currently serves on the Board of Advisors for the Space Frontier Foundation. He lives in western Massachusetts with his wife Linda and their two dogs. His hobbies include building model spacecraft.

Ray Vukcevich (www.sff.net/people/RayV) was a finalist for the 2002 Philip K. Dick Memorial Award for his short-fiction collection *Meet Me in the Moon Room,* from Small Beer Press. His first novel is *The Man of Maybe Half-a-Dozen Faces* from St. Martin's. His short fiction has appeared in many magazines including *Fantasy & Science Fiction, SCIFICTION, Lady Churchill's Rosebud Wristlet, The Infinite Matrix, Talebones,* and *Asimov's,* as well as in several anthologies. He lives in Oregon and works in a couple of university brain labs.

Don Webb, writing teacher, novelist, and journalist, hopes to open a writer's colony with his wife Guiniviere. He lives in Austin, Texas, and has sixty-plus stories on various "Year's Best" lists. At forty-two, he finally picked up his B.A. in English, wearing honor cords that he won bowling. He has made more money from his poetry than from his articles about the paranormal, which is pretty dang paranormal if you think about it. His wife Guiniviere is a painter, filmmaker, and composer, but Don makes the better chili.

Leslie What (www.sff.net/people/leslie.what) is the author of *The Sweet and Sour Tongue* and a pseudonymous trashy novel. She has won awards for nonfiction, dramatic work, and fiction, including a Nebula Award for best short story. Her recent work has appeared in *The Writer, The MacGuffin, The Third Alternative, SCIFICTION,* and in numerous anthologies. She's worked as a psychiatric nurse, managed a low-income nutrition site, and tap-danced professionally; she is an artist and the mother of two.

Acknowledgements

ຣ໑ເ໑ສ

This book would not exist without David Pringle, editor extraordinaire of *Interzone* and founder of the *fictionmags* internet forum, where the coeditors of *Witpunk* met. The editors would like to thank Gary Turner for his generous help and advice; the indefatigable Gordon Van Gelder for always coming through; Ellen Datlow for her time and advice; John Betancourt, John Boston, Paul Di Filippo, Pierre-Paul Durastanti, Peter Halasz, and Dennis Lien for their help; and lastly, Randall W. Scott, for his assistance accessing the Clarion Archives at Michigan State University.

Thanks also to Michael Bishop, Terry Bisson, Eileen Gunn, Lauren Halkon, Jan Lars Jensen, Michael Kandel, Richard A. Lupoff, Kim Newman, Jeff VanderMeer, and Kevin Young – honorary Witpunks all!

Credits

ຂOC໕

This page constitutes an extension of the copyright page.

"Is That Hard Science, or Are You Just Happy to See Me?" copyright © 2003 by Leslie What. Previously unpublished.

"Jumping," copyright © 2003 by Ray Vukcevich. Previously unpublished.

"Kapuzine and the Wolf: A Hortatory Tale," copyright © 2003 by Yves Meynard and Jean-Louis Trudel. Previously unpublished.

"The Lights of Armageddon," copyright © 1994 by William Browning Spencer. First published in *The Argonaut,* Spring 1994.

"Mother's Milt," copyright © 1992 by Pat Cadigan. First published in *OMNI Best Science Fiction Two,* edited by Ellen Datlow, OMNI Books, 1992.

"Savage Brcasts," copyright © 1988 by Nina Kiriki Hoffman. First published in *Pulphouse: The Hardback Magazine: Issue Two,* edited by Kristine Kathryn Rusch, Pulphouse Publishing, 1988.

"Science Fiction," copyright © 2003 by Paul Di Filippo. Previously unpublished.

"The Scuttling *or*, Down by the Sea with Marvin and Pamela," copyright © 1999 by William Sanders. First published in *Are We Having Fun Yet?,* Cascade Mountain Publishing, 1999.

"The Seven-Day Itch," copyright © 2003 by Elise Moser. Previously unpublished.

"Six Gun Loner of the High Butte #6," copyright © 2002 by Jeffrey Ford. First published in *The Journal of Pulse-Pounding Narratives,* Summer 2002.

"Spicy Detective #3," copyright © 2002 by Jeffrey Ford. First published in *The Journal of Pulse-Pounding Narratives,* Summer 2002.

"Tales from the Breast," copyright 1996 by Hiromi Goto. First published in *Ms. Magazine,* September/October 1996.

"The Teb Hunter," copyright © 2003 by Allen M. Steele. Previously unpublished.

"Timmy and Tommy's Thanksgiving Secret," copyright © 2003 by Bradley Denton. Previously unpublished.

"The Wild Girls," copyright © 2003 by Pat Murphy. Previously unpublished.